Praise for Margaret M
Best First T

'Margaret Skea brings sixteenth century Scotland to vivid life in *Turn of the Tide*. I enjoyed travelling back in time with her.'

Sharon K Penman

'The quality of the writing and the research were outstanding.'

Jeffrey Archer speaking on the *Alan Titchmarsh Show*

'A rollicking good read … Skea is definitely a name to watch out for.'

Scottish Field Magazine

'The sheer villainy of some characters will take your breath away.'

Historical Novels Review

'Set against the backdrop of a sixteenth century Scottish clan feud, a wonderful novel of blood, dirt, political manipulation and the cost to a family when one man struggles against the tide. Margaret Skea's style is more down-in-the-dirt than that of Diana Gabaldon and just as meticulously researched as Philippa Gregory. It's touching, fierce and surprising, with a sprinkling of humour.'

The Bookbag

Praise for *A House Divided*

A House Divided

Margaret Skea

sanderling

First published by Sanderling Books in 2015

Printed by Anthony Rowe, Chippenham

Set by www.VAforAuthors.com

Cover Design by www.hayesdesign.co.uk

A CIP catalogue record of this book is available from the British Library.

ISBN: 978-0-9933331-0-1
Sanderling Books
28 Riverside Drive
Kelso
TD5 7RH

Acknowledgements

To the many family, friends and fellow authors who encouraged me while I was writing this novel, especially at those times when I felt like giving up – thank you. Particular thanks must go to those who so generously gave of their time to read and provide constructive criticism on early drafts. Any errors, historical or otherwise, are of course, my own.

Based on Bleau's Atlas of Scotland 1564

Contents

Contents

Main Characters

All characters are real unless specified otherwise. I have followed the convention of referring to earls by their title rather than family name and lesser nobles by their place of residence. This did not however solve the problem of several characters with identical Christian names, who had neither title nor place that could be used as an identifier, so where they are to be found together I have used their surnames to distinguish them.

The Cunninghame Faction

Earl of Glencairn:	head of the Cunninghame clan. Ranked 11th in order of precedence among the Scottish earls. Primary residence – Kilmaurs.
Lady Glencairn:	his wife.
John Cunninghame:	his brother.
William, his eldest son and heir:	Master of Glencairn.
Patrick Maxwell of Newark:	a Cunninghame cousin.
Margaret Maxwell:	his wife.
Patrick, Margaret and Helen:	their children.

The Montgomerie Faction

Earl of Eglintoun:	head of the Montgomerie clan. Ranked 12th in order of precedence among the Scottish earls. Primary residence – Ardrossan.
Hugh Montgomerie:	Laird of Braidstane.
Elizabeth:	his wife.
Catherine and Mary:	their children.
George:	his eldest brother, a cleric at the English court.
Patrick:	2nd brother, an officer in the Scots Gardes in France
John:	3rd brother, a physician in Italy.
Grizel:	Hugh's sister, now married to Sigurd Ivarsen (fictional).
Alexander:	uncle to Hugh, James VI's 'Master Poet'.

The Munro Family
(All members of this family are fictional)

Munro:	serving under Patrick Montgomerie in France.
Kate:	his wife, living at Braidstane under the assumed name of 'Grant'.
Robbie, Maggie and Ellie:	his surviving children.

Others

James VI: King of Scotland, heir to Elizabeth I of England.

Henri of Navarre: Henri IV, King of France.

James Hamilton: courtier and (probable) spy for James VI.

James Fullerton: ditto.

John Cowper: a cleric with a standing commission to conduct witchcraft trials.

Mistress Aitken: known as the 'Blawearie witch', she escaped death following her conviction in return for exposing other supposed witches.

Part One

March–May 1597

Greater love hath no man...

King James Bible, John 15:13

Chapter 1

The bed in the guest chamber at Hillhouse was set hard against the chimney wall, the windows firmly shuttered. Tallow candles guttering in wall sconces flickered light across the painted ceiling beams and caught on gold threads in the looped-up bed-hangings. Kate Munro's first thought, temporarily suppressed – to fling open the shutters and flood the room with light and air, for whatever the ill she didn't hold with maintaining a close atmosphere. The woman in the bed was perhaps twenty-five or six, with a listlessness indicating that whatever her physical problem, there was an issue of the spirit also, and that likely the more serious. A servant sitting by the bedside, a basket of mending at her feet, bobbed an acknowledgement, and gathering her sewing left the room, but the factor who had showed Kate to the chamber hovered in the doorway, as if he didn't trust to leave her.

She waved him away. 'There is no silver to steal here, and as for my patient, she will be quite safe.' – Could folk not be grateful for the plants that carpeted the woods and clung to the hillsides, rather than imbuing them and those who gathered them with a supernatural, and often evil, power? As for her skill at turning babies and the like, it was aye the men, excluded from the birthing chamber, who imagined a frightening magic it didn't contain. And so much superstition surrounding a birth it was a wonder any bairn survived.

The woman stirred, tried to struggle upright. Kate placed a hand on her shoulder. 'Rest easy.' She perched on the side of the bed, her assumed name still weighing heavy, despite the six years she'd carried it. 'I am Kate Grant, called to give you ease.' A painful flush crept up the woman's shoulders and neck. Kate smiled a reassurance. 'There is little I haven't seen, and though there is much in the world only God can help, with women's problems I have some skill and will gladly do what I can.' Guessing at an additional reason for reluctance, she moved to latch the door. 'No one else will know anything of what you tell me. Nor need we fear to be disturbed.'

Without a word the woman shed the covers, raised her shift above her waist, spread her legs. Kate gave a cursory glance to the pad of sheep's wool covered in muslin which lay beneath her, noting that the blood was fresh, the quantity no more than could be expected, indeed perhaps less, given that the woman had travelled a distance so soon after a birth. She had to steel herself, however, not to gasp at the sight of her thighs. They were mottled, the variety of colour indicating an abuse both long-standing and regular, the most recent blooming like a scattering of pansy petals, yellow and purple. The woman allowed her shift to drop.

'How old is the child?' The gentleness of Kate's tone belied her anger.

'Five weeks.'

'Where is he?'

'She. At home. I have done my bit, and not well.' The woman touched her breast. 'And now that the wet nurse better meets the babe's needs, I am sent away.'

Kate smothered her first instinct – if she could encourage the woman to talk of what she had suffered before naming the man who brutalised her, more of the story might emerge. She placed her hand on the woman's arm, ignoring the stiffening, and gently massaged it from elbow to shoulder. 'You were forced ... too soon?'

'I am aye forced: too soon, too often, too hard.' The voice was dull, defeated, increasing Kate's anger. 'Even in the later months there was no respite.' Dull became bitter. 'And how should I expect respite? He is my husband.'

Kate forced briskness into her voice. 'Let's start with the present. The rest can wait. You have the advantage of me. I don't know your name.'

'Margaret Maxwell.'

Tensing, Kate asked, 'Your husband?'

'Patrick. Of Newark.'

Kate shut her eyes, the memory of Maxwell, lip curling as he drew William Cunninghame away from their confrontation at the Queen's entry in Edinburgh in '90, as clear as if it had been but yesterday and not seven years since. In an attempt to smother her dismay, she focused on the practical. 'Is this your first child?'

'I have been married five years, so it is my fourth, though only three live.'

'And when you are pregnant?'

'The first time, he left me alone from the fifth month, and so I prayed to fall again. But with the second I was not so fortunate. Someone assured him he could not harm the

17

babe before the last weeks and so he saw no reason to be deprived.'

It was impossible not to ask. 'You are a long way from home. Your husband ... is he here?'

For the first time Margaret exhibited an animation. 'No, thank God. Though how long a reprieve I shall have I don't know. His mother was to visit to inspect the latest Maxwell and he did not wish me to cast a blight on the proceedings, hence my exile here. To convalesce.' Kate sensed her bitterness. 'Not that he will encourage any great rejoicing over another daughter. I am left in no doubt how far short I have come in that respect.' She dragged her shift off her shoulder, exposing other bruises. 'It isn't only in bed I suffer. He has an evil temper and makes no attempt to rein it in.' Then, as if she misinterpreted Kate's involuntary stiffening, 'Oh, he has not laid a hand on the bairns ... yet, and perhaps will not, at least not while he has me to torment.' A sigh. 'I would be glad enough to escape, if only for a little while, but for the children.' And in a sudden burst of candour, 'I should hate them, as they are his, but find I cannot.'

The litany of abuse aroused Kate's own demons – if Maxwell should find her here... It was unlikely he would have entirely forgotten her, despite that she was supposed dead and buried long since. She watched the play of emotions scudding across Margaret's face and knew she couldn't walk away and leave her. Knew also, of a certainty, that if she'd been told the name of the patient beforehand, she would have declined to come, reckoning it as too great a risk to her children and to the Montgomeries who gave them shelter. A sobering and not altogether comfortable thought.

'I have a soothing cream, a mixture of arnica and aloe,

which will give relief from the bruising, but I would like to examine you more closely, to see if there is anything more serious amiss.'

Margaret shrugged. 'You may poke and prod all you like, though I doubt the point of it. If you bring a measure of relief today, next week I will likely suffer again.'

Kate thought back to her own lying-in, to the care she had been afforded each time, her husband's courtesy and restraint until she felt ready to resume relations. And, knowing her experience was far from the usual, felt twin pangs: that others, and clearly Margaret Maxwell ranked among them, were not so fortunate; her own undiminished desire for Munro and the intimacies they had shared almost a betrayal of the woman in front of her. She scrubbed her hands in the ewer of water in the corner and dried them on a scrap of linen from her bag. 'As to that, I cannot promise protection from your husband, but I can perhaps minimise your pain.' She raised Margaret's shift again and began to palpate her abdomen, moving methodically from right to left, noting each time Margaret winced.

The examination over, Kate perched again on the bed. 'You said the latest child is a girl. And your other children?'

'Another girl, and a boy his father thinks a weakly thing. That also my fault.'

Kate had seen folk in the past turn their face to the wall, her treatments no match for the miseries that gripped their mind. She thought again of Maxwell – if she didn't win this fight for Margaret, it wouldn't be for want of trying.

'Supposing your husband thought he risked the chance of further sons if he continued with the abuse, would that hold him back?' She could see it was a new thought for Margaret. Giving herself no time to consider, she continued, 'I will be back in a day or two and expect to see you up and about. Lying here will not aid your recovery.' She played what she hoped would be a trump card. 'If you fear for your children you must try to find strength. I shall tell Mistress Wallace some gentle exercise is required.' She rummaged in her bag. 'Bayberry will improve your appetite.' Moving across to the window, she unlatched the casement, threw the shutters back. 'As will fresh air: while the weather is suitable, as now, the windows should remain open a fraction. It is much the healthier.

There was at least a glimmer of interest in Margaret Maxwell's face. 'What of noxious night airs? Should I not fear them?'

'There is nothing to fear in the scent of pine. Quite the reverse.' The light outside was beginning to fade, though she reckoned there was perhaps an hour or more before it would be full dark, sufficient time to make for home. 'I'll away now and speak to Mistress Wallace. A day or two of the medications I have left should see you much improved. Tempting as it may be to give in to your despair, you have, as you say, bairns to think on.'

It was the right note, Margaret straightening. 'Thank you, for the medicine … and for listening.'

Chapter 2

Robbie was stretched out on the rough grass below Hill-house's barmkin wall, gazing westwards towards Arran and the snow-covered slopes of Goat Fell. He stirred at Kate's approach, scrambled to his feet.

She smiled. 'Not warming yourself by the fire then?'

'With that old witch for company? Not likely. It was much as I could do not to recoil when she favoured me with her cackling and her gappy smile.'

It was the disdain of youth for old age which Kate was quick to challenge. 'She deserves your sympathy, Robbie, not mockery. Forbye her missing teeth, it likely pains her to be so gnarled. When I return I will bring buckthorn, for though it is too late by far to unknot her, I can at least offer some relief.'

He looked up at the battlements rearing above them. 'This is a Wallace tower, is it not, and with the means to pay you in other than kind?'

'Yes, though I won't set my hopes too high just yet, for those who have the most oft keep the tightest fists. Recognition in this quarter cannot be other than helpful, with perhaps an increased income to follow.' She was determined not to share her misgivings. 'At any rate, I've made a promise to return in the next day or two, but there will be no need for you to accompany me. I know the way well enough, and there is little hazard in it, by day at least.'

He was looking down, picking at burrs stuck to his hose. 'For you this compensates, doesn't it?' And then, abruptly, 'Not for me...'

She saw for the first time how like his father at a similar age he had become: the same set of head, unruly hair corkscrewing in all directions, pewter eyes. Arrested by the resemblance, and caught off guard by his perception, she avoided an answer, swinging into the saddle and clicking for her horse to 'move on'. At the foot of the slope they passed the byres, a substantial match for the goodly flock of sheep, heavy with lamb, dotted across the rough ground. Scattered among them Galloway cattle, barrel-shaped, indicating they too were near to dropping their young. Here and there patches of gorse, the spiked stems winter-dulled, and in the hollows, where sunlight failed to penetrate, pockets of frost still silvered the coarse grass.

Robbie came up beside her, matched his pace to hers.

She forced a smile and, as if it was but a commonplace question, as if the answer might not have the sharpness of an arrow-thrust, asked, 'What is it you want, Robbie?' In the early days, when their coming to Braidstane, aside from the oddity of a midnight ride, had seemed to the bairns like the visit long-promised, he had plagued her with questions. How long would they bide? When would their father return? Could he keep the horse? Yet as the weeks stretched into months and they moved from the castle to the bastle house and began to make of it a home, the constant

22

enquiries had been replaced by a seeming acceptance of Munro's absence that relieved and saddened her in equal measure. Now, the set of his shoulders, the whiteness of his knuckles on the reins, gave birth to a sliver of fear that the acceptance she had schooled herself to believe in had been but a skim of ice on a loch. The answer she now sought perhaps the first crack that, spreading, would expose dangerous waters beneath.

He was upright in the saddle. 'I want to go to France. To join Patrick Montgomerie and Father. I want to be a lancer...'

He had become a man unnoticed, and a stranger. Had she anticipated it, or had time to consider, she might have been able to temper her reaction, to plan how best to play it. As it was she was unable to keep the bitterness out of her voice. 'You want to fight, much like all men.'

Words tumbled from him, a waterfall cascading over rocks, increasing in power. 'I am old enough now not to skulk here in fear of William Cunninghame. It is William, isn't it?' His head was up, his chin jutting forward, his voice gaining in resolution, as if he built up to the kernel of his complaint. 'I am tired of being called "Grant". I want my own name back.'

'And with it danger. Don't you know it was to avoid it that your father left?'

'I know it fine.' His mouth was tight. 'But I'm not convinced he choose aright.'

Anger rose in her, the stronger for her own reservations. 'Don't presume to judge, Robbie. You were only a child. Your father did what he thought was necessary, and none of it easy. We owe him our lives and mustn't forget it.'

'That was then.' He turned the argument. 'We have

23

seen nothing of William Cunninghame, nor any of his kin, for long enough and should surely be safe now. If Father cannot come home to bide, why does he not at least visit? There are others, put to the horn and facing imprisonment if caught on Scottish soil, who still find it possible to slip home from time to time. His exile was voluntary. Should that not make it the easier?'

'Easier?' She was back in her bedchamber at Broomelaw that last night, Munro rousing her from sleep, telling her of Archie and Sybilla, of the tide engulfing them, of his own challenge to William's treachery. 'The Master of Glencairn had no thought of imprisonment when he came riding to Broomelaw to seek us out. The affront too deep.' She injected a certainty into her voice. 'I had rather your father be abroad and alive than risk death by coming here.' She grasped his arm, willed him to understand. 'The danger will never be past while William Cunninghame lives. Nor is there any safety for a Munro. Grants we have become and Grants we must remain, but,' as he tried to wrest free, 'I cannot deny it would be a fine thing to learn how your father fares. If Patrick Montgomerie were a better correspondent...'

'The moon would be made of cheese. You and Elizabeth both have been waiting to hear from him these seven months or more.'

She noted his omission of the courtesy title 'aunt', a signal he thought himself old enough to be above such conventions; the reprimand that yesterday would have sprung instinctively to her lips died in her throat. 'Patrick may have sent and the word gone astray.'

'Or he may be dead and unable to send.'

It was the the cruelty of youth, and likely unintentional.

She focused on countering his original suggestion. 'John Shaw makes for Veere at the end of the month; he could send for word.'

On their left was a small loch, the water stained peat-brown, rushes flourishing on the fringes, tall and straight, the heads firm. Robbie, similarly rigid, said, 'I would rather it was with your blessing, but whether or not, I mean to go.' He was staring past her, towards a rocky promontory capped by an L-shaped tower. The sinews in his neck stood out taut as fine cord, so that Kate suspected it wasn't this tower he thought on, but their old home as they had last seen it, four-square and sturdy, silhouetted in the moonlight, and they galloping away as if the devil was at their heels. She was both right and wrong.

'I went to Broomelaw. Saw it blackened and scarred: the roof gone, windows gaping.'

She found it hard to breathe. 'When?'

'Last month. When you thought me at Greenock. Did you imagine I could forget? Young I may have been, but it didn't make the loss easier. When we first came to Braidstane ... I knew why Elizabeth Montgomerie sent the steward to Renfrew. How could I not? So I quizzed him after, and he was ready enough to talk, the more so perhaps that it was out of turn. He spared me no details and I determined one day I'd see for myself. And now I have.' His voice broke. 'And almost wish I hadn't. I thought if I saw it I could look ahead, not back.' His breathing became ragged. 'But the truth hasn't set me free. Rather the reverse. Now I can think of little else.' He paused, as if unsure whether to continue. 'Parts of the walls are broken, the stone scattered.' A new, bitter twist to his mouth. 'There are no lintels lying ... stolen, I imagine. It should not be so.'

25

Kate, sharing his pain, ached afresh for Munro. It was hard enough to be a mother of daughters, but this son-man was an unmapped country, as foreign as if he had been an Egyptian, to lose him as well as her husband a prospect too painful to contemplate. 'The truth, Robbie? The truth is Broomelaw is no longer our concern. We lived there once, that is all. Gifted to your grandfather: its price allegiance to the Cunninghame cause. On Cunninghame land it was built and on Cunninghame land it will always be. When your father broke with William, it was in full knowledge that to do so risked all.' She weighed her choices, steeled herself to be brutal. 'There is something else you should know.' He looked at her, his eyes the grey of a leaden sky, and so like Munro's it hurt to hold his gaze. 'The Cunninghames did not destroy Broomelaw. At least ... I think not.' A hesitation, for the thought once said could never be unsaid, its effect unpredictable. 'I believe it was your father. A ruse that William might think us all dead and thus be satisfied. Now do you understand why we are "Grant" and no longer "Munro"? How we have had peace these six years past? Why your father does not risk return?'

Into the silence a curlew cry, high and plaintive. Robbie's voice, likewise far off. 'Whatever Father may have done, or not done, it changes nothing. I cannot be other than I am. You should not ask it.'

Kate focused on the crescent-shaped scar below his jawline, gained in a tumble from the barmkin wall. Thought of the child he had been, of the stranger he had become, said, 'I don't know who you are, Robbie.' The questions she had asked herself a thousand times during the six years they had lodged at Braidstane, that she had aye been unable to answer, slipped unbidden into the space between them. 'Would it have been different had you grown up in your own place? If your father had been there to steer you through? If Anna...' She bit back the name – did it all come back to the twin he had lost? For him likely yes, his pain something no one else could truly understand. But for herself, though Anna's death still cut deep, she knew it to be a consequence and not a cause. The root of their ills much further back: at the Ford of Annock and Munro's part in the massacre of the Montgomeries there. Never spoken of, nor fully understood, its shadow a weight she would not share with anyone, least of all her children. Only once, in anger, had she come close to questioning Munro, his answer near enough to an acknowledgement of guilt to cause her retreat: from a knowledge she could not have borne, and from him. Their marriage, their children, their life together threatened. The recovery, partial as it had been, a long and painful thing. Twice at Broomelaw she had thought them free of Annock, each time her hopes dashed. Now, living at Braidstane as 'Grants', under the Montgomeries' protection: willingly given despite the earlier ills, she had hoped the children would grow up without old rivalries stalking them, even if *she* couldn't slough them off. But that, it seemed, had been a foolish notion.

'Elizabeth intends to send word to John Shaw with a list of things to be bought in Veere. You could volunteer to take the message, and once there, add that we would appreciate it greatly if he were to send word on to Patrick. No doubt it will be a simple enough thing to find out where the Gardes are stationed. For where the French King goes, they go also. You could contract to meet him on his return and bring whatever news he garnered back to us.'

'Why should I not cross to Veere myself? I can save

John the time and the expense of paying another messenger. And perhaps Father … you must want to see him… As for the girls, it is as if they have forgot him altogether … is that your wish?'

She thought of Maggie and Ellie, drew in a deep breath. 'Of course not. But I cannot ask him to risk it. Better to be thought dead than to be so.' They had reached a copse of young trees starting to bud, the new growth a sharp reminder of another year gone. 'And besides,' she chose plea over command, 'we depend on you.'

'No you don't. He jerked the reins, startling his horse. 'Oh, I fetch and carry and mind the bairns. Help Hugh. Birth a lamb or two. Feed the cattle. Trail around behind you while you make visits to far-flung patients … and I daresay I would make shift to deter a vagabond if we should happen upon one. But you do not need *me*: a stable lad would do just as well.'

'It isn't so much what you do, Robbie. Looking at you helps me to hold onto the memory of your father, that he will not be a stranger altogether when he does come home.'

'Is that all I am to you? Father's shadow?' Robbie's voice rose, broke again. 'All the more reason then to leave.'

'That wasn't what I meant, just…'

His mouth was tight. 'For all we know…' He met her eyes for the first time.

She saw her own dread reflected in them – that her husband might not be here, not because he was afraid, of the Cunninghames or anyone else, but because he wasn't anywhere at all. Because he mouldered in some foreign ditch, nothing to mark his grave, no one to mourn him. 'Please. Don't say it. I have a fear that to speak it out might make it so.' She caught her lip in her teeth, instinct causing her to give ground. 'You are approaching manhood, but not there yet. There waits but five months till your fifteenth birthday. If you are still of a mind to go then, I will not stand in your way.'

Chapter 3

It was Robbie that, had Kate but known it, occupied her husband's mind as he sat in the dust of the courtyard of the Hotel de Vincennes, rubbing a mixture of lard and ash into the reins spread across his knees. An occupation that owed more to a lack of anything else to do than to their condition, the leather so well worked it could have passed for the finest calfskin rather than the oxhide it was. The French King, Henri, was in the palace at the Louvre, a select few of the Scots Gardes with him, but Munro not one of them. Not that he would normally wish for such an honour, but at the end of a long winter anything would be preferable to the air of lassitude hanging over the quarters. He was ill-suited to doing nothing and what small jobs he could invent for himself left him more than enough time to think. His thoughts of late rarely of anything other than of Kate and the bairns, of Broomelaw and Braidstane, of the Montgomeries. And always, lurking in the shadows, William Cunninghame.

With thought of the children came the accustomed pain, that six years on from his flight from Broomelaw he struggled to visualise them. Not surprising perhaps in the case of Ellie, who had been little more than a babe when he left, but even Maggie and Robbie's features eluded him. Dreaming or awake. A failure which, though sense dictated it was only natural, nevertheless shamed him. As for Kate, though on occasion she appeared in his dreams as vibrant and clear as if she stood at the end of his pallet; waking, he found her image likewise blurred, as if on a poorly printed pamphlet: the edges curled, the ink already beginning to fade.

Now, as he idled away the time, Munro wished with all his heart he might risk taking leave with his family as others did, rather than be stuck here waiting for spring and the chance to go on the offensive once more. And perhaps see the end of the conflict at last. He thought on the previous summer, how the balance of power had shifted backwards and forwards, now Henri, now the Spanish gaining the upper hand. Significant French victories countered by notable defeats. The triumph of La Fère turned to dust by the loss of Calais with three thousand French casualties, the English and Dutch troops arriving as promised, but too late.

He set aside the reins, picked up the bridle – it was hard to believe it had been three years since he had left Norway to join Patrick Montgomerie in the Scots Gardes. Little suited to the life of a merchant in Flekkefjord, and knowing that though he had worked hard since fleeing Scotland, nevertheless he lived on charity: the Ivarsen's need of him rather less than his of them, he had found Patrick's offer too tempting to refuse. And correspondingly a mite disappointing that service in the Scots Gardes hadn't proved quite the excitement and camaraderie he had anticipated. Especially as Patrick Montgomerie was everywhere with the King and so spent little time with the lancers. His company a loss to Munro that served to emphasise his other losses.

A clatter of hooves and a commotion in the gateway. Munro uncurled his legs and scrambled stiffly to his feet as Patrick slid to the ground beside him, wiping away sweat from his forehead with his sleeve. He scanned the courtyard as Gardes began to spill from the doorways of the surrounding buildings.

Munro rotated his shoulders, the click audible.

Patrick grinned. 'Arthritic, are you?

'You'd be stiff if you'd sat as long as I have with nothing more to do than clean tack that wasn't dirty in the first place.'

'Well, you'll have plenty to do now, so you may hope to loosen up.' He raised his voice, addressed the gathering soldiers. 'We're on the move.'

A hubbub of voices, all shouting at once, so that Patrick held up his hand.

'Amiens is taken.'

A collective in-drawing of breath, a weight to the ensuing silence cut by a single voice behind Munro, the tone accusing, 'The folly of leaving an arsenal without a garrison to guard it...' The soldier broke off, arrested by Patrick's glare.

'It isn't ours to question such decisions...'

Another voice, equally truculent, 'Only to pick up the pieces thereafter?'

'Enough!' Patrick's voice was controlled, his gaze freezing those who continued to mutter. 'Be ready to move out in an hour.' His tone became deceptively mild. 'Any comments you may have you may take to de Biron.' A pause. 'Or the King.' A hardening of his voice. 'And send word to others of the company elsewhere. The King has little patience for stragglers.'

The courtyard emptied, save for Patrick and Munro. Patrick bent and picked up Munro's reins, rubbing his thumb along their length. 'Any more rubbing and you'd have rubbed right through. Is it a lady's purse you're aiming for?'

'What else was there to do? The only alternatives the whorehouses or a gaming den. For which I have neither the inclination nor the silver.'

'Or a church.'

Munro wasn't sure whether Patrick was serious, as he continued, 'You could aye pray, for your own sins, or those of others, or, more pertinently in the present case, for the relief of Amiens.' He drew his mouth into a mockery of a smile. 'And you'd be no more stiff from hours on your knees than sitting, and maybe make something of it.'

'What happened?'

'Ah. That's a tale not for the telling, or not at least until we are sure of our privacy.' His mouth tightened into a straight line. 'But Henri's not best pleased. He's sending all who can be immediately mustered with de Biron to make preparations for a siege, while he himself rides out to the garrisons to raise other troops. As it stands at the moment we would be vastly outnumbered, though a sizeable force inside a besieged city can be more of a liability than an asset.'

'Do you ride with us?'

'Not for more than a day or so.' Patrick slapped the reins against his thigh, 'Honour it may be to be a part of Henri's bodyguard, but at a time like this I'd much rather be accompanying de Biron than the King.'

Munro took less than a quarter of the hour allotted to make his preparations, returning to the courtyard to find Patrick lounging against the well head, a chunk of bread in one hand, a pitcher in the other.

He gestured to the spare pitcher balanced beside him. 'You at least will not ride out thirsty.'

Munro took a deep draught, cast a look around at the soldiers criss-crossing the courtyard, queried again, 'Well?'

'We had the news from Amiens in the early hours. And though it didn't make for good listening, I took the messenger straight to the King.' Patrick paused as if considering how much he could or should say, then, 'There were others of the guards rather more reticent, who thought the presence of Gabrielle d'Estrées in the bedchamber should change matters. But awake or asleep it isn't only his bed she shares. When she accompanies the King on his campaigns, it is not just to wash his clothes and prepare his food and keep him warm at night, though that she does and willingly, Marquise or no; she is party to all his concerns. He considers her a better man than many of his advisors, and her counsel sound. Love there is between them, but neither is blind to the more important issues, nor would they put their own comfort before necessary action.'

'You like her?'

'I don't know her well enough to like or not like, but what I know of her I admire.'

'And Amiens?'

Patrick checked no one was in earshot. 'The guards will be a laughing stock when the truth is known. Falling for the trick of a cart capsized in the city gate.' Patrick shook his head. 'And as for the contents, a child with half a brain should have wondered how a group of peasants could come by apples and walnuts at this season.'

'Had it been our ruse, you would have thought better of it.'

'Had it been our ruse, we might have taken La Fère months before we did and been free to support Calais; and Albert trounced there, we might not be marching on Amiens now.'

'True.' Munro's accompanying glance at Patrick was speculative. His unspoken question answered.

'I have to admit, though I would far prefer a battle than a siege at the end of a tiresome winter, there is a certain satisfaction in some real work to do. Which is why I envy you. For you will be in the thick of it, while I...' Patrick broke off as groups of Gardes began to form up around him. He nodded his satisfaction, addressed them. 'We are called to an important task. The relief of Amiens is crucial, and dear to Henri's heart, forbye regaining the arsenal.'

Munro was tracing circles in the dust with the toe of his boot. 'And for the sake of the townsfolk I trust it may be quickly.'

Patrick refocused on him. 'Aye, well, there is little quick about a siege, but at least we have the advantage of terrain, the Somme a natural barrier, the crossing points easy to hold.' He gestured for the men to move off, Munro hanging back by his side.

'What did you mean by "the thick of it"? The digging of trenches isn't the work of a day, you'll surely be back long before we see real action.'

'No we won't. Aside from the preparation of the siege works, diversionary attacks are also planned. I mentioned your name to de Biron. So while we drum up troops and

35

money, you must sharpen your sword.'

36

Chapter 4

Kate had been summoned to a difficult birth in a house near Beith and had considered bringing Maggie with her, but something in the manner of the call had changed her mind. The sun was riding high as she came through the gateway, geese strutting in the barmkin, hissing at her as she passed. Two children hunkered on the cobbles, playing at jacks with small stones and a wooden die. A third stretched out against the warm stone of the tower wall, tatting, the tool flying between her fingers, red wool snaking from a spool tucked by her side – a fourth delivery then, not the most usual time for complications.

She was considering the possibilities as she climbed to the hall and found the master of the house slumped by an unlit fire. At her footfall he raised his eyes for an instant and, as if unseeing, dropped them again – worse than she thought then. Without pausing to speak, she crossed to the spiral stair that wound to the upper floors.

The woman was barely conscious, her face glossed with sweat, hair plastered to her forehead, her shift crumpled around her thighs. Kate threw off her shawl, rolled up her sleeves and grasping both feet slid them back towards the woman's buttocks, splaying the knees wide, exposing the crown of the babe's head in the vulva. Kate touched the scalp, felt it give under her finger like moss. She cast a quick glance at the serving girl by her side. 'Is there anyone else to help?' A younger girl appeared out of the shadows, shaking. Kate kept her tone brisk. 'I need plenty of water, boiled and cooled a little, a swaddling cloth and clean rags.' The eyelids of the woman on the bed flickered, as if in response to the mention of swaddling, Kate shaking her head. 'It has long been too late for the babe, it's you I must concentrate on.' The woman subsided, a single tear trickling down her cheek. Kate placed her hand on her shoulder. 'There was nothing you could have done differently.'

The girl had returned, and Kate, twisting one of the proffered rags, eased it between the woman's teeth, sprinkling the other with a distillation of poppy seeds. 'Press this over her mouth and nose, it should keep her quiet while I remove the babe.' She indicated to the older girl to hold the knees wide-spread. 'Firmly mind, this will be neither easy nor pain-free, but I have no choice.' Taking the forceps from her bag, and ignoring the servant's indrawn breath, she opened the cup-shaped blades, working them around the babe's head until she had as good a grip as was possible in the circumstances. It was difficult, the babe barely crowning, but at least she did not need to fear damage to the child, only that she might not manage to withdraw it cleanly.

She began to pull, her pressure on the forceps even and slow. There was a moment of resistance, then a tearing, as first the babe's head, then the shoulders appeared, and then, in a slither, the rest of the lifeless body. Kate severed the cord, wrapped the bloodied foetus, already partially decomposed, in the swaddling cloth and passed the bundle over to the younger girl, who was gripping the bedframe as if she feared to faint. Kate palpated the abdominal area feeling for the afterbirth. She closed her eyes – dear God: twins, the loss double. She probed again, assessing the possibilities for speeding the second delivery that the woman's ordeal might be ended, her recovery begun. If indeed recovery was possible. Infection of the womb almost inevitable with two dead bairns rotting in it for goodness knew how long. Survival, if it could be achieved, more likely the result of a miracle than of anything she could do. Thank God she had left Maggie behind.

Her examination almost over, she felt a fractional nudge against her wrist, so faint she couldn't be sure. And then she was. The girl was back, hovering at her elbow. Kate spoke decisively. 'There is another one, and maybe live.' We need the fire, and the clean water I asked for, plenty of fresh bedding and a warming pan in the cradle.' She was probing more firmly now, feeling the presentation, searching out the head, knowing time was short. It was breech but small and Kate worked quickly, manipulating and easing until the head slipped round and down. She took a deep breath, thankful for the copy of Paré's treatise on turning babies which John Montgomerie had sent from Florence along with the forceps, and which had been more than useful on many occasions since. 'How long has labour been in progress?'

'Since yesterday, in the forenoon. At first it seemed as normal…' The girl's voice trailed away.

Kate felt a hollow sensation in the pit of her stomach – a day and a half, the chance was slim, but she had felt movement, weak maybe, but definitely there. She gestured to the rag lying across the woman's face and to the bottle beside her head. 'Add another three drops, we must keep her from waking. In other circumstances her assistance in pushing would be helpful, but in this case,' she paused, considered, reaffirmed her decision, 'I think we will do better without. For now it's best she knows nothing.' She touched the older girl's arm, steered her back to the side of the bed. 'Take the knees again, hold them as far apart as you can.' She was edging the forceps in and up. A trickle of sweat ran down the side of her face, dripped onto her hand, tension visible in her arms and shoulders as she pulled. The curve of the forceps was almost clear, the dark head visible within. Another minute and the job was done. The babe's face was a bluish-grey, the limbs flaccid. Kate slid her fingers into the tiny mouth, hooked out a clot of mucus, and, covering the mouth with her own, blew inwards, at the same time gently massaging the tiny chest. There was a flutter under her fingers and she blew again, another flutter, a third gentle puff, before she felt the rise and fall of the tiny ribcage. Lifting the child, she slapped it firmly on the buttocks: the cry, though weak, a triumph. She continued her massaging until the skin took on a roseate tinge, then cut and tied the cord before wrapping the babe and laying it in the warmed cradle. She leant on the side, her weight rocking it lightly, one finger stroking the child's palm, the knot in her stomach uncoiling as tiny fingers curved around hers and gripped tight.

The younger girl was beside her, her chest heaving as if she had been running, her eyes wide. Kate shared her smile. 'Fetch your master, he has a child to greet.' Then, sliding her finger from the child's grip, she turned her attention back to the mother. The breathing was fast, twin spots of colour flushing her cheeks, but as yet she showed no sign of waking – no bad thing. Kate swabbed the tears caused by the first birth, which though sizeable, were at least straight and would be easy stitched. It was not the reason her mother anticipated when she forced the young Kate to spend wearisome hours labouring over a succession of samplers until she was satisfied with the quality of Kate's sewing. An irritation then, and the subject of many disagreements, Kate, and many of her patients, had they but known, had cause to be grateful for it now.

With no way of assessing the condition of the womb, aside from a careful watch over the following days for the common signs of fever and swelling, she began to think on the combination of herbs to leave to counter infection – bayberry, a specific for female problems, certainly, and hyssop … burdock perhaps, for the purification of the blood … aloe, always helpful. No doubt one of the women who had helped her would be competent to follow instructions for the administering of them. Pray God the husband would have care to the comfort of his wife and would allow a proper healing before anything was expected of her.

There was a movement in the cradle, and a snuffling. Kate glanced towards the girl stationed at the mother's head. 'She'll be fine for now. Prepare a little sugar and water as a precaution against the babe waking too soon; it will soothe and ensure there is no need to disturb the mother before time.'

The girl was looking past her shoulder, hesitating.

'Well, girl, don't just stand there, do as you are bid.' There was an edge in the voice, but Kate, turning, ready to do battle on the woman's behalf, saw the real concern

41

for his wife and child which underlaid the irritation, and so suppressed her frown. She gestured towards the cradle.

'She is small, but an unexpected blessing, I imagine, after the last two days.'

'I thought to lose them both,' he corrected himself, 'all,' and then as an explanation, 'We had no idea it was twins she carried. Had I known I would have insisted on outside help from the beginning.' He drew a deep breath, closed his eyes briefly. 'If I had lost her … it would have been my blame.'

'As to that,' Kate took the risk, 'the life of the child is in God's hands, but she has as much a chance as most that she will live and thrive. But in a large measure your wife's recovery is in your own control.'

His forehead puckered. 'What must I do?'

It was her wish to be blunt but yet to avoid indelicacy. 'It is not what you must do that is most critical, but what you must not. For a considerable time at least.' And by his flush saw he understood her.

'I will not press her, not until she is ready.'

Relieved, Kate continued more gently, 'It's not just the length of labour, nor a regaining of strength, nor indeed the loss of the first bairn, that is at issue here. There are grave risks of a poisoning of the womb, and that I cannot gauge. The next few days will be critical, but if there is no fever, if you will see she takes the medicines I leave, given time and peace and God's grace, she may recover fully and be both mother and wife once again.'

He was standing over the bed, stroking his wife's hair, seeming unaware of the sweat that matted it, speaking almost as if to himself. 'We have three healthy bairns and with them there had been no thought of danger, so we had not expected this time to be any different, the women of the house confident.' He turned back to Kate. 'When it went awry … if I had sent for help sooner … would it have saved the other bairn?'

'No.' She weighed the difficult truth. 'It was not the prolonged birth that killed him. He has been dead for some time.'

He turned his head aside. 'But there was no sign…'

'I'm sure. At the end there is little room for movement, and thus hard to recognise a difficulty. With a second child still living, almost impossible.' She inserted conviction into her voice. 'You must not blame yourself, nor your wife, nor indeed the servants. Had I been here, I could have speeded things on a little, that is all. The outcome would have been the same. Concentrate on the child you have, not the one you have not. And help your wife to do the same.'

He was looking past her, towards the failing light framed by the square of window. 'Can I see him?'

It was the question she hadn't wanted; the sight of the tiny body already beginning to rot, swaddled in a bloodied cloth, a memory no one would wish, least of all a father. She had not the right to refuse him, yet something in her face must have revealed her reluctance, for he blanched.

'You think it best not?'

'Yes … yes, I do.' She hesitated, unsure of whether to elaborate, decided there was nothing to be lost and much to be gained by silence.

For a few moments he too was silent, as if he warred within himself, then, 'It is not cowardice?'

'It is but good sense.' This time there was no hesitation. 'For you, and for your wife; better you remember only that he was too poorly to live, not the manner of his death.'

43

Chapter 5

Dusk fell like a curtain across the French countryside. Ahead of him Munro saw Patrick peel aside and head backwards down the line, a signal that they broke to make camp. And not before time. Condemned to move at the speed of the baggage trains, it was likely another three days' march to reach Amiens, but at least on this evening, with Beauvais in their sights, they could rest secure in the knowledge they were firmly in the King's territory. The soldiers spread out, the repartee and curses which flew back and forwards among them as they pitched tents and set fires a polyglot mixture of French, German, English and a smattering of Scots. Munro, in common with the rest of the cavalry, saw to his horse before looking to his own comfort, Patrick joining him as he headed back to the area where the Scots Gardes congregated.

'The decision is made?'

Patrick nodded. 'Once past Beauvais, Henri heads north doing the rounds of the garrisons, while the rest, under de Biron, make straight for Amiens.'

'And you?'

'I must accompany Henri, however little the role of nursemaid suits me.'

'Hardly nursemaid.'

'Bodyguard then, but however you term it, you will be in the front line while I am far from the action.'

'Not for long, surely?'

'For as long as it takes. The Spanish force at Amiens is said to outnumber us almost two to one, though that...' he glanced around, '...isn't knowledge Henri would wish shared. But while we muster all available troops, your first task will be to cut off the supply lines from Doullens. And after, and this I envy you, to harass any nearby towns from which reinforcements might come.' A grin. 'Remember it was I who recommended you. You'd best not let me down. It's my reputation at stake here. Aside from the task itself, of course.' They skirted a group of French cavalry officers already sitting down to a game of cards, Patrick shaking his head in response to the invitation to join them. 'Serious though, failure isn't an option. The arsenal aside, Amiens is a badge of honour to Henri and this an opportunity for you to shine. Succeed and you'll find him not ungrateful.' They settled among the Gardes beside a smoking fire.

Munro, turning his back against the rising wind, said, 'How long do you reckon this siege will take?'

Patrick shrugged. 'It's too early in the season for them to have had opportunity to stockpile food, and if, as we think, there are some seven thousand troops in the city, what supplies they do have shouldn't last long. But that as you know is only the beginning.' And as if he guessed where Munro's thoughts were headed, said, 'Dogs and cats and boiled leather and worse have been known to keep body and soul together for long enough, when the alternative is surrender.' They lapsed into silence, Patrick, perhaps regretting the sombre turn of the conversation, picking up a stick to whittle it into a point to poke life into the embers. 'Make a reputation here and when autumn comes you could ask for leave.' An image of Scotland and Ayrshire, unmentioned, hung between them, the colours sharp.

Munro spread his hands. 'If I thought it safe do you think I'd have spent the winter languishing in Paris with less to do than an ostler in an empty stable? I wish to God I *could* risk going home, but however much I try to convince myself, there is always the memory of William Cunninghame to dissuade me.'

'The risks of creeping back must surely be small. You're a lancer now, and far removed from the Munro who troubled William. And why should you even cross his path at home? He isn't exactly a welcome visitor at Braidstane, or wasn't the last time I heard.'

'He doesn't need to be. Only to have his ear to the ground. It isn't my own safety that holds me back, but rather Kate's and the bairns; a careless word in the wrong circles and they would be threatened.'

Patrick was dismissive. 'There will no doubt have been others who have annoyed William more recently than you. Forbye that he thinks you dead and gone years ago.'

'There is always the risk that some ill-chance will bring him to Braidstane's door. Alone, Kate and the children may pass muster as Grants, but there is no chance of me doing so.'

'Perhaps you should have finished him off when you had the chance.'

'So I have thought a hundred times, but the gain would likely have been outweighed by the loss if I had.' He

46

thought of Kate. 'When you have a wife, you'll know.'

While Patrick and the small group accompanying Henri disappeared to the north, de Biron and the main French force continued west. They moved through village after village, the evidence of the ravages of past conflicts plain to see. Whole swathes of countryside stripped bare, as if by locusts. The hosting of Henri's current force, even for a night, certain to stretch a village's resources well beyond what they could spare. Munro turned to look at the long column straggling back as far as the eye could see. A walking city, it comprised first cavalry, then infantry, and behind them the artillery and spare horses. At the tail the carts and wagons and pack animals, interspersed with smiths and carpenters and other artisans. And at the tail the pioneers and camp followers, some of them whores that aye accompanied a moving army, but others wives and companions, who chose to travel with their menfolk, risking danger and disease to stay by their side. Not something he would wish for Kate, though as he stretched his back to relieve his stiffness, some of her herbs and remedies wouldn't go amiss. There were plenty among their company with potions and liniments to sell, but whether quack or genuine, it was hard to tell and not worth the risking of so much as a sou.

The closer they came to Amiens the more Munro thought on the task ahead. The difficulties faced by a besieging army were considerable in any circumstances: the bombardment of the city only a small part. At least he, if Patrick's recommendation was relied upon, would be spared the weeks of digging the building of the siege works required, along with the duty that fell to the raiding parties: of procuring sufficient supplies of food and drink for the besieging soldiers and all who accompanied them. Clouds were building to the north, the promise of rain in the air. Munro thought on morale, tricky enough to maintain when the sun was shining, all but impossible if the army sank in a morass of mud or froze to the ground as they slept. As he rode on he found himself praying, for good fortune, fine weather, a speedy resolution.

Chapter 6

At Braidstane, Kate was also praying, but for a resolution of a different sort. The Montgomeries were gathered in the solar, Kate and the children with them, the fencing match begun as Robbie and Kate rode home from Hillhouse, become an ongoing contest in which Kate struggled to hold her ground. She had hoped her admission that it was no longer a question of *whether* he could join his father's regiment, but *when*, would be sufficient for him, the five-month reprieve a straw for her to clutch at. But now, as Robbie, targeting Hugh, reopened the discussion, she very much feared even control of the timing of the thing was slipping away from her. The only crumb of comfort, that however he might refer to Elizabeth and Hugh out of their presence, he was not yet confident enough to drop their courtesy titles to their face, evidence that there was still a little of the child in him, though not much.

He came straight to the point. 'Uncle Hugh, do *you* think Patrick would make space for me in his regiment?'

'Why wouldn't he?' Hugh looked up from his perusal of the castle accounts. 'You're young, a fine rider, and without ties to bind you here.' He turned to Kate, raised his hands as if to deflect her protest. 'You cannot expect him to settle for what Braidstane has to offer. He must make his own way, and there are opportunities abroad that can never be found here.' Hugh bundled up the papers. 'I have time and to spare now, and if the lad is wanting to make plans, what harm in that? It may be months away yet, but it is only sense to be well prepared.' Ignoring Kate's frown, he drew Robbie towards the window, began to discuss practicalities.

Something in Hugh's readiness to pursue the conversation made Kate wonder if it had been a discussion planned, on their recent outing to Ayr perhaps, rather than the random thing it was meant to appear. She attempted to reassert control. 'It isn't tomorrow you go, Robbie. You can plague Hugh for information nearer the time.'

Elizabeth weighed in. 'Supposing he has any information of value to give. Whatever experience you once had of France, Hugh, you have been long away. In the last years there has been more of strife than of peace there, and foreigners of any ilk are likely looked on with suspicion. It will be information of the most recent sort Robbie will require.' An obvious attempt to cut short the conversation, and clearly intended to spare Kate, the effect was quite the reverse, reinforcing the potential dangers and pitfalls of such a journey.

Hugh was dismissive. 'Change or no, travellers aye need a bed for the night and food for their bellies, and in my experience innkeepers are the last profession to be choosy, the weight of coin in your purse what matters most.' He turned back to Robbie, began to talk of the route he would choose, the kind of hostelries to look for, those to avoid. 'Pity we have not a horse suitable for you to take, though we may be able to ease a purchase of one. I was little older than you when I first took to soldiering in Holland, and would have been there sooner but that my father insisted on my attendance at the college in Glasgow. Much good it did him or me…' He shot a smile towards Elizabeth. 'Though it was there I made the acquaintance of John Shaw, and that a happy mischance. Still, France is the better prospect at present, and Patrick will see you right I'm sure. I could almost wish…'

Kate cut in. 'By which I take it you mean the French King's position remains precarious and his need for an army correspondingly great.'

Elizabeth gestured Kate to the bench beside her. 'Kings aye want armies, in times of peace or war. And young men aye flock to them. You might as well sit down and leave them to it. When Hugh starts he's hard to stop.' A log flared in the hearth, crumbled to ash. 'Armies are sometimes as useful for preventing battles as for taking part in them. It is three years since the last of the de Guise faction submitted to Henri, and Paris has remained in his control ever since. They say it is only in Brittany he is threatened.'

'And by Spain.' Kate sat down, but she wasn't ready to give up the argument. 'We may not hear all the latest news here, but enough boats slip back and forwards from Irvine to the French ports to make it common knowledge that should you stray into the French countryside you are as likely to meet a Spaniard as a Frenchman. It is not just in the Gardes I fear for him, but the travelling also. Trailing about Ayrshire is hardly preparation for traversing Europe alone.'

'As to that,' Elizabeth, always accurate even when a little lassitude would have been more comfortable, said,

51

'traversing is hardly fair, and when he goes, I doubt Hugh will encourage him to do so alone. It is only sense to travel in company, whatever length the journey. There are always merchants who would welcome an additional sword in their train...' She paused, as if recognising the unfortunate choice of word.

Kate pounced on it. 'I wish Hugh wouldn't encourage him at all. I always knew I couldn't hold him here forever, but soldiering wasn't in my plan. I have been putting a little money aside for the college and hoped he might pay more attention to his studies than his father did.' Then, longing in her voice, 'I would have given almost anything to study; it was aye an annoyance that if I had only been a lad ... but Munro didn't value the opportunity. To him and to Archie...' She broke off, the memory of Archie and of Sybilla as clear in her mind as if they stood in front of her now. And the waste. She forced herself to refocus on the discussion in hand. 'Munro thought college was time that could have been better spent on more physical pursuits.' Nursing her sense of frustration, she allowed it to fill up the cracks in her resolve to make Robbie wait out the five months until his birthday, before he could go to France.

Elizabeth spoke also from the heart. 'Like Hugh, then, and my brother John. I felt it hard that those who appreciated it least could take advantage of what education was available, while I had to make do with their leavings. And in our house, for all that Father was well travelled, books were a scarce commodity. As they are yet. You were more fortunate.'

'In that I suppose I have reason to be thankful.' Kate, her gaze shifting to the corner shelf, the Bible its only occupant, thought of the alcove in the bastle house kitchen

52

and her own treasure trove. 'My mother's interest in herbs and their uses was aye a fascination to me, and the books she left my most treasured possessions.'

'And have proved their value since.'

Kate heard the wistful note in Elizabeth's voice, acknowledged it. 'Without them, I wouldn't be able to make the living that I do. She would, I think, have been proud of me, though for her it was a matter of family health and occasional help to our neighbours, the idea of presenting a bill for her advice unthinkable.'

'She didn't live a seeming widow with young children.' Elizabeth was matter of fact. 'In your position she might also have found the needed spur.'

'Perhaps.' Kate nodded towards the girls. 'When the bairns were born I had a hope they might have better opportunity than I, but all their schooling is likely to achieve is a greater dissatisfaction that college is barred to them.'

'It's not uncommon to place your own ambitions onto your children's shoulders.' A pause, a smile, perhaps to take the sting out of the words. 'Though not always wise.'

'Yet Robbie did show an interest in what I do, so that I hoped he might take to it with serious intent, as a physician or a surgeon perhaps, and for him there would have been no bar. It is to that end I have kept him by me these two years past.'

Hugh had his back turned, and all Kate could gauge of his conversation came from Robbie's reactions to it. He was laughing, his eyes alight, and hearing him, she felt the sharp pang of loss.

'Perhaps it was the freedom and the chance to be away from home he valued. The doctoring a secondary thing. It's hardly surprising the lure of a regiment is stronger than that of the sick room. And besides, if doctoring was Robbie's desire you would likely lose him to Florence or Padua, as we have John.'

'A hospital has not the dangers of an army.' Kate was picking at her thumbnail, edging back the skin around the cuticle. 'The thought that any day Munro...' she broke off. 'To see Robbie also take that road ... perhaps I should be glad the girls aren't likely to have the chance to venture far.'

'At least you have a boy to fear for. While we...' Elizabeth looked towards Hugh, '...he has not said so, but I know Hugh feels the lack of a son. When my time comes,' she touched her stomach, 'if we are blessed with a boy, I will no doubt feel just as you do. But clever though Robbie is, he has never been the most bookish of bairns. College wouldn't suit him well.'

Maggie, though she sat with Ellie and Catherine Montgomerie, occasionally intervening to adjudicate in their game of spillikins, was clearly concentrating on Hugh and Robbie's conversation and equally clearly envious of what she heard.

Elizabeth drew her away from the game. 'You are to become your mother's escort I hear. And that a weighty responsibility, but one of which I'm sure you're capable. And rather more to your taste than standing as Agnes' second-in-command.'

No doubt intended as a distraction, it nevertheless held its own worries for Kate. It was one thing to drag Robbie around with her, or, when the need arose, to send him back to Braidstane alone if she was forced to bide away, quite another to think of making use of Maggie in that way. Despite that there were many younger than she who carried heavier burdens, and whatever else, Maggie was feisty and strong and her tongue a match for most. As Anna had been. A thought she thrust away, along with the equally uncomfortable knowledge that danger could come as easily on your own doorstep as abroad.

Ellie, curled on the floor, awaiting her next turn at the spillikins, began to slip sideways, her eyes drooping. Kate moved to catch her before she fell altogether, and, handing Maggie a candle, said, 'She needs her bed. If you see her safely across the barmkin, I shall follow shortly.'

Ellie, jerked awake again, was shaping up to protest, but Kate pre-empted her.

'Tell Agnes I have promised you a comfit if I receive a good report of you in the morning.'

Silence fell as Maggie left, dragging a still-reluctant Ellie with her. It was broken by Elizabeth. 'You cannot keep Maggie a child just to make the years seem less.'

Kate was thinking of Munro, his lack a vacancy of heart impossible to fill. It was a moment of clarity, an understanding he had been too long away, and that whatever the cost, whatever the risks, it was time he came home, if only for a visit. For all their sakes. And though she would not have admitted it, to Elizabeth or anyone else, Robbie's reference to those who, though banished, found it possible to slip back from time to time had found its mark.

Elizabeth broke into her thoughts again. 'If there is anything I have learnt, it is that the more lightly you hold to someone, the closer they stay. Giving Robbie and Maggie some freedom now may prove a blessing to you in the end.'

'I know. I know. It's just … I hadn't wished to burden them with fears we would all be the better without, but the danger of letting them loose at home or abroad not knowing our full history...'

'They know they must call themselves "Grant", and Robbie knows also that it is William Cunninghame he must be wary of. For the rest, there are some things best left unsaid. One day they will understand and bless you for your silence.'

'I hope so. It's hard to know if I've been fair in the choices I've made.'

Elizabeth nodded towards Robbie. 'Munro trusted you to look after them and would be proud to see what they are now. And will be prouder still when you have steered them through.'

Robbie and Hugh were still deep in conversation by the window, the volume low enough that it failed to carry, but punctuated by occasional bursts of laughter so that Kate knew its content was likely not suitable for all ears. And grateful as she was to the Montgomeries for the sanctuary they provided, she had room for regret that Hugh had been a soldier first, before he was a laird.

Chapter 7

It was almost a week before Kate returned to Hillhouse, Maggie with her. Margaret Maxwell appeared in the doorway swathed in a cloak. Kate turned to Maggie. 'If Mistress Maxwell can manage it, we shall walk a little. Can you see to the horses.' It was a command, not a question, and Maggie, still living in the glow of being allowed to accompany Kate, took a hold of both bridles without protest. Kate smiled her thanks. 'We likely shan't be long, but a little hay and water and a light grooming wouldn't go amiss.'

'You see I have taken you at your word, and feel the better for it.' A shadow crossed Margaret Maxwell's face. 'Though every day's improvement takes me closer to the time when I must return home.'

Kate indicated her saddlebag. 'I have brought other medicines for you to take away with you when you go: salves and compounds of herbs that you may boil and drink. They should lessen your discomfort, for a time at any rate.'

'Thank you.' Margaret's smile was wry. 'I am not so foolish as to think a week away will have changed anything.'

Kate would have liked to offer understanding, to admit her knowledge of Maxwell, but the need to protect her own children was too strong, the precautions that had been the irksome foundation of their lives since first they came to Braidstane, too engrained to be displaced. She took hold of Margaret's arm, glancing up at the open windows above them. 'Shall we? There are things best said without fear of listening ears.'

A path wound round a hillock to the west of the barmkin, the view from the top sufficient to justify the excursion, should anyone be watching. They sat in the lee of a slab of rock facing away from the tower, looking down the valley towards the shore, the water a glint of silver in the far distance. Margaret pulled her cloak tight against her chest, and fixing her gaze on the horizon, began to talk. The details more horrifying even than those previously disclosed. Kate was not sure how long she listened, Margaret's voice washing over her, fierce and fast, turbulent as a river in spate. Instinct held her silent, sensing that to speak of how she felt, possibly for the first time, was itself cathartic for Margaret, though her root of pain remained.

'...I can wish him damned to hell without shame, for God knows he deserves no less, but it is little comfort that is where he will end. Hating him, I cannot but hate God that he does not strike him down, and so damn myself also. And if we are joined in death, it will be hell indeed.'

Kate placed her arm around Margaret's shoulder – it was not the moment for theology, but rather for solace. 'You won't be.' She had been reasoning with herself throughout, but now came to a decision. 'If you are in need of a friend, I hope you may count me as one. There are reasons to keep me from Newark, but you have only to send, and my stock of medicines are at your disposal. Meanwhile, is there anyone among the Wallaces you could confide in? Perhaps they might be able to exert some influence.'

'The salves I will be grateful for, but as to the Wallaces, I may as well talk to the wall. Maxwell listens to no one, excepting William Cunninghame, and I cannot hope for any positive influence there.'

Kate flinched, so that Margaret, glancing at her face, said, 'You know him?'

'A little.' It was dangerous to say more, too late to draw back. 'I had the privilege...' Kate swallowed her sarcasm, thankful that she had stopped herself before making mention of the Queen's entry. She corrected herself. 'I saw him once. He seemed ... not genial.' The sun was beginning to slip below the horizon, the colour to fade. Kate examined her palm. 'And his reputation in our parts does nothing to change my opinion.'

There was a moment of awkwardness, as if each of them had thoughts they would rather not voice. Margaret rose. 'We should go back. It grows cool and I should not keep you longer. There are no doubt others in need of your ministrations.'

Kate smoothed down her skirt, looked towards the sky. 'I will not make any more calls today, unless there is a particular need. But I should go nevertheless,' she injected a lightness into her voice, 'else I may find the supper spoiled for want of supervision.'

Margaret was picking at a rag nail. 'Just to talk ... it has been...'

Kate rescued her. 'I'm glad. And you need not fear that others will hear of what has been said. In my position I

59

hear much and say little. It is by far the best, indeed the only way.'

They were approaching the barmkin wall when Margaret faltered. Kate, thinking the distance had been too much for her, turned to lend her support and so failed to see Patrick Maxwell standing inside the gate.

The voice was as harsh as she remembered. 'Well, wife, I see you are much recovered.'

Kate took a step back, looked down, became the servant; glad, for perhaps the first time, of her coarse worsted skirt and the plain cap imprisoning her hair.

'Patrick.' Margaret seemed to shrink into herself. 'This is my first excursion and has exhausted me. I fear I will have to lie down. Should you be staying for supper, I...' She moved to pass, but he stepped in her path.

'Oh, I'm staying,' he stretched his lips into a thin smile, 'and not just to eat, but for the night also. Tomorrow we are for home. But you may away to your chamber. It wants an hour until supper. Once the courtesies have been observed, I will join you.'

Kate shifted – to intervene, madness, but...

Maxwell turned. 'And you are?'

'Mistress Grant, sir.' She curtsied.

He looked her up and down and, his inspection done, clearly dismissed her as of no account.

'You attend my wife? Well then. Attend her to the bedchamber. And afterwards you may make yourself scarce.'

'She is not a maid, Patrick, nor any servant of the Wallaces. I required some medicines and Mistress Grant was kind enough to provide them.'

'Indeed.'

Kate kept her head down, not wishing to meet Maxwell's

eyes, aware of his increased scrutiny, matched by a contempt he made no effort to conceal.

'My wife has no further need of the services of a wise woman.' He reached into his doublet, withdrew a purse, flipped a coin towards Kate. 'That, I trust, will suffice.'

Kate allowed it to drop onto the cobbles, tilted her chin. 'I have already received all the payment I require. Good day, Mistress Maxwell. I trust your recovery is swift, and that you are allowed the rest and peace it requires.'

Maxwell grasped her arm. 'Do not presume to tell me how to treat my wife.' His eyes narrowed. 'Your face is familiar. Have I had the pleasure?'

She fought for composure, for a suitably subservient tone. 'No, sir.'

Margaret said, 'Don't be ridiculous, Patrick. Mistress Grant is from near Irvine. Those of her station do not travel far.' She glanced at Kate, apology and understanding passing between them, added a curt, 'Good day, mistress, and thank you for your trouble.' She gestured to the stable boy who was watching the exchange, round-eyed. 'Mistress Grant requires her horse, see to it. And call for her daughter.' She swept past Maxwell and disappeared into the tower.

Maggie appeared leading the horses, and Kate, wishing for nothing more than to get away as quickly as possible, moved to help her to mount, but Maxwell was ahead of her. He grasped hold of Maggie's chin, tilted her face upwards.

'Your daughter is it?'

Kate, inwardly seething at his treatment of Maggie, managed a nod.

'Are you sure we haven't met before? There is a look about her that is also familiar.'

61

'You bide near Greenock; my reputation does not stretch so far.' She turned, placed one foot on the stable boy's linked hands and was hoisted into the saddle, then dipped her head in a passable imitation of deference. 'Good day, sir.'

Maggie looked back only once, Kate not at all, her breathing remaining ragged until they had passed beyond the hillock and were hidden from view. Aware of Maggie's scrutiny, she sought to deflect it. 'That was Mistress Maxwell's husband, come to reclaim her. I did not find him amiable.'

'And Mistress Maxwell? Does she find him amiable?'

Kate shot a surprised look at Maggie.

'I'm not a child. Elizabeth and Hugh may like each other well enough, but it isn't hard to see that not all marriages are likewise happy.'

'You do not think we were unhappy, Maggie? Your father is not here, but there isn't a day goes by but that I wish he were. There was no lack of love in our marriage, indeed it is for love your father remains away.' She weighed in her mind the need to reassure Maggie against the danger of saying too much, the turn of the conversation uncomfortably akin to the one with Robbie a few days earlier.

'Why do we not keep to our own name? Avoid any mention of our old home? Scarce talk of Father?' Maggie had drawn to a halt and Kate was forced to do likewise.

'It is the safest course, for us and for the Montgomeries. You were young, and, as children do, accepted the change in our circumstances with little protest. It seemed best not to hark back to what had gone before, for a careless word could have cost us dear, especially in the beginning.'

'Word to who?'

'I had hoped to spare you this knowledge for longer, but the truth is likely easier to bear than any story you might imagine for yourself. You must understand, Maggie, the Munros have been followers of the Cunninghames for generations, but William Cunninghame, Glencairn's heir ... your father crossed swords with him, and in a manner that made it impossible for us to remain at home. William thinks us all dead, and in that lies our safety. The Montgomeries absorbed us into their holding, for what family does not have a widow and bairns to care for, but your father could not have been so easily hidden.'

'Does Robbie know all this? Did you tell *him*?' A pause, a new hard edge to Maggie's voice. 'And when *was* I to know?'

'I told Robbie nothing, or not at least until last week, when he also tackled me, much as you're doing now.' She sensed a fractional relaxation in Maggie, sought to be conciliatory. 'Perhaps I was wrong, but I thought that for all of you to grow up without the old antagonisms was the better way.'

The silence stretched between them, Maggie clearly considering, then, 'Can I come with you another time?'

Glad of the change in topic, Kate was quick to respond. 'Yes, of course. I had once thought Robbie might continue an interest in what I do, but it seems I was mistaken, so if you would care to learn, I should be glad of your company. If you are to be out and about, it is as well you know what not to say and why, but I'd appreciate you keeping such knowledge from Ellie. For all it is a while ago now, one slip and we could still lose everything.'

63

Chapter 8

Mistress Wallace paused in her slopping of porridge. She fixed Maxwell with a glare, her spoon halfway to her mouth, milk dribbling unnoticed onto her bodice. 'Your wife is not bravely yet. Yesterday was the first she went beyond the barmkin, and for only a short stroll. Even that taxing her beyond her strength. You cannot expect she will manage the ride to Newark.'

Margaret, surprised by the intervention, felt a pang of guilt that in her time at Hillhouse all she had noticed of Mistress Wallace was her rotting teeth and her carelessness at the table, the habit she had of picking at her scalp. Grateful for the respite from Newark, she had nevertheless been suspicious of the Wallaces' closeness to Maxwell and so had kept to her chamber more than had been strictly necessary, to avoid the need for social converse. Now, she shot a quick smile of thanks towards her hostess, receiving a wide gape in return.

Maxwell was on his feet. 'She managed to get here. She can manage home again. Though no doubt she will plead exhaustion on our arrival, a few days will see her right, I'm sure.' His mouth was set in a line that brooked no further protest, though his voice became smooth, the sweetness of honey in an insect trap. 'You will make yourself ready, my dear, we leave presently. I have no wish for delay.'

Strengthened by the knowledge of an ally in Mistress Wallace, Margaret drew up her shoulders, began to frame a refusal. 'I do not feel...'

'Your children need you.' His reply was emphatic, a trump card. 'They mope and whine like calves removed from their mother and I can listen no longer. If their behaviour had been other, perhaps you could have lazied yourself here for another week or two, which might have been more convenient all round. Though I have threatened them with a beating if they do not stop their nonsense, they continue to drive me mad and so home you must come.'

She was aware his words were calculated to frighten her into submission, his threats to the children likely for effect, carrying more of bluster than of substance; but they raised enough doubt in her mind to ensure acquiescence.

As they took their leave she turned to Mistress Wallace. 'I am grateful for your hospitality, and for the recuperation you allowed me.' Looking directly into Mistress Wallace's eyes for the first time, she saw a spark of fellow feeling. 'I am sorry I have not been more sociable. Perhaps...'

'Another time.' Mistress Wallace scraped at her head, scabs clinging to her nails, then extended her hand to Maxwell. 'If your husband will allow.'

Margaret saw by his stiffening that the barb had not passed him, saw too his reluctance to touch Mistress Wallace's fingers and smothered a smile, comforted by the growing suspicion that not only the comment, but the accompanying action had been entirely deliberate and designed for her husband's annoyance. She caught the twinkle in the old lady's eyes as Maxwell fulfilled the courtesies, bowing over her hand, a shared amusement that sustained her through the rant begun as soon as they were out of the barmkin.

'Hideous crone. It is to be hoped you have not acquired any of her habits in your time away.'

'I have not been long enough away to acquire anything. Though,' she couldn't resist the temptation to bait him, however foolish it might prove to be, 'as she was forever scraping and scratching at her head, I did have time to wonder if it was lice or the mange she had.'

Maxwell scrubbed his palm on his saddle blanket.

She allowed her hand to stray towards her own scalp. 'I have felt an itch myself since coming here. You would have done well to keep your distance until I had the opportunity to treat my hair.'

It was pleasing to see the effect of suggestion, as he scratched at his head. But little enough to compensate for the bruising she had received the previous evening.

'You would have done well to warn me, Madam; if I have caught anything, it is your blame.'

He sprang ahead of her, and with the increased pace, every bruise she carried, old and new alike, began to ache. Occupied with her own discomfort, it was some time before she realised the direction they took.

Maxwell half-turned in the saddle. 'It is but a small detour to Kilmaurs. I have some business with William Cunninghame. They will no doubt oblige us with a bite, but though we may delay long enough to sup, it is our own bed we lie in tonight. Or I do at least. You may have to make suffice with the bairn's chamber.'

She bent her head in acknowledgement, keeping her face still, ensuring no trace of a smile was apparent – pity she couldn't play on the possibility of unclean hair for more than a day or two at the most, but any respite was welcome, particularly after the recent mauling.

The stop at Kilmaurs proved tedious. Glencairn and his lady away, it was William alone who received them in the great hall. His eyes were red-rimmed, though his speech unslurred.

'Maxwell. And Margaret.'

Even the sound of her name on his lips made her stomach churn.

'This is an unexpected pleasure. I would have thought,' William's eyes swept from her throat to her waist and back again, as if in his head he undressed her, 'you would be looking to your latest bairn and not to gallivant. Still. It is to our advantage, if not to the child's.'

Margaret flushed, her fingernails digging slits across her palms. Knowing William's uncertain temper, especially with drink taken, she contented herself with, 'They are in good hands, and shall see us home today.'

'You do not stay then? What a pity.' He turned back to Maxwell, his dismissal of Margaret obvious. Straightening his doublet, picking off imaginary bits of fluff, he said, 'I have a good hawk which we might have flown this evening. I still can, of course, and it is a bird you would have enjoyed, for nothing he sets his mind to escapes him.'

'Like master, like bird, then?'

A glint of pride in William's face. 'Indeed. I am more

than satisfied.'

Maxwell had moved across to the window and was scanning the sky. A few wisps of cloud hung on the far horizon like stray clumps of sheep's wool.

'The weather looks to be set fair. Perhaps I could stay for a day or two. If,' he directed a glance at Margaret, who kept her gaze firmly fixed on the floor, lest her quickening hope might be noticed, 'you could spare a lad to escort my wife to Newark. She has not the stomach for hawking and has some necessary tasks to undertake besides.' His hand once again strayed to his head.

William strode to the door and bellowed. The lad who scurried up the stair had a bruise on his left cheek and a slight limp, but in the instant before he dropped his eyes Margaret read defiance, quickly masked.

'Saddle the roan and bring Mistress Maxwell's horse. You are to see her safe to Newark. But don't dally on the road home, for I have it timed to a nicety how long it should take.'

For the most part it was a silent ride, the air still, their only halt a pause to watch a hen harrier, the moorland echoing with its courtship call as it climbed and plummeted. The acrobatic display of spirals and twists reinforced Margaret's belief they belonged here, and free, not tied to a man's wrist. Margaret darted a look at the boy who rode beside her. That he was feart of William wasn't in doubt, and likely justified. The world, she thought, is ill-divided. And power a wicked thing. There were those, she supposed, who didn't abuse their position, though her

68

experience was otherwise. Glancing at the bruise on the lad's face, she thought of young Patrick, already the butt of Maxwell's scorn, and prayed she might be able to protect him. She increased her pace. A day alone with her children was aye a pleasure, the more so now for the miss of them this week past.

Despite Maxwell's absence, she felt Newark close around her as they rode into the barmkin, the gate a prison door clanging shut behind her. Nevertheless, she was mistress here, and so said as they dismounted, 'I wish to greet my children, but for all that William Cunninghame claims he has your journey timed, you must take some refreshment before your return.' However unused the lad might be to courtesy, as the bruises he carried suggested, he would receive it from her. To counter his obvious reluctance, and with a smile to soften the force, she said, 'I would take it as a slight if you were to leave without allowing me to offer you hospitality. The kitchens are in the basement, to the right. You will be well looked after there and I'll be with you shortly, to set you on your way.'

She heard the children before she saw them, shrieks issuing from the stable loft as she crossed towards the tower door. She paused, as always, and looked across the firth to the distant shore and the blue smudge of hills, their tops severed by cloud – someday, when the bairns were grown and safe, that was where she would go to find sanctuary, whatever the cost.

A head poked over the top half of the stable door and then it flew open, a small figure hurling herself at Margaret, almost knocking her off her feet. 'Mama!'

She hugged Meg to her, felt the fine bones, the warm flesh, breathed in the scent of horse and hay – it was for this she returned, for this she stayed. The shout had alerted young Patrick, who tumbled from the loft and lined up in front of her to give her formal welcome, his eyes alight, his pleasure unrestrained.

She conjured up a smile – this was how it could be, how it should be, if Maxwell were not his father. 'Hide and seek? In the stable? It's to be hoped you pay attention to your hiding places, else your clothes may be less than savoury.' She was teasing, but Patrick, always less sure, began to brush vigorously at his breeches. She caught at his hand, drew him close. 'It's no matter. What is important is to see you both fine and healthy and happy.' She was looking at the hem of Meg's skirt, which swung uneven above her ankle. 'You cannot have grown with me but a week away?'

Patrick snorted. 'She fell in the cesspit and had to be pulled out, *and* she lost a boot. Jean made her remove her clothes here, for all the world to see, and she wasn't allowed to set foot in the tower until she had been thoroughly dowsed. The dress has shrunk, but Jean says she must wear it still, that it be a lesson to her not to go where she is forbidden.'

Meg's face gained in colour, as if she worked up to a fight, so that Margaret, releasing Patrick, swallowed the amusement she felt and hunkered down to place her face level with the child's.

'Never mind, sweetheart, Jean will relent soon enough, if you can muster a hint of remorse. I have a dress I thought to have cut down for you anyway, for you would likely have had need of it before the summer is past. You are rather too quick for me, that is all.' As she stood up her sleeve fell back, exposing her wrist, mottled blue-black, and despite her hurried pulling at the material, she saw by Patrick's stiffening that he noted the bruising.

'You've seen Father then?'

'He collected me from Hillhouse and we rode together as far as Kilmaurs. He stays with William to go hawking. But I had more important folk to see.' The attempt to deflect him was unsuccessful.

'He should not use you so. You should not let him.'

'Hush, Patrick.' Margaret indicated Meg. 'It's best not talked of. I promise you,' she gripped his arm, 'it shall not be so always.'

'We could run away, all of us.'

Her gaze strayed to the shore, to the mountains beyond. 'We will. One day. Just not yet. When there is not a babe...'

'There will always be a babe ... until you are too old, or dead. What good will flight be then?'

He was but four years old, a child robbed of childhood. 'Enough.' She felt the instinctive flinch, softened her voice to remove the sting. 'Today should be a joyous thing.' She glanced up at the sky, at the high scudding clouds. 'I think the rain will hold off. We'll take our supper outside and make the most of the sunshine.'

Chapter 9

Arras lay in shadow as the small force approached from the south-east. It was Munro's fourth diversionary attack since his arrival with the French force at Amiens, and by far the most important. He called a halt at the edge of the woods, remained in their shelter. They were far enough away from the city itself to be out of any danger from guards manning the walls, yet near enough to see that the gateway leading to the old town remained open. He assessed the possibilities. Little likelihood of anyone being able to slip through the guards on the gate without challenge. And not worth the risk. He rehearsed in his mind his preliminary plan, based on the intelligences they had gathered of the layout and fortifications – in an hour or so the gate would shut for the night. Another hour and the city would slumber.

He thought of himself and his small party of raiders like a cloud of horse flies, a constant irritant to the Spanish forces, holding them in Arras and other of the towns north of Amiens, well away from their own besieging force. He turned, gestured to the youngest member of their party. 'We do nothing here until it is full dark. I will need five men.

For the rest, find a suitable place of concealment near the edge of the woods, but well enough hidden for safety.' The lad melted into the trees, leading his horse, his progress into the depths of the forest sure and silent. Munro nodded in satisfaction – though young, he was shaping up well. Leaving two men behind to keep an eye on the main gate, he sent a pair northwards to circle the city. 'Note the placement and numbers of guards on the wall and whether they appear careless in their duties. If Arras has any weak point save the river I wish to find it. But mind you aren't seen. Only those with something to hide fail to seek the protection of a city's walls when it is within reach.' He turned to the remaining man. 'You're with me.' They threaded westwards through the woods, following the jagged line of Arras' fortifications. The new arrowhead bastions which protected the inner city wall were impressive, the earthworks below them sharp-edged and imposing. There were two main gates to the old town, both of them well protected, likewise the original city walls, the ditch around them straight-sided and deep. Had there not been the extension of the city to enclose the abbey and surrounding grounds, Arras would have been well-nigh impregnable, to attempt any kind of assault likely a wasted effort even as a diversion. As it was, the junction between old and new provided the only point of vulnerability, and even that could scarcely be considered unprotected. He continued his reconnaissance, weighing up the pros and cons of a two-pronged versus a single assault. Whatever, it would have to be done in the space of one night, for in daylight they couldn't hope to conceal any attempt to undermine the walls. He scanned the sky, the cloud cover welcome. If Arras had a point of vulnerability, so did his plan. Moonlight the complication they could do without.

Returning, Munro found his men restive, edgy, their unease the familiar blend of anticipation and fear. Action of any sort was welcome after the long winter in barracks, and nipping at the Spaniard's heels far preferable to the digging of ditches and siege workings that was the lot of the main French force. He briefed them, and in twos and threes they disappeared. He had allowed two hours for those that were to attack from the northern side to reach their position. Even in darkness, the lack of tree cover for the last part of their journey was the main concern. Their only option to hug the base of the outer earthworks, taking especial care when passing under the two smaller gates leading to the abbey precincts. For men to pass unnoticed in the shadows was one thing, carrying the gunpowder and fuses and necessary tools another. The sacking to wrap them had been requisitioned from a sutler in the baggage train and was, he hoped, adequate. As he waited, Munro mentally tracked their passage through the marshland fringing the western side of the town, thankful the night was dry, minimising the danger of them getting bogged down. Once on the northern side, where marsh gave way to cultivated fields, their progress should be faster, if more risky, access to the culverted river relatively straightforward. He edged forward his own men, waiting until each man was swallowed up in the lee of the wall before sending the next across. Last of all the engineer, wading carefully to avoid the sound of splashing, the cask of saltpetre held above his head.

From his vantage point his men were no more than flickering shadows, a blessing some might say, though Munro, however much he wished for the French King's victory, had

74

the uncomfortable feeling that to expect blessing on any of the activities of war, whether in the cause of religion or not, was a presumption. A treacherous thought he banished instantly – there was a task to accomplish and no place in his head for philosophical musings. They had perhaps six hours, little enough time to do the job and regroup in good order.

Across the marshland he heard an owl cry. He counted the repetition, nodding in satisfaction at the third and final call, indicating the fires at the southern perimeter were set: piles of damp scrub ready to produce copious smoke. Another series of calls, this time from the west, indicating the archers were in place. And moments later the echo from the musketeers to the east. It was unlikely the muskets would do much real damage, Spanish armour of high quality and their distance from the walls nearer to four hundred yards than two, but still, surrounding gunfire would add to the illusion of attack and increase the tension for those guarding the city.

A faint splash to the left of Munro. He stiffened, relaxed again as a figure materialised at his elbow. 'Ready for the charges?' The engineer nodded, swung a pack onto his shoulder, melted back into the darkness. Munro followed him into the river, the chill of the water as it reached his thigh giving him pause, thankful his own load was firmly strapped to his back, well away from any danger of a soaking. He waded slowly, taking care to make as little noise as possible, keeping his senses tuned to the night noises all around him. The man in front had almost reached the shelter of the inner wall. A voice above them barked an order in Spanish; the engineer, startled, losing his footing. Munro saw him fight to keep his balance, to protect his load, and in so doing fell onto his knees in the water, the accompanying splash magnified in the silence. They froze.

Raised voices above them, one high-pitched, apprehensive, the other lower, insistent, and though his knowledge of Spanish was rudimentary, it was enough to know they argued over the sound. The spark of a tinder box, the flare of a candle settling into a steady glow. The unmistakeable snap of the nocking of an arrow onto a bowstring. For what seemed like hours they remained motionless, waiting to be caught in the lantern light playing across the surface of the water around them and flickering against the projecting wall. For the shot that would surely come of their carelessness. Three times the light probed the darkness, each sweep wider than the last, the final one touching the water inches from Munro's head.

To the left of him a moorhen protested, wings flapping. The light paused, returned, highlighting the dark body, the red beak, the twin flashes of white on the tail. A twang of the bowstring, the whisper of the arrow arcing downwards, the moorhen rising up and away. A laugh, another order, the light snuffed, the voices, now casual, fading away towards the right.

Munro exhaled, his legs shaking now that the immediate danger was past. The engineer was still on his knees, unmoving, and as Munro reached out to help him up, he toppled, the flight of the arrow that pierced his neck brushing Munro's arm. Munro caught and held him to avoid a second splash, his fingers groping for a pulse. Finding none, he rescued the charges, lowering the body into the water without a sound. He waded to the inner wall, leant against the cool stone, recovered his breath.

A touch on his arm, a chipped tooth grin, a murmur in his ear, 'Supper?'

'Saviour. I thought we were all done for.'

The soldier peered past him into the darkness, queried, 'Pierre?'

Munro shook his head, indicating the charges, and without a word the soldier reached for the load.

Into the silence an owl call. Munro's thrice-repeated response was swift, the answering call equally so. They inched along the wall towards the narrow junction point between old and new city. The soldier halted, turned, indicated the series of cavities packed with corned powder. Munro nodded, satisfied, and together they moved on into the covert, crouching, half-doubled over. Three more pauses to inspect cavities and to send each man back to the shelter of the wall. Munro came last, his movements slowed to compensate for lack of expertise, the task of adding the charges and inserting the fuse along the gap dug out of a line of mortar inches above the surface of the water fallen to him, the loss of the engineer a lack that might yet ruin the whole enterprise. He returned to the ditch, and straightening up, rolled his shoulders, edging along until he reached the waiting soldiers. Munro tapped the first man, the signal passing along the line. He counted as each faded into the darkness, their progress across the ditch marked only by the occasional faint splash, the engineer's earlier stumble and the raising of the moorhen perhaps a blessing after all. When all but one of the soldiers were safely away he made another series of owl calls, waiting for the echo, his head cocked. When it came, he and the remaining soldier, the young man who had earlier impressed him, were crouched, ready. It took three sparks for the match to flare, the youth protecting it as Munro held it to the fuse. A pause, a prayer, and the flicker of light travelling along the cord, disappearing into the culvert entrance and out of sight. Then it was their own retreat across the ditch, to light the final fuse to the charges set against the protecting bastion, before making for the cover of the woods. If the plan worked, good. If the charges failed there was nothing could be done. Either way they needed to retreat and fast.

The youth beside him stirred. 'Something's awry.' Munro reached out for his arm to steady him, a silent caution, but too late. He was weaving back across the marsh towards the lee of the bastion, clearly to check the final charge, his figure blending into the wall just as the first explosion came. In the flare of light Munro saw his body tossed high into the air, saw him land face down in the reeds before being buried under a rain of rubble. There was a low rumble from the river culvert, building in intensity, matched by clouds of smoke billowing from the fires to the south, which, rising in a pall, blew towards the new city. Three more explosions in quick succession and then from the far side of the junction between new and old the echo of others, the sound of one barely dying away before the next.

The city woke in a clamour of bells, those from the priory joined moments later by those of the cathedral. Lights flared along the walls, figures running in all directions, a rising cacophony of high-pitched shouting and barked orders punctuated by screams. From the west, fire-tipped arrows found their mark in buildings clustered against the inner wall, their success indicated by the flames which leapt into the night sky, plumes of black smoke adding to the general confusion. A touch on Munro's shoulder, his second-in-command looking around for the lad.

Munro shook his head. 'He was young, brave, foolhardy. It is a waste best not shared. Suffice it that he died setting charges, that he placed duty before safety.' There was a bitter edge to his voice. 'However misplaced.' A pause, another shake of his head. 'I should have stopped him.'

The soldier waved towards the smouldering city. 'It is a job well done. And any failure in it not your blame.'

Chapter 10

Whether it was the hawking that raised Maxwell's spirits or the drinking that followed, he sat in the solar at Kilmaurs, his legs stretched out towards the fire, becoming garrulous. With both Glencairn and his lady away, William, enjoying his temporary status as host, saw no reason to rein in his natural inclination to excess, and Maxwell was more than happy to match him. William, also clearly pleased with the way his hawk had performed, with the plump pigeons they had eaten for supper the least of what had been taken, was disposed to be generous with his advice.

'You should get a hawk.' He reached out and stroked the bird's head, murmuring. Maxwell, made brave by the drink and by William's obvious ease, followed his example, but pulled back sharply as the hawk fastened his beak on his finger, drawing blood.

William stroked the bird again, waving his other hand in a semblance of apology. 'He doesn't take easily to strangers. A characteristic of the breed. Get your own bird, young enough to train, and you'll see.'

Maxwell sucked on his finger, sufficiently drunk to

contemplate wringing the bird's neck, sufficiently sober to see the danger in such a thought. Self-preservation prevailing, he refrained from complaint and reached for more ale.

William became confiding, one arm around Maxwell's shoulder, his speech slurred. 'I have thoughts of taking a wife. A pretty one, and good in every sphere. If you catch my drift?'

Maxwell expelled his breath in a long sigh, shaking his head. 'They're no good if they're fractious, I can tell you that.'

'Margaret?' A sly smile stretched William's face. 'She's good for one thing at any rate. How many bairns has she dropped now?'

Maxwell poured himself another drink, became confiding in his turn. 'Four, but only three of them healthy, and two of them girls. I had higher hopes of her, for she does not come of a weakly family, but we are not done yet.' He pursed his lips. 'The boy is somewhat lacking, not in physique, in that he follows me, but in spirit, and with a timidity I could wish his mother shared. Of late she has begun to show a mind of her own, and that I will not tolerate.'

'And neither should you. It is not for a wife to doubt her husband's judgement.'

Maxwell flushed, recognising the implied criticism. 'I can manage my own house.' He blinked, as if to clear his vision, admitted, 'Though I sent her to Hillhouse when my mother was expected, for fear that she might speak out of turn.' He hesitated, and the drink talking, added, 'Which may have been a mistake.'

William was dismissive. 'What could she get up to there, with only the old witch for company?'

'Witch indeed, if appearance is anything to go by,

81

and interfering with it. At least she tried to be.' Maxwell slapped his hand on his thigh. 'But I took no nonsense from her, whipping Margaret away when it suited me, despite their protests, and from under the nose of some wise woman they'd brought in to see to her.'

'A wise woman? Any longer in their company and your wife might have been drawn into their ranks. Three witches together makes a quorum, or so they say.'

Maxwell, his head fuzzy, was dimly aware there was something out of kilter in William's words, an insult that fully sober he might have taken exception to, but refilling his ale once more, he fixed instead on the scene at Hillhouse and the vague unease it had produced in him.

'Have you heard tell of a widow-woman in Irvine with a knowledge of herbs and the like and enough of a reputation that the Douglases would send for her?'

William, aye alert at the mention of 'woman', said, 'A widow, eh? They bring the benefits of experience. Or so I've found. Is she pretty? With spirit?'

Maxwell puckered his forehead, tried to picture her clearly, but all he could remember was dowdy clothing and tightly scraped hair hidden under a plain bonnet. 'Not that I noticed. Though she had a familiarity.'

'Seen her in a bawdy house perhaps?'

'A mouse of a thing: unlikely. And thin with it. Not much to get a hold of. I don't imagine she would give much satisfaction. But there was something about her, a look of someone, if I could only think of who. Her daughter had it also, as well as an insolence in the set of her head.'

'Her sort aye have the same look about them.' William made a vague wave of his hand. 'If she'd been a redhead now ... I might have found her of interest.'

Maxwell, still probing his memory through the fug of ale, found an indistinct image of a girl's face, framed by a few strands of auburn hair escaping from her cap. 'The daughter was a redhead,' he mumbled, 'I think…' He was only half-listening to William, William not at all to him, for he was past the maudlin stage and complaining about some girl and a theft and how it was all the fault of Munro, dead these six years past and good riddance to him…

The mention of Munro triggered something else at the edge of Maxwell's consciousness. He shook his head to try to clear it, to blank out the pounding that felt as if a hundred horsemen thundered by.

Without warning he was back in Edinburgh, at the Queen's entry, the cacophony of sound overlaid by a cool taunting voice. 'The Montgomeries must be high in favour.'

He took hold of William's arm. 'Munro's wife. That's who she reminded me of.'

'Who reminded you of who?' William shook him off, as if he took Maxwell's familiarity as an affront.

'The wise woman. From Irvine. She had the sound of Kate Munro.'

'Kate Munro is dead these six years, with her lout of a husband and the brats.' William licked his lips as if in pleasure at the memory. 'All courtesy of reivers. Saved us the bother, and the repercussions. Though,' it was as if something tugged at William's memory also, 'they did have a bairn, red-headed and feisty. She was but a wee bit thing when I saw her,' he rubbed at his shin with his boot, 'and though with a temper to match her hair, I had room to regret *her* passing.'

'A sister, or cousin perhaps?' Maxwell was worrying at the thought like a dog with a bone, unwilling to give it up, unaware of William's increasing irritation, which had sobered him sufficiently to follow Maxwell's train of thought.

'There are none. Ask my father. If there had been it would have been a mite more difficult to reclaim Broomelaw, though much good that has done us, for it lies a ruin still. It is rather too far a distance to trust to builders without supervision, and though I have agitated often, Father keeps putting the restoration off. I would have liked fine to live at Broomelaw while I wait out his demise. It would have been a fitting end to a troublesome family to take their place. Though likely it would require considerable enlargement.'

'You had confirmation of their deaths?'

'Bodies, charred to a cinder as they slept. Is that confirmation enough for you?' Maxwell, recognising the danger signs in William's tone, nodded as if in agreement. William continued, 'Forget it. She cannot be a Munro. What's in a voice? No doubt there are a thousand like her among the common folk.' He returned to fondling the hawk, who opened one eye and shifted his grip on the perch. 'Tomorrow is set to be fair, and if you do not deeve me further with foolish notions, I may let you try your hand with the bird.'

Chapter 11

Without Maxwell's presence there was a holiday atmosphere at Newark, Margaret and the children taking advantage of the fine weather to explore the Clyde shore at low tide. She stationed herself in a sheltered hollow on the grass while the children clambered over the rocks, Meg guddling in the rock pools, Patrick going as far out as possible to fish for minnows with a pin attached to a rod fashioned from a stem of birch. The result a few sprats he relocated in a pool near the high-water mark, his pride in his catch obvious. The childish act gave Margaret pleasure, for it was little enough opportunity either of the children had to play without fear of censure. And when Patrick asked if they might go down to the docks at Greenock to see the fishing fleet unloading their cargo, it was a whim she was minded to indulge. It had been many months since she had taken a cart down into the town, and by the time they reached the hill overlooking the harbour she found herself pleased on her own account to be out and about again and among folk who had no notion of her circumstances, and who wouldn't look on her with carefully concealed pity. It was an unexpected freedom she determined to make the most of, for the day at least.

It was busier than she expected, and she held tight to Meg lest the child should lose her footing and topple into the murky water lapping the harbour wall. Patrick was harder to contain, disappearing here and there, returning every few minutes with some further excitement to report. His main interests lay in the creels of antenna-waving, claw-snapping lobsters hoisted up from the ships' holds and tipped into seawater-filled vats to await purchase; in the men who sat cross-legged mending their nets which sprawled over the cobbles around their feet; and in the masts and sails and ropes, coiled like sleeping snakes. Meg, too, was eager to see everything, but, lacking in serious interest, was keen to keep moving, so that Margaret was grateful for Jean's forethought in pressing a pouch containing comfits into her hand as they left. On the landward side of the harbour a market was in full flow, fleshers and baxters vying with costermongers, the praise of their own goods, the mis-crying of others, largely good-humoured. Here and there an apothecary peddled cures for everything from carbuncles to kidney stones, their claims, it seemed, ever more extravagant. Further back, away from the reek and the dirt, the clothiers and cutlers and cordiners, their stalls piled high, and beyond them a barber, pulling teeth, his latest victim tied to the chair that he might not move. Margaret rummaged in the pouch, chose the two biggest comfits, held one out to Meg. 'There, one for now, and if you can stay still for five minutes and not touch while I examine this cloth, there will be another one after.' She turned to examine a bale of shot silk, running it through her fingers, twisting it in the light to reveal the hidden colours, pinning and tucking in her mind, thinking of length and width and the lie of the cloth. It was long enough since she'd a new gown, and though foolish perhaps to think on it now, the babe but five weeks old, her figure not as it should be, yet…

The voice behind her, as unwelcome as a shower of rain.

'Well, wife, is this what you do when I am not here? I do not recollect giving assent to a frittering of money and time.'

The contrast between her usual pent-up frustration and her enjoyment of the morning's jaunt rendered her reckless.

'It is not your money I think to spend, but only a small fraction of what I brought to this marriage. And as for time, there are plenty of wives of our acquaintance who are abroad much more than I.'

'As for time,' he mimicked her. 'Other wives answer to their own husbands, as you should to me. And whatever you brought to the marriage it is mine by law to dispose of as I see fit.'

Meg's hand found hers, gripped tight. Defeated her. She allowed the cloth to slip from her fingers and cast a quick, apologetic glance at the stallholder who had halted in his patter to watch their altercation. 'The cart is tethered by the wall yonder. We were almost ready for home. Though I thought to pick up herrings for supper while we were here … if you will not think *that* a waste of time?'

She knew it was unwise, that she would likely suffer later for baiting him, but she did not need to anger him to receive the force of his hand, and even a minor rebellion felt like a triumph.

Young Patrick appeared at her side, as if he too had sensed danger, Maxwell's face darkening as the boy stepped between them.

'Your mother requires herrings. See you to it. And be quick about it, for I am fair hungered and have no wish to wait any longer than I need for my supper.'

Margaret groped for her purse, held out two coins, attempted to soften Maxwell's command. 'Don't feel you have to take from the first boat. A few minutes spent looking will be well spent, that you are not fobbed off with the smallest of the catch.'

The herrings bought, from the boat nearest to hand despite Margaret's stricture, Maxwell handed them all into the cart and tossed the reins at Patrick.

'I shall expect you home presently and in good shape.'

Maxwell's mood did not improve as the day progressed. The children kept out of his way and for that Margaret was grateful, for though it was true he had not as yet physically abused them, nevertheless while he was in their company they were constantly on edge, and Margaret with them. She ached to see Patrick in particular withdrawing into himself, startling at the smallest noise, a wary expression in his eyes. There was more than one kind of cruelty, and the physical not necessarily the worst. What Maxwell's breaking point would be was hard to gauge, and so she watched, powerless to advise, as the children trod on eggshells around him.

After supper, having drunk more than was good for either his health or his temper, he began to disparage first

88

their near neighbours and then, running out of folk there, turned to wider afield. Margaret was barely listening, for it was not an unusual occurrence, but mention of the Montgomeries caught her attention.

'Hugh, he that is married on Elizabeth Shaw, now there is a jumped-up creature if ever I saw one, and uncouth with it. He struts about the court as if one of the King's favourites, making much of his connections.' A candle in the tall sconce by the hearth flickered and died. He focused on it for a moment, said, 'He was here once, and offensive. I had him on the run, but that another fellow intervened, name of Munro, who should have known better for he was a follower of Glencairn and therefore with no business protecting a Montgomerie.' He was staring into the fire, as if he saw in it a remembrance of the thing. 'I saw them off. Not that Munro lived long thereafter, for they were attacked by reivers, and the lot of them wiped out, or so William claims. And good riddance.'

He waved his tankard at her for a refill, Margaret quick to oblige, for if he became sufficiently drunk he might be incapable and thus spare her his attentions. He was beginning to ramble, moving on to talk of the Cunninghames, which, though it didn't improve his temper, at least kept him from thinking of others closer to home.

'That wise woman. Who was she? How did you find her?' His head was buried in his tankard so that he mumbled, but she had an instinct that the questions were of more serious import than it might appear.

'What? Oh...' she was dismissive, 'Mistress Wallace heard tell of her. She has gained a reputation for women's problems.'

'A midwife then? I thought she had a sly look about

her, they aye seek to close ranks and keep a husband from his due. Well, you're home now and won't be needing her attentions any more.' He took another swig of ale, slopped it down his jerkin, wiped it in with his sleeve. A moment's silence before he stirred, began again. 'Are you sure we've not seen her before? I thought she had a familiar look.'

'I'd never met her before, so why would you?' Belatedly she recognised the danger of turning the question against him and drew it back to herself. 'Each time I have had need of a midwife it was to Greenock you sent.' She weighed up the risks, decided to chance a further comment, in the hope it would take his attention away from the recent past. 'If you have seen her, it must be other than here; before our marriage perhaps.'

As soon as the word 'marriage' was out of her mouth she regretted it, her stomach turning at the smile sliding across his face. The last thing she wanted was him maudlin.

'That was a fine night.' The smile faded. 'Though you haven't been so welcoming of late. The bairn is five weeks now, it is high time.'

He began to paw at her neck and she remained still, knowing from experience that resistance would inflame him further. She tried another attempt at distraction.

'Perhaps she has the look of someone else,' and, with an inward apology to Kate, 'Those of her class are much of a muchness in appearance and dress.'

He was worrying at it, ferret-like, refusing to let it go. 'There was something ... a look of Munro's wife ... and a right besom she was too ... every bit as uncouth as her husband and with as little respect for those of higher station.'

It was the second time he had mentioned the name

Munro. She tried to sound merely conversational. 'The family that fell foul of reivers?'

'That William says fell foul of reivers, but I wonder...'

In her head Kate's voice, 'There are reasons I cannot come to Newark...' – Yet she had offered friendship and support, risky surely if there had been a connection. A shiver ran through her: Kate hadn't known who she was, not the first time. But she'd returned. A bravery perhaps that deserved recognition.

Maxwell waved his tankard at her, growled, 'Am I not entitled to a wife to fill my cup?' As she poured for him he grasped her wrist. 'And take one for yourself. You're aye abstemious and could do with a little loosening.'

Knowing it would be unwise to rouse him, she acquiesced, sought to calculate how long it might be before he drank himself under the table and if she could keep him here long enough for that. He was mumbling again, talking into his drink, back on the track of the Munros.

'I'll find her out. If she has any connection to Broomelaw there will be someone who knows. A merk or two spread about and I shall have her.' He became expansive. 'William doesn't know everything, though he may think it ... but I'll show him I have a trick or two. That hawk of his, she's a fine bird, and it was good hunting we had, but money hunts also...' His eyes were beginning to glaze, his mouth to slacken. He roused himself twice more, lifted the tankard to his lips, repeated, 'Oh yes ... money hunts...' before his head dropped and the tankard tipped sideways into Margaret's waiting hand.

Chapter 12

The wind that had been southerly for weeks, bringing an early flush of growth, the sheltered valleys lush with fresh grass, the hillsides greening, swung round to the north, in its tail an unwelcome return to winter. Flurries of hail and sleet at Irvine become driving snow at Braidstane, piling in drifts against the barmkin wall, and filling up the barmkin itself, so that they had to carve out paths four feet deep else they would all have been confined indoors. For the children, traversing the barmkin between castle and bastle house was an adventure, travelling through the roofless tunnel of ice, carving patterns and shapes into the packed snow and etching their initials deep into the tunnel walls. Hugh, with Robbie to help him, battled to gather the stock, which had but lately been released onto the slopes around the tower, and bring them back inside. It was a grim task, probing the drifts with a pole searching for buried ewes and lambs, the numbers they brought home scarcely out-numbering those they left where they found them, frozen and lifeless. Packing those they could into the byres was itself a fearsome thing, for disease increased the longer they were kept in close confine; yet to leave them outside was unthinkable. There were aye lambs too small or too feeble to survive, others that found their way into a ditch and, trapped in the puddles of water lying in the bottom, died for lack of rescue. These Hugh accepted as the natural run of things, and though each one a disappointment, most years the losses were no more than should be expected. But this unseasonable weather, coming hard on the heels of the lambing, was a force that couldn't be reckoned with, the consequences severe.

Robbie, for once with more to do than hours in the day, worked with a will beside Hugh from first light until dusk, Kate, though she shared in the distress of the loss of the stock, taking comfort in the occupation it gave him. With little time to eat, and no time for leisure, it seemed all thought of France was buried under the weight of the work required at home. In other circumstances, when remaining indoors was a matter of choice, the bastle house seemed roomy enough, but as the days wore on, the weather failed to improve and, journeys outside limited to those of necessity, irritations built. The bairns had less than usual tolerance and a tendency to exaggerate the smallest of ills. Kate, unable to venture beyond the narrow confines of Braidstane, spent more and more time with the Montgomeries, despite a nagging sense of guilt that the added pressure of her family's presence shrank the available space in the tower house also. A feeling Elizabeth, with a perception likely borne of her own early days when she first came as a wife to Braidstane, seemed at pains to dispel.

'How good it is to have another female to talk to. Hugh isn't the best of company the now, and with good reason, so that I cannot find it in me to chide him, though it doesn't make for comfortable conversation. It is at times like these I most miss Grizel. And sorry as I am for the necessity that brought you to our door, I am grateful for your company.'

The thought of Grizel was a welcome distraction. 'Have you heard from her? The trade from Norway should be well under way by now, for Sigurd was never one to hold back when the season changed.'

'I did think we would've had news by now, but perhaps Flekkefjord is still winter-bound. Grizel talked of making a visit so soon as spring came; it is word of that I wait for.'

'Perhaps the visit will come before the word. I'd like fine to see Grizel again. And her bairns.'

'Aye, though there is noise enough here times without the addition of another three to supplement it, and the smallest but a babe. That is,' Elizabeth pulled at a loose thread on her bodice, 'if all remains well.'

'Why should it not? The first two are healthy enough.'

Above their heads, a scream and a clatter. 'I grant you the noise of extra bairns, but the fighting would likely be less.' Kate glanced upwards at the ceiling. 'At least that was how I found it when we had visitors at Broomelaw; bairns aye squabble more within their own family than with other children.'

'You have the right of it. And it is one of the blessings of having you here. Though,' the corners of Elizabeth's mouth lifted, 'your bairns are now so nearly family, the effect is lessening.'

'And I am grateful...' It was a serious reply to a comment made half in jest, Elizabeth responding in kind.

'This thing with Robbie, it will turn out, and for the better, I'm sure. He has grown up almost without our noticing, and once he is properly a man, a jaunt to France may be just what is needed. When my brother went to the college at Glasgow it made all the difference to him. Boys need their freedom and a chance to spread their wings. John envied Hugh, that I do know, and would have gone himself to the armies of Europe if Father had not put pressure on him to learn the business. It took him long enough to agree, and it might not have been possible at all had he not been allowed to take over most of the travelling. Letting him loose in Holland, even if only to trade, anchored him at home, so that when he is in Greenock it is by choice and not forced, and he is the more settled for it. So it may be with Robbie. Especially if the quarters he encounters on his travels are less than comfortable. And from the tales Hugh told, army barracks are rather less than palaces. It will give him more of an appreciation of the value of what he has at home.'

It was kindly meant and so Kate took it, smiling her thanks, even though what Elizabeth had *not* said lay between them: that in Hugh the desire for adventure had never subsided, his frequent jaunts to court but a poor outlet for his energies; an unacknowledged ache she knew Elizabeth found impossible to dispel. In the pause that followed she debated with herself, and then, with an almost imperceptible stiffening in her shoulders, said, 'It wasn't Robbie I thought on…'

'Munro and Patrick are well able…'

'It's not them either.' Kate hesitated, for once aired, it would be a problem that touched them all. 'There is another issue. At Hillhouse I had an encounter I would rather have avoided.'

Elizabeth's renewed wariness matched her own. 'Who…?'

'Patrick Maxwell. Of Newark. It was his wife I treated,

95

though if I had known at the outset I would likely not have gone.'

'But you went back?'

'He wasn't there the first time, nor expected. And seeing what she suffered and knowing I had medicines to provide relief, I couldn't in all conscience avoid to return.' Kate was twisting at a curl of escaped hair. 'I didn't take to Maxwell when I met him in Edinburgh at the Queen's entry, and I like him less now. He is arrogant and a bully and, I believe, a risk to her health. If it were not for her bairns … there are times when I think allowing someone to die may be the kindest course.'

'You cannot really think that?'

Kate heard the genuine shock in Elizabeth's voice. 'I have no desire to be other than a good Christian, but sometimes, when the suffering is great, it is all I can do to stamp on the idea as the devil's thought it is.'

'How many Maxwell bairns are there?' It was a transparent attempt to bring Kate back to solid ground.

'Three, though I gather there is no pleasure for her in the getting of them, and it appears Maxwell looks for a quiverful. It was as I was leaving the second time he appeared, and was no more pleasant than I remembered him.'

'He didn't recognise you?'

'Not then, though he did suggest a familiarity about me, which his wife dismissed as being preposterous, citing my lesser status and therefore out of his orbit. I was glad of her intervention, though I think she felt guilty at the disparagement, but I have feared since he would think on it further, and my crossing swords with William in Edinburgh come back to haunt me.'

'Your visit to Hillhouse was almost three weeks ago. If

96

Maxwell recognised you, if he had troubled to think on it further, if anything had come of his thinking, there would surely have been repercussions by now. It was a dangerous moment, but you are still here and unchallenged, and may be all the safer for it.'

Kate looked towards the window, to the leaden sky holding the promise of more snow to come, and buried the thought that Maxwell's lack of action might just as easily be explained by the weather.

From above, the sound of a slap and a wail, Maggie's voice, though indistinct, clearly attempting to calm some trouble between the Montgomerie girls.

Elizabeth glanced upwards. 'Maggie has fair come on in these last weeks. Just the thought of helping you has given her sense beyond her years. It is a young lady she is now and not a bairn.'

'I know. And this weather, it is the ideal opportunity to take her through the remedies in the storeroom and see if her interest is more than passing.'

'Tested remedies only? Or some of your more experimental notions?'

Kate laughed. 'There would be little point in only telling her what she might easily learn from any apothecary. It is some of my "experimental notions", as you call them, that have given me my reputation. Though in fairness, I confess to you, if not to others, they are not, for the most part, my notions, but rather ideas that have been tried and tested elsewhere. As you know, I have Hugh's brother to thank for much of my knowledge. It is only that we are in a backwater here that what I do seems new. But at times it is easier to take the credit than to admit to foreign and thus dangerous ideas.'

Maggie was perched on the workbench as Kate lifted down bottle after bottle from the shelves that lined the storeroom. As she handled each one Kate kept up a stream of information: uses, dosage, contra-indications, possible effects, good and bad. She could see Maggie's enthusiasm growing, so felt the need to sound a note of caution. 'It is sometimes better, aye and safer too, to avoid to treat if you cannot be sure of the outcome, at least as far as less serious ailments are concerned. Better to admit a lack of knowledge than to promise what cannot be delivered.'

'But...' Maggie was clearly thinking this through for herself, trying to marry it up to what she knew of her mother's practice. Kate, aware of how her mind was running, said, 'If the patient will die without my intervention, then it is worth trying anything at all, even without much hope. But in those cases I do not hide the dangers, nor exaggerate the chances for improvement. There are always those who will blame you whatever the circumstance, but most folk, I find, can see reason, at least once they are past the first shock.'

'But you are more cautious with minor ailments?'

'There is little point in making a minor problem worse by the wrong treatment. And there are times when I find it best to do nothing at all and allow nature to take its course.'

'Does that not harm your reputation?'

'Most would rather an honesty from the start. I lose little by offering encouragement that the ill will be sorted without treatment, especially when money is tight. Folk appreciate not being cheated out of a groat or two.' She lifted a larger than average jar down from a shelf. It was half-full of a brown liquid with a layer of silt on the bottom. 'But for others this is surprisingly efficacious.'

Maggie was peering at the label on the bottle, deciphering the Latin tag, incredulity spreading across her face.

Kate pre-empted her. 'It may have the whiff of chicanery about it, yet there are occasions when a patient will get better the quicker for the taking of such a remedy, though it be nothing more than bog water.'

Maggie shook the bottle, dispersing the silt through the water, her dissatisfaction clear. 'Does it work better for looking foul? And why keep a jar when it can be got fresh any day of the week?'

'And have someone come for a remedy and make them wait while I run up onto the moors? A consolation only works when the patient does not recognise it as such.'

'But you charge.'

'To those who can afford it, yes. How can I not? If I were to prescribe it without charge, other of my medicines would be thought equally valueless.' Kate, aware this was a moment of crisis, that it was essential she restore Maggie's confidence, in her and in her trade, said, 'Sometimes treating the mind is as useful as treating the body. I do not peddle bog water unless I am convinced the need for it is real, even if the perceived ailment is not.'

Maggie took the jar and shoved it back on the shelf, her whole demeanour confirming Kate's suspicion that what she wanted was to be able to perform miracles, to cure real, not imagined ills, and bog water with no place in her plans. She prepared to convince her otherwise. Over the next few days they spent fruitful hours in the storeroom, while the weather howled about them, Maggie's questions indicating a level of understanding that cheered Kate. The cherished mother-child relationship faded, replaced by the promise of a new companionship, and with it the realisation that the passage of years wasn't all loss. Maggie's was an interest far beyond anything Robbie had ever showed, and Kate reluctantly had to concede, to herself first, and then in the privacy of the solar to Elizabeth, that her hopes for him had been built on the sand of her own desires, his ambitions lying far beyond her control.

But at night, hugging the stone pig that warmed her bed, she found her thoughts turning more and more to Robbie. And to the five-month respite she had gained, which by day stretched far ahead, but at night shrank to no time at all and, sleep eluding her, imagined all manner of ills. Fear for him almost displacing her worries for Munro.

Elizabeth, when she confided in her, was characteristically brisk. 'You do not diminish Munro by concern for his children.' She narrowed her eyes, as if to defy contradiction. 'You will not forget him. I saw from the first that you were life and soul to each other. Distance does not change that. Nor, I think, time.'

Chapter 13

It should have been a call much like any other. And so it began. Kate was tamping down the fire for the night, spreading the logs in the hearth, trickling water on them to douse the remaining flames. Though the heat would have been welcome, the fear of a stray spark far outweighed the additional comfort of allowing the fire to burn itself out. She started at the hammering on the door, moved to the window, squinted out. Behind her, Maggie, stumbling down the ladder from the attic, was rubbing sleep from her eyes, questioning, 'Who is it?'

'A call likely.' To the lad who stood on the doorstep, she said, 'There is no need to break either your fist or our door. Who is it you seek?'

He was tall, though slight, dishevelled, with an air of the exotic about him, a gold ring in one ear, his longer than average hair plastered to his face by sweat. His breathing came in short gasps, and Kate, ignoring his protest, led him to the table and filled a tankard of ale, though she couldn't persuade him to take a seat.

He looked from Kate to Maggie, who, as if belatedly

aware of her state of undress, pulled her shawl close around her.

'I am come from Irvine, to fetch Mistress Grant, if she will come. We have two men with gunshot wounds gone bad.'

Kate said, 'I am Mistress Grant. How long since the injuries were got?'

'Four days.'

A familiar frustration showed in her face, a frustration he clearly recognised, for he added hastily, 'We are a ship's company and were making up the west coast when we were overtaken by a pirate vessel, English by the cut of it.' He made to spit, swallowed it down. Despite his agitation she heard the pride in his voice.

'We gave good account of ourselves and got away, but not without injury. The captain thought we could make it to Glasgow and so we might have done, but that first one and then the second man took bad and so we waited only for the first chance we could find of a safe berth...'

She didn't wait for him to finish, her initial flare of anger at hearing of the length of time before they called for help dispelled by the circumstance. Replaced by the bleak thought that, however speedily she made it now, it would likely be too late. 'I'll be but a few minutes gathering what I need. Take your drink, you need it.'

Maggie said, 'I'll see to the horses.'

Kate hesitated, thought of refusal, but Maggie, already part way up the attic ladder, forestalled her.

'Much use me learning of remedies with no opportunity to see the conditions they are designed to treat.'

'It won't be pleasant, mind.'

'I know that.' Maggie spoke in a you-don't-need-to-tell-me

102

voice. 'But if I am to be of any use to you, I must be ready to face unpleasantness, and besides, I've never been the most squeamish.' There was a hint of scorn. 'Not half as much as Robbie.'

'All right, be as quick as you can.'

The ride to Irvine in the half-dark was as swift as they could manage, which was not swift at all, the ground treacherous, the snow banked up in the lanes freezing in the ruts, the horses slithering and skidding, their shoes sparking on the ice. The moon, though partially obscured by cloud, gave just sufficient light to make the journey possible. Kate, aware of the dangers of the terrain, held her mount firmly in check, despite the need for haste. To have a horse take a fall, not unlikely in the conditions, would be unhelpful at the very least, and maybe disastrous. And so it proved.

They were close to Irvine, the smell of seaweed and salt in the air, when the track turned sharply to the left. Maggie, less experienced than Kate, pulled her horse round a fraction too quickly, and resisting, it skittered sideways, one front hoof catching on the edge of a rut. The crack as he went down as loud as a pistol shot.

The lad, who had been a fraction ahead, pulled up and swivelled in the saddle, fear in his face, the threat of ambush clearly on his mind.

Kate, recognising it, said, 'It wasn't a gunshot.' Maggie, who had managed to slide clear, was on her knees by the horse's head, tears spilling down her cheeks. Kate, her own distress firmly in check, knelt beside her, oblivious to the dampness seeping through her skirts. She ran her hand down the cannon bone, found the jagged edge, and seeing the pain in the horse's eyes, knew there was only one thing

103

to be done. She scrambled to her feet, turned to the lad who stood over them. 'You have a pistol?'

He reached into his jerkin, withdrew the gun, as Maggie, leaping up, grabbed his arm and tried to wrest it from him. 'No!'

'We have no choice.' Kate grasped Maggie's shoulders, pulled her back. 'The leg is broken. Would you wish for Blackie to suffer?' Then, to the lad, 'I'll hold his head.'

'I'll do it.' Maggie freed herself from Kate's grip, dropped to her knees again, cradled the horse's head in her lap, burying her face against the horse's neck.

Kate gave her a moment then nodded at the lad. Maggie was crying in earnest now as she slid back, and taking Blackie's face in both hands, braced herself for the shot. It felt wrong to leave him lying by the side of the track, and as they remounted, the lad handing Maggie up behind Kate, she determined for Maggie's sake to take a different route home once their task was done.

The lad's horse, of a lesser quality than the average hired mount and already tired by the outward journey, faded as they reached the outskirts of the town, so that he was forced to walk the last quarter of a mile or so and was clearly relieved when they reached the ostler's yard.

Kate and Maggie dismounted to leave their one remaining horse in the ostler's care, though Kate's cursory glance into the yard left her in no doubt of his shortcomings. He would likely blame the weather for the careless feeling pervading the yard, but himself slovenly, she felt the need to be specific in her instructions.

'Give him a light feed and water only. We'll likely not return for him tonight, but if we do, I don't wish for him to be sluggish on account of a stomach swelled with oats. If you do not see us by midnight, provide clean bedding and a stronger feed to settle him for the night, and look for us in the forenoon. We will pay whatever is necessary then.'

'Ye'll pay the now.' He stood in the gateway, clearly unwilling to let them go before money changed hands. 'For the night and all, in case of it being necessary.' He spat, as if to emphasise his lack of trust, the gob of spittle blending into the glaur of the yard. 'I dinna give credit, not to my regulars, not to you.'

Kate suppressed her anger and scrabbled in her purse for coins which she dropped into his outstretched hand, and not waiting for him to test their metal, pushed past. 'See that you follow my instructions and do not think to lock us out before midnight, or we will make such a racket as will have all your neighbours cursing you.' She turned on her heel. 'Come, Maggie, we have wasted enough time as it is.' On the lane leading to the harbour she quizzed the lad as to the men's injuries – whether of shot or ball, clean through or remaining in the wounds, what treatment, if any, had been given. And set her teeth not to react to what she heard.

'We couldn't do much at the start, for we were occupied with outrunning the ship that preyed on us, and might not have succeeded except that, being smaller, when the wind dropped a mite we could still take advantage of what remained, while they could not. But it was twelve hours before we left them behind.'

Kate cut him off. 'Never mind the reasons, just tell me what wounds they have, and what has been done.'

'In one the ball went into his shoulder and is lodged somewhere, carrying jerkin and shirt with it. He suffers with a high fever that will not abate.'

105

'Is there inflammation? Heightened colour? Does he complain of aches?'

His voice was uneven. 'He complains of nothing, for he is barely conscious, bar a constant tossing and turning and a moaning, but the skin all around the wound is up like a cow's dug with the heat, and as red, and if you so much as come near it to lift the dressing, he screams like a stuck pig. As for the other, his seemed a clean wound, the ball straight through his leg, and the captain said once cauterised he stood a chance of little more than a limp, but last evening...' he ground his palm with his thumb, 'he also seemed to take a turn for the bad. We were right glad to come in sight of the town, that we could seek help for them both.'

'Cauterised?' A familiar pit opened in Kate's stomach. 'With what?' She knew the answer before she asked it, for it wasn't the first time she had been called to a gunshot wound. It was aye the same, failing a national peril, men honed their skills by warring with their neighbours and sometimes over the most trivial of matters if they didn't have a more deep-seated cause, and there were plenty of them. Their own ills the evidence of one such. She dragged her thoughts away from the Cunninghames and back to the job in hand. However barbaric she thought it to pour boiling oil into an open wound, and the patient as likely to die of the treatment as of the original injury, the practice remained. It was often only with reluctance she would be allowed to try her own more gentle remedy: a healing salve of egg white, oil of roses and turpentine; and that usually when considerable damage had already been done. The frustrating thing: if the patient died it was her treatment the cause of it, if they lived, her only credit that she had not done any harm with her new thinking.

The lad was quick to answer, as if he sought to justify his captain and the whole crew. 'As soon as he felt it safe to turn our attention to other than the danger of pursuit, the captain set the cook to heating the oil and attended to their wounds himself.' He faltered, which Kate mistakenly thought a reaction to her instinctive flinch. 'I was asked to help to hold them down but,' he paused as if struggling for words, then in a rush, 'to my shame I fainted. I am determined not to be so weak again.'

The bravado in him, the obvious desire to redeem himself should they think him feeble, cut Kate, for he was not much past Maggie's age. She choose her words carefully, so as not to patronise him. 'It is no shame to faint at such a moment, and the treatment, though done in good part, is more the killer than the cure.' It took an effort to keep the anger out of her voice, for whoever else she might hold responsible, it wasn't the lad's blame. She quickened her pace, searching for a word of reassurance, however hollow. 'The sooner I can apply a salve the better the chance I may be able to moderate the damage done.'

The stench was indescribable. A mingling of tar and tallow, stinking bilges and sweat, and overlaying it all, burnt flesh and putrefaction. Kate, used to most of it in varying combinations, nevertheless found herself needing to suppress a retching as they followed the captain through the hatch leading below. Maggie, though game enough, was unprepared and, her stomach heaving, fled back onto the deck. When she reappeared a few minutes later her face

107

was ashen, but she climbed down steadily enough, with an apology for her lapse.

The captain, who had stood at the head of the rope ladder to help them aboard when the skiff bumped against the boat's planking, shrugged, as if to indicate lack of surprise at her weakness, and Kate felt a surge of anger, expressed in sarcasm.

'No doubt all your men aye keep the contents of their stomachs, stench or no.'

He regarded her from under heavy-lidded eyes, his expression unreadable, and made no reply, which served only to increase her irritation – it was a brave thing for Maggie to come at all. She was tempted to remind him that there were many who would have refused to venture out in such weather and at such an hour, but the urgency of the matter overrode her personal feelings, so that she bit her tongue and contented herself with smiling encouragement at Maggie.

The captain's hair and beard were close-cropped and drizzled with a grey that matched his eyes, and though he didn't say so, it was clear he had little confidence in a woman for the task in hand. A prejudice likely to be reinforced were she also to disgrace herself by vomiting. Wishing both to maintain her dignity and to win the fight no doubt ahead of her regarding the most appropriate treatment, she swallowed down the bile that rose in her throat as he opened the door to the tiny cabin. Her handkerchief she left in the pouch hanging from her waist, as if the smell affected her not at all, following him in without so much as a break in her step.

It was obvious he had a genuine interest in his men, and more than could be accounted for by the loss he would sustain should they fail to recover. In his favour was both his willingness to delay his own journey to seek treatment for the injured, and that he had clearly given up his own cabin to them. She was aware of his scrutiny as she straightened from her initial examination, and detected a concern underlying his gruff manner, so that she was willing to concede that his attempt at doctoring, however barbarous, was well-intentioned and stemming from years of customary practice. For which, in justice, she could not entirely hold him to blame. Accordingly, she moderated her approach and began by commending his generosity in placing the two men in his own quarters. His reaction: laughter, was entirely unexpected.

'You've not spent much time below decks in a small merchant craft I take it?'

She flushed. 'No.'

Fine lines appeared at the corners of his eyes. 'You need not think too well of me, for there is nowhere else they could lie, without some of their companions having to share their bed. And that unlikely to be popular with either party. We have hammocks enough for half the crew, and that sufficient, for there are never more than half asleep at one time.'

She coloured, awkward, shame at her lack of knowledge followed by an inexplicable feeling of relief that his laughter seemed to hold more of amusement than mockery. And in the smile that remained a hint of something else, producing an answering flash of warmth in her, instantly suppressed – perhaps she would meet with less resistance than she thought. But still, it was as well to establish her credentials before she broached a revolutionary treatment.

'I know you think this is no place for a woman, and no

job either, but I have experience of gunshot wounds and some success with a gentler treatment: it is not only at sea that men place themselves in danger.' It was a half-question, his response blunt.

'It's likely they are lost to me as it is. Whatever you do can hardly make the situation worse.'

The initial flicker of warmth in her was replaced by a renewed resentment, both that he voiced the standard reaction, and for her own foolish notion in hoping for any other. But his tacit agreement, however lacking in confidence, at least gave her a free hand. Though what she saw in the sailors' heightened colour and the heat rising from them, far from contradicting his assessment of the chances for their survival, rather reinforced it. She rummaged in her saddlebag for a sedative to ease the pain of the removal of the dressings. 'Send for some tepid water, in a clean bucket. A jug of boiling water also and a sharp knife … and a dish and spoon for preparing a salve.' She produced two bottles and a bundle of rolled rags, each containing an egg; answered his unspoken query. 'The salve is best made fresh. Egg white is a powerful soother, and blended with rose oil and turpentine can both cleanse and heal.'

He stood back. 'I'll leave you to it then. Anything else you require, if we have it, it is yours.'

She was bending over the older of the two men, the one most in urgent need of attention. 'Assistance to restrain him would be helpful, at least while I remove the dressings and seek out the ball and the cloth your lad says may be trapped inside the wound.'

'I picked out what material I could. But the ball I didn't find, for I was wary of probing too far.'

'There are those who live comfortably enough despite

110

carrying shot within them, but it is a chancy thing and one best avoided. The jerkin I imagine was far from clean? If he is to be saved it must come out. This distillation should render him unconscious while I work.' She soaked a rag in a preparation of valerian and placed it over his nose and mouth, waiting for his tossing to ease. 'It will be helpful that he is restrained, for, unconscious or not, muscles can react to pain, and any movement at all could prove hazardous.'

She focused on the job in hand: passed over the knife and tweezers to be boiled; doused the bandages, stiff with pus, with the tepid water; and began to cleanse the area around the dressing with an unscented soap made from pig fat and wood ash. It was a slow and delicate task to ease the dressing from the wounds, and she prepared herself to find gangrene. But although the flesh was red raw and roaring, the surrounding skin blistered and puckered from the application of the oil, there was no sign of the rotting she expected. She looked up at the captain, a half-smile in her eyes.

'Where did you get the maggots?'

Again the undefined flicker in his gaze which brought a new flush to her cheeks, though his answer was straightforward enough.

'A pair of pheasants, brought aboard in France, which were found to have been hung for rather longer than was necessary, discovered when they dropped unexpectedly from the hooks in the galley. I was a soldier before a sailor, and have seen it done in the field with some success, and so, when I smelled putrefaction, I introduced the maggots to the wound and bound them in. It was as well to get some value for the price of the birds.'

Had it been one of the Montgomeries who made humour of the situation she would have responded in kind,
but made uncomfortable by this stranger, perhaps ten
years her senior, whose gaze she found unsettling, she held
herself in check, allowing him only the smallest of nods
before concentrating on removing the maggots one by one
and placing them into the jar he proffered. She turned her
attention to the delicate task of probing the wound with the
sterilised blade.

Maggie was kneeling by a small chest preparing the
salve. The cabin boy who had brought the implements
stood over her, curious. Kate, pausing a moment, turned
her head to see how Maggie was getting on and caught a
glimpse of the boy's grin and of Maggie's answering smile.
Perhaps it was the residual worm of guilt as a result of her
own reaction to the captain, or her unadmitted reluctance
to accept that Maggie was growing up more quickly than
she would wish, but whatever it was, her tone was sharp.
'Make sure the salve is well mixed, and mind that the proportions are right.'

Maggie looked up, a mixture of surprise and hurt in
her gaze, so that Kate's guilt increased. She turned back to
the captain, sought to channel their conversation into safe
waters. 'Without the maggots he might have lost the use of
the arm, or maybe even the arm itself. If I can find most of
the foreign matter, the herbs will reduce his fever and keep
him quiet, and the salve may do the rest.' She was nosing in
the wound with the point of the dirk, her face close, her lip
caught between her teeth, removing each shred of fibre she
encountered with the tweezers. 'I will leave you yarrow for
the pain, and borage for fever and inflammation. See to it
that they are boiled together and administered every four

hours. If recovery is to come, the improvement will show itself within a day or two.'

He was regarding the wound thoughtfully. 'The maggots have removed the rotting flesh, why then still the inflammation and fever?'

'It is the oil, burning the flesh and skin, which, aside from the pain of it, has caused the body to be in revolt. Some day, and I trust it will be soon, there will be an understanding that wounds of this nature do not require such drastic measures, but rather a clean wound and a soothing salve and sound sleep, to allow the body time to heal itself.' She worked swiftly, probing as deeply as she dared, nodding to the captain to administer more sedative each time there was the faintest stirring of limbs. Fairly certain she had found all the cloth, and just about to give up in her search for the ball, she was directing Maggie to fold clean dressings and to bring the salve, when she felt a resistance to her probing. She looked up. 'Hold him tightly now, I think I may have found it, but it's deep and will be the devil to extract.' Even with the full length of the tweezers buried in the wound she struggled to get a grip on the ball, and just as she captured it he gave a jerk, clearly a reaction to her touching an especially raw nerve, so that she lost it again, the tip of the tweezers pushing the ball further into the wound. She glared her frustration at the captain. 'I said muscles react whether a patient is conscious or not. If I manage to get it again, see your hold on him is firm.'

'Found once, it will surely be easier second time round?'

'Surely nothing. And poking about like this is a gamble at best. I was lucky once, I may not be so again and should perhaps leave it be.'

It was as if he sought to make amends for allowing the

patient to move. 'You have a skill, it is … impressive.' He changed his position in order to get a better grasp of the sailor's shoulders, was close enough to Kate that she felt his breath on her cheek.

Again a glimmer of a smile around his mouth. 'I must admit I was sceptical when I sent for an apothecary and you were brought. I have a different feeling now.' A fractional pause, as if he wished an ambiguity to register.

She was aware of her heartbeat, as if it were a weight rising and falling in her chest, the unruly feelings stirring within her, unwelcome, and mindful of Maggie at her shoulder, sought for an answer that allowed for no equivocation, 'You'd better hope your confidence is not misplaced then.' Realising as his smile broadened how far from successful she was, she was disproportionately pleased by his start of shock when she brought a thin skewer from her bag.

'I had the end filed blunt. It will do less damage as I probe.' She spread the edges of the wound with one hand, seeking for resistance to the probe with the other, found what she was looking for.

To Maggie she said, 'Scrub your hands well. Then hold the skin back.' And to the captain. 'We may thank God it is still within reach.' She withdrew the skewer. 'Have you a firm grip this time? Any movement now and we may not have another chance.' Taking a deep breath, she inserted the tweezers, grasped the ball, wriggled it free. The cabin boy was holding out a small dish, and as she dropped the ball in it was impossible not to smile, at him and the captain both. 'It is misshapen, but all there. If indeed there are no more fragments of cloth lurking, we may still save him.'

The captain nodded. 'Whether or no, you couldn't have done any more. You have my thanks.'

114

Her heartbeat quickened, became more insistent. To suppress it she applied herself to examining the wound, and when she was satisfied there was nothing else visible to remove, she turned to smearing salve onto the clean dressings and bound them over the wound with strips torn from an old, but clean, shift.

Her head was bent low over her patient, her face close to the captain's hands. A stray curl of hair fell over her eyes and she felt him tuck it behind her ear.

'I thought it might disturb your work.'

There was nothing in either the action or the words she could object to, but nevertheless she was discomfited, both by the sense of intimacy in his action, and, more treacherously, by the sudden wish that Maggie did not hover at her shoulder. She turned her attention to the younger sailor, her face puckered as she worried away at the likely cause of his fever.

'You have used maggots here also?'

'No, for they were all bound into Angus' wound.' There was a note of apology in the captain's voice, an acceptance of error at odds with his previous air of self-confidence. 'We thought at the first he had no need of them, and until last night he appeared to be making good headway. When I realised his wound also was going to the bad, I thought the best we could do was to put into shore and pray there might be an apothecary to hand. I considered trying to move the maggots, but feared that, disturbing Jamie's wound, we'd lose them both.'

This at least she could handle, and in a businesslike manner. 'It is not all lost.' She indicated the jar. 'Jamie has no need of these creatures now, and an extra day or two and they will likely make a good job of this wound too. It's

115

grateful we should be there are beasties that find rotting flesh pleasurable, however strange.'

She reached into the jar to capture one of the maggots and felt the familiar squeamishness that touching them always brought, looked towards Maggie, grinned. The captain, clearly aware of an understanding between them, a shared history from which he was excluded, raised his eyebrows. She grasped at the chance to turn his attention away from herself.

'This is one task I will gladly relinquish. It suits Maggie well, for she aye loved to grub about in the dirt for small creatures to torment. Not that she saw it as torment, for in her mind she treated them kindly and was correspondingly upset when they died on her. But she has nimble fingers now and will be able to handle them with more care.'

Maggie straightened up, as if to emphasise her maturity, then grinned back at Kate. 'I suspicion that maggots are a mite more hardy than the worms I used to capture, but I shan't press them too hard.'

The captain, as if to include himself in the exchange, laughed. Not the guffaw that had heralded their arrival, but a gentler thing, and almost against her will, recognising danger, yet lacking the will to fight it, Kate laughed with him.

Professional concern, and the knowledge that the interests of the two injured men would best be served by a repeat visit, warred with a renewed fluttering in her stomach, caused by a lingering expression in the captain's eyes as she repacked her saddlebag. Concern winning, she asked,

'How long can you stay at anchor? It would be best if I return to see how they do and to change the dressings.' Another hesitation. 'Perhaps twice more.' Maggie opened her mouth, as if she was about to volunteer her services, but Kate allowed her no opportunity to speak. 'After that, if they are progressing, they can be safely left in your hands.' She voiced another solution, 'Or it might be possible to arrange a lodging for them ashore until they are quite recovered ... which may be best.'

She felt both guilty and glad when the captain shook his head.

'It won't be necessary to move them. We can wait. Two days? Two visits. Will that suffice?'

Chapter 14

Two days, two visits. Both times Kate went alone. With a moderation in the weather, everyone and his uncle seemed to require her services, many of the requests routine matters that Maggie plagued to be allowed to attend by herself. A request she was happy to grant, though she refused to admit the reason, even to herself, for that would be to admit to feelings she would rather *not* acknowledge. The snow was shifting, the dangers of travel less, Hugh's offer of a stable lad to accompany Maggie the needed excuse for her decision. But thoughts of the ship's captain came to her in odd moments, the remembrance of the warmth in his eyes, the light touch of his hand on her arm, disturbing.

Both men had improved faster than she could have hoped. On the second day they were lucid, cool to the touch, the skin around the wounds paled to a more normal brown, edges of scabs beginning to form. The captain accompanied her to the cabin and stood at her side as she bent to change the dressings and apply fresh salve. She could feel his breath on the back of her neck, sensed his eyes fixed on her. She chastised herself – the boat would be gone tomorrow; it was a foolish, a wrong thing to be so moved, and by a stranger.

'You do a good job, Mistress Grant. I am a convert already to your methods, and would wish that if ever I have need of such ministrations it will be to Irvine I can come for help.'

She bent to lift her saddlebag, he also, the touch of his fingers like a burn. Her patients had lapsed into sleep, their limbs relaxed, their breathing even. Unlike her own. She forced herself to say, 'They should do bravely now. A few more days and the dressings will no longer be necessary. If you are to leave on the tide tonight, I could instruct one of your men...'

'You could instruct me.'

Her heartbeat was so loud in her head she thought he must hear it too. 'If you wish it.'

He set her bag down again, glanced at the drowsing men. 'Instruct away. They look to be settled the now, and are unlikely to be disturbed by us ... or us by them.'

She buried her face in her saddlebag, trusting the muffling to disguise the tremor in her voice. 'I'll show you the proportions of the salve.' Risked an upwards glance at him. 'And if you have an egg to hand I can run through the preparation.'

He shook his head. 'Not here, though if you have time and to spare I will send onshore for one. And in the meantime you can teach me the method?'

There was little room in the cabin, Kate close enough to the captain almost to count the hairs on the back of his hands, fine and golden-coloured, visible only because of the light falling on them through the narrow porthole. She would dearly have liked to sit down, but to reveal any

119

weakness seemed a dangerous thing. 'The other ingredients can be prepared ahead of time and if properly stored will need only the addition of egg to make it effective.'

'Good. What is it you want then?' Again an ambiguity, the sense of it strong.

'A dish and a spoon and a bottle with a tight stopper. It is a simple thing.'

'That even a ship's captain should manage?'

She knew she shouldn't allow herself to be drawn into trading pleasantries, yet found herself saying, laughter in her voice, 'With care perhaps.'

He gestured towards the door. 'Come. The galley is likely the best place for this, and besides,' he looked at his hand, rubbed it on his shirt, 'I take it clean hands are an essential ingredient.'

'Indeed.' She coughed, as if to expel a tickle, tried for a firmer tone. 'The galley will do very well, thank you. This shouldn't take long.'

'As we are to wait on the tide, I'm in no hurry.' A pause, as he unlatched the hatch. 'Are you?'

The strict truth was no. For there remained three hours till suppertime and no calls to make on the road home. The sensible reply, however, the safest course, would be to say, 'I am needed at Braidstane, so must not delay too long.'

Instead, her stomach churning, saliva flooding her mouth, she shook her head, allowed the implication.

'Shall we?' He held out his hand, helped her through the hatch, his grip on her fingers remaining a fraction longer than was necessary.

They were gathered in Braidstane's solar. All evening Kate had been trying to bury the guilty feelings the touch of the ship's captain's calloused palm had aroused in her. And failing. Now, as the Montgomerie children quizzed her as to what like the boat had been, and how many sailors in the crew, and if any had a wooden leg because the other had been eaten by a sea monster, she found it impossible to think of anything other than the fine white lines in his gypsy-brown face as he had smiled down at her, the light in his eyes awakening an answering spark in her own.

And hating herself for it.

She had been six years alone, the ache for Munro, though something she was at pains to hide from the children, no less strong than in the early days. It had not been the first time in all her traipsing about the county she had met with a touch on the wrist or a look that held suggestion. Each time her reaction had been the same: amusement, a hint of pleasure that she had not altogether lost her attractiveness, an easy ability to sidestep the issue without offence on either side. Never a threat, to either her virtue or her heart. Until now.

Maggie took up the tale, revelling in describing the ropes coiled on the deck like snakes, the steepness of the ladder that took them below, the stench in the captain's cabin, which, now it was a memory, she could relate with humour, the cramped quarters, the captain, handsome enough, she supposed, though old.

'Was he really old?' Elizabeth was laughing. 'Or just as old as us?'

Maggie tilted her head to one side, considering. 'His hair was greying and his skin like crumpled canvas, but his eyes looked young.' She gave up. 'Oh, I don't know, ask mother, she saw more of him than me.'

Kate felt her face flush, hoped Elizabeth wouldn't notice, or if she did would refrain from questioning. She had no desire to air her thoughts to anyone. And why should she? It was only that the captain had somehow moved her. Did so still. Intruding into her dreams, he threatened to occupy waking moments also. And even as she told herself there was nothing worth a confession in what had passed between them, the voice of the minister at Renfrew thundered in her head, reminding her that to sin in thought was an equal wrong.

Shaking her head in dismissal, she said, 'Oh, older, definitely. By a considerable margin.' She slid onto the floor beside Ellie and the Montgomerie girls, bent her head to their game. She had never knowingly allowed her children to see her cry and was determined today would not be the day. Not when the tears for the husband she lacked be adulterated by those for a stranger.

Chapter 15

The French force had been encamped outside Amiens for almost a month, the first flurry of activity over, and now settled into the day-to-day routine of what, despite de Biron's earlier optimism, was likely to be a long siege, their stranglehold as yet failing to bite. The weather was kind, the sun holding sufficient heat it served to keep the tracks between the tents passable and to dry up the water pooling in the base of the ditches being dug to encircle the city. For the time being, divisions of the four thousand foot and seven hundred cavalry of the French force were strategically spread along the line of the Somme, the approach from Flanders seen as the greatest danger. De Biron had established himself at Longpré, and both Corbie to the north-east and Pécquigny to the west of the city were heavily occupied. Munro spent little time in the camp, the diversionary attacks to which he was assigned following one after the other. It was as he returned from a successful foray at Abbeville that he paused on a knoll above the French camp, arrested by a column of dust to the east, signalling troop movement of some sort. But whether of their own or an opposing force was impossible at this distance to tell. Below him their camp spread: a tide of tents, seething with movement, and with the defensive network of banks and ditches unfinished, still vulnerable to attack. He ordered his men to take shelter in the lee of the hill, and summoning one to accompany him, set off to make a reconnaissance. Though his own eyesight was keen enough, it was the younger man who first made out the blue and gold of the French King's colours. Relieved, Munro despatched him with orders for the waiting men to proceed to the camp, while he spurred his horse to meet the oncoming troops.

Munro and Patrick retreated to Munro's tent, closing the flap against the cacophony of the surrounding camp. To the neighing of horses, the creaking of axles and the ring of hammer on anvil, was added the hustle and bustle of the sutlers who sold everything from food and drink to second-hand shoes: always most in demand. And constant in the background, like a piper's drone, the arguments and scuffles. Among the soldiers, for whom the tedium of the building of siege works was aye a dangerous thing, and among the camp followers, their usefulness debatable, their permission to remain always in doubt. Not that the canvas did more than dampen the sound, but it gave at least the illusion of privacy. Munro gestured Patrick to sit, hungry for the latest news.

Above the general hubbub there was a high-pitched yelp of a child, choked off. Munro grimaced. 'An army is no place for children. Scavenging like dogs and kicked for their pains.'

'An army is a walking city, and the cruelty within it no more or no less than any such. If it was an urchin in Renfrew would you even take note of it?'

'Perhaps not. But it puts me in mind of my own bairns; and I would die rather than that they be here.'

'It is a way of life, and were Henri to send the camp followers away, morale would suffer. It may not be the pleasantest face of the army, but is a necessary one nonetheless.'

The light in the tent began to dim, an indication of approaching dusk, and accompanying it another sound, building in intensity.

Patrick waved in the direction of the new noise. 'That equally so, however unpalatable.'

They fell silent, listening to the trading of insults between the attacking and defending forces which was the normal closure to a day's proceedings. Threats of rape and plunder once the city's defences fell were countered by those of castration, skinning alive, or decapitation of the besiegers when the relieving forces should arrive. Day by day the volume increased, the threats from each side increasingly virulent.

Munro shook his head. 'I recognise the value of it all, but to hear it every evening would be more than I could stomach. It is an unexpected advantage of my role that I am rarely here.'

Patrick shrugged. 'Morale or lack of it is has as much a part in the eventual victory or defeat as any other tactic. You know that.'

'I know that the threats are real and that many in our ranks will relish the prospect when the city does fall. And I no better than they, for though I may not wish for it, I will likely lack the courage to dissent.'

'You are a soldier and under authority, the responsibility belongs to others.'

'That isn't what Kate would say.'

'There is no place in war for a crisis of conscience. And besides, push any of us to the limits and who can say what we would do. Those women on the walls who threaten us, the same women who load weapons and boil cauldrons of oil to pour on our heads, at home may be a Kate to their husband and children, indeed it is likely the thought of protecting their families that turns them from matrons to she-bears.' Patrick paused, regrouped. 'When you are home again, Kate will not judge you by what you have done abroad, so long, that is, you have the good sense to keep silent.'

Munro thought on the business at Annock and the long shadow it had cast. But that had been close to home. This war a different thing. He got up, poured them each a drink.

Patrick raised his tankard. 'That's more like it. I was beginning to fear you had turned to abstinence.'

Munro settled against his bedroll. 'Are you here to stay?'

Patrick shook his head. 'No. Henri is here to oversee the last of the siege works and then he is for Paris. As you know, where he goes, I must follow.'

'What takes him away again so soon? He isn't known to shirk the front line.'

'Nor is he now. Money *is* the front line. And had you accompanied us to the garrisons you would understand. Everywhere we went we found troops ready to disband for lack of pay, and it took all his persuasive charm to convince them cash would be forthcoming. But until it is, they are not.' There was a grim set to Patrick's mouth. 'And who can blame them? Already hungry, half of them barefoot, their clothes in rags, they weren't in any fit state to be of use here. We are lucky to have brought the reinforcements we have.' He nodded down at his own and Munro's well-shod feet. 'We have little to complain of in the Gardes. For the rest, the King has sent urgent letters to Henri de Mont-morency commanding a sale of new offices and an increase in the gabelle of salt, and there is talk also of forced loans; but there has been a shortfall before, and could well be so again. That's why he goes in person to press parliament to register the edicts he has framed to meet the need. Pray God he succeeds, or the troops we have now, far from be-ing further swelled by the necessary reinforcements, may be decimated, not by the Spanish, but by desertion.'

Another thought struck Munro. 'There is a rumour the Spanish have made overtures of peace. Is there any truth in it?'

'An approach was made, but though Henri would wish for peace, he won't agree while Amiens, Calais and Ardes remain in Spanish hands, and so he told the ambassador. We may expect no respite till the summer is past at the very least.' He hesitated, then said, 'All the intelligences indi-cate the Archduke Albert is gathering a substantial force to counter our offensive.'

'Substantial? Are there any figures that can be relied on?'

'Figures, yes. As to whether they can be relied upon … that is less certain. The talk is of a force some twenty-eight thousand strong.'

Munro whistled.

Patrick ignored the interruption.'But as you know there

is strength in rumour; the reality may be different. As we may hope it is, for to be outnumbered seven to one is not a prospect I'd relish, and I doubt that Henri could pull the "peasants with pitchforks" ruse for a second time, as he did at Besançon. Verification will likely be a job for the scouts, an honour you may be given.'

'What of the English and Dutch?'

'There are promises of troops to assist us here, but no willingness to carry out offensives elsewhere. And promises as you know come cheap. Henri is right to garner support himself, and when we come back, it will hopefully be with a sizeable force, and soon. He has no more desire to sit out the summer in Paris when he could be here and leading the siege himself than I have.' Patrick stood up as the clamour increased, unlacing the tent fastenings. The tone of the catcalls directed towards the city walls became more visceral, and above them, ululating voices, a cut-off scream.

'Useless mouths!' Munro was out of the tent, Patrick with him, heading for the newly dug ditch facing the city gate. Amien's main gates had been pulled back, spewing a ragtag of people onto the open ground in front of it: the old stumbling or leaning on sticks; women, their walk ungainly, ragged shawls stretched around them, failing to hide their swollen bellies; children grasping at their skirts, eyes wide with shock. Behind them, soldiers were driving them forward, kicking, punching and clubbing any that sought to turn back. Munro saw a boy, little more than a child himself, leading another, smaller boy, the second hesitant, his free hand outstretched, sweeping the air around him. 'Patrick.' Munro pointed to the pair, the oasis of space around them. He flung himself down a ladder into the ditch, re-emerged as a surge of people, forced from behind with the pressure of bodies, swallowed the boys, obscuring them from view. He started forward at a run, Patrick by his side, heading for the spot where he had last seen the blind boy and his companion. The Spanish troops were retreating back into the city, the gates closing behind them, cutting off any hope of retreat for those they had expelled. Munro wove through a group of French soldiers fanned out in a thin line, the folk cast out of the city running towards them, hope visible on their faces. Munro saw them falter, hope replaced by horror at the glint of sunlight on steel, as the French soldiers penned them in, cattle destined for slaughter. He drove forward, ignoring the clash of swords all around him, the air cleft with bodies falling, blood bubbling from throats open to the sky, his ears full of the screams of the dying. Grasping hold of a soldier who blocked his way, he was himself knocked backwards, the pommel of the man's sword catching him a glancing blow on the side of his head. He struggled to his feet, staggered forward again, caught a glimpse of the boy, barefoot and ragged, his eyes, as he lifted them to Munro's call, opaque, unseeing. He grabbed hold of the boy's elbow, swung him round behind him, hissing at him not to be afraid, and as Patrick grasped the boy's shoulder, turned back to seek the other child. In the space, a group of women, pressed forward from behind, were cut down, terror in their eyes. He felt a thump between his shoulder-blades, a stinging sensation on the back of his knee and, his leg buckling under him, wondered as he fell whose blood it was that spread like a tide around him.

It was strangely silent, bar a low drumming in his ears, as if temporarily deafened by cannon shot. Someone muttered beside Munro, the accent his own, and he turned his head towards the sound, his eyelids flickering. A different voice, relief-tinged.

'He's coming round.'

Munro, struggling to sit up, found himself held down by straps cutting into his arms.

Patrick grasped his shoulders, halting his attempts at movement, his face close to Munro's, his tone urgent. 'Stay still. You've lost a lot of blood. And though patched, likely to lose more if you don't take care.' And then, with a touch of humour, 'It's as well you lost weight in the training, it was as much as I and the boy could do to get you back here in one piece.'

Munro raised his head experimentally, felt the dull throbbing increase to a hammer beat. He leant back against the grass-filled sack, reconciled himself to an uninterrupted view of the pole disappearing through a hole in the tent roof. Searched backwards for his last memory. 'Did any…?'

Patrick shook his head. 'Only the blind lad who helped in your rescue. I had a hard enough job arguing for him to be allowed to stay, and indeed might not have succeeded had not his more acute sense of smell averted a near disaster in the munitions store. Sunlight and straw and a broken bottle a combination that would have been lethal if he hadn't picked up on the first curls of smoke. As for the rest: the city couldn't feed them and nor could we.'

'We could have let them go.'

'To die in the countryside, or be driven from other doors? What value that, other than to salve our own consciences?' Patrick's mouth was set in an uncompromising line. 'From the moment we set the siege, the useless mouths were already dead. It was only a matter of timing.' A pause. 'You cannot tell me you got no pleasure from your success at Arras, or last year found no exhilaration in the victory at Fontaine-Française. This is but another side to the same coin, and it is hypocrisy to claim otherwise. We all have blood on our hands.' He found a parody of a smile. 'And this latest episode, good news, for it indicates the beginning of a desperation we can surely exploit.' He sat down on the end of Munro's pallet, looked past him along the line of other beds, other injured soldiers. 'Though we aren't near the end yet. Those driven from the city tonight were but the poor and deformed. It is when we see the rich merchants' wives expelled that we can truly take heart.'

It was two weeks before Munro was fit to leave the hospital tent, Patrick long gone, so that the time of his forced rest dragged. He heard snippets of news from soldiers who came for treatment of minor injuries, some received in skirmishes, others in accidents occurring as the artillery were manoeuvred into position in preparation for the bombardment of the city. And just as he was about to be released, the account of a failed assault, the storming troops driven back by cauldrons of boiling pitch cast from the walls. Those who survived the unlucky ones. Which brought to mind Patrick's comment regarding the women

131

whose role it was – could Kate be driven to such a pass as that? It was not a thought to dwell on.

As he limped back to his tent, intending to present himself at de Biron's command post the following morning for further orders, his attention was caught by a larger than usual crowd around one of the sutler's stalls. A bargain to be had? Perhaps the results of a successful foraging party. But as he approached he recognised from the haranguing of the crowd that here was trouble. He wrestled his way to the front. The sutler was in the middle of a circle of women armed with staves and an assortment of domestic implements, being knocked backwards and forwards between them, his legs and arms already bloody, one side of his face reduced to pulp. Ignoring the weakness in his leg, Munro was preparing to wade into the fray on the sutler's behalf, for, whatever his sins, to allow the rule of the mob was a dangerous thing, when he felt an insistent tug on his arm. He half-turned, ready to shake off whoever impeded him, but found himself staring down at the blind lad, whose life he had saved, and who had helped to save him in return. The boy was trying to drag Munro away, babbling in rapid, accented French, Munro struggling to make him out. One word penetrated.

Munro spun round, almost knocking the lad off his feet. 'Typhus?'

The boy nodded, and now that he had Munro's attention, his speech slowed, became comprehensible. Munro turned back, renewed his efforts to breach the circle. In the centre he grasped the sutler, and holding him firmly, fired his pistol into the air. The effect was immediate. He bellowed at the crowd. 'This is insanity. If you wish the typhus to spread, kill him. If you wish it to be stopped, let him live. He has information that will be needed.' Holding firmly to him lest he seek to escape, Munro led him towards the hospital tents, the women falling back, their catcalls fading to a murmur. Dear God, he thought, it isn't just the Spanish we fight.

And so it proved, the typhus racing through the camp despite all efforts to halt its progress. Pioneers were among the first to succumb, arriving in droves at the field hospital, complaining of the light burning their eyes, of joint pain and nausea, of the telltale red rash and a fever setting their bodies on fire. Within a week a quarter of them were dead, many of the soldiers also, the double loss endangering the progress of the siege works. Munro, not yet sufficiently fit to resume his leadership of diversionary forces, volunteered to dig alongside the foot soldiers. And that was where Patrick, sent ahead to alert the commander of Henri's imminent arrival, found him, his amusement clear as he stood on the edge of the ditch in which Munro hefted a shovel. Patrick nodded to the soldier in charge, called Munro away.

As they walked back towards the swarm of tents, Patrick said, 'They could surely have found something better to occupy you than digging a ditch, despite,' he indicated Munro's leg, 'that you aren't fully restored to your usual fitness.'

'You haven't heard then? There was an outbreak of typhus, thankfully now run its course, which decimated the pioneers. If we hadn't pressed every available hand to digging, the lack of activity would have alerted Amiens to our weakened state and doubtless all would have been lost.

133

In the circumstances how could I not help?'

'Your help is needed in another sphere now. One more suited to your abilities. Henri has mustered some eight thousand foot, three thousand horse, and extra pioneers. There must be food enough, else we may not keep the latest recruits long. Your knowledge of areas already stripped bare is essential.' He looked towards Amiens' walls. 'The assault is imminent?'

Munro thought of the previous failed attempt, and the nagging sense of guilt that, stuck in the field hospital recovering from his leg wound, he had been spared participation in it, nodded. 'This time it will be a full-scale bombardment.'

A glint in Patrick's eye, a hint of mockery in his voice. 'And no wound from a friend to keep you from it.' They had reached the edge of the camp, passing the field hospital where Munro had been treated. Patrick jerked his head towards it. 'Would you recommend the treatment?'

'It was as good as may be expected, and perhaps better than I could have hoped. I have at least kept my leg, which is more than can be said for other poor devils.'

The extra troops Henri had brought placed such an additional burden on those tasked with feeding them that for a time it seemed the French force was scarcely better off than those trapped inside Amiens' walls. Henri took no more rations than his men, a tactic that went a long way to avoiding the problems of desertion Patrick had anticipated. The issue was not money, for the French King had wrung an agreement from the parliament in Paris that the soldiers would receive full pay for as long as the siege should last. What consequence it would have for the royal exchequer was a different matter, the problem shelved until another day. The issue was supply. Munro and the others tasked with obtaining food found they had to extend their search further and further away, the extra distances a hazard in themselves, reinforcing as nothing else could the dangers of a lengthy siege. So that it was a relief to all when the order was given for the bombardment to begin in earnest.

From first light till dusk the sound of cannon fire resounded throughout the camp. At first an assault on their eardrums, within a day or two it was the silence at nightfall which made the soldiers uneasy, the sense of security the cannons provided lost to them. Such was the constant pall of smoke it was as if daytime became night, the soldiers manning the guns moving like shadows through the mirk. A shipment of wheat arrived from Paris, so that for the time being bread was in reasonable supply, but as to flavour, it was, as everything else, tainted by sulphur. The wine they drank, likewise. Munro, chancing to glance in a drum of flour and seeing it move, thought on how Kate would react to the weevils, serving to emphasise how far removed from home and ordinary life he was.

Chapter 16

To the relief of all at Braidstane, the weather turned. Kate was balancing on a stool in the bastle house storeroom, clearing the rafters of the last of the previous season's herbs in preparation for a new gathering, when Hugh burst in on her. The stool cowped, tipping her off, and she landed heavily, one leg crumpling under her, the remnants of the dried flowerheads scattering. Hugh returned the flowerless stems to her with an apologetic smile.

She looked at them. Found it impossible to be truly cross. 'You can make amends by bringing the rest down. I don't feel safe climbing back on a stool with you around.'

Once done, Hugh turned to face her, his smile gone.

'This is not a social call, then?'

'No...'

'Spit it out, Hugh. If Robbie is at you again to plead for him, you can save your breath. We have an agreement as to when he can go to France, and I'm not for shifting.'

'This isn't about Robbie.' His reticence unnerved her. 'It may be nothing, but if it *is* true, then you must be on your guard.'

'If what is true? Hugh, you're not making any sense.'

'I came round by Irvine on the road home, and while I waited at the saddler I overheard a snatch of conversation. Maybe misheard...'

'Hugh! It gets no easier the longer I wait.'

'It was a pedlar, and talk of money to be made, of information William Cunninghame was willing to pay for, and handsomely. It seems he makes enquiries about a wise woman in these parts, a widow: who she is, where she hails from.'

'Any reason given?'

'I heard only a fragment.' He was rubbing a track through the rushes on the floor with the toe of his boot. 'Some mention of Maxwell. The pedlar was hopeful that as he went about the county he would pick up enough of a thread that he could spin a good yarn and pocket the money.'

Kate was back at the gateway at Hillhouse, Margaret Maxwell stiff at her side, her own head bent, focusing on Patrick Maxwell's feet.

Hugh's voice came from far away, fading. 'It may be nothing...'

She came to in the chamber off Braidstane's solar, Elizabeth bending over her, the light subdued by half-closed shutters.

'Don't try to move just yet. You have given us all a fright.'

Kate lifted her head, the room beginning to shift. She subsided back onto the pillows.

'It's a fine bump you gave yourself and lucky that you weren't alone when you fell.' An attempt at humour. 'However handsome my husband is, I should have thought you past swooning over him. But at least the table has taken no damage.'

'I've never fainted before. It was the strangest sensation. As to hitting the table, I didn't feel it.' Kate made a face. 'But I certainly do now.'

Elizabeth perched on the edge of the bed, traced the pattern in the brocade with her finger, became serious. 'What was it Hugh said to affect you so?'

'Apparently, William questions who I am, where I came from … at the root of it, Maxwell.'

Elizabeth breathed in, the pressure of her fingers on Kate's shoulder increasing. 'It cannot have been sufficient to threaten you, or he would have been here already.'

'Maxwell recognised me at Hillhouse, I know it, and though he couldn't place me at the time, if he has remembered since… It wasn't only Munro who antagonised him. I did my fair share at the Queen's entry, when I twitted the Cunninghames with the King's interest in you.' Kate was staring at her palm, focusing on the lifeline that traversed it. 'There was little point in telling you before. Besides that I'm not altogether proud of myself, for it wasn't the wisest of moves. Nor did it go down well. When the King invited you into the palace, I commented on your good fortune in having Eglintoun as your lord. And however ill-judged, if I was to have the time over again I do not know that I would behave any differently. William and Maxwell were odious then, and unlikely to be improved now.' Elizabeth shifted, but Kate forestalled her. 'Oh, I well know the dangers of a confrontation, how can I not? William murdered Archie and Sybilla, is responsible for Munro's exile, for our change of name, our fleeing here: there can be little he would not do. And I have not hidden myself and the bairns these six years to throw it all away now. For if he were to find that we escaped what purported to be a reivers call on Broomelaw, no doubt he would wish to finish the job, and there is but a small step from finding us, to seeking out Munro.'

Elizabeth stirred again, but Kate allowed her no chance to interrupt. 'I have my own family to think on, but there is yours as well. Have no fear, I shan't forget that. Though it doesn't stop me wishing William ill... I dream sometimes of repaying him for all the pain he has caused.'

Light footsteps on the stairs. Kate, recognising the footfall, slid back down the bed, closed her eyes.

'Has she stirred?' Maggie was breathless, clearly from running. 'I was as quick as I could.'

Kate made a good play of flickering her eyelids before she opened them fully, and, stretching to the limit her ability to dissemble, managed, 'What happened?'

'You fainted. And Uncle Hugh carried you here, and I...'

Elizabeth stemmed the flow. 'And Maggie has done everything that was needed.'

'You will likely have a sore head for a day or two. It was a right crack you gave it, but I've prepared something for the pain.' She touched her finger against the side of the tankard she carried. 'Still a little warm perhaps, but it'll do.' Her head was up, her body stiff with pride. 'I thought yarrow likely the best.' She held it to Kate's mouth.

Kate took a sip, made a face. 'There is nothing more effective for a headache, however unpleasant the taste.' She felt the back of her head, estimating the extent of the swelling, probing the area around it. Her fingers came away smeared with grease and she sniffed at them. 'Arnica.' She smiled at Maggie. 'Our lessons have been fruitful then.'

It was three days before Kate was fit enough to venture further than the bastle house kitchen, and even there she held her head as still as possible as she moved around, for any sudden turn sent a shaft of pain shooting across her forehead and a wave of dizziness through her.

Elizabeth came calling. 'That story of Hugh's, there could be numerous reasons why William would enquire of a wise woman. Some illness at Kilmaurs that defeats them ... or a woman of William's acquaintance requiring particular services.'

Kate opened her mouth to protest. 'I...'

'Oh I know,' Elizabeth held up her hands, 'you have aye refused to aid in the losing of bairns, and to your credit, but there are many wise women who have no such scruples, indeed who make a goodly portion of their living by it.'

'But why would he have heard of me at all?'

'You have been six years here and your reputation increasing. It shouldn't surprise us if word of your skill has reached Kilmaurs.'

'I had rather be less well known then.'

'Perhaps it is your widowhood. He has a reputation in that direction.'

'Don't. Whatever he may want, if he was to find me...'

'It was a foolishness of Hugh to repeat the gossip, regretted so soon as it was out. As well it might be with you on the floor at his feet. There is little use fretting over

140

what may never happen. With every day that passes, your safety increases. Concentrate on resting, on regaining your strength.'

'It isn't rest I need.'

'Try to enjoy it then, need or no.'

Chapter 17

It was inactivity of a different kind frustrating William Cunninghame. Lady Glencairn looked up as he entered the solar and made straight for the jug of ale.

'Is Father expected from court? I have plans to discuss with him.'

'What plans?'

'The matter of Broomelaw. The renovation there is long overdue, and the word is that its condition worsens month by month.' He leant against the mantel, scraping flakes of dried mud from his boot against the edge of the stone hearth-slab. 'To be canny is one thing, parsimonious another. Besides that Father saves no silver by waiting, quite the reverse.'

'It is your father's stewardship that keeps us in comfort while others find themselves in straits.'

He swept away her protest. 'You cannot deny there are times when you have found Father's carefulness irksome, and in this it is folly.'

'The issue is not just cost. Your father has a doubt as to whether there is any advantage to be gained by laying out money on such a project.'

'The issue is of a promise made. The Munros all gone, that tower was to be mine.' He slammed his tankard down on the mantleshelf. 'Must I wait for Father to die before I have a place to call my own?'

'You are Master of Glencairn. Your place is here. However little pleasure it may give you...' She turned her head aside, irritation spilling. 'Or us.'

The implication hung between them, a corrosive poison further inflaming William's temper. He took a step towards her, enjoyed the frisson of fear evidenced in the widening of her eyes – he wouldn't stoop so low as to hit her, but it did no harm that she think it possible.

She straightened her shoulders. 'It is not only the building work that must be considered, but the additional expense of setting up a household.'

'To buy your peace,' his voice dripped sarcasm, 'that outlay is surely a cost worth paying.'

'What is worth paying?' Glencairn stamped his feet on the rug at the doorway, scattering clarts of mud across the polished floor.

Lady Glencairn accepted his perfunctory embrace. 'I had not expected you till evening, and so took an early bite. Are you hungry?'

He shook his head. 'I've not come from court the now, only from Clonbeith. I travelled there last night, my horse casting a shoe just short of the tower, so I was forced to wait until this morning for the smith to set it right.' He was rubbing his hands together, glanced at the empty hearth. 'Call for the fire to be set. April or not, it is a dreich day and I took a foundering on the way home.' He turned back to William. 'What is this cost worth paying?'

'Broomelaw. It was a Cunninghame stronghold once and should be so again. Besides that it is high time I had my own place.'

'High time you earned it.'

It was an opportunity, William quick to take it. 'This tower, it interests me. And to oversee its repair would be a task I would be happy to undertake. Would that be occupation enough for you?' He intercepted the look his mother directed at his father. Saw that Glencairn weakened, chose another tack. 'It does our reputation no good to leave Broomelaw prey to all those with light fingers, as if we cannot afford to take care of what is ours. Is that what you would have the world think? That we are impoverished?'

Glencairn's face darkened, and for a moment William thought he pushed his father too far, then, 'I will have no one think us poor. But nor will I commit to something I have not seen. If you are ready at dawn, we will look to it.'

Glencairn and William set out at first light, the steward with them. For once William was sober, and as a result his hands shook slightly on the reins, though his head was clear enough. His thoughts full of Broomelaw, he cast a glance at Glencairn, decided a little foreknowledge wouldn't go amiss. His tone was more measured than usual.

'I have to warn you, the damage to the tower is extensive.'

'Not a cheap job then?'

'One that grows more expensive with every passing month. It isn't just the main tower that has suffered, but the ancillary buildings also, forbye the perimeter wall. I have been twice in the last months, and each time I find a deterioration.'

Glencairn half-turned in the saddle, William aware of the surprise in his gaze. He pressed home his advantage.

'We have a family name to uphold and a position to maintain. It ill behoves me to remain at home as if I were still a child.'

'Oh, I know you are no child.'

There was an implication in Glencairn's words that William decided to meet head on. 'I do not spend all my time in hawking and whoring, whatever mother may think. But when I do it is for lack of other occupation.'

It was well past noon when they reached the slope below Broomelaw, the sun on their backs as they climbed, the remnants of the tower standing gaunt against the skyline. William gestured upwards. 'You see? The last time I was here, the west wall still had its windows intact. Another six-month and there may be nothing here.'

It was a not uncommon practice to reuse building materials from crumbling towers, the original ownership of little concern to those who scavenged. The Cunninghames had done their fair share of looting in the past, but that did not lessen the affront now. It was the prod best calculated to sway Glencairn. He turned to the steward.

'We will make a preliminary survey today, and you can return tomorrow to sketch out the bones of what is necessary.' He followed William towards the entrance of the main tower, turned to look at the surroundings. 'It is well set, that I give you.' He bent to make a closer examination of the wall. 'And the stonework competent. A pity so much is lost.'

William was already inside, his voice echoing. 'The stair has survived, though most of the interior has gone.' His steady progress was an indication of the accuracy of his pronouncement, his footfall on the stone stairs punctuated by a periodic scrabbling as he passed the entrance to each storey. As he reappeared on the fraction of wall walk clinging to the eastern corner, he called down, 'There are three floors, forbye the garret, and though the wood is gone, evidence of the height and scale of the rooms remains. More spacious than it appears, it will be well worth the effort of repair.'

Glencairn was non-committal. 'We can make no final decisions until the proper survey is complete. And you'd best come down before you fall down, for little use in you having a four-storey house to call your own and a broken back confining you to a chair.'

William laughed, leaned out past the remnant of parapet, his arms spread in typical William bravado, pretending to teeter on the edge. 'I'll not fall. The stairwell is more or less as it should be. The only difficulty is negotiating where the main floors should join.'

'There have been a fair few collapses by the look of it, and could be another at any time. I have no wish to carry you home across my saddle.'

William decided on acquiescence – rare enough to find his father accommodating, it would be a folly to lose the ground gained, much better to keep him sweet. It was the first time in his life he had been truly enthusiastic about anything, the first in a long while he had still been sober by the afternoon. He hoped the significance of that had not been missed.

The ride back to Kilmaurs was companionable enough, the absence of sparks flying between them a novel and not unpleasant feeling. He reopened the discussion. 'I had thought there would be need of enlargement.'

Glencairn's face clouded. 'It isn't your money to be spent, or not yet.'

William was uncharacteristically reasonable. 'I said I *had* thought. But now I think it might do as it is. A little more light perhaps, but that won't be hard to achieve, and half the walls gone already. We could employ our own stonemasons and carpenters. No doubt they could be persuaded to camp out while the work is done, and the time away from home would encourage them to work the harder. A pity it is a step from Kilmaurs, but whoever we used we would have the issue of supervision, and it will be easier with our own men than those we have no connection with.' He paused, repeated his earlier offer. 'I could watch over them.'

They were passing a clump of gorse, aflame with flower. William, looking at it, thought on Munro and on the fight lost on the shore by Rough Island, and felt a rush of satisfaction – it would be a fitting end to a memory which still rankled.

Supper was a relaxed affair, devoid of any of the usual tensions.

'A successful day then,' Lady Glencairn said.

'Indeed.' Glencairn was expansive. 'William is right. Cunninghame land Broomelaw has always been, and

Cunninghame land it should remain. It's only right our heir should have his own place.'

It was an easiness that lasted well into the evening, amid conversation so ordinary, so much as it might have been in any family of their station, even William was ready to prolong it.

Lady Glencairn began well enough. 'This issue of the furnishing of Broomelaw. It would be a poor show if we couldn't find you some necessities that could be spared. I have been up to the attics and found hangings,' she nodded at Glencairn, 'from your parent's time, and not the latest fashion perhaps, yet still moth-free and sufficiently heavy to keep out the draughts.'

She turned to William, risked a pleasantry. 'It would be a foolish thing in any case to lay out too much in that respect, for, should you take a wife, she might wish some changes made.'

William permitted himself a small smile. 'With a house of my own, I may have opportunity to think on it, and something to offer of more value than my current billet.'

'There is good ground around it?'

Glencairn stretched out his feet towards the fire. 'Some, though much of it hilly, but there is grazing further afield suitable for sheep and a few cattle, and that I'm minded to attach to the holding. The byres, though they have suffered substantial damage, will, when repaired, have space enough, and the stabling is surprisingly generous.'

William nodded in agreement. 'Though why they needed stabling of such extent ... I wouldn't have thought Munro had the wherewithal to keep more than one horse, or at the most two, and the quality likely poor.'

'Now that I come to remember it,' Glencairn was

thoughtful, 'the word at Clonbeith was they would have liked fine to keep Munro's mare, left in place of the horse he borrowed for the trip to Stirling, for they felt they had the better bargain. But as to where or how he came by it, that I don't know.'

'His wife perhaps?' Unwittingly, Lady Glencairn strayed into dangerous territory. 'Did she come of a good family?'

William was dismissive. 'Not so you'd notice.'

'Were those who sacked Broomelaw ever found?'

'No.' Glencairn shrugged. 'Reiving is a national pastime; it could have been any one of a hundred culprits. And once done, it were as well to leave it be, for to do otherwise was to risk further trouble.'

'But all of them ... burned in their beds. Bairns included. It is a horrible thing.'

William kicked at a log spilling out onto the hearth. 'We burn vermin. And I have not heard you protest at that.'

'People are not vermin. Children are not vermin.' Lady Glencairn's head came up, her face flushed. 'Nor should we think of anyone as such, friend or foe.'

William's face darkened. 'I do not need you to tell me how to think. The Munros were not worth our worrying then, and certainly not worth a remembrance now.'

'The drowning of Archie and Sybilla, the sack of Broomelaw, two tragedies in the one month and for the same family; does that mean nothing to you? They were supposed to be our own folk, and if we could not protect them, we should at least have sought justice on their behalf. For all that it is six years since, and I had no knowledge of Munro's wife and bairns, I find there are times I grieve for them still.'

Glencairn poured himself another drink. 'To grieve over what cannot be mended is a foolish thing. And of no good to anyone. Rebuilding Broomelaw, that will be our tribute.'

'Taking it for ourselves, is that a tribute also?'

William allowed his irritation to show. 'There are none left that have a call on Broomelaw, *save* ourselves. How do you wish us to act? If we do nothing, we are unfeeling. If we do something, we are grasping.' He stood up, looked across at Glencairn. 'If we are to discuss this, perhaps it should be elsewhere, for there is little sense to be had here.'

Chapter 18

It was Ellie, who, with no understanding of the sense of what she said, broke the news. She was perched in the window reveal in the dairy, trying to piece together a wooden puzzle, as Kate worked the churn. Despite that it was áye a cold seat however warm the day outside, Ellie often watched as the milk became warm butter, the reward for her patience to be allowed to run her finger around the sides to gather the residue that clung to it. It had been almost an hour now and Kate's face as red and as shiny as a plum. A strand of hair escaped from her cap, stuck to her cheek, and, without pausing in the turning of the churn, she lifted one arm to push it back and to wipe away the trickle of sweat running into her eye.

The difficult spring, when the weather had threatened the loss of much of their stock, had given way to a May of blustery showers that came and went with little predictability, making it hard for Hugh to find two days at a stretch dry enough for the necessary repairs to the stabling and barns. Kate, sympathising, had nevertheless been grateful that, if nothing else, it had produced grass plentiful enough for sheep and cattle both. Hugh's herd, though their numbers were diminished, were yielding well, so that there was plenty of milk, and to spare, for both houses. In previous years, Agnes and Kate had felt guilt in taking milk with nothing to offer in return, but this year they had no such qualms, the work that Robbie did for Hugh more than compensating.

Kate was humming to herself and thinking with pleasure of the round pats of butter that would shortly grace the dairy shelves, when Ellie tossed her puzzle to the floor, the pieces scattering. 'Wish Robbie was here. Now I shall never get it right.'

'No need for temper, miss. It wants but an hour till supper, and no doubt Robbie will sort it then, or perhaps Maggie... Get down and pick up the pieces before you lose any.'

'He won't be here for supper, and Maggie's no use...'

'What do you mean Robbie won't be here? Why will he not? He was to stay but one night at Greenock.'

Ellie shrugged. 'I saw his saddlebags yesterday and they were bursting full, so he could scarce close them, and,' she grinned in remembrance, 'he was pulling the strap so hard the buckle slipped and caught his thumb and he said a bad word.' As if she thought she mightn't be believed, she insisted, 'I did hear him, even though I was in the hayloft. He took something out and stuffed it into his jerkin, and he was swinging into the saddle when I sneezed, and he stopped and looked up and saw me and he snapped his mouth shut, then he waved me down and called me kitten and said he'd bring me something nice if I promised not to spoil his secret...' she faltered, took up again in a wail, '... oh but now I have, and he won't and...'

Kate stopped working the paddle of the churn, colour

152

bleeding out of her cheeks. 'Did he say what his secret was?'

Ellie shook her head. 'Something he had to do. A surprise we'd all enjoy...'

Kate tried to quell her unease – time enough to quiz Ellie further if he didn't appear. She scraped the butter onto the slab, began to work it into pats, and, forgetting both the salt and the dampening of the wood, pressed it into the moulds.

As Ellie had predicted, Robbie didn't appear.

Agnes, ladling broth into bowls, said, 'Has anyone seen Robbie?' And when she got no reply, 'Why is it boys aye expect supper ready when they want it, and take no thought to warn if they're going to be late?'

Kate stroked Ellie's hair. 'Whatever you know of Robbie, Ellie, it's best you tell us. Secrets are all fine, but if food is to spoil, it's as well we know the reason why.'

'But I promised...' Ellie trailed off, looking at the floor.

Kate's voice softened. 'Robbie will know he would be missed at supper.' She made a shrewd guess at what would reassure the child. 'He only meant for you not to run to tell when he was going, in case,' she tried to make light of it, 'I'd have some other job for him which might spoil his own plans.' She caught Ellie's chin, tilted her face upwards, manufactured a smile to cover the chill in her stomach. 'What was it he said?'

'Nothing, only...'

'Only what? It's all right, if you just tell us it will be a help, to us and to Robbie.' And when Ellie remained stubborn, she tried another tack. 'I need an idea as to where he is gone and for how long. And whether he is to want his supper late, or not at all.' She summoned a smile. 'Else I will be having to save a pudding for him just in case, and that would mean less for you.'

Ellie capitulated, a smile breaking. 'He said he might bring Father. And I said, 'But he doesn't know me,' and then he pulled my hair and said I might have been just a wee bit thing when Father left, but nobody could forget me...' Her smile faded. 'I don't remember him...'

It was a knife-thrust in Kate's gut. She pushed back her chair, made for the ladder leading to the attic. The chest under the window was empty, Robbie's spare clothing, what little there was of it, gone. The blanket from his bed also. In her head she had a vision of Munro in the uniform of the Scots Gardes, and in her heart the sinking feeling – where else would Robbie go? And without a word – a cruelty she'd not thought him capable of. Her anger died as quickly as it had arisen, replaced with guilt. For how could he ask, knowing he would be refused. If she had listened to him, if she had given way, just a little, if she had asked John Shaw to take him. Perhaps that would have sufficed and he would have gone to Veere and come home again, content. But now, if he had gone to France, and she could think of no other explanation for his absence, then likely he travelled alone, the dangers great, and if aught should happen to him, the blame would be hers. Banging shut the lid of the chest, she came back to the kitchen and hugged Ellie to her.

'Will he be long?' Ellie was twisting the loose end of her hair ribbon round and round, stroking it against her lip.

Ignoring the spoiling of the ribbon, Kate, making an

effort, smiled down at her. 'We'll know soon enough, I'm sure. And be happy to see him home again.' That at least was true.

Over Ellie's head her eyes met Agnes', her answering unease masked by a brusque, 'Sit down and eat. We shouldn't let the food spoil because Robbie failed to share his plans with us. It's enough to have to keep some hot for Maggie.'

Kate breathed in, a second irrational but no less real fear almost winding her, so that Agnes, perhaps reading her thoughts, continued, 'She is due home anytime and likely starving, for,' she cast a look at the sky and the clouds scudding across the narrow window, 'she has the wind against her.'

'Everyone gets to go places only me.' Ellie's small shoulders stiffened.

Kate slid back onto the bench beside her, indicated the bowl of broth. 'Your turn will come. In the meantime, you need to eat up, or you'll not be strong enough when you are of an age to traipse about on your own.'

Steam rose in curls, dampening Ellie's nose, which she rubbed with her sleeve. 'What's Maggie doing?' She spoke through a mouthful of broth.

Kate's rebuke was automatic. 'Don't speak with your mouth full.'

Agnes said, 'I sent her for salt. She was hanging around under my feet and deeving me and I was glad to see the back of her. Though,' she cast another glance at the window, 'if the wind had been as strong then as it is now, I might have thought better of it.'

Kate, glad of the distraction, said, 'At any rate, it should blow the cobwebs away, and, if it is a hard ride, will perhaps content her for a day or two.'

Agnes humphed. 'It'll take more than a gust or two of wind to put Maggie off. She's aye after being out, and riding her favourite occupation, as Anna...' She broke off, apology in her eyes.

'We cannot always avoid mention of Anna, indeed, it may be better to talk of her. I think they would have been fine friends, though,' the sides of her mouth lifted a fraction, this time in genuine amusement, 'there would likely have been more than a few arguments. Three redheads in the family wouldn't have made for an easy life.'

Ellie was wiping her bowl with a chunk of bread, trying to scoop up a last piece of barley. Agnes indicated the pot on the hearth. 'Are you for more? I think we could spare a little?' She took Ellie's bowl, refilled it, her satisfaction plain. 'Nothing beats a bairn with a good appetite.'

The door burst open, the wind catching it and throwing it back against the wall.

Maggie was framed in the opening, her hair wild. 'Apologies.' For once there seemed to be a real contrition in her voice. 'I hadn't thought to take so long, but the wind was against me all the way there, and then just as I thought the journey home would be more comfortable, it veered to the east and, though with less bite to it, was just as strongly against me as before.' She turned to Agnes. 'But I have your salt, safe and sound, for though it was pelting down as I came away from the town, I left the rain behind so soon as I came inland. Which was just as well, for my left foot is wet through as it is.' She stooped to remove her boot and, turning it up, examined the stitching. 'I knew there was something amiss.' She pulled at a tail of thread and poked her finger through a gap between the upper and sole.

156

Kate took the boot, prodded at the leather around the frayed stitching. 'Likely mendable, which is fortunate, for a pair of boots isn't what I thought of spending money on the now. The word is the new cobbler in Beith is capable and his prices fair.'

Which is more than can be said for the last one.' Agnes cast a glance at her own boots. 'They are moulded to my feet the now, but when first I got them, you'd have thought they were made for a goat, they were that narrow. They pained me for months, until I gave them a right soaking in bog water, and then wore them night and day until they dried to a decent shape. Not that I'd advocate it, mind, for it wasn't the most comfortable of experiences.'

Maggie was looking at her stockinged foot. 'And did you have brown stockings at the end of it?'

'Aye.' It was almost a chuckle. 'But as there is no one but myself to see them, it hardly matters.' Agnes hefted the sack of salt onto her crooked elbow. I'll just put this by and then get you a bite to eat. Wet or not, I'm sure you're famished.'

Maggie squeezed herself onto the bench nearest the fire. 'I am, and a mite chilled.'

'I trust you didn't pay overmuch for the salt?'

'I don't think so.' A glimmer of a smile flitted across Maggie's face. 'I was just loading it into my saddlebag when I overheard a burgess haggling for a similar amount.' There was a trace of pride in her voice. 'And I doubt that she got any more quality than I, but she paid half as much again.'

'The arguments with Robbie have served some useful purpose then. For you were aye tenacious in holding out for your own way. Though whether it is enough to make up for the aggravation of listening to your bickering is another matter altogether.' Agnes, pleased that Maggie's expedition had been successful and mindful of the narrowness of their purse, made mention of Robbie without thought.

'Where is Robbie?' It was an innocent enough question, but one which neither Kate nor Agnes answered. Ellie filled in the pause.

'Gone away. And we don't know where. It's a secret. From all of us. But,' and here she seemed to swell in importance, 'I saw him. And he promised me a present when he comes home,' her voice betrayed a slight wobble, 'but I don't know when and I hope it's soon.'

'It will be.' Kate shook her head at Maggie, who had opened her mouth to query further. 'He'll be back before we know it and,' with another glance at Maggie, 'deeving us all so thoroughly with his adventures we'll no doubt be wishing him away again.'

Maggie took the bowl Agnes offered, and with a swift glance at Kate said to Ellie, 'You know more than me then, for I had no idea of Robbie going anywhere, other than to take Aunt Elizabeth's message to Greenock.' She was rewarded by a half-smile from Kate, and a satisfied grin from Ellie, who subsided back onto her seat and began to concentrate again on eating.

The silence that accompanies good food enveloped them, and Kate, watching the girls as they took care of all put in front of them as efficiently as the pigeons that attacked her vegetables in the small plot by the barmkin wall, forced herself to count her blessings. Whatever Robbie's situation, it was good to see the table well provisioned. There had been times in their early days at Braidstane when they would have found it difficult to survive on what Kate received for the medicines and treatments she provided for the folk of the surrounding area, if it hadn't been for the generosity of Elizabeth and Hugh. And if it wouldn't have been starvation they faced, it might have come gey close. But her reputation building, Kate could now provide for her family herself and in a manner that satisfied. Munro would be proud.

Maggie waited only so long as it took for Ellie to be tucked into the truckle bed and for her eyes to flicker shut, before questioning Kate. 'So what is it with Robbie then?'

With a quick look to be sure Ellie was indeed away, Kate said, 'Ellie saw Robbie setting off yesterday morning, his saddlebags overfull, and was promised a present if she told no one what she had seen. His clothes are all gone, his blanket also. He spoke of your father, so it must be to France he's headed, perhaps with some notion of bringing him home.' She paused, stared into the fire. 'God knows I long to see him, but I have not Robbie's confidence that it's safe.'

'Will he find him?' Maggie homed in on the crucial point.

'The regiment's whereabouts won't be hard to track, once, that is, he makes it to France. But there is the small matter of the channel to cross.'

Maggie was thinking aloud. 'But surely, if John Shaw is heading for Holland … isn't it the most likely thing that Robbie would go with him, and make for France from there? Isn't that what he plagued you for permission to do?'

'If he thought John would take him on his own say-so.'

'Why wouldn't he? He would have no reason to think anything other than what Robbie told him, especially when he came with messages from here.'

'You're right. I suppose I should be grateful the crossing is likely taken care of.'

Maggie, her interest fully aroused, teased at the problem.'Where would he get the money? Once on his way to France, he'd have to pay for food and lodgings. It won't be a day or two's journey just.

'A week or two more like, at the least. And as to money, I've no idea. He must have salted something away.'

Agnes weighed in. 'Praise where praise is due. He has a head on his shoulders, and though often he puts it to uses that would be better left alone, yet in a matter such as this I suspicion he wouldn't go unprepared.' She allowed herself a smile. 'You have only to think of the food he puts away to know he won't allow himself to starve. Oh...'

'What?'

'He has been so helpful to Hugh these last months, perhaps he was paid something for his efforts. Not,' Agnes added hastily, 'that I think Hugh would have anticipated him using any monies for a venture such as this...'

'No?' Kate's scepticism spilled out.

'No. Hugh may think Robbie's interest in the Gardes a positive thing, but he wouldn't go against your wishes in this way, or not until Robbie's birthday is past.'

'Perhaps not. But he might have taken thought to the possible effects of giving Robbie money...'

'At least if Robbie has sufficient funds it lessens the danger of the journey. Think on that.'

'I am thinking, but a pouch full of money can be a danger also, a magnet for all the worst sorts of people.'

'You do not lessen the danger by fretting, only may make yourself ill. Two months from now we may see him home again, and bringing welcome word.' Agnes cleared the remnants of their supper from the table, resting a reassuring hand on Kate's shoulder in the passing. 'With good fortune and a following wind as your father used to say.'

'Pray God then, that is what he gets, though whether it is what he deserves, is another matter.'

'Don't be too hard on the lad.'

Kate looked at Agnes in surprise. 'Since when have you been soft on Robbie? Well-intentioned he might have been, but it is a foolishness nonetheless, and one we may all live to regret.'

'He isn't a child,' Maggie said, and Kate, glancing at her face, knew that, sympathetic as she was towards her brother, it was her own freedom of movement she sought to gain.

Maggie's chin lifted. 'And shouldn't be treated as one. We are neither of us children, and the lack of a father has made us more capable of looking after ourselves, rather than less.'

Chapter 19

The rain that caught Maggie at Irvine was coming down straight at Kilmaurs, turning the tracks into rivers of mud, making any thought of driving a cart impracticable. The enforced rest had William stamping about the castle, growling at everyone who crossed his path, an unwelcome return to his habitual temperament that Lady Glencairn had hoped permanently dispelled by the plans for Broomelaw.

Glencairn, his own return to court frustrated by the weather, had even less sympathy for William's gripes. 'We are well into May, this weather unlikely to last long. Having waited six years, what odds an extra day or two? '

'The men are contracted and will need to be paid whether they have started work or not, is that to your liking?'

'Wasting money is never to my liking. But it is common sense to wait, however unpalatable. If a cart be spilled or a leg is broken for the sake of hurry, that would have its own cost and maybe more than the extra wages.'

William thumped his hand on the table, the candlesticks swaying. 'You were not always so careful. A few years ago, the men would have worked as agreed or lose their wages.

This is an ill change.'

'Ill change indeed.' Glencairn's face darkened, a warning sign that William, focused on his own frustrations, failed to notice. 'A few years ago you would have had more respect. Remember who holds the purse strings and take care you do not push me too far. If you cannot keep a rein on your tongue in private, at least ensure you do so in front of the men. This plan for Broomelaw is not so forward I cannot draw back.'

William took a step towards his father, opened his mouth to respond, thought better of it.

'A wise move.' Glencairn bent to poke life into the fire, as if by turning away from William's anger he could diffuse it. 'It is not all lost, we can make use of the delay to discuss the plans more fully. There are issues the survey has raised that will bear consideration.'

'And I am to be part of these considerations?'

William's sarcasm seemed wasted on Glencairn, his answer deceptively mild. 'Of course. It is, after all, to be your home.' He went to the doorway, shouted on a servant. 'Bring the steward and send for the master mason ... and a jug of ale to wet our deliberations.'

Chapter 20

The weather clearing, they gathered at Kilmaurs at first light on the third day, the master mason summoned to the solar to listen to Glencairn's final orders in private.

'It suits me to allow my son to think he is in charge of this venture, and it will suit you to do the same. But do not allow him to stretch the job beyond the figures we have agreed, or you will find yourself carrying the extra cost. If there is a serious difficulty, you may send to me,' he waved his hand, 'but I do not expect to be troubled with matters of little consequence. I trust you are up to the task.' He produced a semblance of a smile, offered a sop. 'If all is concluded to my satisfaction, and in a timely fashion, there will be an extra payment for you, in accordance with the job done.'

The mason looked Glencairn straight in the eye, though his words betrayed his uneasiness. 'Does the Master of Glencairn remain throughout? Or can we look to ourselves?'

Glencairn snorted. 'He won't settle for a blanket roll in a derelict stable for more than a night or two, you may be sure of that. Once the work is started he will likely lodge at Renfrew ... or he may return here. I do not think you need worry over constant supervision.'

The mason nodded and turned to take his leave, his mind already on the task ahead: the treacherous ground to be negotiated, the materials they would need to take, the possibilities for purchasing others nearer to hand as the job progressed, the unknowns that might yet spiral the cost beyond any profit. He was jolted to a halt as Glencairn continued, 'But do not take it as a licence for shoddy work, nor for slacking. See that you keep to the terms of our agreement, or you will answer to me.' It was an affront to his integrity the mason ignored with difficulty, inwardly seething. Glencairn glanced out the window to where William circled on the cobbles. The dismissal was clear. 'And I suggest you do not mention this conversation to my son, for I doubt he'd take it kindly.'

They headed northwards towards Broomelaw, everywhere they looked evidence of the recent rain: burns which were normally a trickle become rivers, fast-flowing through newly cut gashes in the hillsides; meadows strewn with hay and dead vegetation; the occasional animal carcase trapped in a mess of uprooted trees, their leaves moving in the breeze like tattered flags. Great swathes of water, the remnants of flooding, lay in stagnant pools in every dip and hollow, making the going difficult and requiring wide detours from their normal route to avoid the carts getting bogged down in the soft ground. William, infused with a childish enthusiasm at Kilmaurs, became steadily

165

more truculent, every obstacle to their progress clearly a personal affront. The fact that Glencairn had been right to insist they waited clearly doing nothing to improve his temper. The mason shared his desire to have the journey completed as speedily as possible, though not his irritation, for the sky was the clear rinsed blue that often follows a storm, and all around them, in the warmth of the sun, steam rose, softening the contours of the landscape. On the brow of a hill they passed a coppice of young trees, and issuing from them a burst of birdsong as if every thrush in Ayrshire congregated there. The mason, risking a glance at William's face, decided against comment. Though his spirits were lifted by the singing of the birds, he very much doubted that William felt the same. Nor was he likely to welcome casual conversation.

As if to prove the point, William broke the silence, his focus clear. 'If we do not meet with further obstructions, we should manage Broomelaw with time enough to set the men to work today. You have brought all necessary materials?'

'To begin, yes. After that, how things progress will determine our needs. It's not always possible to predict them with certainty, and best to buy what is required as and when they're needed.' The mason was aware William wasn't impressed by his answer, and steeled himself for rebuke.

'Of what value all your deliberations with my father then, if they did not produce a definite plan?'

Glencairn's warning ringing in the mason's head, he said, 'Your father understands the plan can only be conceived in the most general terms, and so we spoke. This morning he was instructing me to keep a close eye to the

166

budget, that is all.' It was true as far as it went.

'As to budget,' William's tone became combative, 'I have little control over it, and less interest. But as I am here and my father is not, your task will be to give me what I want; how you satisfy my father as to costings is your own concern.'

The mason dipped his head, thought – harder to deal with than his father then, if that be possible, his reputation in the county well-founded. Treacherous ground indeed, and maybe more so than the going underfoot.

To the surprise and chagrin of the master mason, William lasted a full week at Broomelaw, succeeding only in getting in the way and managing to irritate all around him. Wherever the workmen turned, he was there on their tail, querying this and questioning that, allowing nothing past without explanation or justification, so that the master mason feared a mutiny. At the beginning of the second week, when William announced his intention to make for Kilmaurs, for a day or two at least, the mason found it hard to conceal his relief. And wasted no time in calling the men together.

'Now perhaps we can make some real progress, without William Cunninghame aye looking over our shoulders. But how long we will have peace I cannot say, so it's best we make the most of our time.'

Chapter 21

Kate was just about to answer a call to Beith, and in consequence was making up a new compound for rheum, when Catherine Montgomerie came flying across the barmkin waving a letter like a flag of surrender. She was just ahead of Elizabeth, who was smiling as she said, 'I'm glad I caught you. There's news from my brother.'

Kate scanned the proffered note. '...*written in haste, that I might set your minds at rest. The details I trust will wait until I can see you in person, but I'm more than happy to oblige you and to give Robbie passage to Veere, and will set him on his way thereafter, well provisioned, with a suitable mount and in good company. I can't contract to wait for his return, but will instruct my agent in Veere to make all appropriate arrangements when the time is right.*'

'You see. He will be well looked after and likely back before we know.'

'It was a presumption on our friendship Robbie should not have made. What your brother will think of us when the truth of it is known...'

Agnes was brusque. 'It's hardly reasonable, Kate, to

168

blame the boy for doing only what you would likely have done in his place. I don't mind you as a child who aye kept within bounds. You thought he would obey your injunction to wait, and in that you've been proved wrong. But don't say it wasn't in your mind to approach John Shaw to take Robbie with him two months since, for I have lived with you long enough to know. As for Shaw, better he thinks it was an arrangement made with your blessing, than that he comes home and is made to feel guilt for actions not his blame. Be grateful that Robbie's journey is eased, and save your scolding for when he does return.'

'If Robbie has lied to John in one thing, how do we know he hasn't lied in his further plans too?'

'Truth or lies, thinking on it will do none of us any good. There is trouble enough in a day without adding to it by imagining ills that may not come. You have had one encouraging word. Hold to that.'

Out of the corner of her eye Kate saw Ellie and Catherine Montgomerie edging from the door of the pantry towards the bastle house entrance, their hands firmly behind their backs. There was a telltale dusting of sugar on Ellie's bodice and the whiff of cinnamon in the air, and Kate thought of the pastries Agnes had laid on the stone slab to cool and her likely annoyance if they were caught helping themselves. She took a step sideways to block Agnes' view – it was a temptation hard to resist and no harm in it. And though the bastle house was not their own, they were not so straightened they couldn't spare a pastry or two. But she would prefer Agnes to bake other than Robbie's favourites. Perhaps John Shaw wouldn't be long in coming, and the news when he came encouraging.

It was not John Shaw however, but John Montgomerie
who blew in on a bitter north-easterly wind more akin to
winter than early summer, flurries of hail the size of rabbit
droppings mixed into the rain. Ellie and the Montgomerie
girls were moping in a deep window reveal, their faces
pressed against the glass, watching the hail build up on
the ledge outside, then melt and fuse together into a lumpy
slush. Kate, likewise frustrated by the return to unseason-
al weather, was crossing to the tower house in the hope
that Elizabeth's company might go some way to settle her.
Her twin fears: for Robbie, where he might be, whether
he was safe, if his mission to find Munro had been successful, and, this the hardest thought of all, the one about
which she swithered daily, if he had convinced his father
to risk a journey home; and for Maggie, whose attitude at
present was a mite disquieting. She had declined to accompany Kate to the tower, preferring to stay in the confines
of the bastle house, an unexpected choice which left Kate
uneasy. There had been several occasions of late when she
had caught a glimpse of something secretive in Maggie's
eyes, a conversation turned, a question avoided. It was a
new awkwardness Kate wasn't sure how to handle, torn between keeping a close control on Maggie's movements and
allowing her some level of freedom. There were times Kate
thought her a child still, a feeling at odds with the flashes
of new-found maturity evident in her interest in how Kate
dealt with her patients. At odds too with her careful handling of the more dangerous of Kate's remedies.

Agnes, agreeing that Maggie had something to hide, was less inclined to worry; her counsel, to give Maggie more responsibility and freedom, rather than less, and thus provide a safe outlet for her energies. 'Think on your own childhood, and the freedoms you had, which did more good than harm.'

Kate thought instead, but didn't say so, that it was fine for Agnes to talk, for it wasn't her who had one bairn dead and another goodness knew where, and a husband as good as lost to her. In all of this she knew she was unjust, for Agnes' loyalty to the Munros was unquestioned and her willingness to spend of herself on their behalf, unlimited. In every way that mattered they were Agnes' family, and whatever ills they suffered, she shared in them. Recognising that confining Maggie carried its own risks, not least the danger of driving her to some foolishness akin to Robbie's, Kate began to allow Maggie to make longer visits alone if the ailment was minor, trusting it would be enough to satisfy her restlessness. Her best guess was that it was thought of Robbie and his freedom that irked her. Her suspicion both right and wrong.

Kate was halfway across the barmkin when Elizabeth, with a half-strangled shriek, erupted from the tower entrance and flew past her, tramping her shawl into a puddle of slush in her haste. Kate swung round to see her scooped up as if she was but a bairn. Her voice as she cried out, 'John! Where did you spring from?' squeezed by his embrace from her normal well-modulated tones into a breathless squeal. Kate held out her hand – this then was John Montgomerie: physician, home from Italy, and full no doubt of all the latest theories and practices, and if the gift of the Paré he had sent her last year was anything to go by, willing to share his knowledge with her.

He set Elizabeth down and bowed, his touch on Kate's fingers light. 'You must be Mistress Grant?'

Elizabeth, still clinging to his arm, said, 'No need for such formality, she's Kate to us all.'

'Kate, then. Although we haven't met, I feel I already know you well.'

'Likewise.' Her face lit up. 'I must thank you for the Paré, it has proved its usefulness many times over.' She glanced back at the bastle house. 'I should get Maggie. Whatever business occupies her, she won't want to miss you.'

Behind them the tower door banged, spilling out the Montgomerie girls who splashed across the courtyard without any regard to their soft slippers. Elizabeth put an arm round each girl's shoulder. 'As you see, your nieces sprout like weeds, and...' she grimaced at their feet, 'have as little regard for their clothes as their father.'

John bent down and retrieved Elizabeth's dripping shawl. 'Or mother.'

Kate returned to the tower, Maggie in tow, raindrops sparkling on her hair and shoulders, dark splashes around the hem of her skirt. John was in full flow, the Montgomerie girls sitting cross-legged at his feet. He broke off to greet them.

'Maggie.' He bowed. 'Quite the young lady I hear.'

'And fast on the way to becoming my right-hand man, with a fine head for remedies and a deft hand for the mixing of them.' He bowed again and Kate had the suspicion

he hid amusement at how Maggie swelled at the commen-
dation.

They settled to supper and to John's tales of life in Italy,
his mention of the Santa Maria Nuova hospital of particular interest to Kate.

Her expression was wistful. 'It must be satisfying to
work in such a place.'

'Sometimes, yes, at others...' He looked down at the
girls at his feet, paused. 'Perhaps that discussion is best
kept for another time.' A particularly strong gust of wind
rattled the shutters and, as if glad of the interruption, he
turned the conversation. 'I had thought to find summer
here, not an extended winter.'

Elizabeth sighed. 'It's been a strange time. An early
spring, the lambs coming thick and fast and even a calf
or two, which looked to set us up for the year ahead, and
then the return to a winter more severe than it had been all
season. For two weeks we were barricaded in by snow four
foot deep. It hasn't been easy, for the stock, or for Hugh.
We have given up anticipating the weather, tholing what
comes while praying for better.'

I take it we can't expect him in yet awhile?'

'No. He feels the miss of Robbie, who proved his worth
ten times over in the worst of the weather.'

John glanced at Kate. 'Where is Robbie?'

Elizabeth answered, her tone light, conversational. 'In
France, looking for his father, and will, we trust, bring
word of Munro and Patrick both to us.'

Kate's hands were clasped on her lap. 'I had hoped his
usefulness with the stock would have held Robbie here, but
it was not his wish.'

As if John thought to spare her further pain he turned

the conversation again, swallowed his yawn. 'Lost many lambs?'

'A fair few. It is a frustration to Hugh that half the autumn's work has come to nothing, so he isn't his cheeriest the now. He will be in by dark, if you can stay awake that long...'

John patted his stomach. 'I've been dreaming of Ishbel's cooking for months past and perhaps have overindulged.'

Elizabeth voiced the question which had been in Kate's mind also. 'Is this a fleeting visit or might you bide a while?'

John hesitated. 'My time in Florence is done, but...' he shook his head as if to halt the smile spreading over Elizabeth's face, 'I can't stay hereabouts. Besides...' this with a grin towards Kate, 'there is competition now I fear might best me.'

'Serious though,' Elizabeth also smiled at Kate, as if to reassure her she meant no insult by the comment, 'do you have plans?'

Again the glance towards the children, the fractional hesitation, the too hearty, 'When Hugh is here...'

'Oh, but...' Maggie started, but withered under Kate's warning stare. Ishbel reappeared from the kitchens carrying a pastry from which steam rose, sweet and strong.

'Brambles!' John was smiling in earnest now. 'I did think I was full, but I daresay a little space can be found.'

'You're fortunate. They are of last season's preserving and remain only because they had been pushed to the back of the pantry shelf and forgotten until I decided to have a redd-out last week. Remembering how I used to clip your ear for filching from the bowls of fruit I had ready for preserving, I thought you might welcome a tart. It may be a trifle pungent for the bairns, the fruit having sat so long,

174

but I daresay you'll not mind if it's a mite fermented.'

'We'll not mind either,' piped Ellie.

In the ensuing laughter, Kate found herself back at Broomelaw, seeing Anna, having demolished a jar of candied fruits that had been kept overlong, the seal faulty, weave her way from the kitchen to the solar, her giggles punctuated by hiccups. And Munro, struggling to keep his face straight as he carried her to the truckle bed in the attic chamber, where she curled into a ball like a hedgehog and slept the clock round.

With a pain akin to indigestion, Kate declined the tart, an omission that Elizabeth, after a glance at her face, let pass without comment. Instead she said, 'The word is that Dunlop is to have a new minister. Old Hamilton is getting beyond his usefulness, though ousting him remains something of an issue. He holds to the divine right of clergy, his Presbyterian tendencies little more than skin-deep.'

As a distraction it proved effective, Kate's forehead puckering. 'But you have little to do with the church in Dunlop surely?'

'No indeed, but Hugh has little love for the Hamiltons, who are rather too close to the Cunninghames for comfort, particularly old Hamilton's son. If the father is persuaded out to grass there will be little reason for the son to be around these parts. He disparaged Hugh at my mother's funeral and with seeming pleasure, and Hugh has never forgotten it.'

Hugh was in the open doorway, cold air following him up the stair. 'What have I not forgotten?' he began, then broke off. 'John! Where did you spring from?' Kate saw the obvious affection with which the brothers greeted each other. And from nowhere a remembrance of Munro's voice, strong and clear. '…I liked them, Kate, and so would you, for they like each other so well it would be hard to do otherwise…' Her throat constricting, she closed her eyes, as if by so doing she could capture Munro's fleeting image, draw him close. Hugh was laughing at John's story of a patient in Florence who suffered from every ailment known to man, and a few others besides.

Elizabeth said, 'It will be a man of course, They're aye the worst patients.'

'True enough.' John scraped the last remnants of tart from the platter, and with a nod of appreciation for Ishbel, settled back into his chair. 'I have to agree, though it pains me to admit it, that men, when not at war, seem to suffer least, but complain most. If they had to suffer childbirth…'

Kate finished his sentence for him. 'There would be a lot less bairns in the world.'

Elizabeth, perhaps fearing where the conversation might go next, stood up, and amid protests shepherded the Montgomerie children to bed. Kate, following her example, splashed a protesting Ellie across the barmkin and left her in Agnes' hands, with a hurried, 'She will likely take a wee bit while to settle, for everyone was that excited at John's return; my own head is birling.'

'Away you go then.' Agnes shooed her towards the door. 'No doubt he will have plenty to say of doctoring in yon foreign place, though why it should be better than at home I don't know, but you'll not be wanting to miss his speir'

'Yon foreign place, as you call it, is Florence, and one of the foremost cities in Italy for medical advancements and far ahead of anything we have here.' Kate had a distant look. 'And somewhere I'd give my eye teeth to go.'

'Aye well, your teeth are likely more useful to you

where they are.' Agnes relented. 'We can aye learn, and I daresay he is as good a teacher as many and maybe better than most.'

Raising her skirts above her ankle, Kate picked her way through the puddles back to the tower. The door to the hall was ajar, laughter spilling out. Elizabeth, now seated on the settle by the fire, patted the space beside her. John had pulled a chair close to the hearth and sprawled, his legs outstretched, toasting his feet. Maggie was curled on a cushion, her hands clasped around her knees, her gaze fixed on him.

John broke off to smile at Kate. 'I'm glad you found the Paré useful. It is, I think, one of the best books on *gynaec-ologia* that I know of. And I don't say it just because I have met the man. Though to listen to him … his enthusiasm and knowledge was infectious. To be able to discuss his methods here, a bonus previously unthought of.' He nod-ded at Maggie, who beamed in return. 'And to see how your assistant does, that also will be a pleasure.'

Elizabeth said, 'There were a lot of things unthought of when last you were here. And hardly surprising, given the length of time passed.' It was the mildest of rebukes, but brought a serious tone to the conversation that Kate would rather had been avoided.

With a glance this time at both Kate and Elizabeth, John said, 'And the old issues, are they quiet the now?'

'If by that you mean have we seen or heard anything of the Cunninghames, the answer is no.' Maggie's tone was combative. 'Though you wouldn't know it by the way we still skulk about as if we expect to be discovered at any moment.'

'Maggie…' Kate, not wanting to embarrass her by

treating her as a child in front of John, tried to face her down, but she refused to be silenced,

'You cannot deny it. It is the past drives us, not the present.'

'God knows I wish we could forget the past, but we cannot. It threatens us still.' Kate turned to Hugh for support, but Maggie was too quick for her.

'We have been six years here and no sign of trouble. And that the reason Robbie…'

Elizabeth put a restraining hand on Maggie's shoulder. 'Six years, long as it may seem to you, Maggie, is no guarantee. History tells us that. Old enmities may appear to slumber, but much like a dragon in his lair, sleeping with one eye always open, it takes little to wake them and we all do well to remember it. Your mother fears William Cunninghame, and with good reason; it is only that he thinks you dead which has protected you … and us, these past years. It would be more than a foolishness to reignite a flame at present tamped down.'

Maggie subsided, but Kate, seeing how tightly she clasped her hands behind her back, understood it as a tactical withdrawal, rather than acceptance, and worried afresh at the secretive look she glimpsed in Maggie's eyes.

John stretched his feet onto the hearth. 'I'm sorry. I had no notion of stoking any fire other than this one.' He smiled at Elizabeth. 'Now that the bairns are away, you can tell me all the stories they wouldn't want repeated, so that I'll have something to tease them with tomorrow.'

The next hour passed in a blur of reminiscences, punctuated by Hugh's bellows and John's more restrained laughter. Kate, whose mind was buzzing with a hundred questions of the hospital in Florence, stifled a yawn, and

Elizabeth, seeing it, called a halt.

'Good as it is to talk, the morning will be on us all too soon, and while left to ourselves we might take the luxury of lying long, neither the bairns nor the livestock will.'

John handed Kate and Maggie to the door. 'If you are not called away in the forenoon, perhaps we might have time for more detailed discussion. There is much I can tell of the Santa Maria Nuova that you might find of interest.' He gave her a lop-sided grin. 'And besides the Paré, there are other books I have with me that I hope you will enjoy to read, though some are a mite controversial.'

Kate laughed. 'Fitting then. Hugh, supportive as he is, already thinks some of my methods a touch outlandish. Forbye that he is generally too polite to say so.'

'Not the Hugh I remember then. Neither tact nor diplomacy were his strongest suits.'

Hugh was at Kate's shoulder. 'All the time I have spent at court has not been entirely wasted. I can feign a politeness like the best of them, always a useful skill when dealing with women.' And this to John. 'As no doubt you will learn for yourself one day.'

Kate was aware of a stiffening, of a flush of colour suffusing John's neck and ears. She placed her hand on top of his, twisted the door handle. 'Till tomorrow then, I look forward to it.'

Chapter 22

John Montgomerie was as good as his word, arriving at the bastle house before Kate had thought to alert Agnes to the likelihood of a visitor. A mistake, as Agnes had chosen that morning to set to blackening the swee hanging over the hearth, the fire below allowed to go out. A cool day, despite the season, Kate compensated by a burnishing of the pans, attacking the insides with a mixture of wood ash and lye, before, mindful of the brambles Ishbel had unearthed, turning to the contents of the pantry lest anything similar lurked there. And as is often the case, what should have been a small task grew far beyond her intention. She was just squeezing a remnant of a cone of salt onto the table, already piled high with an assortment of smoked meats and cheeses and jars of all shapes and sizes, when the knock came.

Agnes, her arms blackened almost to the elbows, turned, her dismay at being found in such a state clear.

'I hope this is a call for you and not a visitor.'

Kate, wiping her hands on the sackcloth tied around her waist to save her skirt, said, 'Ah … it'll be John, come to make good his promise to show me some books he has brought.' Her apology was heartfelt. 'I didn't think to see him so soon.'

'You didn't think at all, that's the long and the short of it; if you had done, you would have saved us the embarrassment of being found in such a guddle.'

John poked his head around the door and, casting a glance at the table, said, 'If you'd rather I came back another time...'

'And what use would that be?' Agnes was caustic. 'You've seen us at our worst now, not much use our pretending to a better show.'

'It isn't show I have come for, but to bring Kate books and for the chance to air some of the latest medical theories without fear of being laughed out of the room.'

'Hugh...?'

'Has taken himself off on a message to Edinburgh. And expects to be back tomorrow or the next day. I was preparing myself to spend the day entertaining the girls, when Elizabeth, claiming my presence would disrupt their schooling, suggested I disrupt your work instead.'

'You'd best have a seat.' Agnes was working the bellows, breathing life into the fire. 'Though it's little enough heat you'll get for a good while yet, so I wouldn't advise you to remove your jerkin.'

'Perhaps...' Kate was tentative, 'to give time for the fire to draw a little, you might like to see the storeroom...'

Agnes rocked back on her heels. 'To give time for me to make some semblance of order from this mess, more like.'

Kate, aware that the best way to handle Agnes was to allow her to disagree, said, 'Or you could sit here, John, and I could listen as I tidy, for it was I who made "this mess"

181

in the first place. It won't take long to make a clearance.'

'Away with the both of you, little use you'd be, Kate, with John distracting you with talk of ailments and their cures. Besides that, I have no desire to hear a litany of symptoms, else I may find I am at death's door all unknowing, from a multiplicity of ills.'

John looked around at the neat shelves of the storeroom with their rows of tightly stoppered bottles and the baskets underneath containing an assortment of packets labelled in a clear hand. He nodded his acknowledgement. 'Well set I see, and able for most calls that come your way.'

'Not most,' Kate shook her head. 'There are aye conditions I cannot help, either because I do not have the knowledge or the remedies required. Glasgow is a mite far for me to visit the apothecaries myself, and though Hugh is willing enough to fetch and carry on my behalf, that is of little use if I do not know exactly what I want.'

John was moving along the shelves, picking out a jar here, a sachet there. 'Most of these you've gathered and prepared yourself then?'

'Yes. And fortunate that Agnes, despite the haste of our flight from Broomelaw, thought to pack my mother's herbals. At least I can be confident of what I collect and,' with a grin and a nod at the bottle of belladonna in John's hand, 'I haven't poisoned anyone yet, or not that I know of at any rate.'

'You'd know. Bad news aye travels fast, and your reputation only as good as your last patient. Indeed,' he set the bottle back on the shelf, 'when something goes awry, keeping other patients' confidence is like holding water in a sieve, and often the only course is to move elsewhere and start again.'

'And was...' Kate began.

'No,' John chewed on his lip, 'the reason I left Florence is more ... personal.' He stopped.

'You don't need to explain.' Kate gestured to the bench where John had set down the books. 'Whatever your reasons for being here, I cannot but be grateful for the chance to examine these books of yours. Aside from the Paré and Mother's few herbals, my only sources of medical information have been the pamphlets pedlars bring, and you know the value of those.'

Their shared laughter was broken as the door flew open, Maggie sliding to a stop at John's elbow, indignation oozing from her. 'You should have called...'

John vacated the stool. 'Well timed. Your mother was just about to send for you. I thought you'd both like to see these.' He slid two loose pages onto the table.

Maggie gazed at the drawing of a foetus in the womb, then lifted her head, her eyes shining. 'It's beautiful, who drew it?'

'Leonardo da Vinci. There are many such sheets in Florence, at the Santa Maria Nuova and elsewhere. They are well regarded, and, as you can see, with justice. Because of his great talent, he was permitted to dissect corpses there, and no doubt it added greatly to his understanding.'

'Is this a drawing from a dissection?' Maggie's eyes widened.

'Possibly, though more likely an amalgamation of knowledge gained over many years.' He stabbed the page. 'What do you think of the writing? Is it not odd?'

She was turning it this way and that. 'What language is it?'

'Italian, but if you wish to read it, it must be held up to a mirror, and even then, it isn't the clearest of scripts.'

'Why would he do that?'

'No one knows. Some say for secrecy. But,' John shrugged, 'I find that hardly credible, for he was free enough with his ideas in the right quarters, and there are many anatomists since whose works owe much to him. There is a suggestion he wished to protect himself from the church, yet the illustrations are evidence enough to damn him should anyone wish to denounce him for his ideas, and the notes are organised, and often all on a subject brought together on a single page, as here. It does not seem the action of a man who wished to hide his knowledge. Publication was suggested, but nothing was done with them in his lifetime, and though a follower called Melzi spent many years working on them, collecting them into chapters, he also failed to finish.'

Maggie was still holding the sheet, her finger tracing the curve of the foetus. 'And are they all still together?'

'No. Many remain in Florence, but there is much talk of notes and drawings which have found their way into private collections all over Europe. And as you see, even I have acquired a couple.'

'So how...?'

'Did I come by these two?' Kate saw the flicker of a pulse under John's eye.

'It was a ... gift.' A pause, as if he chose his words carefully, a tightness about his mouth. 'That I was prevailed upon to accept. As small compensation for my leaving Florence.'

Kate picked up the second sheet covered in anatomical drawings of an arm: some displaying the skeleton, some the muscles. 'This is so detailed, so clear.'

'I know.' The tension left John's face. 'It is a talent we aren't likely to see again and to which we owe much. And if it has its roots in dissection, what harm cutting a corpse? They are hardly in a position to object. When I am gone I'd rather my body was of some use than that it mouldered in some boggy hollow, pushing up the moss.'

Kate steeled herself not to think of the burial mounds at Broomelaw and the suspicion that her own safety and that of the children had been bought by their desecration. She forced herself to concentrate on the title page of the book *Treatise on Surgery*, the thrill of anticipation warring with a sadness within her. For however much she read and learnt, the opportunity to practise any of it in Ayrshire would forever evade her.

John patted the page. 'This is Paré's later book, building on his *Method of Curing Wounds* ... and much more comprehensive. See...' He indicated the wear on the binding. 'I have found it exceedingly helpful, and no doubt will so again.'

Maggie, absorbed by a woodcut illustration in the second book, Vesalius' *De Fabrica Corporis Humani*, said, 'I'd like to be an anatomist.'

'Why not?' John was smiling. 'There is a precedent. And though it is two hundred years since, they still talk of her in Florence. Her name was Allessandra Giliani, assistant to Mondino de Liuzzi, and although only nineteen, a gifted prosector,' he elaborated, '...a preparer of corpses for dissection. A plaque in a church in Rome honours her name, and who knows what fame she might have achieved

185

had she not died young.'

A tinge of envy in Kate's voice. 'Italy must have long been more open to the talents of women than we are here.'

'True. Santa Maria has female pharmacists and physicians both, held in almost equal regard to their male counterparts. If you were to visit the hospital, you would likely not want to come home.'

Maggie was jigging on her stool, eyes alight, and Kate felt the need to inject a note of realism, however much she shared Maggie's obvious desire.

'Little chance the now, so no use thinking on it.' And then, as Maggie's face fell, she qualified, 'Though who knows what may be possible in years to come.' She ruffled Maggie's hair. 'Mayhap there *will* be a famous anatomist in our family one day.'

John smiled at Maggie, asked, 'And Robbie? How far do his ambitions stretch?'

Maggie was matter of fact: 'He wants to be a lancer, with Uncle Patrick and our father.'

'I hate the thought he may be riding straight into danger, yet I cannot keep him here.' Kate was kneading her palm with her thumb. 'We have had no news from Patrick for months since. For all we know...'

John touched her shoulder. 'Don't think it. Besides, with every month the dangers in France diminish, the populace swinging to Henri's side.'

'The strife in France has continued over many years, as wars over religion tend to do. Are we truly to believe it faltering now?'

'The word is this time Henri's conversion will stand.'

'This time?'

'He converted before, to save himself from the St

Bartholomew massacre. And who could blame him. Two thousand dead on that day alone, and, it is said, some thirty thousand in the year that followed. Who would not wish to escape that carnage?'

Kate nodded. 'I was but a child at the time, but news of the massacres reached even to Renfrew. It was a horror that gave me night terrors, and would still were I to think on it overlong. But I do not remember talk of Henri. Was he long a Catholic?'

'As long as his imprisonment. Once he escaped he became his own man again. And has remained so for almost twenty years. To convert now bears the stamp of serious intent.'

'There is still the war with Spain. This reconciliation Henri seeks within his own borders, what is it but a means to gain more soldiers to fight on his side.' She made no attempt to keep the bitterness out of her voice. 'And has he not enough of ours already?'

'Robbie is not alone in his ambition to join the Scots Gardes, nor,' as if he knew the root of her bitterness, 'can the blame for it be laid entirely at his father's door. The Gardes have an honourable history and have always been well regarded. They are so still. What boy would not wish the excitement such a career might give.'

'You did not choose it.'

'For me it was always healing. But though my focus has for too long been on study, and the gaining of experience under the tutelage of greater men, I may yet get the opportunity to serve in a field hospital, and I will not pass on it should it come my way.'

They had forgotten Maggie. She laid aside the illustration, queried, 'They say the French King rides at the front of his armies to show he believes God is on his side. Do you believe it?'

'Every army in the world thinks God on their side. I think … that God must be above all our differences, religious or otherwise, or he is not God at all. That if we could but understand him properly, we would not divide him so.' There was an unaccustomed vehemence in John's voice, an undertone of some private pain which made Kate wonder afresh at his reasons for leaving Florence. She reached out to him, an instinctive gesture, to which he responded with a smile, but it didn't reach his eyes, so that any thought of probing further died before it had begun – she wasn't family to pry into Montgomerie affairs.

The last of the sunlight painted a lattice pattern across the wall above the fireplace as John once again poked his head around the bastle house door. He had been at Braidstane four days, and Kate, having refused the invitation to join the Montgomeries for supper on the third evening, aware that Agnes' patience with her defection was running thin, smiled her welcome. She gestured to the chair by the hearth. 'I hope Elizabeth doesn't feel I'm stealing you away, only it is so good to talk.'

'With someone who understands. I know.' John settled in the chair. 'It is one thing to show an interest, as Elizabeth has, and Hugh also in his way, but it makes little more sense to them than if I were a thatcher describing the latest techniques. To have you here is a pleasure that cannot be measured.'

She waited, instinct telling her there was more to come.

'And not just in the medical sense.' He was making a careful study of the floor at her feet, offered, 'If I am to talk to anyone, perhaps it could be you...'

'I would be honoured. It is oft easier to say to a stranger what you cannot say to those who know you best.' She crossed to the window ledge, leant her elbows on the sill, where she had stacked the books he had brought, and allowed him the freedom to speak without being directly observed.

'There was a girl, the daughter of a nobleman...' A pause as if he marshalled his thoughts. 'She turned her ankle and I was called to treat her.' Another pause, and then, with a catch in his voice, 'We became ... friends. More than friends. Her mother and brother welcomed me, her father...' She heard the note of bitterness creep into his voice. 'When he knew where my interest lay ... had I been a Mohammedan asking for permission to carry her off to a harem, his reaction couldn't have been worse...' He took a deep breath. 'It seems there are no degrees among heretics, a Scottish Protestant as far beyond the pale as the rest.' The bitterness had been replaced by anguish. 'She was willing to come away, our plans made, when her mother was stricken by a wasting sickness. I could not ask it of her, seeing the pain it would cause.' He came up beside Kate, placed his hand on the pile of books. 'Her father brought these papers, suggested it was best I put distance between us.' He opened the top book, withdrew the drawing of the foetus. 'So you see, it is scarcely an act of generosity to give this to you, for I cannot bear to keep it, but nor, though it was my first inclination, could I destroy such a thing of beauty.'

Kate laid her hand on his, offered, 'Maybe one day...'

'I dare not hope, though she is my first thought when I wake … the last before I sleep. But if use can be made of these, some good may come.'

She took the cue. 'I had a case not long since where Paré's methods for the turning of the babe proved most useful, though I did not precisely follow it.'

'Oh?' There was renewed interest in his voice.

'It seemed to me that if I was to turn a foetus, why not to bring the head down, as is the normal presentation, rather than the feet. So I used his method, but not to the same end.'

'And how was it?'

'Slower, and if I'm honest, an altogether trickier procedure. It required the aid of the forceps to deliver, so I have you to thank for the success of the experiment, but the principle is right, I'm sure.'

'Maybe you should write a pamphlet, share your new knowledge and practice.'

'A pamphlet by a wise woman? And on such a topic? I think not. There are many who already consider what I do as close to witchcraft, without adding fuel to their fire. I shall be content to teach Maggie when the opportunity arises … as once I thought to teach Robbie.'

'If Robbie's heart is elsewhere, it would have been a trial to you both.'

'I know. He once made the accusation, and with justice, that for me this compensates. I sometimes think Munro, in joining the Scots Gardes, is compensated also. And find myself resenting that times, however unfair it might be.'

As if he wished to ease her guilt, John said, 'Men and women feel differently about such things; it is the way of the world. You will not change it. Take Patrick. He never thought of anything other than the Gardes, and our mother, whatever her private feelings, was wise enough to see he would have been only half a man in any other occupation and so chose to send him away with her blessing.'

'Despite the danger?'

It was clear he chose his words carefully. 'Life is full of dangers, at home or abroad. We of all people should know that. We lessen it where we can and learn to live with the rest. It is the most anyone can do.'

Chapter 23

It was a philosophy occupying Munro's mind, as he accompanied Patrick and the French King on a round of the siege workings. He had returned from a foraging sortie to find Patrick lounging in his tent, making free of his wine. The conversation was at first general, of Munro's success in his latest forays, the position with regard to stores, the constant need for extra supplies; but Munro had the feeling Patrick had more on his mind, an instinct reinforced when he began to talk of the French King. He was lying back on Munro's bedroll, his hands linked behind his head.

'Henri is in his element here, and at liberty to get to know his men in a way that is impossible while we are in quarters in Paris. There is much to be gained and little to be lost in ensuring you are one of those whose names he will remember when this campaign is over.'

This then was the core of it. Munro felt a mixture of excitement and trepidation. 'I take it you've a suggestion to make?'

'I expect to be in need of a new adjutant shortly ... for I suspect de Biron of fishing for one of mine ... I thought it might as well be you: better the devil you know, as they say.' He grinned, the glint in his eyes indicating the loss of the adjutant wasn't altogether unwelcome.

Munro poured himself a drink, settled, enquired, 'The man was troublesome? Or with too strong opinions of his own?'

'Strong opinions I can handle,' again the flash of teeth, 'but swagger I cannot. If we must have scions of the French nobility foisted on the Scots Gardes, a lesser sense of their own importance, titled or not, and a greater sense of respect for us, wouldn't go amiss.'

Munro laughed, made a mock obeisance, wondered how to buy himself time. It was a serious offer, and a generous one, and he wasn't quite sure why he didn't jump at it.

'Well?' Patrick was waiting.

Munro sighed. 'You'll likely think it ridiculous, but to have a formal role of that nature, it is a recognition I will never go home, or not to bide at any rate.'

'To be here at all is an admission of that … as was your reluctance to visit Braidstane last winter when the chance was there.' Patrick was clearly finding it hard to understand his hesitation. 'If a return to Scotland, even for a month, is too risky a proposition, you need to make a future elsewhere. For Kate and the bairns as well as yourself. What of the farmhouse at Cayeux? That is a gift you cannot afford to refuse. I certainly wouldn't.'

'I know, I know. It is but good sense.' Munro swept away his reluctance. 'I will be honoured.'

'Tomorrow then, you can join me when I accompany Henri around the workings.'

'Are you here now for the duration?'

Patrick nodded. 'Yes. Henri has every intention of

taking charge himself.'

And so it proved, the French King constantly moving among the troops, daily travelling the length and breadth of the circumvallation, talking and discussing with the pioneers. Munro, watching him, saw for himself how morale soared, and recognised the value of his approach, the encouragement it provided for the troops, spurring them on to greater efforts. Nor was he above removing his jacket and getting his hands dirty. A useful trait in a King who wished to maintain his popularity, and one to be commended.

On the third day of the inspections, Munro found himself beginning to feel at ease in the King's company, his last reservations concerning the formalising of his role within the Gardes melting away. Patrick was right, Cayeux was a gift too good to turn down. An unlooked for bonus from his foraging trips that he hoped would compensate Kate for the loss of Broomelaw, with the advantage that the house and the land would one day be theirs, without reliance on anyone's sufferance. Odd that he stood to inherit land more easily in France than in his own country, but so it was, and the Auld Alliance to thank for it.

Today they were on the north side of the city, the sky steadily lightening to the east of them, the mud underfoot glistening with the remains of an overnight shower. All around them the hustle and bustle of preparations for the continuation of the full-scale bombardment: boys scurrying along the circumvallation, bent under the weight of kegs of powder; soldiers straining to move carts piled with cannon balls into positions convenient for loading; a cacophony of grumbling and cursing and shouted orders in half a dozen languages. And everywhere a shifting and a straightening of shoulders and an increased willingness as the King moved along the line. To the left of them, a babble of voices rose above the general hubbub. Munro turned in time to see a couple of heads appearing at the edge of the ditch, willing hands hauling them up. A pioneer was running towards the spot where the swell of the muzzle of a great culverin could be seen protruding from the ditch, the lip pointing at the sky. Henri's reaction was instant, weaving his way back through the knots of soldiers and artillery, Patrick beside him, Munro in their wake. The culverin lay at a drunken angle, one wheel half-submerged in the mud at the base of the ditch, the men who had scrambled clear peering back down. Lucky devils, Munro thought, it wouldn't be the way I'd choose to go. The pioneer had taken charge, sending two men scurrying along the lines, directing two others down into the ditch, and though he spoke to them in what Munro recognised as Dutch, the words themselves meaningless to him, his intentions were clear. They set to work, one attaching ropes around the wheel, the other packing limbs cross-wise under it in an attempt to find traction. The pioneer turned, a crease of worry on his face, and acknowledged Henri.

'Mon Sire. I've sent for the crane. Once we've lifted the cannon, we can resite it further along and cover the gap it'll leave in the offensive by smaller fire.'

'What happened? No one was hurt?'

He shook his head. 'Non, merci le bon Dieu. The men were getting ready to commence firing when the soil collapsed and the weight of the culverin took it down, and them with it, but fortunately not under the wheels.'

Henri was watching the men in the ditch. 'You have them roped; a sensible precaution.'

'We cannot count on the stability of the ground. If there should be further movement … I want to be able to pull them out fast.'

The offensive had begun, all around them the sound of cannon fire, the protracted boom of the bombards punctuated by the shorter blasts from falcons, the air full of smoke and flashes of flame. The pioneer had his head bent to Henri's ear, elaborating on his intentions for the recovery of the culverin, while keeping one eye on the men working in the ditch, Patrick also focusing on their efforts. There was a temporary lull filled by the creaking of an axle clearly in need of grease, the commonplace sound taking Munro back to the hollow below Broomelaw, as he manoeuvred the cart loaded with bodies up the slope towards the tower, wheels slipping on the moss, the axles protesting – at least that ruse had worked, preventing further deaths. Thus far. He turned his head to watch the approach of the four men guiding the crane over the uneven ground. Although one was stationed at each corner to steady it, the superstructure, tall and unwieldy, rocked from side to side, the twin crosspiece attached to the top of the central shaft swaying madly each time they hit a bump. A wheeled adaptation of a cargo crane, more suited to use on the docks, Munro was doubtful if it would be adequate for the weight of the cannon, given the height it needed to be lifted, the pioneer's expression mirroring his concerns. Henri, stripped down to his shirt, stepped up onto the crane platform and flexed his shoulders ready to add his weight to the turning of the shaft once the signal was given. Patrick was next to Henri, Munro and another man opposite. The pioneer was attaching the ropes and checking the knots, the men in the ditch preparing to assist in starting the momentum.

The pioneer gave the signal and they began to strain. It took a minute or two for the ropes to tauten, for the culverin to begin to inch upwards. Three times they managed to pull it part way up the slope, and three times it slipped back. The pioneer, gesturing for others to join him, dropped down into the ditch, placing his shoulder against the wheel and shouting up to those on the crane, 'Take the strain, now. Pull!'

Munro felt the increased tension in his muscles, the sinews on his arms standing proud like hawsers. His face was turning purple, his breath coming in short gasps, the others likewise. The culverin was moving again, foot by foot, and this time they maintained the force on the pole, their efforts rewarded as first the muzzle, then the neck appeared over the lip of the ditch. There was a lurch and a jolt as they edged it past the tipping point, the wheels beginning to grip on the carpet of branches laid on the surface. Too late Munro saw the danger, as the culverin, gaining momentum, began to roll towards them. He tried to reverse the direction of the pole, to slow the cannon's progress, the others straining likewise. And for a moment it seemed they might be successful, before the pole swung back, knocking Munro and the man beside him off his feet. As he scrambled to his knees, he saw Patrick fling himself sideways, knocking the King off the platform just as the culverin careered into the side of the crane, splintering the outer framework and, its nearside wheel snapping, topple, the barrel catching Patrick diagonally across the chest and thigh, pinning him to the ground.

He was at Patrick's shoulders, screaming orders, men

scrambling to haul on the ropes attached to the culverin, others forcing a beam under the trunnion, prising the barrel up enough to allow Patrick to be pulled clear. His chest was compressed, his breathing forced, his pelvis smashed, a jagged splinter of bone protruding through the skin. Blood seeped from the gash, staining the soil beneath him. Munro knelt by his head as Patrick, groping for his hand, struggled to speak. He bent his ear close, Patrick's words disjointed, barely distinguishable,

'Tell them … I wished … to see bairns … full-grown. I once thought it a foolish thing … so tied …' His eyes were clouding over, blood bubbling from his nostrils with each laboured breath, his grip on Munro's hand slackening. 'Tell them … I was … wrong.' A final sigh, his head falling to the side, his mouth hanging slack. Munro was aware of the King kneeling at Patrick's other side, of him drawing Patrick's lips together, closing the eyes. He placed a hand on Munro's shoulder, his voice infinitely gentle.

'Tell them I owe my life to him, that he will never be forgotten.'

Part Two

June–July 1597

There is a way that seemeth right...

King James Bible, Proverbs 16:25

Chapter 1

It was a relief to step from white sunlight into the green shadows of the trees. Kate set down her basket to release her skirt, snagged on a bramble stem straggling across the path. Already half-full, the basket dragged on her wrist so that she was glad of the moment's respite and took another moment to tuck a stray strand of hair back behind her ear. The coolness of the wood was welcome after the heat which had beaten down upon her, burning the exposed vee of her neck scarlet, and, rising from the packed earth through her thin leather soles, had caused her feet to swell and her shoes to pinch. The plant she sought was almost a 'cure-all', effective for everything from kidney stones and bladder problems to the halting of bleeding, from rashes and rheumatism to skin complaints and broken bones. She preferred the wood horsetail to the field variety, growing as it did in damp shade, protected both from the tramplings of livestock and the scorching effects of the sun. It had been in the spring, when they had passed through these woods on that first, ill-fated visit to Hillhouse, that she spotted the hollow stems poking through the moist carpet of dead leaves and noted their location. Strange that it was the thin barren spikes, produced in the second flush of growth when the fertile stems had withered, that carried medicinal value, but there were many things in nature hard to understand.

She wandered through the woods, enjoying the solitude, a welcome change from the cramped quarters of the bastle house. It was a godsend, of course, and she was grateful, but lately she had felt like a caged bird, enclosed by constant chatter and by the lack of privacy. Maggie, having proved herself an apt pupil as far as herbs and their uses went, added to her interest a desire to talk over every visit made, every diagnosis given, and to dissect every success or failure with equal enthusiasm. It was an unforeseen consequence of allowing her to take over Robbie's role, which Kate, on occasion, found rather more of a trial than a blessing. Yet she hadn't the heart to dim Maggie's enthusiasm, recognising not only the added maturity it brought, but also the real talent it revealed. Had Maggie been able to go to college, there was no knowing what she might have become. As it was, with the only course available to her that of assistant to Kate as the local 'wise woman', it would have been wrong as well as unwise to hold her back.

The almost-silence soothed Kate, the clamour of Braidstane fading from her mind, the only sounds the friendly scuffle of a dormouse disturbed in the undergrowth, the high sweet note of a tree warbler, and the soft scrunch of her footsteps on dead twigs. The trees opened out, the hollow between them filled by a still pool, the surface of the water dimpled by water beetles. And by the side of the water, the clumps of horsetail she sought. She set down her basket and busied herself with the task of stripping the fragile spikes from the tall central stem, humming a little as she worked. Lush green, undamaged by sun or wind, she layered them in the basket with moss, for there was little use in a good crop if she were to crush them on the road home. The job done, she sat down in the dappled shade, resting her shoulders against the trunk of a Scots pine, tilting her head to stare upwards through the branches dissecting the deep blue of the sky. The top was truncated, the final branches curving out and up in a cup shape, emphasising the missing centre. Likely damaged a long time before, yet continuing stubbornly to grow towards the light. Like us, she thought.

Kate felt Munro's absence as a gap at the centre of their lives, an ache that was always with her, a bit, she imagined, like a toothache that nagged whatever remedy you tried. The nights were the worst, her bed a cold and lonely place. Now, lying in the quiet of Braidstane's woods, so like those below Broomelaw, she imagined him coming up behind her, his finger-light touch on the back of her neck, tugging at an unruly curl, his voice whispering in her ear. That it wouldn't be so, she knew, but the pretence was in itself a comfort. She pictured him, his mouth upturned at one corner, the tiny scar beside his eye. The temperature was rising, despite the shade, and she removed her shoes, and then, with a quick glance to make sure she wasn't overlooked, hitched up her skirt and released her stockings also. She slid her feet into the water, wriggling her toes, a cluster of water beetles rocking like miniature boats in the ripples she cast.

Somewhere behind her the snap of a twig, as loud as a pistol shot. Kate looked up, saw a shadow flicker. She froze, holding her breath. For a moment, nothing. Then, barely perceptible, a change in the quality of the light, a scuffling, close, but soft, as if whoever came this way sought to travel unobserved. Carrying the dirk had been a simple precaution urged on her at the first by Hugh Montgomerie, one to which she had acquiesced, albeit reluctantly, not at all certain that she could use it if the need arose. But as time moved on and her confidence in moving about the countryside increased, so had her belief in her ability to defend herself should the need arise. As it had done on several occasions when she'd encountered a sailor, overeager to offer the best of his catch in return for some private favours, or a farmhand who fancied his chances with a woman whose trade would likely involve looser morals. Each time the widening of the eyes, the bluster and speedy retreat when the dirk appeared in her hand, a satisfaction hard to best.

She eased her feet out of the water and, ignoring her stockings, thrust them into her boots – it would be more than folly to face danger in bare feet. She slid into the shadow of the pine, her back hard pressed against it, her free hand tight at her side. Another rustle, another darker shadow. Kate grasped the dirk, her knuckles white, took a deep breath.

He was there, the light behind him, so that for a moment as she squinted upwards she thought it was Munro, her heart, already hammering, fit to burst. But as he lunged for her the illusion vanished. Foetid breath on her cheek, a calloused hand across her mouth. Fear, overlaid by determination – he wouldn't find her easy. She took a firmer grasp of the dirk, and, ignoring the possible danger to herself, thrust it into the gap between his knuckles. She felt the resistance of sinew, wrenched it free and raised it to strike again. Despite the blood beading from the cut, he was too quick for her, grasping her wrist, twisting, the dirk spinning into the undergrowth at her feet. Imprisoning arms circled her waist, and for a fraction of a second she thought of the bairns waiting for her in the bastle house, of Agnes, as near family as made no difference and as loyal ... and of Munro. She raked at the man's face with her free hand and, kicking sideways, heard the satisfying crack of heel on bone. Her sudden release, the chance she needed. She crashed through the undergrowth, overhanging branches whipping against her arms and face. He was coming after her, the tangles of brambles catching at her clothes, impeding her progress. She had a stitch in her side, her breathing reduced to short gasps. To her right was a gap in the trees, a narrow track curving out of sight. She glanced back, ducked sideways through the gap and then plunged immediately off the track into dense cover. She was only just in time, the man running straight past, his breathing also ragged.

She waited until the sound of his progress through the woods faded, then, taking care to move as quietly and swiftly as possible, retraced her steps, retrieving her stockings in the passing. The dirk lay where it had fallen, the basket also, kicked aside in the pursuit, the contents spilling. The man was likely a vagrant. She could still feel his grip on her arm, the wetness of his lips as his face closed on hers, and shuddered. She must tell Maggie to take extra care if she was out alone – perhaps she shouldn't let her. Fast on that thought, the recognition that to confine Maggie now she had a taste of freedom would not be difficult, but rather impossible. And in her six years of traversing the county, this was the first she had come near to grief of this sort. Focused on making speed, she failed to notice the man who had accosted her emerging once more from the woods and,

slipping onto the path far in her wake, trailing her to the
foot of the slope below Braidstane.

Chapter 2

The call came at dawn, the boy blown into the bastle house by an westerly wind that carried in it the promise of rain. Maggie, woken by the voices, appeared in the kitchen doorway, her nightrail pulled tight about her, her hair tumbling loose on her shoulders, in time to hear Kate, concern etched in her face, send him to the tower with a request for John to come. It was a grievance that had been building in Maggie since John Montgomerie's return. Her initial pleasure in listening and learning from him tempered by resentment each time he accompanied Kate, while she was left at home.

Kate pulled the strap of her saddlebag taut, and as if to pre-empt Maggie's protest, said, 'Three of us would lend a seriousness to the situation it may not warrant, besides the fright of the payment we might ask.'

Maggie dismissed the flippancy. 'If it were *not* serious, you wouldn't need John.' She took a deep breath, prepared to do battle. 'And how am I to learn anything of worth if I'm to be allowed only to see those cases that have no complications?'

'You are here always, Maggie, John but for a week or two. It is but courtesy to invite him.' Another pause, then, 'And if another call were to come, and you are here, there will be no need to disappoint. Especially as,' Kate ran her tongue around her lips, a sure sign to Maggie of real concern, 'we may not make it back tonight, or indeed tomorrow.'

For the rest of the day Maggie grumped between the bastle house and the tower, her normal sunny nature driven out by frustration. Agnes, not the most patient of folk at the best of times, snapped altogether when Maggie complained for the third time of the unfairness of the situation.

'Your mother may have made you her assistant, but it wasn't to make you useless for anything else. Moping around here with a face as long as a turfing spade is no help to anybody. I will find you something useful to do if you cannot find some profitable occupation for yourself.'

It was enough to send Maggie scuttling to the storeroom to make a pretence of sorting remedies, a pretence that became a reality when she found a basket full of packets each with one corner nibbled away, the contents spilling through the weave onto the shelf below. She forced herself to set the mousetrap, a task she hated. It reminded her of the time at Broomelaw when the trapping of a mouse had left a motherless litter, their presence revealed by a increasingly plaintive squeaking behind the wainscot in their bedchamber. Ignored at the first, until Kate, pointing out the likely pungency should they be allowed to die behind the panelling, incited Munro to remove the nest and to drown them in a bucket. Now, as always, she sought to dispel the memory of the twitching tails, the muted squeals, and Robbie, tossing the small bodies onto the midden, their fur smoothed by

208

the water to the dull shine of polished oak.

A new thought. Her mother away and likely to be so for two days, it was the ideal opportunity. The focus of her frustration changed to the weather, and to the driving rain battering the windows and running in rivulets across the cobbles – if it would only clear … if Robbie could go to Broomelaw, so could she.

When she woke it was to a watery sunshine penetrating around the shutters, painting narrow lines of light across the rush-strewn floor. Her good fortune that an early call came from Giffen, taking her in the direction she wished to go and avoiding the need for any lies. Suspecting the signs of colic in the description given of the three-month babe's symptoms, she took a preparation of catnip as well as the fail-safe chamomile and watched the child relax into a settled sleep before leaving. It was her first individual triumph, her mood correspondingly improved, despite the high clouds that streaked the horizon, threatening her plan.

She had only a hazy idea of their old home's exact location. The idea festering in her since Robbie's jaunt there, she had quizzed him, but recognising that he would no more approve of her expedition than her mother, had been careful to approach it obliquely. Bringing the conversation around to the frost fair, she talked of the skates their father had made, of the man with the corkscrew hair who had magicked a groat from behind her ear, the card inscribed with her name. And casually asked, 'Near to Renfrew was it?'

He had laughed, ruffled her hair, an action she chose

to ignore, said, 'On the Clyde shore, stretching as far as Greenock.' She had willed him to say how long it took from Broomelaw, the direction they had taken, and hid her disappointment when all he said was, 'Though we didn't go so far. I'd have liked fine to skate across to Dumbarton Castle, and might have persuaded Father but for William Cunninghame's appearance. You wouldn't remember, for you were only little.'

It was the information that had been little, but she hadn't dared ask for more. Now, she decided, if she made for Renfrew, she could strike west and north until she got a clear view of the Clyde. Once she pinpointed Dumbarton Castle, and drew an imaginary line south and east from the near shore, it shouldn't be too hard to find Broomelaw. There couldn't be many ruined tower houses standing out against the skyline within a few of miles of the water. And so it proved, though she had been forced to ask directions to Renfrew more times than she would have liked. From there it was easy. She was following a drover's track when she found herself on a gentle incline, above her the remnants of a tower that brought a rush of saliva to her mouth and a knot in her stomach. There was the ring of chisel on stone and a cheery whistling at odds with Robbie's bitter tale of a tower collapsing in on itself and like to disappear altogether in a year or two, so that for a moment she wondered if she had fetched up at another tower altogether, but the small graveyard at the foot of the slope was enough to show she had not. The sight of Anna's name, half-obscured by moss, dredged up memories she hadn't known she possessed: of creeping down to cover the grave with a blanket to save Anna from the cold; and Robbie's anger as he tore it away, his shouted, 'What use a blanket when she is dead!'

shrivelling her insides so that she fled, first to the byre, and then the sound of the horses reminding her of that other death, unmentioned, unexplained, with only the the empty stall to tell its story, to huddle in the outside privy until the cold drove her back inside.

She climbed upwards through the gorse to gain a vantage point from which to look down into the barmkin. It was not as Robbie had described it. She was assaulted by other memories, piling on top of her, weighing her down: Anna on the sheltie on the track disappearing downwards to the loch and polishing tack in the stable, saying, 'Look, Maggie, you can see your face.' Now, as she turned her head away, she saw the broken walls of the sheep pen Munro had built in the aftermath of Anna's death, which had been used for but a single season's lambs. She shouldn't have come.

She dredged her mind for happier memories, and found some. Of lying stretched out on a rug on the cobbles, her back resting against the tower wall, the sun pouring over her, so that she feared she might melt like the ice they brought back with them from the frost fair. Of picking brambles, more going into her mouth than the basket; and of how, despite that she had scrubbed and scrubbed at her hands, the stains remained, though the taste had gone. Of winter evenings roasting chestnuts by the hall fire; her parents, occupied with guests, unaware that Robbie, whispering, peopled the shadows with ghouls. And she, knowing no better, had shivered, her eyes huge, until he lost interest and taunted her with stupidity, so that she flew at him and tugged so hard a handful of hair came away in her fist. Her mother, refusing to take sides, dismissing them, 'If you must fight, do it where I can't hear you.'

An injustice which had rankled with Maggie, but which now, with the Montgomerie girls, she found herself repeating. The sun was beating on the southern wall, and squinting, she thought she could just make out a faint tracing of the target they had spent endless hours throwing pebbles at. Robbie had always won. Renewed curiosity vied with a desire to take flight. Below her, a man criss-crossed the barmkin barrowing blocks of stone to where ropes dangled by a jagged section of wall. She was back at the time after the great storm, when, thumb in mouth, she had watched other workmen hoisting slabs skywards, hauling them to the wall walk. She couldn't return home without discovering what was happening, for her mother would surely want to know. And hard on that thought, another one – how could she say anything to Kate when she shouldn't be here at all?

She inched back out of the gorse, retraced her steps to the horse, and, checking the reins were well tangled around a trail of bramble, headed down the hill towards the remains of the gate. For the first time, though she could not have named it as such, she felt an instinctive stirring of femininity and brushed the dust of the ride from her bodice, smoothed down her skirts. She put a hand up to her head intending to tuck away a strand of hair escaped from her cap, but thought better of it, instead twisting it round and round her finger so that when released it bounced and curled in front of her ear. She was only dimly aware of the picture she made: silhouetted in the half-formed arch, the sun turning her hair to flame, but was encouraged when the workman nearest to her looked up, his face creasing into a smile.

He straightened, bowed in mock courtesy, wiped the

dust from his hands. 'Who do we have here?' And then, as if he noted her worried expression, 'Are you lost, lass?'

It was a thought, but one that held perhaps too many pitfalls. Better she go for something closer to the truth. 'I heard the sounds of working and wondered...' It came out in a rush, 'Despite that I would likely be reprimanded if my mother knew I was here, for I have aye been warned ruins are dangerous and...' here she dimpled in unconscious coquetry, 'and not to approach strangers.'

He laughed, a loud guffaw that drew the attention of the other men, and Maggie felt the first frisson of apprehension as they gathered around her, aware that she amused them, unsure of how much danger that entailed.

The man who'd first seen her gestured her forward. 'Well now, lass, we'd best satisfy your curiosity, for it would be a shame to risk trouble for no result.'

It was too late to retreat. Stepping into the courtyard, she looked up at the jagged remnants of wall etched into the sky, remembered the tower as she last saw it: gigantic in the moonlight, the shadow of the crow-stepped gable lying like a staircase across the cobbles.

At her shiver the man's grin widened. 'We do not eat children, I promise you.' He waved his hand at the jumble of stone behind him. 'And you are welcome to see how the work is done.'

Her chin came up, and any last vestiges of fear were squashed by her determination not to appear a child in his eyes, the forced formality of her words negating her intent. 'That would be of interest, thank you.' Deciding his amusement was benign, she settled on a large block, as he lifted a chisel and began to chip away slivers from an irregularly shaped lump of stone, producing a neat square.

'We have some hundred of these to cut, besides many more of different sizes, before the tower is righted.' He chose another stone from the heap, rubbed at the moss clinging to it. 'I reuse original stone where I can, but many, like this one, sizeable to begin with,' he indicated a missing corner, 'when the damaged section is cut out are only good for a small one in the end. Come.'

He gripped her arm, raising her to her feet, and led her across to the tower entrance, pointing out the variety of sizes of stone, some no more than an inch or two thick, others a foot or more. She was only half-listening, her attention caught by the sight of the weeds sprouting inside the tower, something she would *not* tell her mother. Another memory, sharp, clear: of squatting near the door to herd slaters into pens made of sticks, and all the while Robbie and Anna taking turns to ride the hobby horse across the cobbles. And overlaying it a picture of the day they carried Anna home, lying across the stable lad's arms like a rag doll, her head drooped, her hair swinging.

The mason was nodding towards the tumble of lower buildings sprawled around the perimeter. 'The byres are not dressed stone but random rubble: less preparation, but requiring more skill in the building of them, that the walls be straight. And those roofs we will thatch, not slab.'

She brushed her hand across her eyes, assaulted by an image of her father straddling the ridge of the byre as he tied in fresh rushes.

The mason's eyes were kindly. 'You would have been too young to remember, I daresay. This has been derelict a good number of years now.'

'Six,' she said, without thinking.

'You knew the folk that bided here?'

214

'Everyone did.' Though she had indeed been too young, she imagined that was true, hoped it would satisfy.

'You live nearby?'

This was dangerous ground. Her tongue flicked across her lips. 'Used to.' She avoided his eyes, smothered a prick of conscience. 'My father died...' – It could be true, for all they knew. '...My mother ... when we were left alone we moved a distance, to bide with another family.' Behind her back she crossed her fingers, to make it less of a lie. She glanced upwards through a curtain of hair, hoping the kernel of truth would outweigh the falsehood.

The kindliness was back. 'You'll know then that this was a Cunninghame tower. And will be so again. William, Glencairn's heir, is to have it.' He was assessing her clothes, her place in life. An impression confirmed, as he said, 'But you'll not know him.'

She had only one memory of him: at the frost fair, talking over her head at her father and mother, the contempt in his voice. The kick she landed on his shin, his obvious pain a matter of satisfaction she had guessed her mother shared despite her chiding. Now, tense as a coiled spring, it took every ounce of effort she had to shrug and answer the mason with a simple 'No'. All she wanted was to get away, to put distance between her and Broomelaw – if any of the Cunninghames were to arrive ... it had been a foolishness indeed to come. Not that William would recognise her, for she had been barely three, and as for other of the family, so far as she knew none of them had ever been at Broomelaw. But from what she had gleaned of William's character, any inquisitive child was unlikely to be popular, and if she led him to Braidstane, to Kate...

'Would you like to see how we make the mortar?'

Instinct told her that to leave now, at the first mention of William Cunninghame, might carry an increased risk, so she pretended an interest as the mason lifted a shovelful of a fine white dust to mix with the sand. It rose into the air, settling on him like a sifting of sugar.

'The lime in the mortar is to make it softer than the stone.' He was adding a trickle of water from a bucket, stirring briskly.

It reminded her of Ellie, making mud pies.

'See.' He turned her attention back to the tower wall, crumbling with his fingers at the line of mortar between two large blocks. 'If this was hard then it would be the blocks between that wore away with the rain, the mortar that remained. Done correctly the stone is mostly untouched, it is the pointing that gives.'

She didn't understand what difference it made, but tried to look as if she followed. It was clear that he realised her confusion.

'Sandstone,' he explained, as if to a yard-full of apprentice masons, 'is gey soft, and left unprotected will soon crumble. Built, it is still at risk, depending on the direction of the wind, the degree of shelter, and the force of the weather. So all that can be done to minimise the damage that rain will do is time well spent.' He was running his hand over a particularly large block in the face of the wall. 'Imagine if this block wore down. It would have to be cut out and replaced. A tricky business, and costly in time and stone. The mortar is much easier repaired. So the idea is to give the rain something to bite on that is least trouble to fix.' Again the swift glance at her clothing. 'Do you live in a stone house?'

'A bastle house.'

'Well then. Look to your own walls when you get home and see if they are well done or no.'

It was the opening she needed. She glanced up at the sun, riding high. 'I'd best be off, for I may be looked for.'

'And I should get back to work, else the day will be gone and little to show for it. The Cunninghames don't pay me to be a teacher.'

'Indeed we do not.'

The voice behind them was familiar. Tinged with contempt. The man addressed the mason, his hand biting into Maggie's shoulder.

'Is this what you do when I am not here? Dally with chits? Who is the brat?'

'A local child, curious to see what work we do. She does no harm.'

'She wastes your time.'

Maggie forced herself to remain still in his grasp. Though it was conceivable she could wriggle free, she had an instinctive understanding that better she be sent away by his choosing, than that she escaped by her own.

The mason shrugged. 'We have a contract for the job. If I take an hour or two longer the loss will be mine, not yours.'

'You are paid to do the job in as timely a fashion as possible. Encourage one child and you may have the half of Renfrew crawling all over the place. It will not be an hour you lose then.' William's grip tightened on Maggie. 'This is our ground and I do not welcome trespassers, be they child or adult. Curiosity is a fine excuse for thieving.'

The mason turned to Maggie. 'You'd best go,' and then in a gruff tone she thought likely for the man's benefit, 'Do not think to come back with your friends, you've had enough of my time as it is.'

She tried to move, but William retained his grip. He spun her round, scanned her face, his eyes narrowed.

'Where do you bide? You have a familiar look about you.'

She scrabbled around in her head for a name, thought of the places she passed on her journey to Broomelaw, chose one a few miles back, muttered, 'Kaimknowe,' praying he would have no knowledge of it.

He gave her a push. 'Be off with you.' The contempt was back in his voice. 'If I am to find you here again...' The threat was clear.

Chapter 3

With Maggie gone, William stayed at Broomelaw less than an hour, his unexpected appearance a result of his desire to assert his authority on the job and to keep the masons from complacency lest their work be shoddy. And just as well, he thought, they won't likely be so friendly to bairns again, be they ever so winsome. The warmth was beginning to bleed out of the sun as he reached the hamlet of Kaim-knowe, and he was nearly past before it registered. The girl, though immature, had not been uncomely and he had been close enough to know that she smelled sweet enough, the curl of hair which escaped her cap clean and shining … and, as the sun caught it, with a hint of auburn. Perhaps he shouldn't have been so churlish. He assessed the sky. Plenty of time yet before it became too dark for safe travel. If he had frighted her … she might have a mother he could favour with an apology…

He rode through the clutter of cottages, made for the smithy. If anyone could direct him right it would be the smith, for the child had a horse. An oddity in the situation hovered at the edge of his mind, an elusive mismatch he couldn't quite grasp. And then he had it. Her clothes indicated servant status, but the horse was one of some quality. Which she had taken steps to conceal. By chance he had glanced across the hillside some five minutes after she had gone, to see her scrambling onto a rock protruding like a bony knuckle from the surrounding gorse to mount the decent-looking bay. He had noted the horse's clean lines, the girl's good seat, but had been so occupied with finding fault in the builder's work that the incongruity had passed him by. Now, as he threaded his way through the cluster of cottages following the sound of the hammer on anvil, he teased at the puzzle – her mother a widow perhaps, or fallen on hard times. And in need of protection. A smile touched his mouth. A pleasing thought. His pleasure short-lived when he discovered there was no red-headed chit at Kaimknowe, nor, as the smith scratched his head, anywhere hereabouts that he could think of.

It was an annoyance that lasted the whole journey home, his frustration increasing the more he thought on it; what had begun as an interesting conundrum, with perhaps a pleasing solution at its core, become an itch that the more he scratched, the greater an irritation it became. By the time he wheeled through the gateway at Kilmaurs he was ready to take out his displeasure on the first person to cross his path. Unfortunate for both of them that it was John Cunninghame, who stood in the doorway of the stable passing the time of day.

'William.' John acknowledged him, but did not immediately move aside, turning his head instead to allow the stable lad to finish his sentence. John's greeting, the bare minimum that courtesy demanded, his perceived lack of deference, an ongoing issue, inflamed William further.

He made a show of addressing the lad, but the irritation contained in the message extended, by implication, to John. 'When you've finished gossiping, perhaps you could attend to your duties, or am I to become a stable hand and do the job myself?'

John was equally curt. 'I asked the lad a question. It is only good manners both for him to answer and for me to listen to his reply.' He shifted sufficiently for William to pass him. 'But by all means see to your horse. A little work never harmed anyone, though for you, I imagine, it will be rather a novelty.'

'You do me wrong, Uncle.' There was a studied insolence in William's pronunciation of the title. 'I have a job in hand, one that takes up much of my time. Though you'll not have heard, your visits to the heart of the family so infrequent we have begun to wonder if your sympathies lie elsewhere.'

'I do not gad about. That does not mean my family feeling is any less. Your father has aye had my allegiance.'

'As he should. As I should too, when the time comes.'

'I am a Cunninghame.' It was an unsatisfactory answer. John turned towards the castle entrance. 'I should greet your parents and the bairns. As you say, it's been a while. But we are all caught up in our own affairs, and though I haven't been here, your father and I oft rub shoulders at court.'

Whether the barb was intentional or not was unclear. But so William took it. 'I have had other more profitable ways of spending my time than loitering about the court fawning on James … whatever you or Father may do.'

'James is quick to remember any perceived slight, but apt to forget a favour, unless it be repeated at regular

221

intervals. All your father does is for the family name, and for you.' John's exasperation showed. 'He neither looks for, nor expects thanks, but a little appreciation wouldn't go amiss.'

They mounted to the hall in silence and found Lady Glencairn ensconced on a window seat making the most of the light as she unpicked a sampler, the youngest of the children hovering at her elbow, mutiny clear in the set of her shoulders and the gathering storm in her face. Lady Glencairn looked up, and with a quick glance at the child's expression, thrust the sampler into her hand. 'There now, I have undone the mistake, and the picture none the worse for it. You have time to redo the lettering before supper. And this time,' she softened her words by stroking the child's hair, 'try to keep the lines straight. The first attempt looked as if you sewed with your eyes shut.' With a gentle push for the child, she turned with a smile to John.

'This is a surprise. Have you news, or is it the social visit we were due three months since?'

'Social only.' John bent over her hand, his smile, that had been no more of a stretching of his lips for William, lighting up his eyes. 'Though I had not thought my neglect of such long-standing.'

The pleasant tone of the exchange was an added irritant. William interrupted with a cursory bow. 'Mother, you'll be pleased to hear the work goes on apace. And that the builders, though I cannot guarantee they keep to speed when no one is checking them, are making a passable job of it.'

'Job of what?' John's gaze flicked from Lady Glencairn to William and back again. 'What is it that I have missed? When last we met Glencairn said nothing of a new project.'

Lady Glencairn looked down at the hand John still held.

222

'We are repairing a tower ... and William has the supervision of it. Once finished, it is to be his.'

'Near hand?' There was a genuine note of interest in John's voice and a look of almost approval in his face.

'Broomelaw.' William said the name with satisfaction.

John dropped Lady Glencairn's hand, straightened.

William, failing to notice John's reaction, continued, 'Forbye the waste, the state of it was an affront to the family name.' It was an oblique, and William thought clever, reference to John's earlier comment. 'Had it been left much longer there would have been no tower to repair. Though not overly spacious, it has a good aspect and is well set. I had not thought, until we surveyed it, that the Munros would have stretched to such a house.'

'They had done much with it, as I remember, over several generations. Is it ours to commandeer?' The question, tossed in at the end of John's sentence, had the hint of censure in it.

'As good as.' William was dismissive. 'Since they all were killed in the reiver's raid, there is no one else to lay claim to it.'

The stillness in John's face, the lack of positive response, refuelled William's annoyance. 'Are you not glad for me, Uncle. Fortunate though it is to have a father whose strength does not fail, I am a spare part here. It suits us all that Broomelaw be restored. Another Cunninghame stronghold cannot be a bad thing, and Mother and Father both are happy to support me in the venture.'

'Indeed.' Lady Glencairn patted the cushion on the window seat by her side, and in a transparent attempt at moving the conversation on, said, 'Take a seat, John. Tell us of your affairs.' She nodded to William. 'Your uncle

223

would no doubt welcome some refreshment, perhaps you could see to it.'

'We have servants…'

'Who are not within earshot.' Lady Glencairn cut William off. 'It is little to ask to carry a message to the kitchens, and will speed the process.' A pause. 'You will not refuse a drink yourself after the long ride, I'm sure.'

Chapter 4

Supper began well enough, the talk ranging from the successful lambing, despite the unseasonable weather that had followed, to the easiest sowing of barley in years, the germination levels high. As Glencairn became more expansive, he regaled them with his latest trip to Edinburgh and the tale of Sorley Buie. 'By his own accounting, a great man in Ireland, coming to complain to James of ill treatment by some of the Lords of the Isles and sent home satisfied: Sir James Mac O'Neil. The King is aye canny: a knighthood and the honour of a cannonade as he left, a cheap peace. If all the Irish were as easily bought, it might be the place to go.'

William picked a shred of beef from his teeth. 'Word is Hamilton of Dunlop has designs on Ulster, which is why he busies himself now on the King's behalf in Dublin.'

Glencairn grunted. 'He and Fullerton both. This charade of a college that James sent them to establish, little more than a front for other, more subtle duties.'

Lady Glencairn paused, her spoon halfway to her mouth. 'James is well known to favour education.'

'James is well known to favour a good spy network.'

Lady Glencairn cast a glance towards the serving girl in the process of clearing empty platters. 'But none of that any concern of ours.'

'Any concern of the King is a concern of ours, as loyal subjects.'

'Indeed, but there are lighter topics for our dinner table, are there not?'

John obliged. 'They say Hugh Rose of Kilravock has died. And left a goodly portion.'

Glencairn sipped his wine. 'Would that we had his opportunities. To fall heir to the lands previously held by the Bishop of Moray is as fine a way as any to sort a problem.'

Lady Glencairn set down her spoon. 'Problem?' John heard the undertone of concern in her voice, thought – it must be an uncomfortable thing to live always on eggshells.

'Seventeen sisters and daughters, all requiring portions. I'd call that a problem.'

William said, 'Had he not the reputation of a difficult man, that made trouble for himself?'

John injected amusement into his voice. 'He had the reputation of a man that made good use of his troubles. It's said when the King visited at Kilravock during his last progress, he asked how Rose could live among such ill-turbulent neighbours. Rose's reply, that they were the best neighbours he could have, for they made him thrice a day go to God upon his knees, when otherwise he would not have gone once.'

It was the right tone. Glencairn guffawed, William spluttered into his wine and even Lady Glencairn rewarded John with a smile as he added, 'Whether it was the effect of his prayers or not, he leaves the estate to his son free of

226

debt, and a parcel of ready money besides.'

'Speaking of money,' Glencairn was carving himself a generous slice of beef, 'did you hear the King's latest proclamation regarding usury?'

John shook his head.

'No one is to lend at more than ten for the hundred, cash or kind, under pain of confiscation of their goods or, if the amount be sufficiently serious, injury to their person.'

'Is James in particular need of money at the moment?'

'James is aye in need of money, it is an expensive business being a King … or a courtier for that matter. Traipsing about following the court is a considerable drain on our finances, and I'm not entirely convinced of its worth. But as the Montgomeries take care to be there or thereabouts, it behoves us to do likewise.' Glencairn returned to the original topic. 'This usury business is a sure way to swell the King's coffers, for there are aye greedy folk stepping forward to lend a helping hand to those in straits.'

'We may be thankful then we do not require such help.'

'Indeed, but handy to know our rights should the need arise.'

The talk drifted: to the witch trials in Athole, following the supposed convention of over two thousand witches and the devil among them; and Margaret Aitken, known as the Blawearie witch, who saved her own skin by travelling the length and breadth of the country denouncing others. How Andrew Melville's fame had brought foreign students flocking to St Andrews, the money they brought no doubt welcome to the university. And despite it, rumours that there were those who wished to see him deposed as rector and Wilkie put in his place. How James Melville claimed that the recent earthquake in the north was a judgement,

227

likening it to God punishing Uzziah, King of Judah for usurping the priestly office.

John said, 'I hear the price of lead has risen.'

'For those who have the chance to sell it. Foulis, a gold-smith in Edinburgh,' Glencairn added, clearly for Lady Glencairn's benefit, 'was at me some time ago to invest in his lead-mining scheme at Crawfurd Muir, and indeed I was thinking on it, as it is as near as makes no difference on our doorstep. But he lost patience and took Bulmer as partner instead, and I'm glad of it now. They were, so it is said, just beginning to turn a profit when reivers relieved them of the lead and the rest en route to Leith: horses, ar-mour, even the clothes off their backs.'

'One way of impeding pursuit.' William was clearly amused.

Lady Glencairn thrust aside her food unfinished. 'The actions of reivers should be no laughing matter. They touch us all.'

William shrugged. 'And sometimes to our benefit.'

There was a moment's silence, a tension in Lady Glen-cairn, a coldness sweeping through John, the memory of Broomelaw, broken and smouldering, if not the work of reivers, well disguised. Glencairn's chair groaned as he shifted. It is in all our minds, John thought, and if William doesn't care, at least Glencairn is not entirely comfortable.

An assessment he questioned as Glencairn said, 'Speak-ing of Broomelaw, you should come and take a look, John.' The Earl was back into his stride, hearty. 'Perhaps we could all take a jaunt in the next day or two, the weather proving clement.' He broke off as the steward appeared at his side. 'What is it that is so important our supper is disturbed?'

'A man who insists he must speak with the Master of

Glencairn.' The steward sniffed. 'Had he been a mite more presentable I would have set him to wait your convenience in the kitchens, a mite less and I should have sent him away altogether, but he is most persistent. He says he has some information that is wanted.'

William thrust back his chair. 'I'll go. I daresay I won't be long.'

William gone, John turned to Lady Glencairn, his gaze shrewd. 'You are not altogether in favour of this plan?'

'It is well enough, and to do William justice, since it was conceived he has given it more attention than I would have expected. There have been other benefits also. His temper and general demeanour changed, his behaviour, inside and out, improved almost beyond measure, his drinking moderated. What is there not to favour?'

'And yet?'

'And yet … I cannot but feel a regret for the Munros, a guilt that we profit by their deaths.'

Glencairn glowered. 'A nonsense I have dismissed before.'

'It does not lessen the way I feel.' She was swivelling her ring, light from the ruby mounted at its centre flashing across the ceiling as she did so.

Glencairn's scowl deepened. 'Take care, madam, that you do not stretch my patience too far.'

John, glancing between them, thought of the comfort that was his to offer. The unspoken pact he had made with Munro, the oblique reference to reivers, the suggestion of flight a dangerous flame of hope burning in him still, but

229

which, like a candle in a potsherd, he had taken care to hide these six years since. And must do yet. One day the jar might be smashed, the truth revealed. In the meantime, the image of Munro dwindling into the distance, heading for Broomelaw and home, his left arm hanging useless by his side, remained with John: a burden that could neither be shed nor shared. He could not be certain the Munros had escaped, though he prayed it was so, and as a result it had not been hard when they had come on the remains of Broomelaw, still smouldering, the stones of the broken walls warm to the touch, the remnants of charred bodies among the ashes of the beds, to fuel the general feeling that reivers had beaten them to it. And indeed it was hard not to believe it, for if it was *not* true, then it was the aftermath of a perfectly staged set, William and the others who rode with him easily convinced. Only he, who had reason to doubt what they had found, noticed, as they laid the burnt bodies in a single grave among the cluster of graves in the hollow below the tower, the slight evidences of ground recently disturbed. And thanked God for the speed with which this new burial was carried out, the trampling of many boots on the moss covering the existing graves, obliterating earlier footsteps and the faint track of a barrow leading away from the mounds. Even now, despite the distance time provided, the Munros continued safety, if indeed it be needed, must depend on a general belief in their deaths. He chose his words with care. 'What happened to the Munros, it is better not to dwell on it. They were not the first to be burned out, and will not be the last. Though God knows we could all wish it were different.'

'Wish what was different?' William had returned, a new light in his eyes.

'We were talking of reivers, expressing the wish that such lawlessness might be curtailed. As you will wish now also, seeing you have a tower of your own to protect. Have you had any trouble with thieving while the work progresses?' It had been meant as a conversational ploy only, the frown settling on William's face a danger sign. 'There's been a problem?'

'Not of that sort, no. Or not yet at any rate.' William was terse. 'But there may be soon.'

A coldness swept through John – had a whisper of some sort reached Kilmaurs and given William cause to doubt the Munro's fate? He tried to pitch his interest at little more than casual. 'Have you a reason to anticipate trouble?'

'Only that when I returned today to check on the masons, I found them entertaining a local brat with an interest in the techniques of building, or so the claim. I sent her packing and set them back to work, but I suspicion learning wasn't her game. And besides, though she gave details of where she bided, they turned out to be false.' William poured himself a second drink. 'I have wondered all the way home if she prospected for materials to pilfer.'

'She, you say? Is it not unlikely thieves would send a lass to gather such information.'

'What other reason would there be for her poking about?'

'Perhaps she was curious. Bairns can aye…'

'Perhaps she was being paid for her curiosity.'

John, though unaware of the specific cause of William's interest, again felt coldness shiver through him.

'Is the tower left unattended at night?'

'No.' Glencairn interrupted as if bored by William's concern. 'The men have made a camp there until the work be done.'

'Well then, there is little cause for concern surely?'

'If they can be trusted to remain and not to slip away into Renfrew when my back is turned.' William shook his head. 'Oh, I daresay they are trustworthy enough, and there is little danger the work be spoiled, but it is the girl I cannot fathom.'

William trailed John to the guest chamber. He turned at the door, his sense of unease increasing as William said, 'There was a wise woman who treated Maxwell's wife some months ago. He said she had a look of familiarity about her, as if she might be some connection of that wife of Munro's...'

John was dismissive, though inwardly his stomach churned. 'If there had been any relatives they would have come forward when the tower was burned, to make claim to anything that survived.'

'So I thought, but I have wondered since … if Maxwell was to prove right…' A hint of satisfaction flitted across William's face. 'At any rate, I offered money to find her out, and it may have been well spent. The man who disturbed our supper was a pedlar, with information to sell.'

'A pedlar?' John sought to raise a doubt in William's mind. 'They're aye keen to make money, and frequently with little regard as to how they come by it.'

'I shall not prove gullible, Uncle. And will take steps to verify his story. He is well warned as to the consequences should it prove false.'

Chapter 5

His family was much on Munro's mind as he stood at the prow of the small merchant ship nosing into a spare berth at Irvine. On either side a fishing boat, their masters already ashore, the tail-end sailors, left to finish the business of unloading the cargo and making the decks shipshape, cursing their luck that they remained while their fellows caroused among the taverns beyond the harbour wall. He grinned as he saw a sailor berating a cabin boy who'd tripped over a neatly coiled rope, unwinding it across the deck on the end of his toe.

The voices drifting up from the quayside caught at Munro's throat and, ashamed of the weakness, he looked past the busy quayside and the jumble of buildings huddled behind it, to the hills beyond: a mottle of green and gold and heather-brown. And nestled in those hills, Braidstane, and Kate and the bairns. A cloud moved across the sun, on the hillside an answering shadow. He wondered, for the hundredth time since he had embarked on this journey, how much of a folly it was to be here if he put them all at risk. But here he was, the sights and sounds and smells a pleasure his apprehension failed to suppress. Not that he would have chosen to come home as the bearer of ill news, but he could do no other, the debt he owed the Montgomeries too great, his sorrow at Patrick's death a personal, as well as a professional one.

Memories crowded in on him. His early meetings with Patrick, and through Patrick with Hugh, the friendship springing up between them a fine thing, despite that he had fallen foul of Maxwell as a result. And through Maxwell, of William, though he didn't doubt the seeds of his disfavour had been sown long before. It would likely have come to the same thing in the end. Now, about to step onto Scottish soil for the first time in six years, his thoughts of Patrick and the message he risked a homecoming to bring mingled with the memories of his own family, his corresponding need to reach Braidstane strong.

The first sight of the tower house was a reassurance. Sturdy and four-square, much like Broomelaw had been, though on a somewhat bigger scale. The surrounding landscape was softer, greener, the tang of salt in the air emphasising the proximity to the sea. And hard on the heels of that thought, another proximity, less comfortable: to the Cunninghames at Kilmaurs. He searched the surrounding buildings for the bastle house and felt his first pang of guilt. Though it too was well cared for, its size emphasised the strictures his confrontation with William had placed on his family. An image of Broomelaw, long buried, surfaced in his mind as clear as if he stood on the slope by the sheep pen, the tower dominating the skyline above him, the comparison with the tiny bastle house perched at the corner of Braidstane's barmkin, stark. A new fear – would Kate's feelings for him likewise have shrunk?

Munro spurred his horse forward. The initial silence in the courtyard was an uneasy thing, the moments stretching, broken by the sound of children's laughter spilling from the attic windows. A new guilt: for the times when, caught up in the life of the regiment, Munro had failed to think of his family and of how they fared. A knowledge that Robbie and Maggie would be bairns no longer, that they might have grown up and away from the memory of their absent father, or worse still, that he might have been supplanted in their affections. In his wife's affections also. And who could blame her? He shut his eyes and tried to picture them all as they had been, as they might be now, and failed in both respects. He slid from his horse, the thought uncomfortable – I'll know soon enough.

The door of the bastle house opened, revealing Maggie, tall and comely, and thrusting past her a child, red-headed and bonny.

She stopped. 'Who's he?'

Despite that he could have expected it, indeed had done so every time he thought of home, her lack of recognition stung Munro. Behind the girls, Kate, emerging into the sunlight, halting, one hand on the door frame, as if without it she might fall.

Her voice was quiet, almost toneless. 'He is your father.'

Munro searched her face for any clue as to her feelings, took a step towards her.

'Robbie found you then?' She looked past him, the smile which hovered on her face fading. 'Where is he?'

'Robbie? No. I came...' Munro paused, sought for a

235

suitable question. 'Did he...?'

It was Maggie who broke in. 'He has been gone almost a month. To seek you out. We thought he had succeeded.'

'If he did not...' Kate's voice broke.

'What route did he take?'

'To Veere, with John Shaw ... from there ... we don't know.'

Munro's shoulders settled. 'It's a fair step from Veere. I came straight from Brittany,' a ghost of a smile flitted across his face, 'along with a cargo of brandy.' He made his voice confident. 'A month you say? He's likely with the regiment now, and cursing the ill luck that made us miss one another. Or maybe on his way home again.'

Kate, as if belatedly aware of the dust covering Munro's clothes, the weariness in him, or perhaps needing the support herself, turned back into the kitchen and subsided onto a chair, gesturing him to do likewise. 'Are you here to bide?'

He hesitated. 'A week, two perhaps.'

'You have not resigned your commission then?'

'No. I came ... to bring news of Patrick.'

'When ... how?'

'Three weeks ago ... he died well.'

'That's all right then.' It was a flash of the old Kate, her disdain of fighting clear. There were two spots of colour in her cheeks.

He stretched across the table towards her, thought better of it. 'I wanted to bring word myself, in the hope it may be of some comfort to the Montgomeries to know his last thoughts were of home. He asked me to give them a message.' There was a softening in her face, but he was unsure if it was for him, or for Elizabeth and Hugh.

236

She looked through the open door towards the tower house, a hint of moisture in her eyes, but her voice was brisk. 'They won't thank me then for keeping you from their company. They're all at home. If there is bad news to share, the sooner it's done the better.'

Ellie was tugging at her arm. She pointed at Munro, her stare accusing.

'If he's our father why doesn't he bide with us? Uncle Hugh bides with Aunt Elizabeth.'

'He is a soldier, with Uncle Patrick. Who doesn't bide with his family either...' Kate broke off. 'Why don't you go and find the girls, while we find Aunt Elizabeth.'

They came upon her in the still room, the girls' voices floating down the stairwell from the hall above. Elizabeth's smile for Kate turned to shock as she glimpsed Munro behind her, turned again to a broader smile of welcome.

'Munro! This is an unexpected pleasure. Can you bide? Or is it a flying visit only?' Then as the seriousness of his expression clearly penetrated, her hand bunched against her chest as if she struggled to breath. 'Patrick?'

'I'm sorry.' Then, in an attempt to soften the blow. 'I was with him at the end.'

The jar in her hand crashed to the floor, the oil spilling across the flags.

Munro offered, 'His last thoughts were of you all.'

She managed a nod. 'Thank you.'

'He charged me...'

She shook her head. 'Hugh ... there is no use in you saying all twice. If you could spare this evening...'

'Of course.' Kate was by her side, gripping her hand. 'We will come and stay as long as you need or want us.'

The sombre supper over and the bairns released into the barmkin with permission to amuse themselves, Elizabeth turned to Munro. 'We must thank you. It cannot have been easy to come.'

'There are some things worth the risk. I owe much to you all. This is little enough I can do to repay you.'

'As to that, the past is a complicated business and were we to tease it out would find obligation on both sides. Forbye that friendship isn't a matter of debt...'

Hugh said, 'You were with Patrick to the end?'

'Yes. His last words ... "Tell them I would have wished to see their bairns full-grown. That I once thought it a foolish thing to be so tied ... but I was wrong."'

Elizabeth, her voice catching, said, 'He was a good brother and would no doubt have made a good father when the time came.'

In the silence that followed, Munro thought of the image which would remain with him always, one he would *not* share: of kneeling beside Patrick in a welter of mud and blood, his death a merciful thing despite the waste. How he cradled the mangled body until his own anger cooled, before he carried what remained of Patrick back to the camp.

As if he divined his thoughts, Hugh said, 'He was a soldier always and from a child wished to die one. And if it is sooner than any of us would have hoped, at least he got his wish.'

Elizabeth stirred, as if about to contradict him, but Kate laid a steadying hand on her arm.

'Let's not concentrate on his death, but think rather of his life.' She ran her tongue across her lips. 'There are many die beforetime, but from the little I knew of him, I think he would have said that he had lived.'

It was the the right note, a cue for family reminiscence. Munro touched Kate's arm, tilted his head towards the door.

Hugh accompanied them down the stairwell, and, as Kate stepped outside, held Munro back a fraction. 'Thank you, for coming and for sparing them detail.'

'Kate's right, it's the picture of Patrick as they last saw him, and not as I did, they want to keep.' Munro glanced towards her, waiting part way across the barmkin. He lowered his voice. 'He died as he had lived, with bravery and a reckless disregard for his own safety, and perhaps it was for the better. There are many maimed who would wish to be as he is, rather than suffer the half-life that is left to them. Besides that the French King owes his life to Patrick. Perhaps, in a day or two, I can tell you some of that.'

Hugh nodded, looked in his turn at Kate, asked, 'How long will you remain?'

'I'm not sure. Now that I am here part of me wishes to stay, to take what time I can with my own family, lest my life too be cut short, lest my children … it pains me that I am a stranger to them.'

'And the other part?'

'A fear that I put them all at risk by being here, that it is a selfish thing to want to stay.'

If he hoped Hugh would dismiss his fears he was disappointed.

'For the moment I think they are safe, as are you, if you do not stray beyond the barmkin, but there is talk, and Kate has had a couple of closer shaves than any of us would have liked.'

'William?'

'Not as yet or I would be counselling you to leave without delay, but she has met Maxwell, and though he didn't recognise her, I suspect he has blabbed, perhaps when drunk, for questions as to her origins have been asked in Ayr.'

'And answers?'

Hugh permitted himself a grin. 'We have been somewhat disingenuous and I think have satisfied the gossips, though the reputation of "Mr Grant" has suffered somewhat as a result. I wouldn't advise that you advertise yourself as such in the fishmarket, for Kate is well thought of, and there are plenty among the fishwives I wouldn't wish to fall foul of.'

Kate was walking back towards them. Hugh smiled at her. 'I won't keep your husband any longer. I daresay he has better things to do with his time than talk on our doorstep.'

Kate stood in the pool of moonlight spilling into the small chamber behind the bastle house kitchen, waiting for Munro. It was a moment she had wished for countless times, but now that it had arrived it wasn't altogether the simple, joyous thing she had anticipated. Perhaps if she had flung herself into his arms when he first appeared through the barmkin gate it might have been different, but the hours since had brought an awkwardness between them she could neither explain nor dissipate. She devoured him with her eyes when he was looking elsewhere, but found it difficult to meet his gaze when he turned to her, more difficult still to reach out to him. Longing for his touch, yet afraid she might fail to move him … or he her. She shook herself – they had been farther estranged in the past and with more cause, and yet had overcome the distance. This was only a matter of the awkwardness of a long separation, and not likely a lack of desire on either part.

His voice behind her, husky, scarcely audible, the touch of his fingers light upon her neck. 'Kate?'

She recognised it as a question, a symptom of his equal uncertainty.

'All the time I was away,' he was twisting a curl of her hair around his fingers, 'I feared for you: that William might find you, that he might take his revenge. And each time word came from Elizabeth, though it brought a temporary reassurance, those fears were replaced by a new, a more insidious thought, that you might imagine me lost to you, and…' she leaned back against him, felt the beating of his heart through her shift, '…that you might have found someone else to warm your bed.'

'I promised I would wait.' Into her mind, unbidden, an image of the harbour at Irvine, of the ship's captain's eyes, the warmth of his hand on her wrist, the twist in her stomach as he bent his head towards hers. And though only a few months past, a lifetime since, and with Munro home, of no relevance at all.

A pause in which a desire for total honesty warred with the understanding that to confess to the momentary weakness would be but to salve her own conscience, that there were some things better *not* said. She turned and pressed her face into his chest. 'I had my own fears: that when you

241

did come you would find me other than you remembered, and want me less.' She was crying, but whether for what she hid from him, or what she revealed, she couldn't tell, only that now he was here she found her need of him undiminished.

He slid his arms around her, drew her to the bed, and she forgot the narrow confines, the coarse sheets, the horsehair mattress that however much she pummelled it stubbornly refused to lie flat, and afterwards clung to him as if her heart might break.

Chapter 6

Munro had been at Braidstane three days, the renewal of his relationship with Kate a fragile thing, when Alexander Montgomerie appeared from court. Hugh brought him straight to the bastle house and it was clear that though he might be an infrequent visitor to Braidstane, he was a familiar and welcome one nonetheless. The epitome of courtesy, he bent over Kate's hand.

'You are as well as you look?'

Munro felt a stab of almost jealousy at the readiness of her smile and immediately chastised himself – why wouldn't she be comfortable with those she lived among?

Kate's tone was warm. 'Is this a family visit? Or a mission from court?'

'A little of both, for I like fine to see family and how the children grow, and Hugh has promised an afternoon's archery, should the weather hold. But,' his expression became more serious, 'I'm glad to find you here, for it was primarily you I came to see. To ask a favour, on the King's behalf.'

'A favour of me?' She looked surprised. 'What can I do

243

for the King?'

'The Queen, though well enough in general terms, has a woman's problem. The court physicians and several of the Edinburgh apothecaries have done their best, but to no avail. Hugh has spoken highly of your skill in such matters, hence James' request for your attendance. Of course, it is a request in name only, for he expects a speedy response.'

Munro felt a tightness grip his chest. He looked towards the gable window and noted the single cloud, the size of a man's hand, marring the clear sky, heard Alexander say, 'And I believe to be absent from Braidstane for a day or two might suit you very well.'

Munro brought his gaze back to rest on Alexander's face, aware of a dangerous undercurrent. And catching Hugh's eye got the distinct impression Hugh would rather he hadn't. 'Has there been trouble?'

Hugh downplayed it. 'William has renewed his curiosity. Not yet enough to bring him to our door. But I think I have discovered who stirs the pot.'

Maggie blanched and reached for the window ledge as if for support. Kate subsided onto the bench, queried, 'Maxwell?'

'I'm afraid so.'

'From the moment Maggie and I saw him at Hillhouse...'

Munro moved to stand beside her, as if in protection.

'At first I feared, we all did. But as the weeks passed, I assumed any thought he had of recognition had been forgot. What is it he has done now?'

'It is not so much what he has done, as the memories he has stirred...' Hugh was rubbing his boot on the floor as if to remove an imaginary stain, while behind him Maggie relaxed a fraction.

Alexander was focused on Kate. 'The talk is that Maxwell cited you as having the look of a Munro...' He hesitated at Munro's sharp intake of breath, finished, 'It is that has likely unsettled William, caused him to renew his enquiries.'

Kate said, 'So I would be better away?'

Munro's fingers were biting into her shoulder.

'I think so, yes...' Alexander's gaze was steady. 'For a time at least.'

'And the bairns?'

'Will be safe with Agnes.'

In the background, the children's voices and high-pitched chatter mingled with Elizabeth's more measured tones. There was the screech of the stable door opening, then a squeal and running footsteps across the cobbles. The door banged as the two Montgomerie girls flung themselves on Alexander, Elizabeth close behind, Ellie coming to nestle against Kate.

Elizabeth echoed Kate's question. 'Alexander! To what do we owe this pleasure?'

'The Queen has need of Kate's expertise, so I took the chance of a jaunt.' He squeezed the girls. 'And am glad I did, for if I had been much longer away I might not have recognised these pair.'

Kate lifted her hand to her shoulder, imprisoning Munro's. 'And if I cannot do anything for the Queen? Is there not risk in trying?'

Alexander's answer seemed only half in jest. 'Ours is not the English court, where failure may cost your head. Many have treated the Queen and achieved nothing, the only consequence a loss of reputation.' A smile. 'And if you have no pretensions to remain, word of how you do there will have little impact on your usual customers.'

She breathed in, out again. 'When does the King expect my attendance?'

'I bought a little time in case I should come and find you off on some other errand of mercy. But as you aren't, if you can be ready to travel tomorrow, it would be politic to do so. On several counts.'

Again a glance flashed between Alexander and Hugh.

Munro intercepted it. 'Can I be of use?'

Kate was leaning into him. 'While I make ready you can talk to me.'

Elizabeth shooed Hugh and Alexander out, gathered up the girls. 'Ellie and Maggie can have supper with us. Agnes too if she's a mind. This is to be John's last evening with us, for he travels to Edinburgh also, so Maggie may wish a final chance to pick his brains.'

Munro smiled his thanks. Alone he turned to Kate.

'I know,' she said, as if to pre-empt him. 'It's hard to be called away when we had just begun…'

'It is an honour to be so sought, and who knows when the patronage of the Queen may prove useful.' He cupped her face in his hands, answered her unspoken question. 'You haven't seen the back of me yet. I will not leave without saying goodbye.'

'And the regiment?'

'Can do without me a while longer. The French King was fond of Patrick and gave me leave of absence willingly, with permission to return when I could, when my duty to the Montgomeries was done. Besides his bravery and charisma, Henri is a kindly man, with a care for his troops. Easy to serve…'

They were at a crossroads, Kate very still.

Munro took a deep breath. 'There is a farmhouse ... I wrote of it...'

It was a question.

She shook her head. 'We didn't hear. The letter perhaps gone astray.'

He heard her uncertainty, had an inkling of the effort she made.

'Tell me now.'

'Modest, but pretty, and well set, in a valley not far from the sea...' He was looking past her, focusing on the unseen vista. 'I came on it while out foraging for hay for the horses. I was a good two days' ride from Amiens, for we had exhausted all the resources nearer to hand, so that it was a welcome sight to see the fields uncut, but the farmyard sprouted weeds, and the house was smothered in ivy. I thought it derelict and was halfway through a broken window thinking to find shelter for the night, when the lady of the house herself appeared.' He felt Kate stir, as if she worried that it wasn't an altogether unpleasant memory, so hastened to reassure her. 'She was smaller than Maggie, as round as she was tall, and wrinkled like a crab apple that has been too long in store, a wheel-lock pistol wavering in each hand. I didn't know whether to go forward or back, the chances of being shot, either by design or accident, seeming equally likely either way. The longer I hesitated the more it seemed her hands shook, so that as I dropped to the ground I held my own hands well away from pistol and sword both. I think even then she might have shot me just to be on the safe side, but that I caught my breeks on a loose nail on the way out and ripped the backside out of them. It's hard to be threatening with your rear as naked as the day you were born.'

He sensed Kate relaxing.

'Not one of your better moments then?'

'No. Though I think it may have saved my life. Whatever the reason, she lowered her guns and said if I hadn't come to rape and pillage I was most welcome, but that the custom in those parts was to knock at the door. In the end she fed and clothed me and gave me a bed for the night, which was at least lice-free, if a mite fusty.' He grinned. 'And in the morning she furnished me with a change of clothing. Her long-deceased husband had clearly been of a height with her, but any clothes are better than none. She didn't laugh to my face, but I suspicion she did behind my back. As I would have done in other circumstances. It was when I returned for the second time, with a team to see to the cutting of the hay, that we talked. Her husband and sons gone, it pains her to see what her farm has become. You would all be welcome there.'

A shadow flickered across Kate's face. Munro cursed his thoughtlessness, attempted reassurance. 'Her triple loss was some years ago, when the whole countryside was afire.'

Kate was nibbling at her lip. 'Had you thought to take us back with you now?'

'I hoped so, yes.'

She brushed her hand across her eyes.

He placed his hands on her shoulders. 'But now there is the Queen.' He was aware of a hint of reluctance in his voice, sought to moderate it. 'When the time is right … it is near enough the coast to have the smell of the sea, but much like Braidstane…' the hesitation was fractional, 'it is removed from the thick of things and the surrounding

248

countryside not overrun with either doctors or apothecaries. I would not stand in your way if you wished to work as you do here, though I would hope it would be from choice and not by necessity.'

Her tears were flowing freely now, so that he pulled her towards him and suppressing his own pain, said, 'Kate? I will not force you to come...'

She reached up and took his face in both hands. 'Of course we will come. It is not at that I cry. Only, if Robbie had waited, we might have travelled together.'

He slid his arms about her waist. 'We'll all be together soon.'

'But in the meantime...'

'In the meantime,' he finished her sentence, offering affirmation, 'you must go to court.'

They were in the stable, Munro saddling Kate's horse. 'I wish...'

He touched her cheek. 'The dangers are too great, besides that Hugh would likely shoot me sooner than...'

'Sooner than what?' Hugh stuck his head through the doorway.

'Take the risk of me accompanying Kate to Edinburgh.'

Hugh rose to the bait. 'Glencairn's attendances at court are regular and frequent, and though I am at pains to avoid him whenever possible, our paths do cross. With civility on both sides,' he added, a sardonic twist to his mouth, 'which I hold to for family's sake, however much it sticks in my craw. To take Kate is one thing, a risk we cannot avoid when the King demands it, but you are a step too far,

249

even for me.'

Munro laughed. 'Credit me with some wit,' then, more soberly, 'I have not spent six years apart from my family to throw caution away now.'

'Well then,' Hugh nodded, 'I'll take care of Kate, if you'll take care of my family and my stock, though who has the better bargain, I'm not sure.'

Chapter 7

Church bells were ringing the hour as Kate and Hugh entered Edinburgh, Alexander and John Montgomerie a fraction to the rear. Some in unison, some an echo, Kate counted them out, concentrating on the present to quell other thoughts, other memories. 'Is it to Holyrood we go?'

It was Alexander who answered. 'Yes. James finds it more comfortable than the castle, and I don't blame him. Aside from the wind, which is like to take your head away every time you cross the castle courtyard, the refurbishments of the interior at Holyrood, made for Queen Anne's arrival, provide every convenience. And the garden I know she finds a sanctuary, and the chance to take the air with some measure of privacy.'

'Is there any privacy for a queen?' Kate was sceptical.

'Precious little, but there would be none at all in the castle precincts, which are aye thronging.'

Unbidden, the vision came to Kate of the house the Montgomeries had taken on the Canongate, the walnut tree in blossom, the sunlight slanting along the narrow paths. 'Where do we bide?'

As if he divined her fear, Alexander said, 'I have lodgings on the Cowgate: not grand like those Robert Montgomerie favoured, but convenient, and space enough for us.' He allowed himself a smile. 'And a pie shop near hand, that we might not starve. We should perhaps eat something before we head to Holyrood, for it's hard to say how long it might be before we have the chance again. With luck we may be able to get something hot.'

Again the memory: the smell of the pies on the stall on the High Street on the way to their first visit to the Montgomeries, Munro wrinkling his nose, toying with the idea of purchase, her refusal to be softened. And all that came after. She took a deep breath, relaxed her shoulders. She was here now, and with a chance to make an impression on the Queen, and if it proved favourable, who knew where it might lead. Though Queen Anne had produced but two bairns in the seven years of her marriage, their health did not seem to be in doubt … well, she would know soon enough.

The pie was surprisingly good: the gravy full-flavoured, the pastry sweet, the meat tender, if a little in short supply. Hugh grinned at Kate. 'Now you see why I do not come home a shadow. The quantity may be a mite deficient, but the quality is there, and if I need to take two rather than one, that is an ill I can handle.'

Kate grinned back, aware it was an attempt to distract her, but succumbing nonetheless. 'Do you never think of anything other than your stomach?'

'Occasionally. If I have to. Though it is an inconvenience

I seek to avoid.'

Kate followed the courtier along the wooden gallery to the sheltered north-facing walled garden, where the Queen sat, her ladies around her. Embroideries laid out on their laps, Kate suspected, from the way in which some of them busied themselves with their needles as she approached, that perhaps their attention had been focused on gossip rather than industry.

The courtier announced her. 'Mistress Grant, come from Braidstane.'

The Queen nodded in acknowledgement of Kate's curtsey, motioned to her ladies to leave. They rose in unison: butterflies, taking flight.

Anne patted the bench beside her. 'You may sit. It will be the easier to talk if we are close.' Sadness settled on her face. 'I have heard good reports of your skill. They are not exaggerated?' A pause, as if she weighed her words, and Kate, mindful of the Queen's youth, felt a stab of pity, quite unrelated to whatever the physical ailment might be. 'There are many in my husband's train who make great claims without substance, and I have suffered the attentions of some such. Though your relatives,' and here a glimmer of a smile touched the corners of Anne's mouth, 'do not seem pressed from that mould.'

Kate was feeling her way, unsure of the desired response. She chose to be direct. 'Hugh Montgomerie is an honest and, I think, a good man. But he is a man nonetheless, and with a scant understanding of female ailments. I have some skill and will do what I can. But until I know what the problems are, I cannot make promise of how much that will be.'

'That,' said Anne, with a dryness far beyond her years, 'will make a refreshing change.'

Kate looked down at the tips of her shoes, peeping out below her hem, the worn leather in startling contrast to the embroidered brocade of the Queen's slippers. It must be an uncomfortable thing to constantly question both folk's motives and the truthfulness of anything they said to her, but so was the lot of a queen, and had aye been so. 'Better a laird than a lord,' Munro had said long ago, and nothing Kate had seen since had caused her to doubt his opinion. It was clear the Queen found it hard to come to the kernel of the matter. Kate, instinct counselling patience, waited in silence.

'You have children, Mistress Grant?'

'Three remaining. I had four, but one died.' Kate paused, swallowed the familiar lump. 'A needless accident, almost seven years ago, and I should have put it behind me, for I am not the only mother to lose a child, but I still feel blame for it.'

'The living children?'

'One boy, itching for a soldier's life, and two younger girls.'

'Did you have any difficulties in the...' again a slight hesitation, '...bearing of them?'

For a moment Kate wished that she had, for it would have made the conversation easier on the Queen. But to be less than truthful would be to break with her usual habit, and a breach of faith. She looked up at the tower windows, catching a glimpse of a face pressed against the glass, as quickly withdrawn. 'No. And for that I will always be grateful. But

I have attended sufficient who have had problems, both in the bearing and,' it was her turn to hesitate, 'the conceiving of bairns, to have an understanding of the pain it brings.' Another pause. 'And not just of the physical.'

She was close enough to feel the Queen's involuntary shiver, and again allowed her instinct for silence to take over. In the moments while she waited she became aware of birdsong from beyond the wall, where parkland merged into the gorse-covered slope stretching towards the red crags dominating the skyline. She picked out a thrush and the soft chirrup of sparrows and, soaring above them all, a skylark, its voice pure and clear.

Anne was fingering the black diamonds at her throat. 'Our two children are healthy, and for that I thank God, and that our firstborn is a son and heir. But it is not the expected tally for seven years of marriage, for is not a fine brood my primary task?' She seemed unaware of the undercurrent of bitterness in her words, and continued, 'It is not in the conceiving that I fall short, but in the carrying of a bairn. And each time it fails it is as if a part of me dies with the child. The King, for all that he shares my desire for a quiverful of healthy offspring, seems not to understand how I feel.' A haunted look slid onto her face, as if she regretted the reference to James, or perhaps was apprehensive that it might be repeated in the wrong company.

Instinctively Kate reached out her hand to place it on Anne's arm, drew it back, afraid of presumption, kept her voice soft, sympathetic. 'It is not in men to feel the same way for a bairn they haven't seen. I do not think it lives for them from the start as it does for us who carry it within.' Then, choosing her words with care and thinking again of Margaret Maxwell, with the same desire for secrecy, though in a different cause, said, 'Women's work is best discussed between women, and the details kept private. There is much I will say to a woman that I will not share with her husband, whether commanded or no.'

Anne's face cleared.

Kate moved onto the practical. 'The other physicians, what have they suggested? It will be the easier for me to offer treatment if I know what has already been tried and failed.'

'It is a lengthy list, and if efficacy was in inverse proportion to the unpleasantness of the treatments, I would have been well cured long since. I have eaten crushed orchid leaves, powdered fox's lungs and crab's eyes; drunk wolf oil and tincture of foxglove; been bled and leeched till I think I have little blood left; told to lie on my side and on my stomach, even upside down. Few treatments convenient, and none effective. Forgive me if I think them all quackery. Prince Henry was not the first conception, nor Princess Elizabeth the second. To be candid, I had no thought that you would have anything more to offer other than that which I'd already suffered, but the King was set on sending for you.'

'And happy I am to come, for though I cannot promise anything, there are treatments I have found efficacious in women's problems. But...'

Anne looked up. 'But?'

'Forgive me, but the herbs I would prescribe are most effective when a pregnancy is already begun. If your loss was but recent...'

'I thought perhaps there would be something could be done beforehand, and did not wish to miss the opportunity.'

Kate shook her head. 'Nothing, bar a healthy diet, for

which you need no advice from me. As to herbs, some I have with me, others I will need to obtain from an apothecary. And if I cannot find all I need, I can have them sent. I can leave instructions for their storage and mixing when the time comes, and a promise to return when you should have need of me.'

For the first time, Kate saw hauteur in Anne's gaze. 'Whatever you need, you shall have it, and if we must need send elsewhere for it, it will be done. But there is an apothecary who serves the court physicians, and he will be told all that he has is to be at your disposal.'

'Kate hesitated. 'That I may chose aright, I need to ask some more personal questions.'

'Ask away. I am well used to having my affairs the subject of interest and gossip among high and low alike.'

'Is there a pattern to when the pregnancy fails? A certain month perhaps?'

'Always before the fourth month, but otherwise no set time. And nor, before you ask, is there any pattern to my actions that could be thought to explain the cause of the problem. I have done nothing I should not, and everything that is suggested, however unlikely it sounds.'

The next was a more sensitive question. Kate thought of how best to phrase it. 'After a miscarriage, does the next pregnancy follow on, or do you have some respite?'

'Respite?' A wry smile. 'Disappointment leads to desire, and I have not the heart to refuse the King his rightful dues. I was not so brought up.'

Kate was moving onto difficult ground. 'If I were to recommend a period of recuperation, of abstinence. Could that be accomplished?'

'Do you recommend it?'

'Yes. There is little doubt that to miscarry weakens a woman, and if the body is given time to recover, the chance of another failure is lessened. But it is a delicate issue and one not easily broached with a husband.'

Anne was silent, clearly thinking on what Kate said. 'When Elizabeth was conceived ... it was after rest, for the King was away. I remained behind because of a pregnancy, then with the loss ... it was some weeks before we were together. Perhaps if I can remind him of that...'

Another brief silence in which Kate focused her gaze on the flickering shadows cast by the branches of an almond tree.

The Queen spoke again. 'I will send someone to accompany you to the apothecary. And ... thank you.' It was the gentlest of dismissals, but unmistakeable. Kate rose, curtsied, and stepped back three paces before turning to leave.

Chapter 8

There was a stiff breeze blowing in off the sea. Hugh and
Kate were making for Leith to attempt to persuade Grizel
to come back with them to Braidstane rather than stifling
in the city through the summer. It was a thoughtfulness
on Hugh's part which made Kate both regret she had no
brother of her own and be grateful for the way in which the
Montgomeries had absorbed her into their family. It was
the first time she had been in Leith, the slap, slap of the
tide against the harbour wall and the creaking of timbers
as boats jostled for position a musical counterpoint to the
call of the gulls.

Sigurd's house, set back from the sea down a narrow
wynd, and thus sheltered from the worst of weathers, nevertheless showed signs of the ravages of salt in the peeling
paintwork surrounding the narrow door set into the wynd
wall.

Kate was thinking aloud. 'Odd that Sigurd didn't choose
to lodge hard by the port.'

Hugh laughed, and, though it was no doubt unintentional, Kate felt diminished, as if a child who spoke out of

ignorance.

'A sea view would likely have come at a price, and I'm not talking money. It'll be to avoid the sweet scent of seaweed and rotting fish-heads that Sigurd has chosen to bide a wee way from the shore. If Grizel is to keep the contents of her stomach down in her current condition, the further she is from fish-heads the better.'

He swung down to hand Kate onto the cobbles, then hammered on the door. There was a shuffling and a grumbling and the grating of a bolt before it opened to reveal an elderly man bent almost in two. He squinted up at them.

'Wha is't ye want?'

'To see Mistress Ivarsen.'

'Ye're no expected.' He stood his ground in the doorway.

'I am her brother and have a standing invitation.'

'And a'm the king o' Scotland.' The man picked at his ear with a long, yellowed nail, much like a fish hook, and flicked a gob of wax onto the cobbles at their feet. 'Fancy as ye are, ye'll need to do mair as talk. Wha proof can ye gie me?'

Kate intervened. 'Is Mistress Ivarsen within? Perhaps you could call her?'

He made no move. 'Perhaps ah could.'

'And perhaps we could wait inside while you enquire.'

He appeared to think, then shuffled backwards leaving just enough space for Kate to squeeze through the doorway. He jerked his head towards the landward end of the wynd. 'There's nae stabling here, ye'll hae to take they horses to the livery yard, and,' he shook his head, 'ye'll likely pay, for he's a rogue.'

He leaned past Kate to shut the door. 'The lady maun

wait here while I enquire o' the mistress.'

'Kate!' Grizel, giving Kate as much of a hug as she could manage with her increased girth, led her through a dim passageway into a room surprisingly light, given the alleyway the windows looked out onto. 'It's good to see you. I have been lonely of late. When Sigurd is here I wish to be also, and the older bairns find plenty to do around the docks and are favourites everywhere. But endearing as Gerda is, she hardly counts as company, and as you can see, I am close to a beached whale. This is the third time I have suffered through the hottest months, and each time determined not to do so again. But November nights are gey cold in Flekkefjord, and thus too tempting a prospect to lie close in bed at night without thought of the consequences.'

Kate laughed. 'It's early in a marriage to be only the cold driving you into your husband's arms. And I had thought yours a love match...'

'Oh it is, but at the moment it's hard not to think the inconveniences of carrying a bairn outweigh the pleasures of begetting one.' Grizel shifted in an attempt to find a more comfortable position. 'Though perhaps it's as well we do forget, else the world would soon be empty.'

'There will aye be love, inconvenient or not,' Kate's smile faded, 'and a husband's will whether in love or no.' And then, to reassure Grizel, 'Oh I do not think of you, or indeed of myself, only that I had a patient recently whose husband is not kind.' She placed her hand on Grizel's swollen belly. 'The world is ill-divided, but it will be a fine

261

thing for this bairn to grow up where love is … to have the benefit of both her parents.'

There was sympathy in Grizel's eyes. 'These last six years, I cannot conceive how hard they must have been for you. And to be summoned here, now, with Munro at Braidstane, must be harder still, when every day is precious to you.'

'Hardest of all is the risk of exposure.'

'You have been Mistress Grant for long enough now surely that the risks are few?'

'Word is that the Cunninghames are much about the court. If their suspicion is aroused…'

'Hot-headed William may be, but not I think foolish enough to risk the King's displeasure for suspicion's sake. Or not at least with Glencairn to hold him in check. And besides, you are in service to the Queen, does that not guarantee your safety?'

'In her presence yes. On the High Street, no…'

There was a low growl, as if from a mastiff pup, below the window, followed by a whoop and a shriek. Grizel, distracted, thrust her head out through the narrow casement, then ducked back again. 'It's Ivar and Isabella; Hugh must have seen them coming and lain in wait like a bogey man. I don't know who is the greater child.'

Hugh breezed in, one child hanging on each arm. He raised his arms as high as possible, lifting their feet off the floor, but if he intended to silence them, he failed, their chatter turning to squeals as he swung them round.

Grizel covered her ears. 'Put them down, Hugh! You may not mind the racket, but I have no wish to disturb the entire neighbourhood. Not forgetting the mite upstairs who isn't best pleased if her sleep is broken.'

'Moder, Moder, we saw a monster...' Isabella had detached herself from Hugh and was tugging at Grizel's hand. Then, seeing Kate, she rushed at her and wound her arms around her legs, burying her head in her skirts. Her voice was muffled. 'Are Kate and Ellie and Mary here?'

Kate hunkered down and hugged her. 'No, sweetheart, just me and Uncle Hugh.'

'Oh.' Her head came up, the disappointment clear.

'I am summoned to see the Queen. Is that not exciting?'

Ivar, dismissing his sister with all the assurance of his five years, said, 'It wasn't a monster, Moder, it was a man, all in black, with a hat like a pie on a plate and a bird-mask, with a long, pointed beak.'

Grizel blanched, Kate instinctively tightening her hold on Isabella, who protested, 'Aowh, you're hurting.'

'I'm sorry, sweetheart.' Kate relaxed her grip and bent to drop a kiss on Isabella's hair, but she backed away, her lip quivering.

Hugh, with a swift look at Isabella, dropped onto all fours and moved towards her, sniffing at the floor as if following a scent, and when he reached her he rubbed his head against her leg, his 'Ruff, ruff, ruff!' turning her tremor into a giggle.

Ivar was also edging towards Hugh, attracted by his mock-barking. Grizel reached out for him, clearly making an effort to keep her voice calm. 'Where did you see the plag...' She bit off the word, changed it to 'strange man?'

Ivar shrugged, as if he discarded the memory as he might a toy in favour of something better. 'Oh ... at the far end of the harbour, climbing up onto one of the boats.'

Kate scrambled to her feet, and grasping Grizel's arm, urged her to a seat. 'We came to persuade you to come back to Braidstane with us, to see out the wait till the bairn is due in comfort and fresher air. Perhaps it is more timely than we thought.'

Grizel was adamant. 'Timely or not, I cannot leave now. For Sigurd to return and find me gone, it would not be fitting.'

'But if there is...' Kate, looking at the children who were now crawling all over Hugh, also avoided the word, '...sickness, he would want you safe.'

'And so I will be.' She shivered. 'At the first confirmation I will come, I promise you, whether Sigurd is returned or no. How could I not? For the meantime, I shall take care to remain indoors. When do you expect to leave?'

'As soon as possible, within a day or two certainly.'

Grizel stood up again, a decision made. 'Take the bairns, for me to stay inside is nothing, but for them, impossible. If there is danger they would be better away, and if it comes to nothing, they are ahead of me, that's all.'

Hugh, setting the children aside, began to rise, but whatever he had been about to say, Kate pre-empted him,

'Of course we'll take them.'

Grizel addressed Ivar. 'You'd like fine to go with Uncle Hugh, I'm sure.' And to Isabella, 'If the girls cannot come to you, you shall go to them. I shall follow, just so soon as I've seen your father.'

Isabella skipped across the floor. 'And the baby will come?'

'And the baby will come.'

Chapter 9

The voice was unmistakeable. Munro was forking hay into racks hanging on the stable wall as William Cunninghame and Patrick Maxwell clattered into Braidstane's barmkin, calling for service. Munro tapped the boy sweeping out the empty box beside him, jerked his head towards the door, and, indicating first himself, then the loft above, placed his finger against his lips. The boy nodded and scuttled out. The loft ladder was on the other side of the open doorway and Munro edged towards the shaft of light splitting the stable in two – if he should be seen...

William's voice again. 'Here, boy, take our horses. And send for your master.'

'H-he's n-not h-here, s-sir.'

'Your mistress then.'

Munro heard the creak of the saddle, followed by twin thumps as the visitors dismounted.

'A-ah'm a-alone h-here, s-sir, will a-ah s-see to the h-horses f-first?' The boy's voice betrayed an uneasiness that Munro prayed would be thought but a feature of his stammer.

There was a jingle of harness, a horse snorting, as if in defiance, the boy's instinctive, 'Easy now, easy,' soft and stammer-free.

A moment of silence, then the sound of the boy's boots scraping on the cobbles and a final snort as the horse he gentled shifted, cutting off the light spilling through the open door. Munro, blessing him, took a deep breath, darted the few feet to the foot of the ladder and began to climb. A rung groaned and he froze, holding his breath. Released it again as William snapped, 'We'll see ourselves to the tower. You look to the horses, and properly mind. We shall know if you shirk your duties.'

Munro, stepping carefully to keep his tread light, crossed the loft to where the last of the previous season's bales lay. The gap behind them was small, but he had little option. As he eased himself over, a cat shot up a bale onto his arm and, claws extended, scrabbled up to his shoulder, yowling. Munro heard Maxwell's 'What was that?' then footsteps heading back towards the stable. He disengaged the cat's claws and setting it on the floor dived behind the bales.

The boy was blocking the stable door. 'O-only a c-cat, s-sir. I st-stood on h-him, s-sir.'

'You should take more care then.' There was little of sympathy for either the boy or the cat in Maxwell's tone.

Munro, wedged under the slope of the roof, listened as William and Maxwell recrossed the barmkin to hammer on the tower door.

Another creak of the ladder, a rustle and a thump as the boy pulled himself through the hatch.

'Y-ye're n-no ... w-wanting to be s-seen th-then?' His whisper seemed unnaturally loud, and Munro, lifting his

266

head to signal him to be silent, cracked it against a beam, smothering the oath springing to his own lips.

Another whisper, 'A-ah f-felt th-that,' accompanied by a grin and, then, 'A-ah c-could th-think of a b-b-better hi-hiding p-place … e-except ye c-canna get th-there … or no th-the n-now.'

William's voice rang out across the barmkin. 'Your mistress isn't to be disturbed? Where's her courtesy?'

Ishbel's answer was indistinct, Munro straining to make her out. 'They have lately had a loss and the mistress feels it sorely.'

'Indeed. And the condolences of a near neighbour are not welcome? I think you take too much upon yourself. Stand aside, woman.'

'Indeed I will not.' Ishbel's voice rose. 'You have no right to force your way…'

'You dare refuse the Master of Glencairn?'

Elizabeth calm and conciliatory. 'William … and Patrick. I had not realised you were here. This is an unexpected visit.' Munro sensed she took care that her normally soft voice carried. 'You have caught us at an ill time, and Hugh in Glasgow, but I would not wish to be inhospitable. Can I offer you refreshment?'

William had lost some of his stridency. 'That would be welcome. We heard word of your brother-in-law's death. It is no doubt a sad blow.'

Munro imagined his expression, the sympathy painted on like limewash hiding a rot beneath, prayed Elizabeth wouldn't be taken in.

'I came but to convey my family's condolences, as a good neighbour should.'

'And I, as a long-standing friend who wouldn't wish to

267

fail in his duty.' That was Maxwell.

'I thank you. Please…' Elizabeth's voice faded, the tower door shutting. Munro eased himself up – thank God for the call from the Queen that had taken Kate back to court. Alexander had the right of it: she was safer away. But if he was to be found, all the sacrifices of the last six years would have been for nothing, besides that it would be an ill way to repay the Montgomeries.

The boy was sitting on the edge of the hatch, swinging his legs.

Munro flexed his back, breathed out. 'Where is this better hiding place? I trust it is more comfortable than here.'

The boy's lop-sided grin reappeared. 'C-comfortable? Maybe no, b-but s-safer for s-sure.' His pride was obvious. 'We h-hae a d-dungeon.'

Comfortable it most certainly wasn't. The best that could be said, that it was vermin-free. Munro paced out the dimensions, his foot slipping in the glaur smearing the floor so that he landed heavily in what he hoped was merely rotting leaves, though to judge by the smell, it could very well be worse. He reached out to pull himself up, seeking a grip on a wall which ran with damp, clumps of moss which sprouted in the cracks coming away in his hand. The light was dim, filtered through the iron grill stoppering the narrow opening above his head. Enough to take the edge off the darkness, but little more, the dank atmosphere proof, if any were needed, that sunlight never penetrated – at least it wasn't raining. There was sufficient space for a body to sit, but not to lie down – you could go mad in such a place.

No doubt the original intention. He tried hunkering, until his knees began to pain him, then straightened as far as he was able, his neck and shoulders bent under the curving roof. The boy had promised to return to release him once the visitors were safely away – it surely couldn't be long.

Chapter 10

William and Maxwell had followed Elizabeth up the stair and into the hall, repeating their expressions of sympathy for her loss. She injected as much sincerity as she could muster into her thanks, all the while aware of their appraisal of the room, of the measure of surprise they were unable to conceal at the comfort of the furnishings, the high polish on the oak table, the decorated beams. The pattern on them was bold, the colours vibrant, the paint fresh.

She looked up at them, thought – we aren't the peasants you imagined, but said only, 'You admire the beams I see, they are but lately retouched.' She wondered how long she must keep them occupied, how much time Munro needed, if the boy would think of the dungeon. And in an attempt to disarm, gestured towards the seat by the inglenook. 'Please, one of the servants will see to us shortly.'

'If it is the servant who opened the door to me, I trust she can keep a more civil tongue in her head.'

'Loyalty is an attribute we value highly in this house.'

'Do you value impertinence also?'

She forced herself to ignore the edge of sarcasm. 'Her

thought was of my well-being, I value that.' She waved her hand at the plasterwork between the beams, to distract from Ishbel's perceived shortcomings. 'Do you not think the colours rather fine? The artist came well recommended; he has a following in Edinburgh and has worked for the King.'

She had backed them into a corner from which they couldn't retreat without discourtesy, to her and to James.

William nodded his acknowledgement. 'Indeed, I have intentions of similar myself at the tower I'm restoring.'

She prepared to discuss the practicalities of the maintenance of a house, the relative merits of thatch and slab, the ravages of winter weather, determined that he wouldn't find her lacking in understanding – it would be as fine a way as any to delay them for long enough to ensure Munro's safety. Found the muscles of her stomach contracting as he continued, 'You may have heard of it: Broomelaw, over by Renfrew, a Cunninghame stronghold, destroyed by reivers … but well set and with the makings of a fine house.'

She swallowed, summoned a deprecatory smile. 'I hear little, for I don't go much about, and without many visitors am generally quiet … as you find me now.' She moved to the door, apologised, 'I don't know what has become of Ishbel, I'll see to your ale myself.'

At the foot of the stair she leaned against the wall, took a deep breath, and as Ishbel emerged from the kitchen, took the ale from her, whispered her instructions.

Munro heard the scrape of iron on stone, the grill above

his head disappearing, the tightening in his gut relieved as the steward hissed his name. A rope snaked down through the circle of light to coil at his feet and he moved under the opening, squinting upwards, queried, 'Angus? They've gone?'

'No. But you must.'

Munro grasped the rope and hauled himself up, his thigh muscles protesting, the palms of his hands burning.

'The Master of Glencairn and Maxwell are still closeted with Mistress Montgomerie, but how long she can hold them I don't know. I'm to lead you to a safer hiding place. There is a risk crossing the barmkin, but you have no choice. The boy will meet us at the gate with the horses.' He thrust a bonnet and a cloak at Munro. 'Here, put these on and keep your head down.' A grim smile. 'And if nothing else, your sojourn in the dungeon has made a right mess of your hose. Likely a blessing in this circumstance, for if we are seen there's little fear of you being mistaken for quality.'

William radiated impatience as Elizabeth re-entered the hall with the ale, belying the casual nature of his question. 'You did not wish to accompany Hugh to Glasgow?'

'There are the bairns to consider.'

'Ah, yes, the bairns … you have girls, I hear?' His gaze slid to her stomach. 'Still, there is no doubt time yet for a boy.'

She dug her nails into her palms, sought to hide her irritation. An irritation that turned to fear as the door bounced on its hinges, Ellie and the Montgomerie girls spilling in,

Ivar close behind, Isabella puffing up the stairs in their rear. They skidded to a halt at the sight of visitors.

William said, 'Five children? I thought you had but two.'

This was dangerous water, and no time to concoct a story. 'We do. Two are Hugh's sister's bairns, and one the daughter of a relative who bides here.'

'The wise woman, that treats the Queen?' Maxwell's tone was sharp.

Elizabeth, suddenly cold, thought – it is for this they have come. She shooed the children towards the door. 'Ishbel is baking, no doubt there'll be leavings for you.'

'No need to send them away on our account.' The words were fine, the expression in William's eyes offensive. He ignored Ivar, lingered on the girls. 'Pretty little things, which are yours?'

Kate and Mary gravitated to Elizabeth, cooried in. 'These two.'

'And names to match?'

'Catherine, and Mary,' then, too quickly, 'Family names.' She had no idea if he believed her.

'And this chit?' Maxwell was staring at Ellie, who glared back at him.

Elizabeth thought – he searches for a resemblance. If she puts him in mind of Kate… She disentangled herself from her own girls, rested her hands on Ellie's shoulders. 'This is Eleanor.'

'A relation on your side?'

'Far out.' She cast about in her head for a suitable location. 'Up Fife way.'

'By mother or father?'

She was the accused in a trial, they the prosecutors. To say 'mother' would require a surname, to say 'father' …

she dredged her memory, searching for a Grant connection among the Shaws, risked, 'Her father,' then to muddy the waters, 'though a generation or two back I believe it *was* through the female line.'

There was a curve to William's mouth, though the forward thrust of his chest and shoulders was far from benign. 'Been here long?'

'Some years now.' She puckered her forehead, as if attempting to count back, shook her head. 'No matter … widowhood is…' It was not an outright lie, though the intention was the same. 'Mistress Grant was, as oftimes happens, left without support.'

'She is not without support now. The Queen's patronage no doubt welcome. Hugh is a good friend to her in that respect.'

'We have but done what any family would do.'

'His tongue flicked across his lips, a snake preparing to strike. 'Not all families would feel such obligation. What relation did you say her husband was?'

'Oh, some kind of third cousin, I believe.'

Ellie, with the instinct of a young animal, wriggled free, and stationing herself at Maxwell's elbow, began, 'I don't like…'

'Shush, child, it isn't fitting to interrupt.' Elizabeth caught hold of her again, shot a glance at her own girls, prayed for their silence likewise.

William took a half-step forward, bringing him within arm's length. 'And does your *cousin* have this child only, or is there a clutch to be accommodated?'

The emphasis was clear, his disbelief equally so. It was as if she was being driven back towards the edge of a cliff, the smallest falsehood as likely to tip them all over into disaster as the truth. 'She has three bairns, though the eldest is away the now.'

Ellie thrust out her chest. 'Robbie is gone to find...'

Elizabeth finished her sentence, ignoring the telltale tapping of the child's foot, the snap in her eyes. '...To find adventure, as young lads aye do.'

'Indeed.' William's attention switched to Ellie. He reached out and touched her hair. 'Attractive colouring. Not a Shaw trait, I think.'

She shrugged. 'Perhaps there is the Irish in her.'

He continued to probe. 'Mistress Grant's other child, is it a lad or lass?'

'Another lass.'

'And *her* colouring?'

She thought – not a snake, a terrier, harrying a bone. An answer imperative. 'The other girl is auburn also.' Afraid of where his thoughts might be taking him, she sought to fill the silence, her desire for William and Maxwell to be gone warring with a need for them to remain until she was sure that Munro was safely away. 'A pity Hugh is not at home, but I will pass on your family's good wishes. It is a kindness in you both to call.'

Outside, a door banged, accompanied by a muffled oath. William swivelled towards the window, his eyes, as he glanced back at her, calculating. She heard rapid footsteps crossing the barmkin, the creak of leather, a snorting, then the clip-clop of hooves – dear God, could they not have managed more quietly?

Maxwell's face was pressed against the glass, craning to see the movement below. William regarded her thoughtfully, waved towards the window. 'The men who are leaving, you don't wish to give them farewell?'

'No need. It is but the steward and a companion with a message or two to fulfil.' And then, as if it had been her intention from the start, 'I expect Hugh's return at any time, perhaps early this afternoon ... you are more than welcome to stay for a bite, indeed you would doing me a kindness by saving me from my own company.'

The look in Maxwell's eyes belied the apparent courtesy. 'Another time perhaps, we have trespassed on your time long enough.' He set down his tankard, took William by the arm, headed for the door. 'But rest assured the visit has been *most* instructive.'

She moved as if to open it for them, and contriving to catch her foot on the threshold of the door, sprawled at their feet. Her grimace as she looked up to them for help, genuine, pain shooting through her ankle. She was aware of William's flash of irritation, quickly masked, of Maxwell's barely suppressed tension, thought – pray God it's not broken ... but if I can only delay them for long enough it will have been worth it, said, 'I'm sorry, that was careless of me, could you...?' She allowed William to help her to stand, and, leaning heavily on his arm, hopped towards the settle, unable to put her other foot down. 'If I could trouble you to call Ishbel...' He was on the stairwell, shouting down, Maxwell back at the window, radiating annoyance in the set of his shoulders and the repetitive slap, slap of his folded bonnet against his thigh. Elizabeth, biting her lip against the pain, counted down the seconds, prayed for Ishbel to be slow to respond to William's call – now would be a fine time to display her thrawn streak, ten minutes, even five, could make the difference. Then Ishbel was there, kneeling in front of her, gripping her ankle. A wave of pain, the room receding, the last thing Elizabeth was aware of, William looming over her, his voice fractured, his face dissolving.

Chapter 11

As they reached the foot of the slope below Braidstane, Angus pulled to a halt, Munro, every muscle tense, stopping beside him.

'You *do* have a plan?'

Angus nodded. 'There are caves by Auchenskeigh, on the Dusk Water.'

'How well known are they?'

'Well enough, but so cloaked in rumour and superstition folks are wary. They refer to them as "Elf-hame", and legends abound of little folk and hidden treasure and unexpected rockfalls to trap those foolish enough to seek it. Contraband more likely, or the spoils of thieving, and the rumours of danger useful to keep prying eyes away, but whatever, few will venture. And though the main chamber has space for a small army, there are plenty side passages to lose yourself in. I spent a fair few hours there as a lad when I didn't choose to be found, and in consequence I know every nook and cranny.' A glimmer of a smile. 'But in all my adventuring I had nary a whiff of anything more than animal bones and the remnants of small fires. You won't be the first, nor likely the last to shelter there.'

'How far is it?'

'Five or six miles as the crow flies.'

'Why do we stop then?'

'The caves are almost due west, but we cannot head straight for them, for we'd hit the Lugton Water where the ravine is too steep to navigate on horseback.' He was pondering aloud. 'And the best way, by Auchentiber, crosses open upland, with little cover to speak of. But if we go south, which would take us through more gentle and well-wooded country, it is a long road round.' He looked back to Braidstane rearing on the skyline, his forehead puckered. 'It's hard to know what's best.'

'The choice won't get any easier the longer we hesitate. I'm in your hands.'

They headed south, making an easy crossing of the Lugton at Wardlaw, then struck west, threading their way through the countryside, skirting the small hills littering the landscape. Among them cottages, nestling in hollows for protection from the wind, and perhaps other, more capricious, enemies. At one, a child, gaunt-eyed and stick-thin, perched on a crumbling wall enclosing a square of ground striped with the rotting stumps of last year's cabbages. She stared at them, silent, knuckle in mouth, as if committing them to memory, so that Munro, placing a finger against his lips, tossed her a bawbee. She failed to catch it, but looking back he saw her scramble down from her perch and scrabble on the ground. He hoped she would keep her side of the bargain. They were making good time, the going sufficiently soft to make for a comfortable ride, yet firm enough to avoid the fear of getting bogged down. Angus paused again at the edge of a ribbon of woodland, gestured towards a tall building off to the right.

'Blair Mill, aye busy, and with all the usual comings and goings. We should slow down. With luck, anyone who sees us will think us part of the normal traffic.'

And so it seemed at the first, a carter they passed on the track giving them good day without any sign of suspicion, so that both Angus and Munro relaxed a fraction. Too soon. They were barely past the mill when they heard the sound of hoofbeats, faint at first, and far away, but coming closer with every passing moment. Angus dug his heels into his horse's flank and it sprang away, Munro by his side. Neck and neck they rode until, skidding to a halt at the river's edge, Angus said, 'You away in, but once past the main chamber mind your head, it's gey low in places. There are clefts off to the left with room enough to hide. When it's safe I'll come back for you. In the meantime, if I take both horses, I can maybes draw them after me.'

Munro, his eyes becoming accustomed to the gloom, had reached the central chamber and was picking his way across it, avoiding the stalagmites sticking up from the cave floor, when he heard William and Maxwell's voices echoing behind him – Angus' ruse had failed then. He slid into a narrow passage, pressed himself against the wall, strained to listen. He tracked William and Maxwell's progress by their footfall, now closing in, now receding, as they checked out the side passages one by one, each time returning to the main chamber. Their movements were punctuated by periods of silence, in which he assumed they listened for him, each one a seeming eternity. He edged further up the passageway, moving when they did, freezing when they stopped, and, finding a smaller cleft off to the side, squeezed himself into it as far as he could go, praying it was far enough that any light they shone wouldn't reach him. The walls were crusted with salts and running with water, the moisture seeping through his hose, dripping onto his head.

Their voices were nearer now, William's obstinate. 'The carter was clear enough. Two riders, making this way, and on horses that had been driven hard. Forbye the child. To wriggle more than a worm on a pin surely signifies something. You may give up if you like, but I'm not leaving until I've checked thoroughly.'

He heard Maxwell begin, 'Aye well, there cannot be...' his words choked off by a low rumble, followed by William's 'What's that?'

The rumble became a rattle of loose stones, dust eddying along the cleft towards Munro.

William shouted, 'Let's get out of here. If it *was* Munro we chased, the rockfall will do for him, we need worry no longer. And if some other poor devil, I'm not for risking my neck by looking further.' The sound of their running footsteps was swallowed in the noise of falling rocks, the volume building until the air was full of it.

Then silence.

He edged out of the cleft into the narrow passageway, choking on the dust filling his mouth and throat and stinging his nostrils. Stumbling over loose stones underfoot, he pitched forward, and, stretching out his hand, met a wall of stone. He rocked back on his knees, fumbled for his tinderbox, struck a light. He was in a space some four foot square, the passageway in front of him solidly blocked. He began to haul away at the rubble, but the more he pulled away the more tumbled into its place, and behind the barrier the sound of further falling, the dust rising again in a choking cloud. He had no idea if Angus would be able to find him, nor how long the air would last. He thought of Kate and the bairns, tackled the stones again, the sounds echoing from beyond the rockfall louder than before. After two more attempts, in which the bare space around him shrank, he forced himself to stop. There was nothing to do but wait. And pray.

Part Three

July–September 1597.

Woe to them that call evil good.

King James Bible, Isaiah 5:20

Chapter 1

The cottage stood in a clearing beside a pool, sunlight filtering through the canopy of the sheltering trees. It had been six days since the rockfall in the caves at Auchenskeigh, three since Munro had been carried out, semi-conscious and delirious, suffering from dehydration, his skin, what could be seen of it, a uniform grey. They had brought him to Giffen, as safer than returning to Braidstane, and settled him in the empty cottage, well away from prying eyes, with Agnes to tend to him. Maggie and Ellie had also decamped, Maggie insisting their place was with their father, that their mother would expect it. Now he sat on a blanket, leaning against the cottage wall, absorbing the sunshine. Not altogether to rights yet, he was well on the way, and as Agnes repeatedly told him, with blessings to count.

He was drifting in and out of sleep, half-aware of Ellie's childish babble as she played by the edge of the pool, but was jerked awake by her sudden scream. He levered himself to his feet and handed his way along the cottage wall, cursing his lack of strength. Reaching the corner, he sagged against it. Saw Ellie hanging on Kate's arm, her small face alight. Relief washed over him, as refreshing as if he stood under the Spout Linn at Stewarton – William hadn't found her then. He half-stumbled, Kate catching him around the waist, supporting him.

His voice still croaky, he said, 'See, I kept my promise.'

'Almost. I had not thought to have to trek to Giffen to find my family.' Kate's eyes were dark with unshed tears. 'Angus said they nearly lost you.'

She guided him into the single room, settled him onto the chair by the window, knelt at his side.

'I won't deny at times I despaired of rescue, but,' he touched her hair, 'I'd rather not think on it now.'

She was laughing and crying all at once. 'I neither.'

'A pact then. For tonight at least.'

As if she'd only just noticed the lack, she asked, 'Where's Maggie?'

Agnes paused in the scrubbing of the table. 'Off to treat a bairn by Beith: measles, she thought.'

'Is she long away?'

'Since early morning.'

'Just the one call? Surely she should have returned by now?'

'She talked of herb-gathering, though I suspect it was more of a jaunt on the moor she was after: these past few days have fretted her sore.'

'As they did us all.' Munro pulled Kate close.

She leant into him in an unconscious return to the old ease, chided, 'A shave wouldn't go amiss.'

He rubbed his chin. 'Had I known I was to have my wife back today, I would have, of course.'

She answered the question that hovered, unspoken, between them. 'There was little I could do for the Queen...'

He stiffened, relaxed again at her reassurance. 'Oh, not in that way. Only that she must needs be pregnant before any treatments I offer could have effect. I am to be called as soon as the need arises … I liked her.'

'More to the point, did she take to you?'

'I think so, yes. She was at any rate open with me, which I think a good sign.'

'And the King?'

'I didn't have that pleasure. And perhaps just as well, for Alexander heard a rumour Glencairn had been summoned, so thought it politic to leave as soon as my business with the Queen was done. And here I am.'

'And am I made penniless by the visit?' It was safe ground.

'I had no time to dally in the cloth market, so nothing was spent, not so much as a groat.'

'One blessing then.' Munro stood up, supporting himself against the hearth, and held Kate at arm's length, his gaze mock-critical. 'The addition of a ribbon or two or other such frippery might have been an improvement, I admit … but you do for me.' And as she smiled up at him, thought – whatever the risks, it is good to be here.

Maggie appeared. 'Mother! You're back.'

'So it seems. And your patient?'

'Measles. I left a salve of chamomile to help with the itch.'

'You've been away a while. Agnes almost thought to send out a search party.'

'I waited until I saw the bairn's temperature falling, and the mother reassured, before I left, and then I took my picnic up onto the moor. It was such a fine day and Blackie needed the exercise.'

Kate smiled back at her. 'It's all right, you don't have to justify wanting to spend time outdoors on a day like this. At your age I was aye glad of the chance to break free from home from time to time, and I know fine the value of a good gallop to blow away the cobwebs.'

It was a childish question that came without warning as they sat crushed around the table at supper.

Ellie, finished first, said, 'What's Broomelaw?'

Kate, with a quick glance towards Munro, said, 'It was a house … we lived there once … you were very little.'

'Why was Robbie there?'

'He just wanted to see it.'

'When was that?' Munro dropped his knife with a clatter.

'Some months before he went chasing you in France.' It came out as an accusation, Kate placing her hand on top of his as if in apology.

'Did he say how he found it?'

'In a sad state, the walls broken down, the windows gone.' Kate hesitated. 'I think there's been much thieving.'

Maggie said, 'Not any more.'

Munro felt pressure building in his chest. 'Maggie?'

'I went there too, a while ago, before you came, when Mother and Uncle John were called to Ardrossan and bided away. I needed to properly remember who I was, who I am.' She slowed. 'After what Robbie said, I expected to see it a ruin and instead…'

'What?' His voice was quiet, as if he spoke to a horse he feared to startle.

'There were stonemasons and carpenters working there, and materials everywhere, the air full of dust and the smell of fresh-cut wood. They were kind, at least until...' She broke off.

'Until?'

'Another man came. He sent me away.'

'What man?'

Maggie bit at her lip. 'He didn't say, but the workmen said it was a Cunninghame tower, and it was for them they laboured... They seemed ... almost feart of him ... I was glad to leave.'

Kate breathed out. 'William?'

Munro shook his head. 'We don't know that.' There are many answer to the Cunninghame name and Glencairn generous when he's a mind.'

Colour was creeping up Maggie's neck, reached her jawline. 'He said his father didn't pay the men to slack.'

Munro sought to keep his voice even. 'Did he say anything else?'

Maggie's cheeks crimsoned and she looked down at the floor.

'He asked what I was doing there, where I bided.'

'And you said?'

'I chose a place along the route, near to Renfrew. He seemed to accept it.'

Munro, noting that Maggie still looked uncomfortable, asked, 'Is there anything you aren't telling us?'

It came out as a whisper. 'He thought I reminded him of someone.' A pause, drawn out. 'I'm sorry. I thought if I saw for myself it would be easier.'

Kate was sitting up in the box bed when Munro returned from the privy. Through the open doorway the last remnants of the fire flickered, faded to a red glow. She came straight to the point. 'It must be William, else...'

He tried to deflect her, his intention to protect. 'As I said to Maggie, the renovation will likely be for some minor connection.'

'To reassure a child is one thing. I am *not* a child.'

'I don't imagine Broomelaw is grand enough for William.'

'Grand or no, spite might lend it attraction.'

He sat down on the edge of the bed, rested his hands on her shoulders, hoped he made a sort of sense, to Kate if not to himself. 'Spite is only attractive if those you seek to hurt are aware of it. William thought us dead, what advantage would it have been to spite us now?' The implication in what he said washed over him, ice cold – the realisation there was but one explanation for William's visit to Braidstane.

'What is it you're not telling me?'

'Kate...' He tried to pull her close, but she resisted. 'Whatever it is...' Her eyes were dark, her pupils enlarged. 'You told me once that if there was not honesty between us, we had nothing...' He had the sense that she battled with herself as much as him. 'I need to know.'

His sigh was deep and heartfelt. 'When William came to Braidstane he quizzed Elizabeth about you and the children. About Ellie's colouring, her hair, as if *she* reminded him of someone. If it was Maggie he thought of...'

Under his fingers he felt her quiver, like a trapped bird, then still, the fight gone out of her.

He sought for words to provide some comfort, but found

none, her expression moving through sadness to resignation.

'You *do* believe it was William at Broomelaw.'

There was little point in denial. He nodded. 'I thought Elizabeth held something back, but didn't feel it right to press, for it could have been some personal slight she suffered, but...'

'But now you think he boasted of repairs to our house?'

He nodded. 'It's the only thing that makes sense: of her reluctance to tell me, of what Maggie saw.' A new thought, sharp as a cattle goad, a need to know if Kate shared it. 'For you, does this make it worse?'

She met his eyes squarely. 'I cannot deny I feel it.' A pause in which the past hung between them, a long shadow impossible to dispel, then, her voice gaining in firmness, 'Your mother once said it was a foolish thing to fret over what cannot be mended.' Another pause, a paradigm shift. 'We are alive, that is what matters ... nor do we need a grave to mourn our dead.'

He wrapped his arms around her, rested his face on her hair. 'We are not the only folk to lose a child. When I think of Anna she is always in the light, other bairns surrounding her...'

She reached up to touch his cheek, her voice catching. 'Doing her bidding.'

291

Chapter 2

Dinner past, William was lolling in the hall at Kilmaurs, a glow about him that was neither the result of strong drink, nor the effect of the sunlight spilling through the long windows, bathing him in light. 'Well, Uncle? The job is well done, is it not?'

'Indeed.' John Cunninghame chose his words with care. 'I cannot fault the workmanship, nor the time taken.'

'Credit where credit is due. It is mostly William's doing.' Glencairn stretched backwards in his chair, which creaked under the strain. 'I must admit I wondered if he could sustain his interest, and have been pleasantly surprised.' He nodded at William. 'It is a fitting end to the project that you will make it your own.'

'How much longer before you move in?' John sought to cover his distaste.

'Perhaps the end of next week, once the cleaning is sorted and the furnishings carted across. I had thought when the hay is in would be most convenient all round. When there are men to spare.'

Thought for anyone's convenience other than his own

was so uncharacteristic of William it took John by surprise.

'But first,' Glencairn nodded to John, 'I am bid return to court and thought to take William with me before he becomes busy with the sorting of his own place. You will accompany us?'

'I scarcely think James would notice my presence. I am too small a fish.'

'It cannot hurt the Cunninghame cause to make an appearance at court in numbers. There are others aye supported.'

'There are others that cannot stand, unless by numbers.' There was a contemptuous edge to William's comment, a combative spark in his eye.

John dusted crumbs from his doublet. 'Is this a new antagonism or the tail end of an old one?'

'The business of precedence that I thought well sorted, and in our favour, has become an issue once again. And the Montgomeries are never far from the King. If it is not Eglintoun it is Braidstane, and behind both, Alexander. And now a wise woman Braidstane introduced has the ear of the Queen. If we are not careful our position may be damaged beyond repair. So if you don't have any more pressing engagements...'

John shook his head. 'Nothing that can't wait.'

'That's settled then.' Glencairn rubbed at the base of his back. 'I wish to leave early, the distance grows no less the older I get.'

William said, 'It may be more than precedence that is threatened.'

Glencairn paused, half out of his chair. 'If you have heard aught to our ill...'

'Not directly. But this wise woman come from

293

Braidstane … rumour has it she may be a Munro connection.'

In the window reveal, John saw Lady Glencairn stiffen.

Glencairn was dismissive. 'There are no Munros left. Thank God. Else all our money and effort on Broomelaw would be wasted.'

William shrugged. 'Likely not, but as well to check. This jaunt to Edinburgh will provide the opportunity to settle the matter.'

The chill in John's stomach spread to his chest. 'Is there any reason to suspect the woman is at court the now?'

'Rumour has it the Queen carries another bairn, so it isn't beyond possibility. Like many of her ilk, her primary skills lie in that direction, or so it seems. And if she is, I shall find her out.'

John concealed his sharp intake of breath with a yawn. 'If we are to leave early, I should retire also.' Thought – if it is Kate … if she and William were to meet…

Chapter 3

Kate was indeed in Edinburgh. It had been a matter of much debate, argued out in the clearing in front of the cottage, lacking sufficient space indoors. Munro, despite that he hadn't regained full strength, wanted to leave immediately for France, citing the danger that William might return at any time, and all of them, including the Montgomeries, be put at risk. It was an argument hard to gainsay, yet Kate, though she saw the reason in it, was torn between a desire to run for safety and her promise to the Queen.

'I gave my word. To go back on it, it is not Christian.'

It was a scruple no one else shared. Alexander, though clearly sympathetic, was blunt. 'You have a family of your own to consider, their well-being dependent on yours. Much as I wouldn't relish explaining your absence to the Queen, you should go. She will not blame you when the circumstances are known.'

'You cannot traduce the Cunninghames when they have as yet done nothing to be pointed at. That would surely endear you to the King.'

'I have not been a courtier all these years without

learning when, and more importantly what, to speak. That part you may safely leave to me. And you have not left the Queen helpless, your remedies already prescribed.'

Hugh was more forthright. 'William Cunninghame has you in his sights, and with every day that passes, the danger increases. I will send to John Shaw.'

It seemed it was the end of the argument, but when word came back from Greenock that John was abroad and not expected home for upwards of a week or more, the debate began again. Munro was for taking their chances with the first vessel they could find, but this time Kate found herself on the same side as the Montgomeries.

'If we must go, it would be best to take passage with someone we can trust. And it will give you time to fully recover. We are safe enough here, for a while longer.'

Elizabeth backed her up. 'Do you think William would allow a few miles of water to stop him from following you, if the trail was clear? Money talks, and William, it seems, has money.'

Hugh agreed. 'Sailors are aye short, and a little extra for a word in the right quarter, easy money. It would be folly to do other than wait for John Shaw.'

'I don't like it.'

'This isn't about like, Munro, but rather expediency. The risks of waiting outweighed by the risk of disclosure.'

Kate placed her hand on Munro's arm, played her trump card. 'If we are followed to France, we have nowhere else to run. A week or ten days, it is not so long to wait, and if we take care...'

She sensed his capitulation through the vehemence of his 'Oh, we'll take care: we will none of us step a foot out of sight of the cottage, however irksome those restrictions may be.'

'There is no reason for William to come here. Whatever suspicions he harboured that Munro lived, the rockfall will have convinced him otherwise.' Hugh's smile was apologetic. 'It is Kate we must protect now. And if we are to preserve the fiction of her place in our family, I think she and the girls must return to Braidstane.'

Alexander nodded his agreement. 'And I shall remain until I see you all safely away.'

And so it might have been, but that a message came from court. The Queen had missed her courses and requested Mistress Grant's presence.

Munro was brusque. 'Send word with Alexander that you cannot come.'

Kate shook her head. 'I can be there and back in three days and my duty done. Had we been already away it would have been one thing, but we are here and like to be for five or six days yet. It is the least I can do, to keep my promise.'

'And if William is at court?'

Alexander was reassuring. 'I have enquired of the messenger.' Then, 'Subtley, I promise you. The court is quiet the now, and no sign of the Cunninghames, father or son. Word is William divides his time between home and this new tower of his,' he broke off...

Munro was brusque. 'We know about Broomelaw.'

Alexander continued, 'Either way, the danger may be greater here. To attend the Queen is as good a way as any to fill the time, and who knows what good may come of it.'

Inwardly Kate shared Munro's concern, outwardly she

prepared to go, as if it was a commonplace journey and not one fraught with hazards she didn't care to contemplate. At the last she took his hands in hers. 'Three days, no more, and by then John Shaw should be returned and we can all leave.'

It was a promise she was unable to keep, for on the third morning she was summoned to the King. At the threshold of the presence chamber, Hugh paused, his hand on Kate's arm, a pucker of worry on his forehead.

'Your ministrations *will* help the Queen? James hasn't summoned you to pass the time of day and will expect an answer in the affirmative. I would hate to be the means of bringing you to his attention should things go awry.'

'I have promised to try. More than that I cannot say, but the Queen welcomes my honesty.'

'We may trust James is equally accommodating.'

They wove their way through the clusters of courtiers. Ahead of her Kate saw Hugh stiffen. She followed his gaze towards the group in close conversation with James. The man standing with his back to her, though she couldn't immediately place him, had a familiarity in the way he held his head. As he half-turned she felt her legs give way beneath her – John Cunninghame. For a fraction of a second she caught his eye, saw an answering flash of recognition. Hugh grasped her arm, holding her up, and she willed herself to walk steadily beside him as they threaded their way across the room. She was aware of a stirring further down the hall, a muffled exclamation, cut off, felt a second frisson of fear, Glencairn, and William – dear God, let them not recognise me.

'Ah, Braidstane!' James extended his hand.

She swept a low curtsey, kept her head bowed as Hugh made the introduction.

'Mistress Grant, Sire.'

It was impossible not to look up as the King queried, 'You have seen the Queen?'

'Yes, Sire. We spoke at length.'

There was a spark in his eyes she couldn't define: concern, certainly; a hint of exasperation, perhaps. 'Speech is cheap. I trust you have something more tangible to offer?'

'I have sent for new remedies which may help and will leave instructions for their preparation...'

'*May* help?'

She swallowed, offered, 'I have found them generally to be effective, and so I told the Queen, but I will not make false promises.'

He dipped his head towards hers, spoke for her benefit alone. 'You will find us grateful for your attendance, and you need not fear to do whatever you can.' There was an extra dryness as he raised his voice, casting a glance at several men clustered by the window clad in the distinctive dark-cloaked garb of the physician. 'And if you fail, you will be but the last in a long line of failures. None of whom have paid with their head.'

She was unsure if it was a wry pleasantry, if he expected an acknowledgement, but knowing that the laughter threatening inside her owed more to hysteria than anything else, confined herself to a simple, 'Thank you, Sire.'

Her relief, as it appeared she was about to be dismissed, changed to apprehension as he said, 'Montgomerie made some mention of you leaving Edinburgh. Not soon, I take it?'

It was not a question. Kate dipped her head again. 'Sire.' She thought of Munro, of the girls, of William and Glencairn, fought to keep her face impassive.

'When the Queen is confident, when her ladies are fully conversant in the handling of your medicines, when the point of danger is past, then you may go.' He nodded in dismissal, turned to Hugh. 'Is there any fresh news from London? Gossip that can be substantiated? Despite Cecil's promises, I am starved of information. Times I do not know if I can trust the man. Can your brother do better?'

Kate, feeling the change in atmosphere as if a draught from an ill-fitting window, recognised the caution in Hugh's response.

'I expect word daily.'

'I hope he will not disappoint.'

Out of the corner of her eye Kate saw William heading in their direction. She pressed Hugh's arm, saw him glance over the crowd, recognise the danger. He bowed to the King, said, 'I'm sure not, Sire,' before beginning to back away. Kate kept her head down, matched her pace to his, their retreat from James steady and slow.

Outside the chamber she leant against the passage wall, waiting for her breathing to return to normal, for the thudding of her heart against her ribs to stop.

Hugh gave her a minute only. 'It is as well we do not linger. Glencairn may not have paid you much attention thus far, but it would be a needless folly to give him further opportunity to notice you. And as for William ... if we had known he was expected...'

'We would not have brought her.' Alexander had followed them out of the chamber. 'My apologies, Kate, I feel responsible.'

'It isn't your blame. I pressed to come … Will the Cunninghames stay long?'

'As long as Glencairn feels it useful. And that we cannot guess at. As for William, his presence here now, with a new home to his credit, is surprising to say the least.'

Kate's fear crystallised. 'And if it is because he suspects me?'

'We must take good care your paths don't cross.'

'Is that possible?'

'I think yes.' Alexander was hurrying them across the courtyard, towards the gate leading to the foot of the Cowgate. 'They are not of the Queen's circle, and there is little reason for the King to grant you a further audience.'

Hugh backed him up. 'Nor do the Cunninghames seek our company. The truce we signed in '86 is unpalatable to both sides, but thus far it has held, largely because we strive *not* to meet. James has marked you as important, so even if William has some interest in you, I do not think Glencairn would allow the risk.'

Kate was still worrying away at this new danger as they emerged from the palace. 'I have contracted to return to the apothecary tomorrow, and if he does indeed provide what is promised, it will be a matter of explaining their use to the Queen, and perhaps then she'll be happy for me to leave.'

Hugh shook his head. 'Not when James has expressed his wish for you to stay. How long until the pregnancy is safe?'

'It will be months yet, I cannot wait…'

'You may have to. In the meantime I'll send word to Braidstane and will remain with you as long as need be.'

301

'And if Hugh has a call to answer, rest assured I will be your escort. And irksome though it may be, I suggest you remain indoors, aside from your visits to the Queen.'

Kate's stomach was churning, her breathing fast – *I should not have come.*

They had almost reached their lodging. Behind them running footsteps, the clatter of a collapsing stall, the vendor's voice raised in anger, a tethered cow bellowing. And above it all the clash of steel on steel. She flinched, instinctively pressing herself against Alexander. He glanced backwards, thrust her under the overhang, relief clear in his voice.

'Buccleugh, wouldn't you know? And Ker and a few henchmen apiece. The word about court was that they had taken lodgings within yards of each other, which shows a singular lack of sense on both sides.'

'Why must men aye look to stir up old wrongs. Have we learnt nothing in the last hundred years?'

'Some of us, perhaps.' Alexander was sanguine. 'James may have done something of a job on Ayrshire, but Borderers are a law unto themselves. What it will take to subdue them, Kate, is anyone's guess.'

'Another war, or threat of one.' Hugh sounded so relaxed about the prospect she was hard put not to scream.

Instead she said, her sarcasm heavy, 'This is how they keep to the rule of law?'

'Might is the only law in the Debatable Lands. And has ever been so.'

The fight faded up the Cowgate, the sound dwindling. Alexander drew her back onto the thoroughfare, and as if he thought her owed an explanation, said, 'It is not that we take these things lightly, but what we cannot control

302

isn't worth fretting over. I had rather spend my efforts in ensuring Eglintoun and Hugh do nothing to rock our own present peace. And that, I may tell you, is job enough for me.'

The same thought was in Kate's mind from the moment she woke, along with the knottier question of how much, if any, of her reservations regarding the quality of the remedies she had procured from the apothecary to communicate to the Queen. Her second visit to his shop accomplished without fuss, she nevertheless suspected, from the ease with which some of the herbs crumbled between her fingers, that they might be rather older than last season's preparation, their potency diminished. Say nothing, and any blame for their lack of efficacy would be hers. Say something and the King would likely require her to remain to search out fresh supplies. A prospect she didn't relish, the risk she might come face to face with Glencairn or William an ever-increasing danger.

Time hung heavy on her, for though she attended the Queen daily, it was often for no more than a few minutes at a time. In a happier circumstance she would have spent her free time browsing the stalls of the Lawnmarket, but fear of encountering the Cunninghames far outweighed the boredom, so while Hugh and Alexander attended on the King, the most she risked was a seat by the window in their lodgings. Several times Alexander accompanied her to Leith to visit Grizel, but as the days wore on, the thought that she was living on borrowed time, that she couldn't hope to avoid the Cunninghames forever, increased her fear, so that those visits also dwindled. It was impossible to entirely relax, and as she perched on a stool in a patch of sun-warmed floor listening to the hustle and bustle below, she wondered how Maggie and Ellie might be faring, how they were coping with their own enforced confinement. The realisation that, but for her stubbornness, they could all, should all, have by now been safely en route to France, something she preferred not to dwell on.

She opened the window a fraction, resting her elbows on the cill, the calling of the stallholders, as they sought to entice customers, mingling with the background low-ing of cattle, the bleating of sheep, the squawking of hens. Her smile turned to a grimace at a drawn-out high-pitched squeal. Used to the slaughter of animals for home consumption, she was no stranger to the sound of animal death, her only discomfort if the kill was not cleanly made. As seemed likely in this case. The work of an apprentice perhaps, with a deal still to learn.

There was a commotion below her, a string of oaths cut off by a pistol shot, and in the momentary silence the skittering of horseshoe on cobble, followed by a thump and a loud hammering at her door. The maid's grumble as she pulled back the bolt become a cry of outrage, as it was suddenly stifled. Kate grabbed her bonnet, stuffed it onto her head and thanked God her hair was already scraped back. Not before time.

The chamber door bounced against the wall, the hinges groaning in protest.

'Mistress *Grant*.' William Cunninghame filled the en-trance, his gaze on Kate, calculating, and behind him an-other man, tall and angular with a long face, made longer by his beard. He had a certain familiarity, but the name, if indeed she'd ever known it, eluded her.

She rubbed her hands on the apron tied about her waist, dipped a curtsey, inserted a question into her voice. 'You have the advantage of me, sirs.'

William ignored her query, omitted the courtesies, continued on his own track. 'A Montgomerie cousin, eh? From far afield?'

Dangerous to say no. Perhaps equally so to say yes. She prevaricated. 'A fair way, and not strictly a cousin, rather by marriage only.' She cast about in her mind for a family name near enough to convince but far enough to take them outside William's ken. Thought – we should have prepared for this.

'The Grants of Clayhouse?'

She took a risk. 'No, indeed,' then hesitated, as if deliberately, contriving to look embarrassed. 'The Montgomeries, though they have been good to me, don't go out of their way to share my origins,' again the slight hesitation, 'seeing as I hail from across the border, Berwick direction … as my late husband did also.' She saw his eyes narrow, as if he found something out of kilter.

His companion said, 'A foot in both camps. I should have thought that might suit Braidstane very well…'

His voice was also familiar, tugging at her memory, William's lack of response to his comment clear evidence that the insult offered to Hugh wasn't the only thought her answer had triggered. She forced herself to meet their eyes, kept her voice even.

'Was it Braidstane you came to find? I don't expect him much before suppertime.'

'On the contrary. It was you I wanted to quiz.' A belated, perfunctory bow. 'William Cunninghame, Master of Glencairn. Cousin to Patrick Maxwell … with whom I believe you have acquaintance.'

His words ran through her, ice cold. 'I treated his wife, yes.'

'Successfully?'

She bit her lip. To say yes would be to imply Margaret Maxwell should have no further need of her, to say no, that her ministrations were worthless. 'She is on the mend, supposing she is allowed to fully recuperate.' It was a commentary on her marriage that William, to judge by his reaction, understood very well.

'Not how Maxwell tells it, but I haven't come to argue the merits or otherwise of your dealings with Mistress Maxwell, but rather to tease out our own acquaintance. You looked gey familiar when Braidstane presented you to the King, and rather better dressed than the average wise woman. I feel sure we must have met before.'

He came close, as if to look over her shoulder into the street below, clearly not his main intention. His breath was warm on her neck.

'You must be mistaken, sir. Since I came to Ayrshire I have not been out of the county,' – that at least was true. 'Forbye this attendance on the Queen. And as for the clothes: they are but borrowed finery. As befits a visit to court. I am not myself in them.'

His gaze flicked over her. 'You do yourself down, they suit you well. What think you, Hamilton?'

She dipped her head, remembering him now, the man who had disparaged Hugh at Jean Shaw's funeral, to whom Elizabeth said Hugh harboured a long-standing antipathy.

William continued, a studied insolence in his tone. 'Perhaps it is the common clothes you should discard. And why not.' A pause, as if to allow the innuendo, then, 'With the ear of the Queen you surely have a right.'

She edged sideways, trying to secure a pathway to the door should she need to call a servant. 'Right? I think not. Nor inclination either. I have a station in life and no desire to rise above it.'

He sprung the trap. 'But not the voice to match. Where, I wonder, did that come from? Not the gutter, that's for sure.' The warning. 'I have a good ear for voices.'

An emptiness swelled inside her and she found herself praying for Hugh or Alexander to come ... praying for Hugh *not* to come.

Another rap at the door, this time polite.

William turned his head, momentarily distracted, and she ducked past him, giddy with relief. 'It is the Queen's man, come to escort me to Holyrood. I must not dally.'

'Another time then.' His bow was exaggerated. 'Come, Hamilton. We look forward to it ... Mistress *Grant.*'

Chapter 4

Kate was barely five minutes returned from Holyrood when there was another knock at the door. Although scarcely any distance, it had been an uneasy walk to and from the palace with only the lad the Queen had sent for protection. She gripped the edge of the table, straining to make out the muffled conversation between the servant girl and the latest visitor – Grizel perhaps? The footsteps on the stair were light, but rapid – not Grizel then.

Margaret Maxwell hesitated in the doorway.

Kate moved to greet her, at once pleased to see her gaunt look diminished, yet wishing her anywhere but here. She was aware of her tension, as of a tightly wound spring. 'Mistress Maxwell. I had no idea you were in Edinburgh. I didn't see you in the palace with your husband.'

Margaret's voice was breathless, her words disjointed. 'He has no idea I am here … I have no right … but when I heard of your service to the Queen … I hoped…'

'Won't you sit down?' Kate focused on the courtesies as much to calm herself as Margaret. 'I will call for some wine.' She found herself saying, 'Whatever the favour you have to ask of me, if I can I will do it.'

Margaret subsided onto the settle, clasped her hands to-gether, took a deep breath. 'I am here to ask of the King…' She stopped, started again, her voice cracking, '…that he order that Maxwell cannot approach me against my will.'

It was shocking in it's audacity. Kate waited, instinc-tively knowing there was more to come, afraid of what it might be. It was not what Kate had expected.

Margaret pulled at a loose embroidery thread on her sleeve. 'I am not here alone. Maxwell's mother accompa-nies me … supports me in this. Indeed it is at her sugges-tion I have come.'

Kate's hand went to her throat, forced herself not to react as Margaret continued, 'Mistress Maxwell has asked for an audience with the Queen, thinking that if we can make the appeal through her good graces, there might be some hope. We thought…'

'Yes?'

It came out in a rush. 'We wondered if you would speak to the Queen on my behalf?'

'To tell her of what you have suffered?'

Margaret nodded. 'So that it isn't only my word against his.'

'And if you fail?'

'What do I have to lose?'

'Your children? If he was to make the case that you are mad…'

'You do not think it?'

'No! Of course not. But others might.'

'With his mother speaking for me, with you also, that case surely could not stand.'

'If you are not mad, then you are wilfully withholding

his rightful dues. Do you expect the King to countenance that?'

'I hope, with the Queen's encouragement, he will not countenance the cruelty I suffer, and I am willing to bare myself to him that he might see for himself. I have nowhere else to go, nothing else to try,' her shoulders slumped, 'but I will understand if you wish no part of it.'

Conflicting thoughts chased each other through Kate's mind – I cannot risk it … to put my children in danger … how can she ask it … yet if it were me … if Munro was as Maxwell is…

Margaret rose. 'I'm sorry, I shouldn't have come.'

'No. Wait.' Kate rose also. 'I will speak to the Queen.'

Hugh spun round. 'You promised what? Are you out of your mind?'

'She suffers, Hugh, more than you can conceive.'

'Many women suffer, they do not all appeal to the King to help them defraud their husbands. Nor drag in others to support them. You were at risk already in being here, this can only compound it. All this time you have hidden indoors to avoid risk, and you will throw it away now?' He was marching up and down the chamber, the floor reverberating under his feet. A momentary pause, a regathering of breath, another explosion. 'God in Heaven, Kate, I knew you to be generous, I did not think you a fool. Have you no thought to your children, to Munro … And what of Elizabeth … my girls. The kindness we have done to you?'

'Hugh…' Alexander put out a hand, but Hugh flung him off.

Kate said, 'I have thought of little else since she made the request. But Elizabeth would have done the same. And so would you if you were faced with her pain. It is to the Queen we go, and she has shown herself sympathetic to me...'

'And when you have to face Maxwell, give evidence against him before the King. Have you thought on that?'

'Knowing what I know, if I do not face Maxwell, I will not be able to face myself.'

Alexander stepped forward again, this time succeeding in halting Hugh's marching. 'The promise is made and cannot be unmade, however lacking in sense it was.' And to Kate, 'When do you see the Queen?'

'In the forenoon. Maxwell's mother is to send word of when I should present myself.'

'Well then, we may pray no ill comes of it.'

Hugh balled his fists. 'We may prepare for a fight.'

They were ranged on either side of the Queen's bed-chamber, the door firmly shut against all gawkers. Maxwell, his face like thunder, and with him William Cunninghame; opposite them, Margaret, and Maxwell's mother, behind them, Kate. Hugh stood by the window, Alexander close by to keep him in check. The Queen was seated, James standing at her shoulder, his expression unreadable.

The King indicated to Margaret to step forward. 'It is by request of our Queen that we will hear you, but know you the decision is mine and mine alone.'

It was a veiled warning, a reminder not to overstep the mark. Maxwell smirked.

Margaret swept a deep curtsey, her voice very quiet. 'I am conscious, Sire, of the honour you do me in listening...'

'Speak up, madame. If your case is good you have no need to whisper it.'

The Queen began, 'If I may...'

'You may not.' James' feeling on the matter was beginning to show. 'You have done your bit. If Mistress Maxwell has a case she must present it herself.'

Margaret straightened, looked directly at Maxwell, as if to strengthen her resolve. 'I have come, seeking your good grace, recognising your wisdom, counting on your impartiality...'

'Yes, yes.' James remained brusque, but Kate saw the flattery was having an effect.

'I have come to show the cruelty I suffer.' Margaret unhooked her collar and began on her buttons.

Maxwell tried to intervene. 'Is my wife to disrobe in public like a common whore?'

'This is not public, and I am no whore. Only a wife who is much abused, who seeks the King's judgement.' She slid her sleeve off her shoulder. Kate, knowing what was to come, was prepared for the mottled bruises flowering across her neck and down towards her breasts. Others were not. The Queen, although she too had already had sight of them, drew back a fraction, the King turning his head away with a moue of distaste. She wastes her time, Kate thought, he will not look on anything unpleasant. Margaret was unlacing her chemise as if in a trance, as if, having begun, she was determined to carry it through. Maxwell made another effort to protest, but to Kate's surprise James halted him with a glare, indicated for Margaret to continue. She turned, exposing the raised weals that criss-crossed her back from shoulder to waist. Kate was aware of Alexander's gasp, of Hugh's distaste. And of James staring fixedly, as if fascinated by the still-raw skin, something in his face allowing her to hope – perhaps there is a chance.

The Queen stood up, placing a shawl about Margaret's shoulders, and with a look at James said, 'That I think will do.' She deferred to him. 'The King will no doubt wish to hear your other witnesses.'

James nodded at Kate. 'Mistress Grant?'

She took a deep breath, sucked in courage. 'I was called to attend Mistress Maxwell in the weeks following the birth of her latest child. I found her much distressed,' she paused, considered how best to phrase it, 'and covered with bruises even in the most delicate of areas, so much so I feared for her...' about to say sanity, she changed her mind, '...recovery. I prescribed for the bruising, counselled restraint, a recommendation that as you have seen was clearly ignored.' She knew instantly it was the wrong thing to say, remembering too late her suggestion to the Queen. As James' face clouded, Maxwell's mother stepped forward.

'He is my son, and it pains me much to say it, but I do not think Margaret safe in his house. If it please you, Sire, I would offer sanctuary to her and my grandchildren...'

Maxwell burst out. 'This is intolerable. Is a husband to be refused his rights? I did only what any man would do when faced with a wife who knew not her duty.'

'Duty?' Kate's voice rose, all her intentions of a reasoned argument, of restraint, washed away by the remembrance of Margaret Maxwell as she first saw her, battered, defeated, and wishing only to die. 'A wife should expect respect and consideration from her husband. Not be mauled and beaten, be treated like a chattel with no rights...'

313

William was gazing at Kate, his hand gripping his chin, his forefinger tap-tapping against his lips.

'Enough!' James cut her short. 'I have heard and seen all that is necessary. And will give my judgement in due course.'

Chapter 5

'William knows.' Kate was slumped over the table, her head in her hands. 'If it had not been for the presence of the Queen...'

'If he was sure,' Alexander spoke firmly, 'Queen or not, he would have denounced you.'

'Suspects then. It was clear in the way he looked at me. Just as when he came here. As if he played with me, like a cat with a mouse, enjoying to torture before moving in for the kill.'

'We must give him no chance to move in then. When you attend the Queen, I will accompany you. For the rest, as long as you remain here, either Hugh or I will endeavour to be with you at all times.'

The afternoon heat was oppressive as Alexander and Kate approached the entrance to the palace. Kate's face was flushed, a trickle of sweat running between her breasts. Her feet were swollen in her shoes, her hair, rolled into a coil, a dead weight on the back of her neck, her bonnet jammed on so tight it made her head ache. She longed for Ayrshire, for the cool wind that came in off the sea, for the shade of the woods.

Patrick Maxwell halted them at the gateway, his bow to Alexander the minimum courtesy demanded, his focus all on Kate. He remained mounted as if he enjoyed to look down on them.

'Mistress *Grant*. I believe I may have misjudged you. I took you for a peasant woman of little knowledge and less breeding. It seems I may have been wrong … on both counts.'

Kate had a moment to be grateful for Munro's absence.

'No doubt you will wish to know James has ruled. My wife is to return home with me and resume her rightful place. He wasn't taken by that display of yours. Indeed it may have gone against her.' He gathered the reins, as if to turn away, then, relish in his voice, 'To show your true colours in that fashion and before the King, it was a foolishness that may go against *you* also.' The emphasis was clear, his smile a travesty. 'But you have one success to your credit: you have caught the attention of the Master of Glencairn. He hopes to take your acquaintance further. If not here, then in Ayrshire. Kilmaurs is no great distance from Braidstane, no doubt he can renew the courtesies at his leisure.'

Alexander cast a glance towards the palace. 'If you'll excuse us, we are expected within and shouldn't delay.'

Maxwell bowed, pulled his horse to the side to allow them passage. 'Indeed. Though the Queen may not have much further need of your services.'

Kate's hand strayed to her stomach, ashamed of the

ungenerous thought – if she has lost the child, we are free to go, said, 'The Queen remains well?'

'Very well. And the bairn she carries. But I suspicion James thinks your influence less than benign.'

As a parting shot it was effective.

Kate repeated her fears as they reached the palace door. 'He and William must have talked. What do you suppose they'll do?'

'Nothing here. Whatever he says, or tried to imply, you still have the ear of the Queen. To risk her displeasure would be a step too far, certainly for Glencairn. But at Braidstane, that is another matter altogether.'

'And the King? Maxwell's threat…'

'Was likely bluster. James wants another healthy child; if you can be the means of bringing that about, he won't risk your dismissal to please Patrick Maxwell.'

Chapter 6

While Kate and Alexander were closeted with the Queen, Hugh was in the presence chamber. Wishing himself anywhere but there, stuffed as it was to the gills with folk who hoped to attract the King's favour, he was considering for the hundredth time whether the price of patronage was not too great. His life was now a far cry from the freedoms of his soldiering days, and though in the eleven years since first coming to court, practice in the art of donning and doffing a mask of interest in the affairs of state meant he could make a passable stab at it when the need arose, it wouldn't have been his first choice to spend his days sweltering here. Only that, as Alexander kept reminding him, there were prizes to be won when the English Queen died, and it was as well to keep ahead of the game. Not that he was altogether sure he fancied moving to England as brother George had done, though undoubtedly that was where the richest pickings were to be made. For if the Scottish court was tiresome, the English one would be more so, with a wider cast of sycophants all vying for the King's favour. Ireland now, that was a more pleasant prospect, and one that would suit his talents rather better than standing in this airless chamber, a smile glued to his face, while James played the nobles as if they were a discordant band requiring to be brought in tune.

There was a stirring among those closest to the King. Hugh, recognising Thomas Hamilton of Haddington, and with him Elphinstone, Seton, and Stewart of Blantyre, wondered what had become of the remainder of the Octavians, for they aye roamed in a pack. Perhaps there was truth in the rumour that some of the group had fallen from grace. Hardly surprising if their failure to raise the funds James was seeking were more than hearsay. As Hugh hovered towards the rear of the room, taking advantage of what little air penetrated through an open casement, there was a momentary lull in the general hubbub, and, breaking into it, a burst of laughter. Hugh felt the familiar tightening in his chest that aye accompanied any sighting of William Cunninghame. At his side, Maxwell. Not a welcome sight, bringing to mind Margaret Maxwell and her plea to the King. A brave move, though he could have wished she hadn't thought to involve Kate. A danger they could well have done without. Maxwell's arm was draped around William's shoulder, whatever he said clearly pleasing, a self-satisfied smirk spreading across his face. Hugh stifled a sigh. The King has ruled then, and in Maxwell's favour. The upside of that coin, perhaps now he would release Kate, her discredit a price worth paying.

Outside, the light was fading, servants squeezing their way through the melée to light candles. Everywhere flames flickered and flared, more than one guttering out, figures in the darker corners blending into the shadows, while those in the light cast their own grotesques against the walls. The folk nearest to the King were shifting, separating, opening a path to the door. The effect a ripple of backwards movement that forced Hugh into the window reveal to avoid being crushed. The King gone, the crowd thinned, slipping towards the entrance like a falling tide, the success or otherwise of their petitions visible in their faces. Hugh saw William and Maxwell elbowing through the remaining courtiers, and held back a fraction, thankful they appeared not to have noticed his presence. He had no wish to reawaken the antagonisms of their last meeting in the Queen's chamber. Nor would Eglintoun thank him for it.

He had reckoned without William.

Leaving the palace precincts by a narrow gateway opening onto the park, Hugh kept one hand on his sword hilt, the other on his purse, his ears tuned to the slightest sound. It was barely more than a step to their lodgings, but however short the distance, risks remained: vagabonds, cutpurses, or worse. He turned onto the Cowgate, two figures materialising from the shadows, flanking him.

William, deceptively jovial. 'Ah, Braidstane, have you heard? The King has made his judgement, and in Maxwell's favour.'

Hugh made a non-committal grunt.

'What? Nothing to say? No doubt you expected friendship with the Queen would give that witch of yours the edge...'

Despite that the taunt was intended to provoke, that the best, the safest policy was to ignore it, Hugh ground out, 'Mistress Grant is no witch.'

'No? I wonder.' William spoke across Hugh to Maxwell. 'Do you not think she has the look of Kate Munro?

An *uncanny* resemblance? But of course *she* is dead and buried these six years since...' A pause as if he pondered. 'Though some spirits lie unquiet in their graves. I wonder did her husband likewise walk?'

The implication lay between them, a challenge Hugh once again failed to ignore, though he held to their story. 'Mistress Grant is the widow of a far out connection and has no truck with spirits, unquiet or otherwise. You would do well to watch your tongue. Your father wouldn't favour a charge of slander against you. And as you saw, the Queen favours her.'

'As *you* saw, the King is less credulous.' Maxwell jostled Hugh so that he stumbled into the waste channel edging the thoroughfare: a running sore of excrement, animal entrails and the mingled detritus of too many people living in close confine. He took an extra step forward in an attempt to break clear, William and Maxwell lengthening their stride to match. They pressed in on him like a pair of pincers, William leaning further towards Maxwell. 'The world is awash with witches just now, or so it seems...' a pause, 'and Cowper and the Blawearie witch between them clever at finding them out. James, they say, follows their progress with interest. No doubt to add detail to the treatise begun when the Queen's barge was threatened...'

Maxwell's reply was tinged with malice. 'It behoves us all to be vigilant, to pass on any concerns we may have. If the Queen were to be placed at risk...' A malicious smile spread over his face. 'James has one male heir, but I daresay wouldn't wish a changeling as a spare.'

Something snapped in Hugh. With a heave he thrust William aside, drew his sword, turned on Maxwell. He was aware of the danger of William taking him from behind

321

and so sidestepped to place the luckenbooths at his back. Concentrating on keeping them both within his line of vision, he feinted with his sword and drew his dirk, already regretting the impulse that had catapulted him into this unequal fight. His breathing shortened, his instinct for tactics took over – if I can keep my own footing, force Maxwell into the gutter … William alone I could easily best.

William was swinging at him, his sword arcing downwards, and Hugh parried, blades clashing. Out of the corner of his eye he saw Maxwell closing, risked a quick glance behind him, and then, dropping almost to his knees, threw himself sideways, Maxwell's thrust carrying his sword deep into a door jamb. As he attempted to wrest it free, Hugh, rising, slashed at his thigh with the dirk, the ribbon of red blooming on the buff of Maxwell's hose a momentary satisfaction. Maxwell went down, and Hugh, swinging back, was himself caught off guard, the point of William's sword nicking his neck. He felt the sharp sting, the warm trickle of blood running down towards his shirt, and redoubled his efforts. William drew him into the open street, allowing room to swing and dodge, cut and thrust, the sound of blade on blade magnified in the gloaming.

There was the ring of horseshoes on the cobbles, and a blow to Hugh's head sent him spinning backwards, to trip over the edge of the pavement and land sprawling against the stone steps of a forestair, his sword clattering out of reach. He struggled to get up, lunging for his sword hilt, but was halted by arms pinioning him, a knee on his chest, a voice in his ear. 'I wouldn't advise it…'

Hugh glared up into his assailant's face, collapsed back against the step. John Cunninghame, without any relaxation of his grip, jerked his head towards the street. Hugh followed his gaze, saw William likewise held, Glencairn kneeling over him, and, off to the right, Maxwell, dragging himself into a sitting position under the overhang.

Glencairn's voice sliced through the silence, his venom directed equally at all three. 'This is how you keep the King's peace? Are you mad?'

William lifted his head, spat out, 'Braidstane is the aggressor here, not I.'

'I care little for who started this fight. Only that we do not suffer the King's displeasure should he hear of it. I did not bring you to court, William, to open old wounds, whatever the cause.' Glencairn rocked back on his heels, ordered John, 'And get Braidstane out of here before I'm tempted to run him through myself.'

It should have been the end of it, and perhaps would have been had Alexander been in their lodgings when Hugh woke on the following morning. As it was, Hugh woke with a throbbing head and a smouldering resentment and no one to counsel caution. Underlying his resentment was the fear that William, deprived of satisfaction in the fight, might yet denounce Kate, to all their ill. The mention of Munro, recalling as it did William's visit to Braidstane, an added concern. Along with the rumour Hugh'd heard that there were those around the King who thought the wise woman summoned to treat the Queen was not all she seemed. A rumour grown in the telling, so that the vague enquiry of Holyrood became the certainty of a hanging by the Mercat Cross, the ripple of anticipation of a new spectacle a pleasure, so Hugh thought, visible in every face he passed.

There was only one possible course of action, one way to halt the thing. He brushed aside thought of the illegality, for they wouldn't be the first to break the embargo on duelling, nor likely the last. And at least it would be one on one, not two to one as in their evening encounter. And whatever William's sins, no doubt many, he had enough of a reputation to maintain to abide by the outcome, or at any rate, not to wish to be exposed as a cheat. Hugh, knowing that Alexander wouldn't support him, found himself a less scrupulous second, and sent the challenge.

The response came promptly. 'There is, he says, no case to answer.'

'And the rumours, the slur on Mistress Grant's character?'

'If she is innocent, she has nothing to fear, if guilty, you do well to distance yourself, lest you and yours be likewise tainted.'

Hugh smashed his hand against the mantleshelf. 'Go back. Tell him again: I will have satisfaction. Tell him I always thought him a coward, now I know it.'

'He has what?' Hugh swept his arm across the table sending his dinner flying: platters, food, drink, cascaded onto the floor to land in a mess of chicken bones and gravy, pastries and cheese and fruit, and over it all a rich burgundy wine seeping through the rush mat to stain the wood beneath. 'When did he go? And where?'

The second stepped back out of arm's reach. 'They say an hour ago, bound for Ayrshire.'

Hugh bellowed for a servant. 'Fetch my horse.' And as the man hesitated, 'Fetch my horse!'

Chapter 7

Alexander was furious. 'Hugh has little more control than a bairn. And less sense. Had I thought him capable of such foolishness I wouldn't have let him out of my sight. We may pray God he fails to catch up with William, else who knows what the end of it may be.'

Kate was by the window, a cushion clutched against her chest. 'What should we do?'

'Stay put. Unless the Queen is to release you, we have little choice.'

'But if the rumours are true?'

'Then you are safest close to the Queen, until we can spirit you away.'

'Don't.' There was a catch in her voice, evidence of her very real fear.

He came to stand beside her. 'Perhaps I can speak to the Queen, cite Maxwell as an issue.'

Whatever the dangers in Hugh's actions, all were

eclipsed by morning with word of more serious import: the pestilence was in Leith. The King lost no time in ordering a move to Linlithgow, and by halfway through the afternoon, he, the Queen, their children, and the closest of his advisors had gone, leaving a bevy of servants to make preparations to follow on behind with all that would be required for a lengthy visit. Kate took the opportunity when the news first broke to seek an audience with the Queen to request permission to return to Braidstane and to her children. A request readily granted.

'I am perfectly well, thank God, and so versed in the medicines you have prescribed I see no real reason to trail you to Linlithgow. Besides that there will be pressure enough on the palace, and the accommodation so cramped I do not think the King will notice your absence. And if he does, I shall inform him it was my decision to send you away.'

Alexander and Kate hurried to Leith, their progress halted at the end of a wynd leading down to the docks by a man pushing a handcart, his black cloak reaching his toes, his bird-mask grotesque, a boy at his side ringing a handbell. Alexander pulled his horse back, barging into a sailor in the process, who cursed him roundly in three languages. The handcart was past, all that was visible from the rear, an arm dangling from under the coarse blanket covering it. Kate found her throat constricting, the first flutterings of panic in her breast. They found Grizel kneeling on the floor squeezing clothing into a pair of saddlebags. Her expression was grim.

'There have been five cases today within a stone's throw of here, and more they say in the poorer quarters of the town. 'I should have left when first you suggested it.'

'You haven't been out?' Alexander's tone was harsher than he intended.

'No. Not since the bairns appeared with a story of a monster, for true or not, I thought it safest to bide in. I had hoped that rumour would be the height of it, and so it seemed until yesterday, when news of the first death came.'

'If you're ready, we should leave. The more distance we can put between us and Edinburgh today, the better.'

The first part of the journey accomplished without incident, they had begun to relax as they rode into Falas. Kate came alongside Alexander. 'Can we not take a lodging for the night here? We are all tired, and surely far enough from Edinburgh now to be beyond risk. Forbye that the roads to come are more treacherous than those we have passed.' She sensed Grizel's relief, pressed the point. 'Better we arrive at Braidstane tomorrow than that we fail to arrive at all.' They pulled to a halt outside a smithy, where the furnace still flamed, silhouetting the outline of the smith bent over the anvil. Alexander dismounted and tossed his reins to Kate.

He re-emerged, one side of his face flushed. 'There is a miller's house at the end of the village where you ladies can lodge. Though I am well warned not to expect the miller to be over-friendly and to make sure my purse is prominently displayed. But there is ample stabling for the horses, and I will do well enough in the hayloft.'

The miller was indeed surly, but didn't refuse them shelter; what was lacking in his welcome was amply supplied by his wife, who bustled about setting food.

'If we canna do right by travellers in need,' she darted a poisonous look at her husband, 'we would be poor creatures indeed.'

Carrying their saddlebags up to the room under the eaves, Alexander expressed caution. 'I didn't say it was from Edinburgh we came, lest we be turned away, best we leave it that way. Though we aren't any risk to them, they might think different.'

Kate woke to a sense of unease, a quality in the silence she couldn't define, but which rendered her unable to turn over and go back to sleep without first checking on Grizel. She slipped from the straw mattress and padded across the floor towards the pallet lying to the right of the window, instinct causing her to peer out. A cloaked figure was edging along the base of the mill. He hesitated at the corner, then darted across the open ground to be swallowed by the stable. Saliva flooded her mouth – if William was ahead of them, who was in pursuit? Maxwell, perhaps? Behind her, Grizel stirred, muttered, subsided again into sleep. Kate turned back to the window, recognised Star's soft whinny and the muted clip of swathed horseshoes as a figure emerged from the stable leading three horses. A thief? Less personal perhaps, but equally inconvenient. If they were to be left without mounts... She had a vision of Alexander lying on the hay wrapped in a blanket, a dirk protruding from the coarse weave, knew if it *was* a thief the best she could do was to hammer on the window and perhaps scare him away. In the passageway a floorboard creaked. She looked towards the door, saw the latch lift, and snatching up her girdle, she twisted the ends around her palms, flattening herself against the wall, to take the intruder from behind as he entered. She rocked forward onto her toes, poised to launch herself at his back, prayed her weight would be enough to stumble him, that she could reach around his neck.

The door opened a fraction, the figure slipping in. She careered into him, knocking him off balance, and falling with him, looped the girdle over his head, pulling it against his throat.

He rolled, his hands grasping at it, gasped, 'Kate.'

She released her grip, slumped back, a mixture of relief and fear flooding through her.

'Alexander!' Mindful of the miller and his family, she kept her voice to a hiss. 'What are you doing? I nearly killed you.'

'I doubt that, though it was a good try.' He pulled himself up to sit beside her, rubbing at his neck. 'We need to leave. Now.'

'We can't just leave. What of the miller? His wife was kind to us.'

'Better we are thought rude, or worse, than we embroil them in your troubles. When it is safe to do so, I will return to make amends.' He scrambled to his feet, reached out to pull her up.

'What's happened?'

'William may be headed this way.'

'But he left Edinburgh a day ahead of us, and Hugh on his tail.'

'Not according to John Cunninghame.'

She grasped the door latch for support, only half-hearing what he said next.

'William put it about he was leaving in the hope of drawing Hugh away, and apparently he had some intention of sending me off on a wild goose chase also, so that you would be without protection, the pestilence putting paid to his plans. When he found we were gone … well, you can imagine. John has come in some haste, and in secret, to give us warning.' He moved across to Grizel, was shaking her awake.

Kate stepped into her dress and buttoned the bodice. 'Why would John Cunninghame…? This could be a trick. What if it's for secrecy of a different kind he has come upon us like a thief, and William lies in wait to ambush us?'

'God knows there is no reason, barring instinct, but I trust him, Kate.'

Behind her, Grizel was bundling up their belongings, lacing her boots. Alexander stopped her. 'Carry them. The stair is noisy enough in stockings.'

Kate looked at his feet, saw he too was boot-less. And though she couldn't have put it into words, that he would render himself thus vulnerable was enough to propel her to the doorway and down the stair in his wake. John Cunninghame was holding the horses, their hooves bound in sacking. As he threw the reins to Alexander and bent to offer his linked hands as a step for her, she found herself asking, 'Why are you doing this? You are a Cunninghame.'

He straightened. 'For my sins.' Then, 'Your husband once said, "Glencairn's man I was born, but I will not die William's".' A pause. 'I think I am of the same mind.'

There were too many questions still unanswered. 'If William left before you, how come you are here and he is not?'

331

'A small matter of a misdirection and...' he ran his tongue around his lips, 'I drugged his horse. Oh,' as her eyes widened and she took an involuntary step backwards, 'not enough to do permanent damage, but enough to make him sluggish; a day or two and the effect will have worn off. Kate,' her name was a sigh, 'please believe me, I wish you no harm, but there is no time to lose, William may already be back on your tail.'

She wanted to believe him, asked, 'Why does he pursue us now?'

'Because he cannot bear to be thwarted. Whether he knows who you truly are, or merely suspects, I don't know. But the rumour about the court, that you are not what you seem, is likely his doing.' Kate recognised the apology in his hesitation, nodded an acknowledgement as he continued, 'And rumours, as you know, can flow faster than a river in spate, and gain much force in the passing. I suspicion he means to make use of it to your ill.'

'On what grounds?'

'Does anyone need grounds to cry a wise woman as a witch?'

'Then this is madness. If we are to disappear in the middle of the night it will but give credence to the claims. Better we wait for morning and leave with my reputation intact. For reputation, as you know, is halfway to safety. Besides that to travel at night is too much of a risk for Grizel.'

Alexander was brutal. 'And William is not? Cunninghame's right, and we're leaving. Now.'

Another thought, more chilling. 'What if you're wrong. What if William has taken another route, if it is Munro he chases?' She appealed to John, 'We cannot travel so fast

as we might wish, with Grizel to consider. Would you…?'
He nodded. 'I'll go to Braidstane.'

Chapter 8

John had paused only once to change horse, the ostler's complaints at being dragged from his bed at such an unholy hour, voluble. His first offering, a sorry nag, fit only for the knacker's yard, quickly replaced, at the sight of John's purse, by a chestnut with bright eyes and sound legs. As he slewed through the gateway at Braidstane, the open tower door and the tuneless whistling emanating from the stables released the tension in his neck and shoulders – no William then.

Ishbel answered his knock, her expression sharpening as he asked for Hugh. He was quick to offer reassurance. 'I mean no harm. I've come from Alexander and Kate with an urgent message.'

Perhaps it was the open use of the name, but whatever convinced her, she gestured towards the stair. 'Hugh's … away, but Elizabeth's within.' She clamped her mouth shut as if there was more she might say but chose not to.

The colour drained from Elizabeth's face when she saw him, but she heard him out in silence, the pause when he finished, stretching. He was unsure whether she believed him or not, had no idea how to convince her. Finally he reached out, touched her arm. 'As God is my witness, Mistress Montgomerie, I mean them no harm.'

'I believe you.' She took a deep breath. 'They are at Giffen, I'll take you there.'

As they approached the cottage, they heard Munro say, 'If I am alive it will put paid to any claim of witchcraft.'

And Hugh's reply, 'William needs you dead. Now more than ever. With Broomelaw in his sights...'

'Perhaps it's time I faced him. Make an end of it.'

'And you think it would end with you?'

John halted in the doorway holding up his hands as if to show he meant them no threat. He unbuckled his sword, placed it on the table, addressed Munro. 'You took my advice once before. Take it again. Leave, while you still can. And this time take Kate and the bairns with you.'

Hugh was glaring at him. 'What is this? Are you William's messenger, or is it some trick of your own?' He balled his fists. 'Do you wish to floor me again?'

Munro shot a puzzled glance at Hugh.

John answered the unspoken question. 'Glencairn and I came on Hugh and William fighting the piece out on the Cowgate three days ago, and fortunate we did, for it would have suited none of us to be clapped in the Tolbooth.'

'But what...'

'It doesn't matter what it was about. Nor,' as Hugh moved to protest, 'who started it. All that matters now is that there is danger for you all. The truce between our families is a fragile thing at best and, whatever way you look at it, threatened now.'

'And your aim is to maintain it? Why should we believe someone who is our enemy?'

Munro halted Hugh. 'John is no enemy, Hugh. I can testify to that.' And to John, 'How long do we have?'

'I don't know. But if you do not wish to stir a hornet's nest, the wisest course is to go, and go quickly. William was still in Edinburgh when you left, Hugh, the word of his leaving a ruse to draw you away, but I believe it is Kate he seeks. She left Edinburgh yesterday with Alexander and Mistress Ivarsen, fleeing the pestilence, like most of the court, and so soon as William realised they had gone, he followed. Though his direction was somewhat awry and his horse without the usual turn of speed.' A smile flickered on his face, disappeared again. 'Kate troubles him and Maxwell stokes the fire.'

Hugh spoke more quietly, his antagonism not entirely assuaged. 'And you? What is your role in all of this?'

'Someone has to stop this madness, this constant aggravation that can only end in more blood spilt. And God knows there has been enough of that. Mistress Ivarsen, as you know, is in no condition to travel at speed, so Kate asked me to ride ahead in case it is for here he makes.'

'You talked to Kate?' A note of doubt crept into Hugh's voice, matched by John's exasperation,

'Yes, I talked to Kate. How else … God's truth, Hugh, I caught up with them at Falas, and if I could follow their trail, so can William, despite my misdirection. But unlike him, I do not desire her ill. If I did, would I be here?'

Munro said, 'So, soon as she arrives we will head for Greenock.'

'I'd suggest you don't wait, not here at any rate. They

may be several hours yet.'

John gone, heading for Kilmaurs, Elizabeth settled the argument. ' If Cunninghame risked coming here to warn you, the danger is great. You must go.'

Munro was obdurate. 'I cannot leave without Kate.'

'Delay here and you may not get the chance to leave at all.'

Hugh was equally firm. 'Elizabeth's right. I can retrace John's route, head Kate off and bring her to meet you at Greenock.'

Munro was thinking aloud. 'Ellie can ride with me ... what like is Maggie's horse?'

'Not fast enough.' Elizabeth spoke firmly. 'Nor would you be with Ellie on your pommel. Besides the time you would waste going to Braidstane to collect them. They will both be fine with us for the time being. And plenty of opportunity to bring them to you. Wherever you go.'

'But William has seen Maggie once already, Ellie too.'

'Then we'll take care he doesn't again.' She was pushing Munro towards the door. 'Now go. Go!'

Hugh was tightening the girth, checking his stirrups. 'Where will you go?'

Munro swung into the saddle. 'Cayeux. Though the area isn't as settled as I'd like, it is at least far outside William's orbit. And Madame Picarde is kindness itself.'

'Well then.' Elizabeth stood back. 'If you leave now

337

you may catch tonight's tide. As for Kate, if she is delayed, there is always tomorrow. And to travel separately may be the safest thing. My brother has four ships, and all, I'm sure, at your disposal.'

338

Chapter 9

William was seated at the table in the centre of the great hall at Newark, sunlight from the west window spilling across the polished oak, ruining the remains of a fine breakfast, as yet uncleared. It had gone some way to moderating the foul mood of his arrival: a product of the knowledge that Kate had given him the slip, travelling God only knew where, but not, as John had said, to Linlithgow, combined with the poor showing of his horse. But he was not yet ready to relinquish altogether his frustration. A servant had twice come to see to the clearance, and twice been sent away by Maxwell with a growl, so that slices of ham and beef lay, their edges curling, and alongside them cut cheeses forming dry crusts, and a loaf, fresh that morning, growing hard and stale. Only the apricots, newly off a ship from Italy, drank in the sunshine without ill effect. Margaret Maxwell, annoyed at the waste of it, had also made an attempt at rescue, and had likewise been given short shrift.

Maxwell leaned back, pushing his chair away from the table, and hooking his hands together behind his head, picked up the threads of an earlier discussion. 'This

Mistress Grant. She cannot *be* Kate Munro?'

'I'm not so sure.' William clenched one fist. 'I thought them finished with the reivers raid. But...'

'You saw the bodies.'

'I saw bodies. Which is a very different thing. If there were others in the tower, if she were elsewhere when the reivers pounced...'

'Why would she not have laid claim to Broomelaw then? Your father made enquiries.'

'Perhaps it suited her to be dead ... or to be thought so...' He broke off, clenched his fist. 'That chit of a girl at Broomelaw ... I know now who she reminded me of ... who *she* likely is ... God's blood, but they have played us for fools!'

He had lost Maxwell. 'Who has played you?'

'Kate Munro, and her brat of a daughter ... They both live.' He stopped again, 'And the other one. At Braidstane. Little wonder I found her familiar. Her insolence alone should have alerted me. A far-off relative indeed, an orphan child.' His mouth tightened. 'The Montgomeries have colluded in the deception. Mistress Grant claimed to hail from Berwick, Elizabeth, that she came from Fife. They are Munros, all three of them, I'm sure of it.' He slammed his fist on the table, the platters jumping. 'But not for long.'

'You cannot be certain?'

'Oh, I'm certain.' William rose to his feet, buckling on his sword.

'What will you do? Your father won't countenance a killing.'

'He won't need to. Kate Munro is dead. Let her stay so. But if her spirit walks, if she inhabits another...' A hint of a smile. 'The King has no truck with witchcraft. We have but

340

to feed the rumour that already exists. And as for the girls, if they are a witch's spawn, they also can be dealt with. Word is John Cowper is at Garnerstoun. And the Blawearie witch with him.' The smile faded as another thought struck him. 'That man we chased from Braidstane, it must have been Munro. Though how they hid him all these years...'

Maxwell was dismissive. 'They didn't. To hide a woman is easy: widows are two-a-penny, every family cursed with them; but to conceal Munro, that would have been a harder task altogether, and a risk I do not think Braidstane would have run. For my money, he's been abroad. Not that it matters, for if it was him, the rockfall did for him for sure.'

The anteroom was narrow, the only natural light coming from a small gable window set within a deep embrasure, so that despite it was almost noon, a candle burned behind the man attempting to work at a desk in the corner. William was pacing up and down, pulling his sword part out of the scabbard, dropping it back, raising it again. Each time he plunged it home the man flinched, a series of blots marring the parchment in front of him.

William halted his pacing, towered over him. 'What's keeping them?'

The man shrugged. 'The Blawearie witch is much in demand with every person, lord or loon, who has some score to settle.'

William raised his fist. 'Insolent pup...'

Maxwell grabbed his arm. 'Leave it, William, he's not worth it, nor do we wish to give the wrong impression

341

to Cowper.' And to the man, 'I take it Mistress Aitken is worth the wait?'

The man bobbed his head three times in quick succession, as a simpleton might, but his reply was clear enough. 'Her talent is a byword the length and breadth of the country. I do not think there are above two or three of those she has cried "witch" who have escaped with their lives, and those only because they in turn have cried others. If the Great Witch of Blawearie names your Mistress Grant, even the patronage of the Queen would not save her.'

It was an exaggeration likely spoken for effect, but it stopped William in his tracks. 'You have heard of Mistress Grant?'

'No.' The denial was instant. 'I merely meant to illustrate the value of Mistress Aitken's testimony.' His tongue flicked over his upper lip, 'You have only to supply the information and the deed is done.'

Behind them the door swung open, the draught coiling around their feet. The woman Cowper ushered in wore a ragged skirt, her long hair trailing free down her back. William felt the first stirrings of unease – it was to be hoped her evidence would be more impressive than her appearance, that she could be depended upon.

As if he read William's mind, Cowper, who now stood in what was clearly an habitual pose, his head thrown back, his arms tucked close into his side, both hands grasping the edges of his cloak, said, 'You needn't worry.' He jerked his head towards the door, the man at the desk rising and scurrying out. 'I have found Mistress Aitken to be a credible witness.' He delved into an inner pocket, dropped an empty pouch on the desk. 'But do not take my word for it. You will no doubt have questions to ask of her?' A pause. 'And answers to give.' He fingered the pouch. 'A commission is not lacking in expense … we understand each other, I'm sure.'

William picked up the pouch, tossed it from hand to hand, set it down again. 'Supposing the expenses are not extortionate.'

Cowper acknowledged the warning with a nod. He took the seat behind the desk, gestured William to the facing chair. 'As you know I have a general commission. Which avoids the need for an individual application to the Privy Council.' His voice was smooth. 'And though a device intended to save the Council time and money, it can facilitate matters in other ways also. Make your accusation, and so soon as the accused is apprehended we will face her with Mistress Aitken. If she be guilty it is but a small step from trial to execution. It *is* a female I take it?'

William nodded. 'A wise woman.'

'Ah. She has caused you ill?'

'Me personally? No.' William contrived to sound shocked at the implication. 'But it has come to my attention that she threatens the well-being of the Queen, and I would fail in my duty if I did not seek to verify such claims.'

Cowper's expression was unreadable, his tone also. 'The smallest of rumours, left unchecked, may fast grow to a monster.'

'It is my belief she is possessed.'

'Indeed. Well then, Mistress Aitken is well versed in such.' He waved the woman forward.

William indicated the door. 'I imagine you find it best not to be party to the interrogation. You will have no wish to prejudice any trial.'

A tight smile. 'I shall be in the room beyond this one.

343

When you are done,' Cowper indicated a staff leaning against the wall, 'three sharp taps on the wall will suffice.' Again he fingered the pouch. 'You will find Mistress Aitken most co-operative.'

He found her stillness unnerving. She was staring at him, a quirk to her mouth as if he amused her. As if it were she who came to assess him, rather than the other way round. Irritated, he said, 'Well? Do you have a gift in finding out witches?'

She inclined her head. 'Where there is evil, I can aye root it out.' Her voice was husky, her words like dry leaves blowing through a vennel, the sense equivocal. He felt a crawling sensation in his stomach, felt himself threatened, sought to regain control. 'It isn't merely evil I seek to root out, but an unquiet spirit.'

'That, too, I can bring to light.'

'What do you need?'

'Nothing.' Her eyes were fixed on him, the grey of a restless sea, the expression unsettling. 'Bar the opportunity to confront the accused. And to know from whence she comes, what charge is laid at her door.' She lapsed into silence, and he found himself talking to fill the void.

'I have no wish for this to go awry. The woman calling herself Mistress Grant is, I believe, possessed of the spirit of another woman, one Kate Munro, who is dead these six years. She has the look of her, and the voice...'

'You knew the first?' There was a spark of interest in her eyes.

'Aye. And saw her corpse, watched her placed under the

sod. But in Mistress Grant, it is as if Kate Munro walks and talks yet.'

'You have no need of me then. You are your own witness.'

He understood her game, was prepared to play it. 'I have not the credentials in this.' He picked up the pouch, counted coins into it, set it on the table in front of her. 'You on the other hand...'

She was staring past him, as if in a trance. 'I cannot yet see her...'

He reopened the pouch, added more money.

She began to speak, her voice high and fluting, as different from her normal tone as could be. It was an impressive charade. 'I see a woman ... with raven's hair...' She opened one eye, her face tilted towards him as if seeking some kind of confirmation.

William filled in, 'Slender, blue eyes, a mole on her left cheek.'

'I see...' the words uncoiled from her mouth, 'I see a witch's mark...'

She cocked her head to one side, as if listening. 'She talks of healing ... but I see death ... and on her shoulder,' her voice rose a notch, 'the devil sits.' A pause, as if in expectation, another clink of coin as William added to the purse for the third time.

She opened her eyes fully, scooped up the pouch, nodded. 'I have her.'

345

Chapter 10

If John Shaw was surprised by Munro's arrival, he hid it well. With a sharp glance at the sweat-soaked jerkin, he pulled him inside and led him up to the solar. 'You're fortunate I'm here. I was just about to leave for Glasgow, but no matter. This is not, I imagine, a social call.'

'No.'

Janet appeared in the doorway, curtsied to Munro. 'You'll take some refreshment?'

He shook his head as if to clear it, as if he didn't follow the question.

Shaw said, 'Whatever it is, there is time for a bite, surely?'

'When is high tide?'

'You need a ship?'

'Can you be ready to sail?'

'If need be, but to where?'

'France: Brittany for preference.'

Shaw gave Janet the nod. 'An early bite then, but hearty.' He pulled up a chair, and turning it round sat, resting his arms on the back. 'If I'm to drop everything and take you south, you'd best tell me all.' He waved at the opposite chair. 'Sit yourself down. There are three hours yet to high tide, plenty of time in which to convince me of the urgency of the thing.'

'Three minutes will suffice.' Munro perched on the edge of the table, as if unable or unwilling to settle. 'Kate was called to court to treat the Queen, and she ran into the Cunninghames there. Which she might have weathered, but that Maxwell's wife came seeking a paper from James to ban her husband from approaching her...'

'What has that to do with Kate?'

'She treated Margaret Maxwell some months ago, following the birth of their latest child,' and as Shaw exhaled, he added, 'Folly, I know, but it was at the Wallace tower at Hillhouse, so she didn't at the first know to whom she was called. When she did, her sympathies were already roused ... and, well, you know Kate. At any rate, she continued, and as a result Mistress Maxwell asked her to testify to the cruelty.'

Shaw was incredulous. 'Folly enough to treat her, though perhaps understandable, but to allow herself to be drawn into contention with Maxwell, and at the court...'

'There's more.' Munro took a deep breath. 'John Cunninghame arrived at Braidstane this morning, warning of rumours flying around Edinburgh that the wise woman treating the Queen is tainted, and William, whether the originator or not, rides on the back of them, and may appear at any moment to denounce her.'

'He has guessed the truth then?'

'We don't know for sure, and nor does Cunninghame, but suspicion is enough. Glencairn, father or son, if they were to find us out, would not take it lightly to have been

347

deceived and in so thorough a fashion. Besides that, they have rebuilt Broomelaw for William. Any of us alive threaten their title to it, so we cannot risk remaining, but this time we leave together.'

'Where is Kate?'

'On her way back from Edinburgh. The pestilence is there, and the court moved to Linlithgow. Hugh has gone to cut her off and bring her here. I thought they might have beaten me. The hope was to make today's tide, but…'

'Whatever happens, you should go today. The captain of the *Marion* is well used to French waters. If Kate is not in time, I will remain, and bring her on the *Christian* tomorrow.'

'No! I left her once, I will not do so again.'

'If William finds *you*, the risk to Kate is double. You have been apart six years, what is another day or two?'

Munro, recognising an element of truth in the assessment, nevertheless refused to be swayed. 'It isn't a day or two at issue here. Six years ago, the safest course, for Kate and the bairns, was for me to go alone. Now she is threatened, it is a very different game. And one I will not leave to chance. William isn't looking for me, nor is he looking here. If he thinks of me at all, he thinks me dead and buried a second time in the caves at Auchenskeigh. Lock me in the dungeon if you must, for safety's sake, but do not press me to desert Kate again.'

Chapter 11

It was mid-morning when Kate spied Hugh riding up the rocky knoll to meet them. They had followed the Clyde valley, stopping at Rutherglen for breakfast, the delay while a change of horses was found providing a welcome rest to Grizel and Kate both, though neither would have admitted it. Kate's immediate thought was for Munro. Hugh's first words a temporary reassurance.

'Your husband is safely away, to John Shaw and a passage to France.'

'Thank God.' She turned to Grizel, a smile beginning to form, then, aware Hugh was not smiling, said, 'What else?'

'It's too dangerous for you to return to Braidstane. I'm to take you to Greenock.'

'Are Maggie and Ellie with their father?'

'There wasn't time. But they aren't at risk the now. I'll bring them to France myself in week or two. In the meantime you'll have a chance to get sorted.'

Kate cut him off. 'They are neither of them safe. William knows Ellie is my daughter, and Maggie...' Two spots of high colour bloomed on her cheeks. 'She had a run-in with him herself at Broomelaw some weeks ago.'

'So Munro said. But we'll take care that should William return to Braidstane he won't find either of them. Nor will we let Maggie roam about the countryside putting herself at risk.'

She waved away his words. 'I know you all wish it for the best, but you are wrong. My husband included. When William saw Maggie he questioned her familiarity, and we feared for the consequences, but time passing we thought it nothing, but now, whether he sees her again or no, it is but a step from suspecting me to minding her. And he wouldn't need to be overly smart to put two and two together and make five. Forbye that making a family home elsewhere might be presented, however falsely, as an adventure. But to leave without them, Ellie would not understand, nor Maggie forgive.'

'You cannot risk coming to Braidstane.'

'I know.' She took a deep breath. 'I'll head straight for Greenock while you fetch the girls.'

Hugh looked towards Alexander. 'Will you...?'

Kate was decisive. 'No. Alexander must stay with Grizel. She cannot travel fast. But you must. I am well used to riding alone.'

'The shortest route passes Newark. You cannot risk it.'

'I won't take the coast road. Maxwell was at the court with William and likely accompanies him to Ayrshire.'

Unexpectedly, Alexander intervened. 'Kate has criss-crossed the county on her own many times, Hugh. She travels in daylight and every mile will take her further from Braidstane and Kilmaurs.'

A moment of silence, a decision hanging in the balance,

then, 'I don't like it, Kate.'

'No more do I.' Her gaze was steady, her voice firm. 'But it is the most sensible course.'

It was a confidence that evaporated so soon as Hugh disappeared from view, but Kate took care not to allow her apprehension to show as she bade Grizel and Alexander farewell. 'I'm sorry, Grizel, I had hoped to be the one to welcome your newest bairn into the world, but no matter, Elizabeth will have that pleasure.' She was twisting the ring on her finger, aware this was, in all probability, a final goodbye.

Grizel, as if she read her mind, reached out to grasp her hand. 'Sigurd runs cargoes to France also; in a year or two, a summer there would not be unwelcome.'

Once past Elderslie it was a solitary ride, the only other travellers a packman following a track southwards and a lad whistling as he shepherded his small flock towards new pasture. She was grateful neither had been close enough to require the courtesy of an acknowledgement, nor, it seemed, sufficiently interested to give her more than a passing glance. Above her the sky stretched, blue, unbroken, but far to the west she could see clouds teased out like strands of embroidery silks, some white, some rose-tinted, a few edged with pale gold. It augured well for a sea voyage. Munro should already be safely away while she would wait for the morrow … and the girls. The farmhouse in

Brittany would be a fine start. Though perhaps there would be other options. She allowed her mind to drift: to Florence, and John's tales of the Santa Maria Nuova hospital, of the liberty women had to practise there … to Maggie's dreams of anatomy. To the armies of Europe, each a polyglot mix of nationalities; surely Munro could be a soldier in Italy as easily as France, and likely less danger in it. To olive groves and vineyards … the sunshine and the sea. There were more ways than one of making a living, and farming of any sort would surely be less uncertain in a kinder clime… She was smiling, even as she chided herself that it would be time enough to make plans once they were all safely on French soil.

She reached the headwater of the Gryffe and turned to follow a track northwards, the climb, though not taxing on horseback, one she was glad not to have to undertake on foot. Outcrops of whinstone, gorse-covered, cut into the swell of the hill, the shadowed pockets of grass in between lush and damp. Cresting the rise she saw Greenock town in the distance, smoke from the tanneries coiling upwards, coalescing into dark smudges, like thumbprints on the clear blue of the sky. Further still, Wester Greenock Castle etched against the skyline, a beacon to guide her to John Shaw and safety. She should be there in fine time for supper. Off to the right the Clyde, a ribbon of silver stippled by sunlight, on it a line of fishing boats strung out like beads, bobbing towards open water. The tide was clearly on the ebb, which settled the issue. This time tomorrow… She bent over the horse's neck to encourage him and so failed to see the horseman who halted on the track below her, shading his eyes against the glare of the sun. Failed also to see him wheel around and take off towards the shore road, whipping his horse into a gallop.

Chapter 12

William and Cowper were closeted together when Maxwell burst in on them.

'You have news?'

'Yes.' His pleasure was obvious. 'You've no need to trail to Braidstane. I've just come on Mistress Grant. Making, I think, for Greenock.'

'Are you sure?'

'I have seen enough of her to know.'

'I don't doubt your recognition, only, are you sure she makes for Greenock? Where did you see her and how long ago?'

'No more than half an hour. This side of Murdiestoun, heading west, and where else would her sights be set but on Greenock? The Shaws are thick with the Montgomeries, as you know. If we go now, we may catch her before she makes it.'

'*We* cannot. Remember I also have a connection to the Shaws, however little they appear to take account of it. My father would not favour any new antagonism in that direction. And if even a whiff of what we do were to reach my mother…' He turned to Cowper. 'But *you* can.'

Maxwell produced his trump card. 'She travels alone. It is the perfect opportunity.'

Kate was little more than a mile from Greenock Castle when Cowper and his man caught up with her. She turned, apprehension fading at the sight of his clerical garb, despite that he failed to return her smile.

'Mistress Grant?'

She countered with a query of her own, her gaze steady. 'Should I know you, sir?'

'My name is John Cowper.' He waited as if for a reaction, blustered on. 'I must ask you to come with me.'

'Is someone ill? I have little medicine with me, but will be happy to assist if I can.'

Cowper nodded to the man with him who reached across to take hold of her reins.

'I am quite capable…'

'It is neither your horsemanship nor your medical expertise which interests us, Mistress Grant. But rather the source from whence it comes.'

It was as if a cloud had covered the sun.

'There have been accusations made. You will come with us to be formally examined.'

'On what charge? And am I to know my accuser?'

He turned his horse. 'All in good time.'

'And if I refuse?'

'That would be unwise. If you are innocent you have nothing to fear.'

'Where am I to be taken? I have bairns without a father.

May I send word?'

A pause, an appraising glance at her clothes. 'There is the expense of the thing to consider...'

'I can pay.'

'Well then. When we reach Bishopton it can be arranged.'

Chapter 13

It was noon on the following day when Hugh and the girls arrived at the wooded slope below Greenock Castle. Maggie had been for setting off straight away when Hugh appeared at Braidstane with Kate's instructions, but Elizabeth was firm.

'It would be a madness your mother would neither approve nor expect. Better by far to leave at first light than to risk injury or worse by riding halfway across the country in the dark.'

Ellie rode in front of Hugh, grasping the pommel with both hands, her feet dangling by Hugh's knees. They wound through the trees, the dappled shade a welcome respite from the heat rising from the sun-baked track they had followed alongside the Gryffe Water. Hugh looked down at Ellie's pigtails lifting and falling on her shoulders with every jolt, and was reminded of Gillis, of other visits to the Shaws: most of them pleasant memories, a few less so, but none more important than today. Relief swept through him: that Ellie and Maggie were safely delivered, that the next stage of their journey could begin.

They broke from the trees onto the terrace. The gate stood open and what sounds issued from the barmkin were so ordinary Hugh felt the tension slipping from him.

Ellie had been unusually subdued on the journey, indicating that despite all the efforts to turn it into an outing, something of the seriousness of the situation had penetrated. 'Uncle Hugh?' She swivelled to look up at him, her green eyes dark, her forehead puckered. 'Mama will be here, won't she?'

'So she told me, and I have never had cause to doubt her.'

'Nothing bad will have happened?'

'She'll be here.' His smile was genuine, and she relaxed against him, yawning.

'Don't fall asleep on us now.' Maggie, also smiling, reached across to tug at one of Ellie's plaits. 'We are nearly there, and look,' she pointed towards the castellations of the barmkin wall, 'there is Gillis, looking out for us.'

As if on cue, Gillis appeared in the gateway, a girl on the cusp of womanhood, suddenly shy. She dipped a curtsey, 'Uncle Hugh,' then turned to Maggie, grasping her bridle. 'Your father is here. Closeted with John in the solar, some secret between them I am not allowed to share. Perhaps you can wrest it from them.'

Maggie was out of the saddle before Gillis had finished speaking, and making for the castle entrance. 'Not mother?'

'No.' Gillis caught up with her at the foot of the turnpike stair. 'Was she expected?'

'She should have been here. Long before us.' Maggie's words were punctuated by quick indrawn breaths as she ran upwards. 'She was coming yesterday, and thought to arrive in the late afternoon.'

The door of the solar opened above them, light spilling onto the stairwell.

'Maggie.' John Shaw grasped both her hands and drew her inside. 'Where did you spring from?

'Mother sent Uncle Hugh to fetch us from Braidstane. We were...'

'We were to meet her here.' Hugh filled the doorway, his voice grim.

Ellie squeezed past him, flung herself at Munro. 'He promised, he promised mother would be here.'

Munro hugged her to him, sought to soothe her. 'I'm sure there's a reason for her delay, poppet.' And in an obvious attempt to distract, said, 'You girls need something to eat, I'm sure.'

John took Gillis' arm, propelled her towards the door. 'Take them to Janet and ask that food be brought. You can all help carry.'

Maggie looked as if she was about to protest, Munro halting her with a glance towards Ellie and a fractional shake of his head. She said, 'Come Ellie, perhaps if we help to set things out, Mother will smell it and be here in no time.'

The door shut, Munro rounded on Hugh. 'What happened? Where did you leave her? Why...'

'She insisted on it, fearing for the girls because of Maggie's run-in with William. Alexander backed her up.' He was aware of John Shaw's sharp intake of breath, of Munro's white knuckles. 'She thought...'

'What?'

'That you would be safely away, that she and the girls could follow.'

'We need to find her.' Munro was on his feet, thrusting past Hugh.

'You need to stay here.' Hugh caught at his arm. 'I will go. She intended to make by Elderslie. It's likely a commonplace delay: her horse gone lame, a strap snapped…'

John Shaw was holding Munro's other arm, but addressed Hugh. 'If you follow her route, I'll send into the town. She is enough of a stranger in these parts for her passing to be noticed.' He tightened his grip on Munro. 'Think of Maggie and Ellie. Bad enough Kate is missing, without us losing you also. I have no wish to make our jest a reality, but if you cannot see sense I *will* lock you in the dungeon.' Then, his tone softening, 'Rest easy. I have plenty friends in Greenock who have their ear to the ground. If she was there, they will know.'

Hugh was returning from his own fruitless search when he caught up with Shaw at the outskirts of the town. It was clear the news wasn't good. 'You have word of her then?'

'I suspect so. There was a woman apprehended by Cowper yesterday, not a mile from our door. Word is she has been taken to Bishopton, charged with witchcraft.'

'Was there a name given?'

'No, but who else would it be? We had no thought of any other visitor beating a track to our door.'

'Do you know this Cowper? Can he be bought?'

'I've heard of him, and from what is said he purports to be an honest man, though some would doubt it. But as to the Blawearie witch whom he trails about the countryside, she has a fearsome reputation. Few of those she accuses escape, her victims already amounting to above two hundred. I have set enquiries in motion to ascertain if it is Kate and where precisely she is held. We should know by tomorrow at the latest. Though how we will contain Munro tonight, I don't know.'

'You may well have to resort to the dungeon. He will not wish to sit back and do nothing.'

'If it *is* her, he must, for the time being at least.'

Chapter 14

William and Maxwell were leaning on the barmkin wall at Broomelaw enjoying the last of the sunshine as John Cunninghame picked his way across the gorse-covered hillside towards the tower. A knot formed in his stomach as he saw William's self-satisfied smile, but he schooled his own face to show nothing.

'Uncle. Come to enjoy the hospitality of the latest Cunninghame stronghold?'

John inclined his head. 'I won't deny my thirst.' That at least was true. 'Nor would I refuse, were you to offer me supper also.'

William waved towards the tower. 'Supper, a bed for the night, whatever you wish. Maxwell is staying, having escaped from the stour the builders are creating at Newark, and I have another guest or two: we will be quite the party.'

'Celebrating?' John strove to keep his tone light, though his mind raced.

'In a manner of speaking, yes.'

That William hadn't made for Braidstane once he found Kate not to be at Linlithgow was a conundrum which had continued to trouble John; Glencairn's charge to visit Broomelaw to check on him, an opportunity he had been quick to accept. This new William, free of truculence, the epitome of a generous host, niggled.

William led the way into the hall, Maxwell following close behind, John at the rear. Despite his visit to the tower when the repairs were almost complete, it was the earlier picture, when Broomelaw had been destroyed, that was uppermost in his mind; this new comfort a startling contrast to the blackened roof timbers, the blown-out windows, the collapsing floors of that terrible time. He waved at the painted ceiling and at the wall hangings, found a compliment.

'Fine handiwork, William, and the furnishings more than adequate. You and your mother between you have made a job of it.'

'It's well enough.' William shrugged as if to pretend the surroundings mattered little to him, but pride was visible in his eyes. He introduced the man who rose from the settle. 'You'll not know Cowper?'

John bowed, smothered his instinctive distaste. 'By reputation only, but that, impressive.'

Cowper dipped his head in acknowledgement, his tone studiously humble. 'It is the Lord's work I do.'

'You have business hereabouts?'

He permitted himself a smile. 'The Master of Glencairn has uncovered a witch, who is a threat not only to common folk, but to the Queen and to her unborn child.'

John had a vision of Cowper and William arriving at Braidstane to denounce Kate, thanked God he had been able to forewarn them of the danger. Aware a response was expected, he affected mild curiosity. 'You know where to find her?'

'Already found, and safely under lock and key. All that remains, to prove her guilty.' As William ran his tongue around his lips as if in anticipation, John felt a mix of guilt and relief that there must be some other poor unfortunate fallen foul of William, a relief short-lived.

'It is Mistress Grant, that hanger-on of the Montgomeries, she that is treating the Queen.' William's expression was virtuosity itself. 'It was our duty to raise the action against her. When the preliminaries are done she will be faced with the Blawearie witch. That, I imagine, all the corroboration required.'

'Is she to be tried in Edinburgh, at the judiciary court?'

'No need. Cowper here has a standing commission. Maxwell and I are witnesses, and if Mistress Aitken of Blawearie also cries her, all that will remain is for a jury to be formed.' William nodded towards his other guests: 'Hamilton and Fullerton, recently home on a visit from Dublin, have agreed to serve.'

'The other jurors?'

'Three is a quorum.' Cowper's tone was smooth.

Despite it, John sensed a measure of unease in Cowper, thought to stoke it. 'You are sure of her guilt?'

'Thus far there is no reason to doubt it, but I will take pains to examine her thoroughly. The commission is set for four days' hence. The Master of Glencairn's hospitality an opportunity to clarify the evidence.'

'And her defence is…?'

'She offers none.'

'Is that usual?'

Cowper shifted in his seat, as if he suffered from piles. 'Why the catechism, Uncle?' There was a dangerous glint in William's eyes, his earlier bonhomie evaporating. 'Do you doubt my testimony? Or Maxwell's?'

'I questioned only that the case is solid. You would not wish it to fail?'

'It won't.'

'Have you also interrogated her, Nephew?'

'Not as yet.'

Again the sense that Cowper squirmed, as if there was something that gave him pause, as if he lacked certainty. 'There is little point, for she refuses to speak, save for repeated requests her family be informed.'

'And have they?'

Cowper cracked his knuckles. 'It appears she has none, saving a bairn or two, but there is little point in seeking them out, their testimony, should they offer it, of no validity.'

They sat down for supper, John unwilling to raise any suspicion by a haste to leave, despite the need to get word to the Montgomeries, and to John Shaw. He had little appetite, but made a good show of appreciation of the meal, which in any other circumstance would have been genuine. The ham was succulent, the spiced sauce with enough of a bite to it to please the most discerning palate, the vegetables accompanying it, plentiful. The syllabub that followed, served with candied fruits, a credit to the cook. Cowper, sitting next to him, his appetite for a good claret clearly matching his enthusiasm for witch-finding, became confidential.

'I have found Mistress Grant unusually cunning. She puts on a good face, and if I had not had the evidence of the Master and Maxwell here, I might have thought her innocent.'

John leaned back in his chair, his voice low. 'How so?'

'An intelligence about her, a lack of hysteria, a pretended dignity.' He laughed as if to show he thought it all a studied ruse. 'But she does not fool me, nor, if she be guilty,' he added hurriedly, 'will she fool Mistress Aitken.'

'Where's she held?'

'In the belfry tower at Bishopton.'

'Securely, I hope.'

'Guarded round the clock, the gaolers local, so no fear of any prior knowledge of her, nor sympathy.'

'Taking no chances then.' John settled himself to wait an appropriate moment to take his leave, surprised to see the moderation in William's drinking that Lady Glencairn had reported seemed to continue. In the circumstances, a curse rather than a blessing, a clear-headed William more dangerous than a befuddled one.

Chapter 15

The confirmation that Kate was indeed taken by Cowper came to Greenock by John Cunninghame, and with him, Alexander, who he had chanced upon on the outskirts of the town. They entered the solar together, Cunninghame a fraction to the rear, head bowed.

'It is true then?' Munro was pacing.

Alexander nodded.

'Who's doing is it?'

'Need you ask?' Cunninghame was bitter. 'My nephew, ably assisted by Patrick Maxwell.'

'And the charge?' Munro held onto the mantle as if he would fall.

'Possession. Consorting with the devil. Conspiring with him to the Queen's ill and that of her unborn child.'

Hugh was hoarse. 'Witnesses?'

'William, Maxwell and Mistress Aitken, the Blawearie witch.'

Munro pushed himself away from the fireplace, stood ramrod straight. 'When will it be heard?'

'The commission is set for Friday forenoon. William, I

believe, forces the pace.' For the first time in the conversation Cunninghame looked Munro fully in the eye. 'There are times when I wish I had any name but my own.'

Munro spared him a smile, though it failed to reach his eyes. 'You may be a Cunninghame, but you are not William. You never were. I was indebted to you once before. I am again. I know what you risked to warn us. That it has gone awry is not your blame.' He held out his hand, Cunninghame's answering grip firm.

Hugh said, 'What should we do?'

It was Alexander who answered. 'There is only one thing we can do.'

It was a hard-fought battle. Munro and Hugh ranged against Alexander and Maggie, Shaw caught in the middle, his opinion wavering from moment to moment. John Cunninghame stationed himself by Greenock's east window and refrained from comment. It hadn't been hard for Alexander to convince them Kate's best chance lay in an intervention by the Queen. What was in contention was Maggie's place in it all.

Munro was adamant. 'No. To involve the child. I will not do it.'

Maggie bridled. 'I am not a child, and besides…'

'We need her testimony.' Alexander was blunt. 'Not in court perhaps, but certainly before the Queen. The fact that she is barely more than a child, her look of innocence, will be in our favour. Yet she was of an age to know her parents when you left, to remember her own name, to understand she carried it no longer.'

Maggie broke in again. 'I hated to be called *Grant,* hate it still.'

'And that in itself adds weight to your testimony.'

Munro argued, 'Surely if I am in court and can testify that Kate is my living wife, the charge of possession cannot stand?'

'You also have been presumed dead, and could likewise be tainted.' Alexander paused to allow that thought to sink in, continued, 'Besides, there are the two other charges, and those the weightier, in that they threaten the Crown itself.'

'And Maggie's testimony will stand against those?'

'A counter charge of slander is oft the best chance.' Alexander was patient, as if to add weight to his argument. 'She can show malice in William and Maxwell, that they have a reason to lie. With the Queen, at least, that will tell. She knows Kate and, her pregnancy holding, has reason to wish her well. If she will speak on Kate's behalf, there is a chance the King will listen.'

Hugh suggested, 'What if we requested the trial to be held in the judiciary court? She is entitled to representation.'

Alexander shook his head. 'Entitled, yes, but it's unlikely either King or Council would look with favour on such an application. It is a pricy business and both are aye keen to cut costs. Hence the granting of commissions to the burghs.'

Munro asked, 'How many commissioners?'

John Cunninghame, remaining by the window, as if he thought he had no right to penetrate the family circle, said, 'Eight, by rights, though the quorum, so they claim, is three.'

'If we could touch them…'

There was a tinge of optimism in Munro's voice, instantly quashed by Cunninghame.

'William has seen to the commission: bringing in Hamilton and Fullerton, and while Fullerton may seek to be impartial, friendship with the Montgomeries is, as you know, quite enough to damn anyone in Hamilton's eyes.'

Hugh shifted, his tone resigned. 'No quarter there then.'

'Kate would not wish to put Maggie at risk.' It was Munro's final card.

Alexander dismissed it. 'She is already at risk. Do you think if William wins this he will stop at Kate? Aside from past history there is Broomelaw to think of.'

'Broomelaw was lost to us six years ago. I am not so foolish as to think we could ever recover it. And nor is William.'

John Cunninghame stepped fully into the pool of light cast by the twin-tiered candleholder suspended from the central beam, Alexander, noting the pallor of his face, fearing what he might say.

'No indeed. But the raising of your ghosts would taint William's title to Broomelaw and therefore be a problem, if not for him, then for Lady Glencairn and, I think, Glencairn himself. Your children are no safer than Kate. The best chance is that with the Queen's help you engineer Kate's release without the publicity of a trial.'

'And if the Queen cannot move James?' Munro voiced all their thoughts.

'Then Kate must escape, while there is still time. And that,' Cunninghame said, 'is not unheard of. Gaolers are often unwilling participants in the matter and aye poorly paid. I have word of where she is held and will do what I can.'

'And then what?'

'Either way, go, as you had intended, and as far from Scotland as is practical. Far enough at any rate to make it not worth William's while to pursue you.'

'Do you think he would let it lie, even if they are abroad?' Hugh's doubts were clear. 'Alive, there is always the chance they might decide to come home, claim what is rightfully theirs.'

Cunninghame's reply was firm, well thought out, a clear indication to Alexander that he had not been wasting the time he hovered in the shadows.

'Provide a letter of affirmation withdrawing all claim to Broomelaw. William is aye keen to save face, and if you aren't here, he may be content to leave you be.' A pause as if to allow Munro a chance to respond, then, 'I will contract to take the letter, to persuade him it is the best choice for all.'

Munro's breathing was fast, as if from running. 'You put aside your loyalties again on our behalf. It is...'

Cunninghame interrupted him. 'There are higher loyalties, as you and I both know. I would wish they were not in conflict with my family name, but though William I must see from time to time, conscience is with me always, and as a consequence is the more troublesome.'

It was simultaneously a confession of friendship and of faith, for which, Alexander thought, I trust he is not martyred.

371

Chapter 16

They left in the half-light that comes before the dawn, the Montgomeries, Munro and Maggie intent on making Linlithgow before supper time, John Cunninghame heading to Bishopton, to fulfil his promise to seek to attempt her escape. A promise Alexander doubted he would be able to keep, however much they all wished it. Riding east, the sun warm on their faces, he pondered the events of the last weeks, guilt that it had been he who had brought Kate to Edinburgh, gnawing at him. Small consolation that it had been compassion for the Queen driving them both. That once the King had word of Kate, they had no choice. It was a silent journey, even Maggie subdued, and all equally relieved when they reached the lochside below the palace unscathed.

The audience did not begin well, though if the Queen was startled by Alexander's request for a private hearing, she didn't show it. With a glance at Munro and Maggie, she dismissed all but one of her ladies, ordering her to remain in the corridor outside the chamber and refuse all entry, bar the King. She heard Alexander out without comment, her hand fluttering over the slight swell of her abdomen and the colour coming and going in her cheeks. 'So. Mistress Grant is not all she seemed.'

'It was a necessary evil, Your Grace.' Alexander contrived to sound contrite.

'I am to believe you now? And to petition the King on behalf of someone who has proved themselves deceitful?'

Alexander risked, 'It is an innocent woman who stands falsely accused, and in your power to aid her.'

'You flatter me.'

Munro's face reddened, Alexander putting out a hand to stay him, keeping his gaze fixed on the Queen. 'All know the importance of the bairn you carry, that Mistress Munro has been instrumental in bringing you thus far. It isn't flattery to think you would wish her ministrations to continue to a successful outcome.'

'You say she is innocent, convince me then...' A pause. 'If I am to persuade the King I will need more than your testimonial, however well disposed he is towards you. Witchcraft is, as you know, his obsession.' She shifted her attention to Maggie. 'Come here, child.'

Alexander, recognising the danger of Maggie bridling at the reference to child, pulled her forward, his hand on her shoulder encouraging her into a curtsey. The Queen raised her up.

'The King is not unkind, but will not listen well to a stuttering or a stammering. Can you speak plainly?'

Maggie nodded.

'Tell me then.'

Alexander saw the flicker of distaste on the Queen's face at Maggie's first mention of Maxwell. As the words spilled out he was aware of her growing confidence, of a perception that took him by surprise.

The Queen seemed equally impressed. 'You can swear to all this before God?'

Maggie's head came up. 'And the King.'

It brought a ghost of a smile to the Queen's face, a dry note to her voice. 'Well then. The King is not insensible to Mistress Grant's,' she corrected herself, 'Mistress Munro's worth, let us hope it will outweigh the deception. However, His Grace is at Craigmillar and not expected to return until Thursday.' And then, more gently, as if in response to Munro's indrawn breath, 'If the trial is to be Saturday there is still time.' She rose. 'When I have spoken to the King I will send word.' And this to Alexander. 'Do not think to presume on past favour. Make sure your story is straight. There will be no room for any uncertainty.' She touched Maggie's shoulder, spoke over her head to Munro. 'You may be proud of the child. I see the mother's clarity in her. You did right to bring her to me.'

Chapter 17

It was late afternoon before the call came. The King was seated before the empty fireplace, the Queen at his shoulder. Maggie could tell nothing from his tone as he greeted Alexander and Hugh. 'Ah, Montgomerie. Braidstane.' As they bowed, Hugh tugged at her and belatedly she remembered to curtsey. Lifting her gaze she darted a look at the Queen, but could tell nothing from her expression either.

Despite the cold hearth, James stretched out his legs, his accompanying pleasantry a clear signal the business would have to wait to the moment of his choosing. 'And how is the hunting in Ayrshire these days? Not worked out, I hope, before I have another opportunity of sampling it.'

'No indeed.' Hugh bowed again. 'Though the winter was harsh and there was some wastage, the herds are recovering and one or two of the older bucks have the makings of a fine chase. When your time permits...' He paused to allow James opportunity to cut in.

'Aye, well, we are oft about the east coast, our subjects in the west are less fortunate.' His sudden shift to the matter in hand took Maggie by surprise. 'This business of

Mistress *Grant, or Munro* as you now maintain,' the emphasis was unmistakeable, 'I trust you have a sound case to make.'

Alexander said. 'If it please you, Sire, I could perhaps explain the need for the deception.'

'Deception of any sort is not to our pleasing, especially so when it touches our Queen.'

Alexander acknowledged the reprimand, waited.

'Well, well, get on with it, man. You will not sway me by silence.'

Maggie watched the cat and mouse game playing out in front of her, fearing for the end result.

Alexander was choosing his words with care. 'It is a problem of six years standing, the root of it lying with the Cunninghames.'

James' eyes narrowed. 'The letters of affirmation stand, and Glencairn has proved himself peaceable. If you are to traduce him, it must be with solid proof.'

Alexander shook his head. 'Not the Earl. The problem lies with William, the Master of Glencairn.'

Hugh seemed about to interrupt, but Alexander placed a restraining hand on his arm, continued, 'Mistress Munro's husband, with whom we formed a friendship during the joyous festivities surrounding your marriage,' he bowed to the Queen, 'put himself at risk to preserve the truce between ourselves and the Cunninghames, and fell foul of William as a result.'

'Indeed.' A pause, James' expression unaltered.

'Munro left his family at Braidstane for safety's sake and there they have remained, taking the name of Grant, while he, as the harder to hide, joined the Scots Gardes in France.'

376

'And now?' There was a bored note in James' voice.

'My nephew, Patrick, also in the Scots Gardes...'

Maggie sensed James' impatience, a lack of sympathy, and guessed by the Queen's tightly clasped hands that she felt it too.

'He saved the French King's life, and in the process lost his own.'

They had James' full attention now. 'He sacrificed himself? At least you have the consolation it was a worthy death.'

Alexander pressed his advantage. 'We would not have known of it save that Munro, risking his own life, his family security, came to bring the news; the manner of Patrick's death, his last words, indeed a consolation.' He glanced towards the Queen. 'It was because Mistress Munro, out of a love and loyalty for Your Grace, answered the summons here, that William found her out, and it was here I believe he determined with Patrick Maxwell to hound her to her death. And he has chosen to claim witchcraft as his justification. We believe he knows full well her true identity, this charade but a way of safeguarding his claim to their tower, which he has taken as his own.'

It was not entirely accurate, Maggie aware Alexander was moving onto ground as treacherous as the marshland they'd traversed to reach the palace.

'The charges he brings?' James was upright in his seat, his expression sharp.

'Maxwell claims malefice, contending that Mistress Grant, as she is called, incites his wife to unnatural behaviours. But the more serious claims,' Alexander was moving on, clearly not wanting to give Maxwell's charge a chance to fester, 'those that William makes, are that she is possessed of the spirit of Mistress Munro, and therefore by the devil.

'You say William Cunninghame has made charges against her. That is one. What is the other?'

Alexander drew a deep breath. 'That she conspires to harm the Queen and her unborn child, which,' he said hurriedly, 'we can show to be wholly false.'

'Why appeal to me?' James was becoming restive again. 'It is to the Privy Council you should go. Without sufficient evidence, they will refuse a commission.'

'It is not to the Privy Council William has gone, but to Cowper, that he may make use of his standing commission, and of the Blawearie witch. I believe,' Maggie sensed Alexander's hesitation, 'money may have changed hands.'

It was the wrong thing to say. James was abrupt. 'Take your evidence to Cowper then. You do not charge him with falsity?'

'No indeed...' Alexander was clearly wrestling with how much to say.

James took control of the conversation. 'This charge of possession, what is William Cunninghame's basis for that?'

'That the Munros were killed in a reivers raid some six years ago, and Mistress Grant's close resemblance to Kate Munro, clear proof of a diabolical cause.'

A pucker appeared on James' brow.

Once again Hugh made to intervene and once again Alexander stopped him, as if afraid of what Hugh might say, or perhaps, Maggie thought, his manner, for Alexander's own words were blunt.

'The raid was a ruse, the burning carried out by Munro himself, that they might all be thought dead. We are

378

convinced William now knows Kate Munro escaped the fire, and so uses Munro's ploy against her.'

'Her husband will testify on her behalf?'

'Of course. But as he is reputed dead also, there is the risk he also will be claimed possessed.'

Hugh, refusing to be silenced, cut in. 'They cannot win. As Grants they are possessed, as Munros they are a threat to William, and therefore in equal danger.'

James pounced on the word. 'Threat? I am heartily sick of threat and counter-threat. I will not be part of it.'

Alexander glared at Hugh to silence him, sought to repair the damage done. 'William has laid claim to the Munro's old home, and though they have no thought of challenging his title to it, if he knows them both to be alive he will perceive them as a threat. Kate Munro is innocent, but if this trial goes ahead, win or lose, there will likely be blood spilt. William will blame us for the deception, and the truce we have sought to uphold these six years since may founder. That is why we seek your intervention, Sire, for the word of the King is the best, indeed the only chance of halting the trial, and, more importantly, preserving the peace in Ayrshire.'

Maggie saw her father flinch, the muscle pulsing at the corner of his eye, the knuckles of his balled fists standing out white, understood what it cost him to allow Alexander's assertion to remain unchallenged. In the silence that followed, she watched James' face, saw the issue hanging in the balance. The Queen moved closer to him, one hand massaging his shoulder, the other resting against her stomach, and weighed in on Kate's behalf.

'If Mistress Munro is cried a witch, even though she be proved innocent, our child is tainted. Would you wish that?'

It was the tipping point for James. 'I will halt the trial.'

Chapter 18

Kate had not thought it possible to fall asleep standing, but so it seemed. Though she was never allowed to remain so. Held in the belfry tower of the kirk at Bishopton, it seemed every time she looked as if she might fall into a stupor she was forced to trudge round and round the small space as if on a treadmill, until her legs felt like tree trunks and she could barely lift her feet. And when her eyelids flickered and her head dropped onto her chest so that she stumbled, she was jerked fully awake by the prick of a goad in her buttocks, as if she were a cow. She counted the hours and the days by the changing light and by her gaolers that she mentally named, in lieu of any better information, as *Surly*, *Bald*, *Fat*. They worked in rotation, their physical appearance so diverse it was easy for her to track the time, and each evening, when she slopped the watery porridge which was all that was provided, she used the handle of the spoon to scratch a mark on the wall, much to the amusement of the fat one, whose turn it was. At the first she had asked their names, volunteered hers, tried to engage them in conversation, aware that if she could somehow gain their sympathy, an opportunity for escape might follow, but all three had remained as silent as if they were both deaf and dumb, as indeed they might be for all she knew – useful attributes for a gaoler, no doubt.

Cowper came to her daily: persistent, questioning, his tone almost gentle, his assurances of her better treatment if she would only confess, renounce her friendship with the devil, re-affirm her faith in the true God, nibbling away at her resistance. Her resolve weakened in pace with her waning strength, so that she bit on her lip until it bled to stop herself from crying out what he wanted to hear.

She tried to blank him out with thoughts of the children, of Munro, of Broomelaw, to fill her mind with pictures of them to mask the other images threatening to overwhelm her: devils and cauldrons and black sabbaths, drawn, she knew, in her most lucid moments, from the pamphlets on daemonology which flooded the streets to fright more credulous folk. She had never given them much credence herself, not the caricatures at any rate, though she would not dispute the existence of the devil, for how else to explain the undoubted evils in the world. But she had never seen him, nor sold herself to him, and that she clung to, for if she would not confess, then surely there was nothing on which to convict.

It was the third day, when blinking failed to dislodge the grit which had become a constant irritant in her eyes, and the hollow in her stomach had settled into a dull ache, that she found herself falling. Everything around her, walls, rafters, ceiling, even the floor under her feet, was fracturing, dissolving, losing substance. A blessed blackness rising up to meet her, the pain of the goad fading. When she came to, she was below the surface of the lake by Broomelaw, choking, and then wrenched into the air again, water streaming down her face and hair into a bucket between her knees. Figures clustered around her, light pouring through the newly opened shutters, assaulting her eyes afresh, voices, fading in and out: Cowper's and another, that try as she might she couldn't name, though she shivered at the sound. She began to crumple again and was forced back onto her knees, the gaoler's fingers digging into her shoulders, her skin crawling at his touch. He turned her round, dragging her head back by the hair, the faces of her antagonists swimming into the centre of her vision: Cowper, and behind him William Cunninghame and Maxwell; and to the side a man holding a prick and a woman who stared through her as if unseeing.

'Bring her a chair.' That was Cowper. 'She is little use to us unconscious.'

'Scots law does not require a confession. Evidence can be presented conscious or not, and evidence we have.' That was William. She tried to bring her mind to order, to concentrate on what was said, to make a choice: silence or defence. A verse of scripture came to her: 'When he was reviled, reviled not again...' She would not make a good martyr. Lifting her head she focused on William, his features blurring in front of her, forced out, 'Lies. All lies.'

'On whose part, Mistress *Grant*. Yours?' Maxwell gestured to the pricker to step forward, but Cowper forestalled him.

'This is a preliminary hearing, and will be done decently and in order that there be no cause for dispute.' He cleared his throat, read out the charges. 'That on the 13th June in the year of our Lord 1597, you did...' Kate kept her head raised, refusing to be cowed, despite the weight of the words: 'Maleficence … possession … consorting with the devil, conspiring to harm the Queen and her unborn child.'

'No!' The denial burst from her. 'As God is my witness, no!'

Cowper's eyes were fixed on hers. 'Name?' he asked.

She hesitated – to say *Grant* would be a lie, and one they might could use against her, to say *Munro*, likely equally dangerous. She switched her gaze back to William, saw the mockery of a smile playing about his lips, found the needed courage. 'Mistress Munro, of Broomelaw, in the parish of Renfrew.'

'Need we hear more?' William, the smile gone, towered over Cowper. 'Either she lies or she is possessed. Mistress Munro is dead and buried these six years since, as I can testify. Let her be pricked.'

Cowper nodded and the pricker approached her. It was the first time Kate had seen a prick at close hand, and despite the horror of it she found herself admiring the workmanship: the geometric carving on the hexagonal wooden handle, the slender three-inch pin – a pity that beauty should be so abused. The pricker bound a rag tight about her eyes, her stomach revolting against the mingled smells of sweat and vomit. She was aware of her shift thrust aside, of hands massaging her neck and throat, moving downwards over her shoulders and breasts, of another smell, faint but distinct – honey. So that is how they do it. A preparation of honey and laurel seeds, the poor man's theriac, was something she had often used as an anaesthetic to dull sensation before lancing a boil. Though she wouldn't have thought it effective against a pricker's tool.

'If you are innocent,' It was Cowper again, his voice detached, 'you have only to tell us how many times you are pricked and where.'

It was impossible. Twice, three times she felt a momentary coolness, as if the pricker had touched her skin with a coin, the sensation so light and of such short duration she had no chance of marking the source. It was not what she expected, for anaesthetic or not, she should have felt the pin driven home. From the depths of her memory an illustration of an assassin's blade, an accompanying flash of understanding – the prick was retractable, the lack of pain nothing more than evidence of the fraudulent nature of the whole charade. Was Cowper part of it? Or himself a dupe?

William again. 'You see. No pain. No blood. She is no innocent. We have a quorum, why should we not finish the business now?'

'You cannot be both witness and jury.' Cowper was surprisingly firm. The blindfold removed, Kate saw him look across at the woman. 'Mistress Aitken, do you recognise this person?'

'Aye, that I do.'

William barked, 'Is this the one you told us of?'

'She is.' Mistress Aitken recoiled as if from an apparition, her voice rising an octave, her finger outstretched, pointing at Kate. 'I see the devil, crouching on her shoulder,' she brought her hand down, 'and there, by her side, her familiar.' She grasped at her neck, shrieking, pulling aside her blouse, and when she removed her hand they could see scratches with blood beading from them. 'See where her cat attacked me.'

Cowper said, 'It is enough. The commission will be held on Saturday. All evidence will be presented then.'

Towards noon the belfry door opened again, the surly gaoler flexing his shoulders, preparing to leave. He registered a surprise Kate also felt, as instead of the usual fat gaoler, a lumpier figure entered, a rough cloak bundled around him, his breeches worn, a flat bonnet pulled down over his forehead. He gestured towards the door, answered the unspoken question, 'Duncan is as spiked as a pig on a spit, and I am forced to take his turn.' And with a scowl, 'To be dragged out on a dirty day such as this, he'll pay, see if he doesn't.' Then, contempt in his voice, 'Is she troublesome?'

'Nothing you can't handle,' the gaoler winked, 'if you've a mind to handle, my preference is for a bit more beef.' He handed over the keys, clumped away, the hinges of the door protesting as it shut behind him.

Kate waited, tense, until they heard the outer door at the foot of the stair also shut. She crossed her arms over her chest as John Cunninghame removed his bonnet.

'How did you...?'

'Don't ask.' He shook off his cloak, revealing a bundle tucked under his arm. 'Here. We don't have a lot of time. There is a funeral coming. A big one. If we can mingle with it you've a chance.' His gaze flicked towards the window. 'And the dirty day, though not the most pleasant, may yet play to our advantage.'

She was trying to wrestle into the dress, her arms refusing to co-operate. With an apologetic glance, she said, 'Can you...'

He worked the sleeves up over her arms, straightened the shoulders.

She looked down at the line of buttons on the bodice, and at her fingers, chapped with cold and shaking. 'I'm sorry, these aren't much use the now.'

Avoiding her eyes, he bent down to fasten the buttons, waving aside her thanks. He drew a woollen cloak around her shoulders, produced a cap and set it on her head, bunching up her hair inside it, said, with a glimmer of a smile, 'I'm not much better, it's as well you don't have a glass.' The bucket in which her head had been ducked still stood in the middle of the floor, the rag with which she'd been blindfolded, discarded beside it. He picked it up and plunged it into the water. 'A white face you'll get away with in the circumstances, one streaked with grime you likely wouldn't.'

He was gentle as he scrubbed at her cheeks and her hands, the pressure bringing warmth back into them. You can get used to anything, she thought, breathing in again the sour smell of the rag, managing not to gag. As he cleaned her up, he outlined the plan: the layout of the church, the best position to stand, the direction they should take as they filed out. 'I've no idea how long we'll have to stand, but the chief mourners don't look as if they've paid for any more than the most rudimentary of services. And with luck thereafter all will disperse in different directions. The drizzle I trust a help to us and not a hindrance.' A smile, a grimace towards their clothing. 'Not the most fashionable, I know, but by what I saw of others, suitable attire.' She looked down, a mistake, the floor beginning to move beneath her. He grasped her arm, steadied her, steered her onto the chair, and kneeling, eased her feet into a pair of soft slippers. A flicker of concern crossed his face. 'These were the best I could manage under my cloak. It's a step to where I have horses waiting. Will you be able for walking in them?'

She straightened her shoulders. 'Oh, I've had plenty of practice at walking in the last few days, and without the benefit of any footwear. At least this time there will be a purpose to it.'

'The horses are hidden in a copse at the foot of the hill, if we can make it to them...'

Below they could hear the church door groaning, the clack of pattens on flagstones, a muted hubbub. 'Ready?' He opened the door, allowed her to precede him, locked it behind them. 'With luck we'll have an hour or two before they discover your loss.'

The church was packed tight, folk pressed into every alcove, the drone of the minister lost in the shuffling of feet and the scratchings and scufflings that came from the crumbling walls behind Kate. Her back was against a bulge in the stone, the irregularity digging into her spine. She shifted sideways to relieve the pressure, stepping on a piece of string, had a moment to wonder why it was there, to lift her foot before she felt it whip across her slipper, a sharp pain in her ankle, the scrabbling of claws on her leg. That the church was mouse infested was so commonplace, the pain of the bite so trivial, compared to what she had suffered in the past days, she found it hard to choke down the laugh that rose in her throat, to turn it into a sob. John Cunninghame, as if aware of the hysteria threatening to engulf her, put his arm about her shoulder, buried her face against his chest.

At the front of the kirk the minister pronounced the benediction, the mourners squeezing back to allow the shrouded body to be carried shoulder-high down the nave and out into the mirk. And then the pressure eased, those who had come to watch, to mourn, perhaps to gloat, straggling out after them.

'Come on, we mustn't lag too far behind.'

The drizzle was still falling, fine, but persistent, the air damp enough to ensure folk weren't tempted to linger about the entrance gossiping. As they emerged from the kirk, Kate paused under the overhang of the porch to pull the cloak more tightly around her, Cunninghame, placing his hand under her elbow, encouraging her onwards. The majority of mourners were following the cart carrying the body, but others drifted away in twos and threes in all directions.

'Come on,' he said again, and then, with a swift glance at her face, 'Let me help.' He placed his arm around her waist and half-supported her, half-led her down the hill and across the field towards a clump of trees, his relief visible when they came upon the horses tethered among the birches.

As he linked his fingers to make a step for her to mount, she asked, 'Where are we headed?'

'Ardrossan. When they discover you've gone it will be to Greenock Castle they'll look. Or Braidstane. John Shaw took a vessel round the coast when first you were taken and has waited in the lee of the castle since. He will get you to France.

'Are Munro and the girls already away?'

'Ellie is with John Shaw, Munro, Maggie and the Montgomeries are at Linlithgow, making an appeal to the Queen on your behalf.'

'And you? If William hears of this...'

'I can take care of myself. When I heard you were taken, the charges William was bringing, I could do no other than go to Greenock to pass the warning on.'

She put out her hand, touched his arm. 'How can we ever repay...?'

'No need. There is no reason William should learn of this.' He was swinging into the saddle, closing the conversation. 'If we should be pursued ... I pray not, but, if we should, make for Beith, and then Dalry. From there it is but a few miles to the shore. If need be, I will draw them off your tail.'

She wasn't fooled by his optimism, but recognising there was nothing to be gained by dwelling on difficulties, offered, 'I am grateful. I know what this might cost you.' It was little enough to say.

His eyes belied his brusque response. 'You've enough troubles of your own to think on, without wasting thought on mine.'

They were past Dalry, the isolated lights of the farms around Dalgarven in the valley below them, pinpricks in a dark sky, when the fog struck. A blanket of white silence, blotting out the surrounding landscape as if it had never been. Kate could make out Cunninghame off to her left, and the ground a few feet ahead of them, nothing more. It was as if they were the only two people in the world. She felt her horse bunch under her, knew he prepared to bolt. Instinctively she leant forward, turning him sideways onto the wind, laying her head against his neck, murmuring into his ear, aware that Cunninghame did the same. With the fog came rain: silent, vertical. Fear coursed through her. She looked across at Cunninghame. Although only two feet away, he was haloed in white, ghostly, insubstantial, her own apprehension mirrored in his face.

'What do we do?'

'We must keep moving or we and the horses alike will take a chill.' He ran his hand down the horse's neck. 'And though this isn't pleasant, at least we are safe from pursuit. We have made good time, and no more than an hour should see us safe to Ardrossan. You at least will be welcomed at the castle.'

She forced herself to think of practicalities, to block out the images of Maggie and Munro, perhaps similarly caught, which threatened to unman her. The wind had dropped, the stillness unnerving. Another fear taking her. 'How can we be sure we're going in the right direction?'

'The river was below us to the left. We should be able to follow it along.' An attempt at a grin. 'Provided we turn downstream and not up.'

Kate, still battling the images of her family, had a more hopeful thought. 'Perhaps the mist is only up here. The valley may be clear.'

'Perhaps.' Cunninghame gathered the reins, clicked to his horse to move on. Without response. Kate pressed firmly with her heels and, with a wry smile of apology for her success where he had failed, moved off. It was the lead his horse required, and side by side they picked their way down the hillside. It was an odd sensation moving through the mist, as disorientating as a child's game of blind man's buff. She was concentrating on holding her direction, her grip on the reins so tight her fingers cramped. Cautiously she flexed them, one at a time, forced herself to relax her hold. Visibility was down to almost nil, the rain increasing in intensity. She bent her head, focusing on scouring the ground beneath them for hazards. Sought to smother the image of Anna lying like a rag doll on the slope above Broomelaw, her neck broken, her horse cropping at the grass nearby. Impossible not to fear a similar fate might befall them. It would be ironic indeed to be put beyond the reach of William Cunninghame by death of a different sort. Her horse stumbled, one hoof catching in a tangle of bramble. She slipped sideways, and, hauling herself back upright, halted to steady him. Cunninghame looked round, questioning, but she mouthed, 'I'm fine.' He nodded, took a firmer grip of his own reins. The changing ground cover, from rough moorland to grassy tussocks, was if anything more hazardous than it had been higher up. On any normal journey Kate would have thought little of crossing similar ground, only refraining from pushing her horse too hard. But now, with visibility one to two feet at most, difficulties were hard to anticipate, impossible to prepare for. Nor was there any thinning of the mist to encourage them. She halted again, waited for him to come close, fought down a rising panic. 'We should surely have reached the river by now.'

He made a good show of certainty. 'We are still a wee way from the valley floor. Once there, even if we have strayed, it won't have been far.'

He was right. It was a matter of a few minutes only before Kate sensed the ground levelling out, becoming soft. Optimism surged through her, reinforced by the trickling of water, the muted clicking of hoof on gravel, signifying their proximity to a river bed. Cunninghame gestured her to a halt, and swinging down from the saddle threw her his reins.

She bent down to catch what he said.

'It will take but a moment to check the direction of the flow.' He nodded at the mist. 'Once done, I shall call out, guide you to join me.'

She saw the shift of his shoulders, indicating the release of a tension he wouldn't have admitted to, and relaxed a fraction in response. He disappeared, the mist swallowing him whole, muting his footfall on the gravel, the only sound the occasional soft scuffle as if he slipped.

Her clothes were sodden, weighed down by the rain; the cold seeping through her. On impulse she dismounted, and, looping both sets of reins over her arm, attempted to wring out her skirt. Difficult as it was she worked around it, twisting it tightly, trying to avoid dripping the water onto her already sodden slippers. And having made the best job she could, had time to be thankful for her lack of underskirts. The call came, and following Cunninghame's voice she led both horses into the river bed. He summoned a smile as she reached him. 'The water level is surprisingly low, especially with the rain we've had, but that's to our advantage.' As he handed her into the saddle she returned his smile, allowed herself to think: this time tomorrow we will be safe away.

A low rumble from behind them barely registered before her smile turned to a soundless scream as the wall of water hit. She felt the horse's legs buckle under her, and instinctively clung on, tangling her hands in the mane as the reins were ripped away. She had no time to see what was happening to John Cunninghame, all her efforts concentrated on holding on, as the water lifted and carried them. She lay close along the horse's neck, gripping with knee and thigh

393

in an attempt to cheat the water of a target. Branches from an overhanging tree whipped across her face, snagged on her saddle, the mane, the trailing reins. Blood was trickling into her open mouth, and she raised her arm to brush it aside, then grasped at the mane again as they reached a bend in the river course and were flung first to one side then the other. The horse's limbs were flailing as he tried to find footing and she heard his leg snap. He crumpled under her and she was thrown over his head, landing in a rush of water that tumbled and pummelled her, carrying her along in a boiling cauldron of branches and greenery and rolling boulders. She had no thought, only to try to keep her head above water, to force herself not to fight the power of it, to let it take her where it would.

Something soft dunted against her, spun her round: a sheep, sodden and cold, and though she recoiled from the lifeless eyes, she wrapped her fingers in the tight curled hair, wrapping herself around its body. On the periphery of her vision a tree overhung the river. She reached out, grabbed, ignoring the searing pain as her hand scraped along the bark, lost her grip, reached again, but too late. Thoughts of the children made her redouble her efforts to keep afloat. She was swept past another one, and a third, and each time she tried to get sufficient grip to allow her to haul herself to the bank. Then they were past the copse, her opportunity gone. She felt the cold seeping into her, sapping her strength, knew that with every moment she remained in the water her chance of survival diminished. Still she fought to avoid being sucked under, fought her own creeping inertia. The river swung to the right, and on the turn the sheep snagged on a mound of debris, and losing her grip, Kate was catapulted high onto a bank of gravel above the curve of the bend.

Chapter 19

John Cunninghame, closer to the centre of the watercourse when the flash flood hit, was swept past Kate in an instant and still upright as he lost his hold on the reins. He was torn from the saddle and tossed in the rush of water, with barely time to draw air before he was sucked under by the swirling current. He shot back to the surface, his lungs bursting, gulped in more air, was sucked under again, resurfaced. He was fighting the force of the water, trying to make for the bank, looking for something to cling onto. Thought of Kate – useless to expect to see her, the mist shrouding all but a few feet in either direction, but if he could only hear her voice, know she was still alive... He tried to shout for her, but as soon as he opened his mouth water surged in, choking him, and with it the realisation there was little enough he could do to save himself, nothing at all he could do for her. As the current swung him sideways, a half-submerged gate tumbled past, trailing a bundle of bulrushes, but before he could grasp it, the submerged portion took his legs from under him and he was once again plunged downwards. It took every ounce of his strength to break the surface of the water, his leg twisted at an odd angle, his foot trapped in the angle between diagonal and upright. Carried along on his side, bouncing off rocks, one minute under, one minute his face clear, he concentrated on gasping in air when he could, holding his breath when he couldn't. Focused on his breathing, he failed to see the overhanging tree, his first knowledge of it the crack on his head which knocked him senseless. His only good fortune, had he but known it, that the strength of the blow freed his foot and flung him face up into the centre of the river. He came to with the detritus of the flood in his hair and his mouth and stuck to his clothing: straw and twigs, cow-pat and sheep droppings. The mist had lifted a foot or so above the surface of the water, and as the flood swept him on he could see meadow, the bases of trees, a dirt track leading off into the distance. Ahead of him the river took another sweep, the current taking him into an undercut in the curve of the bend and to a rotten tree trunk jammed up against the banking. He lunged and caught and held, while the surging water sucked at him, and when he had recovered his breath, began to inch his way along the tree trunk towards the side and safety.

Landed, his first thought was for the track, but standing up he could see no further than a few feet. It was only as he dropped back onto his stomach it was revealed, stretching some fifty yards away to his right. He took his bearings, stood up and made for it. Twice more he dropped down, checked he was still going in the right direction, adjusted his path, stood up again, moved on. Finally he reached it, tripping over the ridged edging into the rut beyond. He had no idea which direction to turn but was past caring, for both ways must lead somewhere.

Instinct drove him uphill. He was tired, every muscle aching, the rush of relief almost winding him as a wall reared on his left-hand side. He followed it along, stumbled through a gateway, tried to call out, his voice a croak. There were people around him, supporting him up a steep wooden stair and through a low doorway, setting him down on a settle beside a roaring fire. A girl knelt at his feet, pulling at his boots. A woman pressed a drink into his hand.

Chapter 20

Winded, Kate lay for what seemed like hours, aware of little except the damp embrace of the mist and the muted roar of the water surging past. Her clothes were torn, her face scratched and stinging, and as she put up her hand to her hair she felt a tangle of weed and small twigs protruding in all directions – stand up, that was what she must do. But when she tried, a stab of pain shot through her ankle. Crawl then. Important to move in the right direction, to avoid tipping herself back into the foaming water. She had been fortunate once, she might not be so again. Drawing as wide a circle as she could with her hand, she found the edge of the banking, mud crumbling under her fingers, and edged backwards, gritting her teeth against the pain. When she judged it safe, she eased herself around, and, heading away from the river, came up against a tree. She hauled herself into a sitting position against the trunk, began a systematic exploration of her injuries.

Aside from her foot, it seemed she had escaped lightly, though when she drew up her sleeve her arm was a maze of scratches and grazes, the exposed flesh a shining pink, the surrounding skin pitted with grit. And from the feel of it the rest of her body was a match for her arm. Her face was on fire, water running down her cheek. She brushed at it with her hand, and discovering it was blood, not water, traced it back to its source: a wide gash on her forehead. Raising her skirt she tore a strip from her shift and, folding it into a wad, pressed it against the cut, temporarily staunching the flow. Then thought better of it. If she allowed it to bleed out a little it would help to clean the wound, and that likely more important than the loss of a little blood. Working blind to clean the cut would be difficult, gauging the length of time to allow the flow of blood impossible, but a few minutes would do no harm.

While she waited, she hitched her skirt and used the the tail of her damp shift to take the worst of the dirt from her hands, then sucked hard on her fingers, grimacing at the taste. She tore another strip of cloth and spat on it, thankful for the antiseptic properties of saliva. She dabbed at the edges of the wound on her forehead, careful, despite her attempt at disinfecting them, to keep her fingers out of the cut, wincing at every touch. She would be more sympathetic in future to the reactions of others to her ministrations, having had opportunity to experience them for herself. If she had a future. A thought immediately stifled. Her cheek was swollen, her left eye beginning to close. She would be a pretty picture tomorrow. Not that it would count for anything if she couldn't find shelter and quickly. And how to accomplish that with her ankle, sprained at the least and more likely broken, she had no idea. Nor was there much likelihood of anyone finding her unless the mist lifted. For who would be foolish enough to be out in this.

She rubbed her hands up and down her arms as briskly

as she could to try to stop her shivering, clamping her teeth together to avoid their chattering. Marshalled her thoughts. Where there was one tree there would likely be more and perhaps a gathering of leaves in the lee of a fallen trunk she could burrow into to provide some heat. A more immediate need struck her. Lying against this tree she faced the water still roaring a few feet away. Should there be another surge … the last thing she wanted was to be swept away for a second time. She inched around the trunk until it was between her and the river bed, then lay on her stomach and began to inch forward, sweeping her arms from side to side to test the ground ahead of her. The greater the distance she could put between herself and the water, the safer she would be. She had heard talk of flash floods and from the warmth of Broomelaw's fireside had spared a thought for the safety of those caught in them, but had never understood the full horror of it until now.

She crawled from tree to tree, the carpet of leaf mould under her at least soft. One hand knocked against the stem of a stinkhorn, and as it snapped she gagged, tried not to breath in. After what seemed like hours she emerged from the wood, the grass under her hands short, as if well-grazed. Her fingers found the round hard droppings of sheep, relief flooding her. Where there was stock, there would be habitation and people. If she could only walk… She made another attempt at standing, but once again her foot gave way under her, and she reconciled herself to slow progress. At least crawling she wouldn't stumble into another hazard.

The track cut across the slight rise, sharp stones digging into Kate's palm as she swept the ground in front of her. She turned to follow the edge of it, hope leaping. It led, not to a house, but to a small sheepfold, the rough wooden gate tied shut. As she sagged against it, trying to quell her disappointment, Kate heard the soft mehing of sheep, smelled the damp wool, felt the gate butted from the inside. She inched further along, stretched her hand up to gauge the height of the wall. It would at least be shelter, and that her primary need. The light was failing, adding the dangers of night to the mist, no thinner than before. Ignoring the pain in her ankle and trying to place all her weight on her other foot, she pulled herself up until she straddled the top of the wall and hitched her leg over. Her foot came up against a sheep which shifted backwards, bleating, the movement sufficient to topple her so that she found herself on the ground, jammed between a sheep and the wall, her good leg bent under her. She was aware of pain, of breath being squeezed out of her, of slipping into a darkness that seemed like relief.

And that was how the shepherd found her, semi-conscious, her head buried against the belly of a sheep. As he picked her up she began to come round, struggling against his grasp, but he shushed her as if a child. She was dimly aware of a face, creased, like old leather, startling blue eyes staring at her, blurring. For the second time she fainted. And came to again to the smell of cooked cabbage and a roughness against her cheek. Her hand explored the space around her, found the edge of the horsehair blanket, the stitching under her fingers uneven. A voice above her, an arm supporting her, a cup held to her lips. She began to drink, but got only halfway through before her eyelids drooped and the room receded again.

When she next woke it was to the soft light of a single rushlight, shadows chasing around plain walls. She grasped the edge of the pallet, pulled herself to a sitting position, tried to speak.

'Wheest. There's no need for speech yet.' There was a soft highland burr to the woman's voice. 'Time enough for that when you are full awake.' She was stirring a pot over a fire that smoked in the corner of the room. 'Will you take some broth? You likely haven't eaten in a while.'

Kate managed a nod and a croak. 'Thank you … yes.' Looking down she noted the shift she wore, which though of a coarse material was clean enough and dry. She gestured to it. 'My clothes?'

The woman laughed. 'My mother is but lately dead and her clothes lying spare.' A pause, an oblique glance. 'Seeing the state of your own, I suspicioned you'd neither be too proud, nor superstitious, to borrow what we had.'

Kate smiled in return, though a tightness in her face made it an effort.

'I am grateful, but…'

As if she read her mind, the woman said, 'There will be no need to think of repayment, now or ever. Here. Take this. It may not look much, but it will strengthen you, none the less.' She passed over a bowl from which steam rose. 'It is little enough we have done and no more than anybody would, my man finding you lying there among the sheep, half-dead, and covered in debris like so much flotsam left behind by the tide.'

It was a question of sorts, and Kate, doubly grateful not to be directly quizzed, offered, 'Flotsam is right: we were en route to Ardrossan when the fog hit, and thinking it safest to follow the river down to Dalgarven we were caught in a flash flood and...' She stopped, her hand flying to her mouth. 'Oh dear God ... John.' She swung her leg over the edge of the pallet, put her foot to the floor, and, attempting to stand, crumpled again, pain shooting from her ankle to her knee.

The woman supported her back onto the pallet. 'You'd best bide where you are the now while I take a look at your ankle. Whoever you've lost, you're no use to him if you canna walk. It isna a bairn?'

'No. A friend to our family.'

'Well then. You have survived, no reason why he shouldn't also. And as for Ardrossan, if there's someone we can send to, Archie'll take a message for you in the morn.' And then, as if she sensed Kate's desire for action now, 'Forbye that it's gone midnight, the fog is still thick and there'll be no one going anywhere until it lifts. Or no if they've any wit.' Her fingers were probing the swollen flesh around Kate's ankle, clearly looking for an edge of bone. She nodded. 'You may be grateful, it's a sprain, no a break. Bound, you may be fit to hobble in a day or two.' She busied herself stirring a powder into a glass of water. 'It's sleep you're needing the now. A dose of this will see you through till morning.'

Kate, more used to giving decoctions than to taking them, allowed herself to be supported as she drank from the bowl. She grimaced; aniseed she recognised and vinegar, vervain perhaps, but there was an undertone in it she couldn't place.

The woman smiled. ''Tis laurel, a wee pickle only, but as effective for bruising on the inside as arnica is on the outside, and catnip for its sedative properties.'

Kate opened her mouth to query further: the proportions, the specific method of preparation, but found instead her speech slurring, her eyes closing. As she gave into the sleep stealing over her, she promised herself not to leave without discussing the remedy in detail.

Chapter 21

William Cunninghame, about to spike a lump of cheese with his dirk, swung around, the blade slicing past the ear of the lad who hovered by his shoulder.

He snarled, 'How could this happen?'

Cowper remained standing beyond arm's length. 'There was a funeral. She must have slipped away among the mourners.'

'A woman with little clothing and no footwear manages to walk out of a locked belfry and into a funeral! Where was the gaoler?'

'One has disappeared. Whether paid or despatched we don't know...'

As William sprang to his feet the lad retreated further, tried to make himself inconspicuous.

Cowper also stepped back. 'When it came to the changing of the watch the first gaoler was relieved by a man who claimed to be standing in for Duncan. He had no reason to doubt it.'

William's dirk clattered onto the table. 'He had every reason. You do not pay him to allow a stranger to sail in on his own say-so. Or if you do you're less competent than I thought you.' He strode to the window, grasped the cill. 'When was this?'

'Today, around noon.'

William slammed his fist against the window frame, rattling the sash. 'Three hours march on us: she could be anywhere by now.'

Cowper cleared his throat. 'She's unlikely to have got far, for the fog struck not long after, and would have put paid to travel for all but the most foolhardy.'

'Or desperate.' William's mouth was set in a thin line. 'As we may assume she was.' He spun round, took a step towards Cowper, the expression on his face causing the boy to edge towards the door. 'What measures have you taken to find her?'

'Enquiries are being made among the mourners and I have sent to Greenock; if it is to the Shaws she has gone, we will know of it.'

'If it is to the Shaws she has gone then she has less brain than a peahen, and I don't recollect stupidity among the charges brought against her...' William broke off. 'Though the whereabouts of John Shaw's ships, now *that* would be useful intelligence.' He snapped his fingers, turned to the boy who halted his sideways shuffle. 'Have you subtlety, boy?'

It was safest to nod, though he didn't understand the word.

William spelt it out. 'Go to Renfrew, enquire of ships trading to Veere. The cargoes they carry, the frequency of their voyages, the names of the owners. The story is you have a master with business to put someone's way. That the man your master seeks will be reliable and have more than one vessel at his disposal. I wish to know the numbers of those ships and where they are, that I might examine them for myself.' He tossed a purse at him. 'This is for information, mind. And make sure you get what you pay for.'

The boy picked his way through the clutter of broken fishing creels and trails of net. Below him a line of small vessels listed against the harbour wall, their hulls protruding from the mud beneath, waiting the rising tide. He hailed the first boat, the only response the gulls which rose from the deck, protesting. He tried the second and the third, with equal failure.

'Ye'r wasting ye'r time, boy.' The man's teeth were yellowed, his breath strong. He jerked his head towards the taverns lining the landward side of the harbour. 'If there's anybody to be found, that's where they'll be, but,' he grinned, 'if it's sense ye'r wanting, ye'r likely chapping, for wi' the haar, the drinkin' has started early and runs late, and it'll be sore heids all round and no much else the day.' A sly look crept across the man's face. 'But there's no much I dinnae ken aboot the ships that harbour here. I could maybes gie ye the information yer after.' He extended his hand, palm upwards.

The boy shook his head.

'Nae coin, nae clack.' The man spat, his aim perfect, the phlegm glistening on the toe of the boy's boot.

That it had been a mistake to refuse him became clear to the boy when he dipped his head into the first tavern. Though there were a handful of men spread about, none of them were awake. A few were sprawled on benches, mouths hanging slack, snoring, others lay stretched across the table tops, heads pillowed on their arms, and from all of them fumes rolled in waves, keeping time with their breathing. He ducked back into the air, the thought of William, the likely consequence of returning without news, a fear gnawing at his belly.

'I tell't ye.' The man was at his side again. 'Hae ye money or hae ye no?'

The boy fished in his jerkin. 'For the right information, aye.' He tried to make his voice firm. 'But I willna pay for gossip just.'

'Will ye no? Well now, let's see what information ye'r needin.'

The man was mocking him, but there was little choice. 'My master seeks a ship or two trading to Veere, regular-like and reliable. Does Renfrew hae any such?'

The man extended his hand, waited.

The boy removed a groat from his jerkin, fingered it, but as the man reached for it, closed his fist. 'When I hae yer answer, ye'll hae your money.'

'If it's mair as one ship ye'r wanting, then John Shaw's yer man.'

'Which ships are his then?'

The man thrust his hand forward, rubbing his thumb against his fingers, and grasping the groat the boy proffered, bit it, then, 'They're no here and nor is John Shaw.'

The boy lunged to reclaim the groat, but the man stepped back, clutching it to his chest.

Again the sly look. 'But I maybes ken whaur he is.'

'Where?'

'It'll cost ye.'

The boy produced another groat, held it tighter than

before. 'Ye'll get nae mair out o' me until ye tell me all I want to know.'

They were like a pair of dogs, sniffing around each other, the man backing down first.

'Word is ye'll find Shaw and yin o' his ships by Ardrossan Castle, a commission ah dare say; the others are all awa, twa to Veere and yin, they say to France.'

The boy nodded, trying to hide his satisfaction, flipped the coin into the air for the man to catch. 'No point in waiting here then.'

William received him in the solar.

'Ardrossan eh? You're sure?'

The boy nodded. 'He seemed to know; at any rate, he was the best to be had, most of the sailors the worse for wear, the haar having laid all the ships up.'

'He'd better be.'

It seemed a dismissal, and so the boy took it, scuttling towards the stair.

'Aren't you forgetting something?' William caught his shoulder. 'Did you spend all I gave you, or did you think to keep some for yourself?'

'No!' The boy was shaking as he thrust his hand into his jerkin. 'I didna mean…'

'I trust not.' William took the proffered coins and released the boy with a push towards the door. 'Next time make sure you remember…'

Maxwell halted the boy in the doorway. 'News?'

Satisfaction sparked in William's eyes. 'John Shaw has taken a ship to Ardrossan.'

'Hardly his normal practice, it cannot be for any other purpose than to aid in Mistress Munro's escape. And no doubt Eglintoun in on it.'

'Indeed. We'll need to move fast to have a chance of catching up with her.'

'Shall I send word to Cowper?'

'Time enough for that once Kate Munro is safely back in our hands, and it will be a particular pleasure,' William's eyes were alight, 'to take her from under Eglintoun's nose.'

'Do you know who helped her to escape?'

'No. but when I do…' William left the sentence hanging.

'When you do,' Maxwell fingered his sword, 'I'd enjoy to deal with him.'

'We may both have that gratification.' William snapped his fingers again, indicated to the boy. 'Perhaps now is the time to send for Cowper. Not even the Earl of Eglintoun himself could dispute *his* right of rearrest.' A smile spread across his face. 'Nor, if the trial were to be at Saltcoats, could anyone dispute Hamilton's position as a juror. If we send now the whole can be wrapped up before the Sabbath.'

411

Chapter 22

Towards afternoon the haar lifted from the inland valleys, though strands still clung along the shoreline, the ships docked at Saltcoats riding the mist as they would normally the sea. To Kate, jolting along in the cart the shepherd had borrowed from a near neighbour for the journey to Ardrossan, the sight of the masts reaching straight up into the sky was a welcome one, their angle indicating the tide was well up. Off to the right, in the distance, she could see Ardrossan Castle, rearing proud on the skyline, and though she had never been there, she took a moment to be thankful for the kindness of the Montgomeries, one and all. She was thinking of Ellie, of France, whether she or the girls would prove good sailors, and if they did not ... well, seven or eight days at sea could be borne and safety at the end of it. She thought of the farmhouse at Cayeux. Though Maggie might take more persuading. But it would be a fine thing if they could all be together again, even if Munro and Robbie would likely only blow in and out as their service for the French King dictated. She would settle for that. She looked down at her wrists, still bearing the marks of her confinement – I will settle for anything, if so be it is a chance for my family to be free of William Cunninghame. There were those of her patients she would miss, and some she knew would feel her loss, but so be it. She would have liked to see John Cunninghame once more, to know if he too survived the flash flood, to thank him for what he had done, but to go looking for him would be a foolishness, and selfish besides. If he had survived, and she prayed God that he had, the less contact between them the better, for him, and for his place within his own family.

They covered the ground in less time than she expected, no more than half a mile ahead, spanning the gulley, a narrow bridge leading to the castle. In the bay a single ship moored in easy reach of the shore.

'Nearly there, mistress.' The shepherd turned his head to smile at her as he steered the cart towards the bridge. She saw his smile turn to apprehension, and glancing round in her turn, saw the riders approaching fast from the rear, knew that it wasn't in friendship they came. The first rider leant across, dragged the cart to a standstill.

'Mistress *Grant*.' It was Cowper, his tone no longer the semi-apologetic one of his earlier interrogations, but abrupt, cold. 'You've given us considerable trouble, rest assured that will not play in your favour.' And to the shepherd, 'This woman has been cried a witch and was awaiting trial. Give her up without protest and you may go on your way. Resist the Lord's work and you too will be taken.'

Kate met Cowper's gaze. 'This man is innocent of all knowledge. He rescued me from the flood, that is all. And though, as God is my witness, I am innocent of the charges brought against me, I will not be the cause of trouble to him or his family. Where is it you take me? Back to Bishopton?'

413

She didn't look at the shepherd, but willed him to understand what she wanted of him.

'It's not for you to question,' Cowper began, but William drowned him out, his satisfaction plain.

'You'll have no further opportunity to use your devilish wiles to escape. The commission will be held in Saltcoats. The time is set, the jury called.'

Kate turned to the shepherd. 'This is neither your quarrel nor your blame, hand me down.' She chose her next words carefully. 'Though innocent, I am not afraid to be tried, but trust I will have friends to speak for me.' It was all she could risk.

He was dropping the tail of the cart, pulling her towards the edge as if eager to be shot of her, growling, 'I'll have no truck with the devil's spawn.' But as he hauled her down he squeezed her wrist a fraction, so that she understood his roughness was for Cowper's benefit and his quick upward glance seemed to indicate her plea had been understood – pray God it had, that he would go to the castle, pass the word on.

There was no belfry tower this time, Kate cast into the Tolbooth, the cries and moans of those mad, or bad, whether before their imprisonment or as a result of it, echoing along the narrow corridor leading to the cell. Kate, used as she thought she was to odours of the worst kind, nevertheless found herself retching as they approached. She hesitated, and the gaoler, impatient, shoved her from behind, so that she stumbled, grazing the right side of her face against the stone wall as she fell. As he dragged her to her feet, she

414

felt her stomach turn at the reek of vomit and excrement on her hands and her clothes. The cries were louder now, more distinct, and as she was pushed against the cell gate, hands reached out through the bars to tear at her clothing.

The gaoler bawled at the prisoners to get back, then forced the gate open just far enough to shove Kate in. Hands grabbed her, bodies crowding her, faces with broken teeth and foetid breath leering into hers, voices taunting. For the fourth time in her life she fainted.

The cell was dim, the only light coming from a single candle flickering in the corridor. Kate came round to the feel of a boot in her side, a voice hissing in her ear. 'A witch, are ye?'

'No.' It came out as a croak. 'I am falsely accused.'

'Oh aye.' He kicked her again. Other hands were hauling her up, pressing her against the gate, fingers clawing at her clothes.

A second voice, in which she thought she detected an element of sympathy. 'Ye'd be as well to admit to it, there's no many here would want to mount a witch.'

A high-pitched cackle in the shadows to her right. 'Lest their bits shrivel…'

An answering burst of laughter, directed this time at the man who had kicked Kate. 'Not that we'd be complaining.'

'There's naethin' here.' Long fingers pinched Kate's cheek, the nails biting into her. 'She's nae mair quality as us.' As the woman tightened her grip, Kate steeled herself not to react – give them no satisfaction, and perhaps they'll stop. Her legs were shaking, and she grasped the bar behind her to avoid falling, held her head up, her expression calm.

The woman grasping Kate's cheek gave it a final twist and thrust her face into Kate's, her gaping mouth revealing gums covered in sores. 'Too good for the likes o' us, eh? Ye'll soon reek like the rest.'

True enough, Kate thought – perhaps it's as well the trial won't be long delayed.

She was sent for again. Cowper, clearly determined to make another attempt at wringing a confession from her, sat behind a deal table, William, Maxwell and Mistress Aitken beside him. He held a cambric handkerchief to his nose as she entered, her dress torn, the ripped hem trailing the stench of ordure. She saw him glance at her face, glance away again quickly, as if unwilling to acknowledge the bruising on her forehead, the scabs where nails had raked her cheek – not altogether comfortable with her treatment then. She swilled saliva around her mouth to take away the dryness, took the initiative.

'You sent for me? I have nothing to say.'

'You surprise me.' Maxwell smirked at William's sarcasm. 'You were not always so reticent, if I recall. In the past you had rather too much to say … and do.'

Twin memories flashed into Kate's mind: the angry flush on William's face as she twitted him with the favour the Montgomeries were receiving at the Queen's entry in '91, and the crack of her hand as she slapped his face at the frost fair. Though neither the most sensible of choices, both held a kind of satisfaction, then and now, despite the danger she found herself in. She straightened, her mouth curling a fraction at the thought. 'I do not care to waste my breath.'

'Once the commission is done you may find you have no breath to waste.' There was relish in William's tone. 'You survived one fire ... and that perhaps evidence enough to damn you. But do not think to escape the tar barrel,' a pause, 'if the garotte doesn't finish you off first.'

She suppressed her shiver. 'I am innocent and will be found so. If so be the commission is sound.' It was a confidence she didn't feel, but she wouldn't give William the satisfaction of seeing her fear.

'That is not what the witnesses have said.'

'Witnesses? Other than these?' The contempt in her voice was clear as she indicated William, Maxwell and Mistress Aitken.

Cowper was examining an ink spot on his index finger, but she suspected her point hit home. A feeling reinforced when he said, 'There is still a chance to recant and renounce your evil, and it may be that mercy will be afforded you.'

'I cannot renounce what I have neither thought nor said, for that would be perjury.'

'Have we not heard enough?' William's face was the colour of an overripe plum. 'It isn't for her to lecture us.' He thrust his face into Cowper's. 'Let the trial be Saturday.'

Chapter 23

He had to find Kate. It was Cunninghame's first thought as he swam back to consciousness, light pricking at his eyelids. He had no idea how far the river might have carried her, how long she could have survived the ordeal, but the alternative didn't bear thinking on. He stretched out his legs experimentally, ignoring the discomfort, forced himself into a sitting position. Not yet fully awake, he nevertheless noted the strength of the light from the unshuttered window cutting a swathe across the floor – what time was it? And where was he? Behind him a swee creaked, and he turned his head to speak to the bent back which was all he could see of the person who tended the fire. His voice was a croak. 'How long have I been asleep?'

The woman turned. 'Long enough to do you some good, I hope. More as a day.'And then, as if she thought a clarification might be required, ''Tis Friday.'

He swung his legs over the edge of the pallet, only partly aware that she was still speaking.

'You'd be advised to stay where you are, at least until you've eaten something. You were a pretty sight when you landed on our doorstep, and though some of the purple and yellow on your hands and face turned out to be nothing more than a scattering of flag iris petals, you have bruises and to spare elsewhere likely to give you grief for days to come.' There was a hint of mischief in her smile. 'But all things considered you were fortunate, it seems.'

'I wasn't alone.' He shut his eyes against the image of Kate, moving forward on her horse, smiling back at him as the wall of water hit. 'I need to find her.'

'Your wife?'

'No. The wife of a friend, and I responsible to see her safe, I cannot...' He was fully on his feet. 'I must go.'

'You will do better with food in your belly. It will put strength in your legs, and I daresay you'd rather be dressed as not.'

He looked down at his bare legs, at the crumpled shirt barely past his thigh. The woman was at his side, steering him towards the table, pressing a bowl into his hands, openly laughing at him now. 'No doubt you can down a bowl of broth in the time it will take me to gather up your clothes.' Her expression sobered. 'I hope you find her.'

It was not Kate he found, but William, and Maxwell with him. Or rather they found him. The tower where he had taken refuge was inland of Saltcoats, and failing any knowledge to the contrary that was where he headed. To spend a fruitless hour limping around the taverns and hostelries fringing the shoreline, asking for a woman caught in the flash flood, before deciding to make for Ardrossan, to seek John Shaw.

A voice behind him, familiar, unwelcome. 'Uncle! You're far from home. And injured I see. What are you doing here?'

John was evasive. 'Some business I had, of little importance or interest to any but myself.'

William grinned. 'Is she pretty?'

He allowed the implication, turned the conversation with a question of his own. 'I thought you at Broomelaw. Have you tired of your own place already?'

William expanded his chest. 'Mistress Grant, that we were to give evidence against...'

'Was helped to escape from Bishopton.' Maxwell's interruption indicated a personal affront, as indeed, John thought, with momentary satisfaction, it probably was.

'When we find whoever was responsible...'

William nodded in agreement, but, clearly impatient with Maxwell, continued his own train of thought. 'She is taken again, and the commission set.'

A flicker of a frown overlaid his satisfaction. 'It was our intention to proceed immediately, and indeed the trial will be tomorrow, but Cowper is insisting that once,' he corrected himself, '*if* convicted, the preachings must follow, the execution delayed past the Sabbath.'

'What of the period of indictment? Is there not a set time frame?' John kept his voice deliberately light, as if it was a matter of curiosity only.

William was dismissive. 'She had her indictment when we took her at the first, Cowper saw to that. And if we are a day or two short of the normal requirement, who will object?'

'The Montgomeries? Your father will not thank you to rouse them, nor the King, come to that.'

Maxwell cut in again. 'Unimportant if we get a confession from her.' It was clear he relished the possibility.

'Torture?'

'Only of the most safe and gentle sort. Cowper would allow none else.'

'Which is?'

'The weights. And that even the Earls of Eglintoun, past and present, have been known to sanction.'

It was a partial lie John chose not to challenge.

William's smile was salacious. 'Though I admit it a pity to mark such pretty legs so.'

'She has not yet succumbed?'

'We have a bar or two still in hand. Few wish to be crippled.' A narrowing of his eyes. 'Why this interest, Uncle?'

John lifted one shoulder. 'Only that I do not wish you to fall foul of the King by being premature. There is talk he begins to doubt some of the accusations that have flown about of late.'

'He will not doubt me.' There was a hard edge to William's voice, as if he dared John to contradict.

'She will not escape again?'

'No fear of that.' William gave him the information he sought. 'Bishopton's belfry may have been vulnerable, Saltcoats Tolbooth isn't. And aside from the weights, the conditions there are conducive to an admission of guilt, which would negate the need for a trial, though,' William contrived to look virtuous, 'I am more than happy to aid in God's work.'

John's teeth were clenched tight, a tension in his jaw, but William, full of his own satisfaction, seemed oblivious. He draped an arm around John's shoulder. 'If you will not share your secret with us, Uncle, at least join us in a bite.

Word is there's an alewife nearby who makes an exceedingly good pie.'

'I will, thank you, if you'll allow me but an hour to look to my own business.'

'Perhaps we could accompany you?'

It was a mockery, reinforced as William winked at Maxwell. A pause long enough to give John concern, then, 'Don't worry, Uncle, we won't spoil your little piece, but do not take overlong, else you'll be forced to eat on your own, for I'm already famished.'

It had been a simple matter to follow the shore from Saltcoats to the small bay below Ardrossan Castle. A single ship rode at anchor, sails neatly furled, two dorys floating at the stern. John whistled, relieved to see Shaw emerging from the stairway leading below decks. It was a matter of minutes before the dory grounded a yard from the shore, John splashing through the shallows to meet it. A few swift strokes and they were bumping against the ship's side, John wincing at the pain in his ankle as he climbed the ladder and swung himself onto the deck.

Shaw dispensed with the courtesies. 'Kate's been taken.'

'I know.' John leant against the wheel, flexed the rogue ankle. 'I ran into William and Maxwell in the town.' He waved his arm in the direction of Saltcoats.

Shaw, glancing at John's foot, indicated the bulkhead. 'Sit down. Tell me what you know.'

'She escaped from Bishopton on Wednesday, and we would have made it here but for the fog and then the flood.

422

We were on the last leg of the journey, but, unable to see much past the end of our noses, thought it safest to follow the river. A mistake as it turned out. Separated when the water hit, I landed in a small tower at the back of Saltcoats with little memory of how I got there and woke to find I'd lost more than a day. But no word of Kate, until I met William, gloating over her recapture.' He wrinkled his forehead. 'How did you know?'

A shepherd found her, fetched up in his sheep pen, and took her home. He was bringing her here yesterday when she was retaken. Though how William knew where to look...'

John's face was grim. 'There are aye folk who can be bought ... and William a past master at finding them out.' He followed Shaw below decks and took the proffered drink, his face set. 'They're holding Kate in Saltcoats Tolbooth and the trial is to be there also. The commission is called.'

'How much time do we have?'

'None as far as the trial is concerned, that is to be tomorrow, and I don't hold any hope for a good outcome. But a delay will follow, for all the ministers from the surrounding parishes are commanded to attend, and to add their weight to the thing by preachings on the Sabbath, the execution, should she be convicted, to follow on Monday. They have not allowed the allotted time, but they do not care overmuch for due process. Maxwell claims word has gone to the Montgomeries, but if it has, it will have been to Braidstane, not Linlithgow. I'm trapped into supping with William, for if I don't go his suspicions will be aroused, but once I've passed myself and found a horse I'll head for the court. Much use it will be James having intervened and the word go to Bishopton. Your ship is ready to sail?'

Shaw nodded. 'Since first I brought her round. Though moored here, we are dependent on the tides.' He scratched his cheek. 'Thank God for the season. It if were winter the risk would be considerable, but the weather as it is the now, I'll be safe enough anchoring off Horse Isle, so that whatever the state of the tide I'll be ready.'

'How will I contact you?'

In answer Shaw stuck his head onto the stairway and bellowed. The lad who had rowed the dory reappeared, favouring John with an impudent grin.

'He may have the look of a rapscallion,' John heard the affection in Shaw's voice, 'but he's bright enough and his loyalty not in doubt, nor is he a blabbermouth. There is a house in Saltcoats overlooking the shore, folk by the name of Barclay. They are old friends and honest, and will oblige me by keeping him for as long as is needed.'

John rose, unable to avoid wincing as he put his weight on his foot. 'I'd best be off, the sooner I sup with William, the sooner I can head for Linlithgow.' He was thinking aloud. 'Three good horses and I should be able to make it sometime tonight. With luck and a following wind, as my father used to say, we could be back by late afternoon tomorrow. We may be thankful Cowper is more of an owl than a lark, and that Kate is to be the climax of a parcel of cases.'

'A clever way to hide personal motive.'

'Indeed. But however William seeks to hide it, he sees little but his obsession with the Munros. Sometimes I wish...'

'What?'

John thought of the moment on the shore by Rough

Island when Munro had allowed William to live, and his own acquiescence in it. He shook his head. 'There are some things best not said, and regret changes nothing.'

'William will not think it strange you don't bide?'

A glimmer of a smile lit John's eyes. 'He chose to believe I have an assignation, and I chose to let him. It's as handy a reason as any to spend the night elsewhere.'

That drew an answering smile from Shaw, and a grin from the boy who hovered at his elbow. He listened to his instructions, his head tilted to one side like a robin, before darting away. They heard his feet pattering above their heads and then the creak of a rope as he pulled in the dory, his surprisingly tuneful whistling.

Shaw said, 'You needn't fear, by the time you've supped there'll be a horse waiting for you. Is there anything else *I* can do? Any way of delaying the trial?'

'Besides turning to brigandry and lying in wait for Hamilton and Fullerton? I think it best not. Besides that William knows it was you Kate sought. If he was to think that you're no longer here, that is perhaps the most help you can be.'

'If you do not return in time … is escape possible?'

'From the Tolbooth?' John shook his head. 'Unlikely. I bribed the gaoler at Bishopton. Cowper will take care it cannot happen again. And if he does not, William certainly will.'

'William isn't the only person with contacts in the town, nor money either. There is Eglintoun.'

'Neither money nor contacts will help Kate now. I suspicion Munro's appeal to the King is her only hope.'

'And the chances of success?'

A shrug. 'We lose nothing by trying. But win or lose,

the Munros cannot stay. Your ship will be needed in either case and likely fast. If William cannot see her burn, I trust he will accept their exile and their land. And that finally be an end to it.'

'Pray God it is.'

Chapter 24

It was gone two in the afternoon when John managed to escape the alehouse and head for the south side of the town. After enduring nigh on three hours of William's self-satisfaction regarding the forthcoming trial, interspersed with ribaldry and interrogation regarding the identity of the lady to whom John pleaded a prior engagement, he counted himself fortunate he had survived without coming to blows. Maxwell had become steadily more drunk as the hours passed, but William had remained disconcertingly sober, delaying John's release. The sky was clear, the wind light, so that he felt relief on two counts as he headed along the shore road and found the Barclay's door. The journey ahead a long one and likely hard on man and horse both, even without the additional hazard of inclement conditions.

The girl who answered his knock led him through to a small parlour overlooking the sea, and disappeared, giving the impression that unknown visitors were not unusual in this house and no questions asked. As indeed might be expected in a seaboard town with an accessible shoreline, but without the benefit of the neighbouring Irvine's

427

burgh status. An impression confirmed when the man who came to greet him exhibited no surprise, sweeping away both John's apologies for taking immediate leave, and his thanks for the offered horse and the parcel of food to see him on his way.

'If Shaw is putting himself out for you, that's good enough for me.' And then, as if he guessed at John's discomfort at the need for secrecy. 'I don't need to know your business.'

John paused at the edge of the town, considered the alternatives. The easiest route, and indeed the safest, would be to strike directly east, towards Kilmaurs, and from there take a wide sweep round by Crindledyke and Ochiltree. But on home territory, especially in daylight hours, there was aye the danger he would be recognised and forced to accept hospitality, with all the consequent delay that would entail. To head northwards by Beith would mean cutting across Eaglesham Moor, difficult riding at any time, the ground broken and boulder-strewn, foolhardy and downright dangerous to attempt to take it at speed. And Montgomerie land to boot. He headed east, but the sight of the ruin of Eglintoun Castle gave him pause. The jagged remains a travesty of the once great house, it was a chilling reminder of the senseless killings that punctuated his family's history, of which Kate's impending trial was the latest vindictiveness. He'd been a part of it long enough; they all had. Decision reversed, he turned north, as if by turning his back on Cunninghame land he could purge himself of past ills. The King was right, a nobility at peace would be to all their gain, that they might ride where they pleased without thought to whose land they crossed, and journeying be the safer for it.

The sun was riding high, the air warm as he picked his way along the side of a burn, the sound as it eddied and flowed, one moment slow, the surface mirroring the sky, the next broken, a rush of white water funnelled through a jumble of rocks, a painful reminder of the Annock Water not far to the east, of the bodies lying in the river bed, of his own part in the massacre there. And Munro's. Loyal to Glencairn then, however little he liked it, Munro was William's enemy now, his wife bearing the brunt. As wives generally did.

He was nearing the hamlet of Dunlop, the dusty track ahead of him deserted, as if the inhabitants also slumbered, sapped by the heat rising in waves from the hard-packed mud – best to give it a wide berth, lest Hamilton had chosen to lodge with his family there. There was aye an inconvenient dog sleeping with one eye open, ready to rouse the neighbourhood, and he'd be hard put to explain his presence here. Past Lugton he turned east, reining in his thoughts along with the horse, the need to concentrate on the terrain increasing with every mile he traversed. His instinctive reaction, as he struck out across the wide stretch of undulating moorland, a treacherous place where bog and stream and hidden hazards lay in wait to trip the unwary, was that it was a fine match for those whose land it was. A sobering thought on several counts – that antipathy to the Montgomeries was as mother's milk to a Cunninghame, and he at bottom as tainted as the rest. That this wean-ing, this new-found sympathy, would likely be a lengthy and dangerous process. And, most sobering of all, that as things stood he was no more welcome in these parts than his father or grandfather before him. He glanced up at the sky, thankful for the sunlight, which glinted on the myriad of lochans and watercourses, directing his weaving path across the moor.

The temperature dropped steadily as he climbed, clouds driving down from the north sweeping across the sun. He reached the highest part: the ground springing with bracken and heather, tufts of bog cotton interspersed with the occasional stunted gorse, the Ballagioch Hill dominating the skyline on his right. The wind was coming in gusts, and rain in it, at first no more than a smirr, then heavy, slanting into them, so that he redoubled his efforts to hold the horse steady. And perhaps might have managed, had not a moss-covered boulder shifted, his horse stumbling and, almost downed, unseating him. He picked himself up and crossed to the horse, which stood, reins dangling, his hoof raised onto the front edge as if it pained him to take weight. To the east the ground levelled, Polnoon likely no more than three or four miles away, and Montgomerie territory or no, he'd take his chance.

Dusk was drifting towards full dark, the midges still biting despite the rain. Polnoon must have been further than he thought, or, and this a concern that plagued as much as the midges, the fear that without the moonlight to guide he might be headed in the wrong direction altogether. A new problem: to disturb folk in the middle of the night, especially those who had no reason to trust him, would be folly. Perhaps he should find a byre or somesuch to wait out the night and start again at first light. With the Sabbath in hand there would would still be time to halt the execution. He would settle for that.

The bothy lay open, the door propped against the wall as if drunk. A half-full stone trough was set against the outer wall, and when he ducked his head inside he saw a pile of new straw heaped against the gable end – not derelict then, despite the door. He allowed the horse to drink his fill before leading him inside, and spreading out the straw encouraged him to lie down, then curled himself into the space between the horse's legs, his head resting against the belly. If not the most spacious accommodation, it was at least dry and protected from the wind. He'd likely not sleep, but rest would do no harm…

He woke to sunlight spiking across the hard-tramped floor, and to the mehing of sheep, accompanied by a low whistling, broken abruptly as a lad appeared in the doorway. John scrambled to his feet, inwardly cursing his tardiness. Outwardly he fixed a smile on his face, indicated the horse. 'He fell lame, last night, so I thought to rest him a little before trying to walk him any further. How far is it to Polnoon?'

'Leading him?' The boy glanced up at the roof timbers, as if to find the answer, 'Upwards of an hour maybe, but you'll no find a smith…'

'It's not a smith I'm needing, it's a sprain he has, not a cast shoe, so it's accommodation for him and a poultice perhaps and the loan of a horse to continue my journey. The tower will have all that, I daresay?' And when he got no answer, 'Well, I'd best get on, the sooner I get there, the sooner I'm on my way.' He encouraged the horse to his feet, and, noting that he still refused to put weight on his front leg, led him out the door.

The boy said, 'You'll no find awbody, for they're all awa.'

'A stable lad surely?'

A shrug. 'I suppose.' A pause, as if he struggled to form his thoughts into some semblance of order. 'There'll be nae horses ... ye'll maybes do better at Cathcart.' And with that he recommenced his tuneless whistling and ambled away, waving his stick in a kind of farewell.

John's halt at Cathcart was mercifully brief, the lady of the house obliging, and though his protests of haste were clearly somewhat of a slight to her hospitality, she didn't seek to dissuade him, instead forcing a jug of ale on him and calling on a servant to prepare a parcel of cold meat and bread and plums fresh-picked from the south-facing wall. The mare the lad led from the stable was skittish, dancing sideways as John swung into the saddle. At the last the woman smiled up at him, a hint of coquetry in her gaze, resting one hand on the mare's neck. 'You'll bring her back safe?'

'If I can leave her at Linlithgow for a day or two, for I have a way to go further ... and return her on my road home?' Not exactly truthful, but in the circumstances as much as he would risk.

'A few days, a week, a fortnight even, for we are well set for horseflesh.' A pause, a wider smile. 'Next time our hospitality will not be so meagre, I promise you.'

He dipped his head, touched her hand. 'I'm indebted, mistress.'

Chapter 25

The chamber was crammed, the press of bodies ensuring the door to the street couldn't be shut. Kate, with a tightening of her chest, surveyed the crowd – seeking a friendly face or anyone betraying sympathy. Curiosity she saw, and malevolence, a lust for blood, but not sympathy. Cowper was heading for the table on the temporary dais, acknowledging the ripple of approval as he squeezed through the narrow gap opening for him – no doubt proud that it was God's work he did.

He called the proceedings to order, the murmur of conversation dying away, the only sound a hacking cough issuing from a slattern called as a witness in the first case of the day, against a woman who'd put the evil eye on her neighbour's cattle so that their milk failed.

'And the calves all lost, for lack of it.' The complainant's voice rose in a wail, 'And we now paupers.' She pointed at the woman who stood accused. 'It was for spite, for that she lusted after my man, and when he turned her aside she put a curse on our cattle, God rot her.'

Kate's case was the last in a long line, Mistress Aitken well into her stride. Each denunciation had been more virulent than the last, the details more lurid. Deluded or self-seeking? Kate couldn't decide. Not that it mattered; if the tribunal believed her, the result would be the same. And why wouldn't they, when William had them in his pocket. The crowd had thinned in the middle of the day, likely with more interest in filling their bellies than in listening to yet another neighbour dispute cloaked as witchcraft, but built again with the prospect of a more meaty charge, the buzz of anticipation matching the increasing temperature. Cowper ran his handkerchief around his neck, shuffled the parchments on the desk, rapped the gavel. He nodded to the sheriff's clerk who read out the charges: first, possession, and then, when the murmurs had died down, conspiring with the devil to injure the Queen and her unborn child. There was an angry growl from the crowd, and they began to press towards the makeshift dock where Kate stood, barefoot and shackled.

'Back!' Cowper rapped with the gavel again. 'Or I will clear the court. I do not preside over a rabble.' His gaze raked the crowd. 'You'll have your chance if the woman is guilty.'

Antagonism flowed towards Kate, a wave that would not be halted, and she felt her legs begin to tremble. She had seen a witch taken once, in Ayr, the stake for the garotte driven hard into a gap in the cobbles, the attached metal band tightened inexorably, until the whites of the woman's

eyes filled with blood, the body convulsing like a mario-
nette, so that Kate had found herself praying for a speedy
death to spare the poor creature the burning to follow. Her
prayer answered, the crowd, cheated of entertainment,
had turned ugly and dragged the executioner through the
streets, his hands and feet tied together, the rope looped up
and around the horse's tail, until his clothes were in shreds,
his back running red – dear God, where were Munro and
Hugh? She'd thought the shepherd had understood, but
maybe she'd been mistaken. Or perhaps John Shaw hadn't
been able to get word to them. Was this how it was to end?
Squashed three in a tar barrel, the flames feeding on her
flesh? She thought on William's taunt, prayed God the garotte would finish her. Her hands were shaking, rattling the
chain binding the shackles together.

Cowper called the first witness. Maxwell appeared in
the doorway, the crowd parting for him, his eyes as they
met hers alive with malice. His testimony was clear and
unequivocal, spoken with the confidence of a practised liar
and, as with all the best lies, with a grain of truth at its
heart.

'On the 1st of March last, I travelled to Hillhouse in the
parish of Ayr, there to collect my wife, and found Mistress
Grant closeted with her. On our return home, my wife, on
the advice of the said Mistress Grant, refused natural relations claiming they would be injurious to her person and
that...'

'Yes, yes,' Cowper cut in. 'The injury she has done to
your domestic affairs is no doubt distressing, but of more
moment to this commission is your testimony concerning
the Queen. Do you have first-hand evidence in that respect?'

435

'I do.' Again a glance directed at Kate, his obvious satisfaction. 'The selfsame advice tendered to my wife was offered to the Queen also, though the effect there I know not. Only that Mistress Grant incited my wife to enlist the Queen's help in refusing my rightful dues and attempted to bring a charge before the King. I will not repeat,' his expression turned virtuous, 'the foul language in which she expressed her disdain, nor the unnatural affections she claimed...' The murmurs in the crowd were building towards a climax, Maxwell fuelling their fears as he would a fire. 'Suffice it to say that, seeing the results of her consort with my wife, I fear for the malignant effect of Mistress Grant's ministrations on the Queen, and on the bairn she carries. The more so when I heard her talk of threat to the pregnancy. It is for this court to decide from whence the threat comes.'

Cowper betrayed irritation. 'And when we hear all the evidence, we will make judgement accordingly.' Kate felt the first stirring of hope. Dashed by Cowper's cold tone as he commanded, 'Call the next witness.'

Conspicuous in a doublet of black velvet, slashed with the Cunninghame silver, a ruffle of lace at the cuffs, the tooling on the scabbard of his sword casting light spinning across the ceiling, William surveyed the crowd, cowing them into silence. 'To the charge of maleficence towards the Queen, I add that of possession.'

A collective gasp, a renewed surge of interest. Kate clenched her fists to still the shaking of her hands – she would not look away.

'Mistress Grant, when questioned in my presence, claimed the name of Mistress Munro,' William paused, dropped his words like stones, 'that I saw dead and buried these six years since. And indeed she is so very like, there can be no other explanation aside from the diabolical.' The crowd were with him, pressing forward, a pack of dogs scenting a kill.

Hamilton said, his voice betraying boredom, 'These men are of good repute. Need we hear more?'

Cowper reasserted control. 'The cause of justice demands we hear all the evidence. Call Mistress Aitken.'

Another stir among the spectators.

Cowper began quietly. 'Do you know this woman?'

'Aye, that I do.'

'How so?'

'As the devil's handmaiden.' Her index finger was extended, pointing straight at Kate. It was a repetition of the charade at Bishopton, with a new climax when she tore aside the neck of her gown to show the parallel lines of scabs running from just under her ear to her shoulder. 'This,' she rotated so all could see, 'the result when first I cried her; her familiar springing on me, drawing blood. I see him now.' Her eyes widened as if in terror and she clutched at her throat, collapsing to the floor in what seemed to Kate a well-simulated faint.

There was a perceptible shift in the crowd, a gathering in on themselves, retreat, followed by a forward surge, onlookers become a mob.

This is it, Kate thought – is this how Christ felt, the crowd baying for blood...? She shut her eyes, prayed, dear God let me not add blasphemy to my sins. There was a numbness in her wrists, her legs, a sensation of falling, before she was dragged again to her feet.

Cowper was bending over Mistress Aitken, shouting, 'Air, give her air I say.' Then, as she stirred, 'Thank you,

437

Mistress Aitken, you are dismissed.' He returned to the dais, indicated silence, began the preamble to the judgement. 'By the powers invested in me...'

'Do not our courts require the right of reply?' The interruption came from somewhere near the rear of the chamber. Kate, craning, like everyone else, to find the source, saw a young man in a blue doublet thrusting his way through the crowd, flanked by two men-at-arms. He reminded her of someone ... the Montgomerie boys by the lake in Holyrood park ... this must be the new Earl of Eglintoun. The shepherd had done his best then.

Cowper ran a finger around the inside of his collar. 'She has no advocate, though the opportunity was given.'

'I will be her advocate.'

Kate was aware of movement all around the perimeter of the room, a shifting and a shuffling as the crowd were ringed by newcomers, conspicuous by their Montgomerie colours and by hands resting on sword hilts. William stepped forward, his face puce. 'By what right, Eglintoun, do you speak? You have no knowledge of this woman.'

'I have knowledge of the law. This court is illegal.'

Cowper was on his feet, puffing himself up, a turkeycock preparing to fight. 'You dare challenge the authority of the King's Commissioner?'

'I challenge the timing. There was not the full fifteen days between indictment and trial, nor have her family been summoned to speak on her behalf.'

'She has no family, barring bairns, and those under whose protection she lived have not come.'

'She was under the protection of Braidstane, and therefore of me, and I am here.' His men were radiating inwards towards Kate.

William took another step. Kate, focusing on him, saw the fractional flick of his head, before he fixed his eyes on Eglintoun.

'And you learnt of the indictment when?'

'This morning, on my return from Giffen.'

'Well then,' it was almost a drawl, Kate feeling a renewed coldness sweeping through her, 'you will not be aware that the indictment was raised not here, but at Bishopton, when first she was taken. The trial is here because she has already escaped justice once. She shall not do so again. I say the timing is legal. If you doubt it, present your proof.' William's head was up, his colour returned to normal, a smile playing about his mouth. He cast a glance around the chamber, brought his gaze back to rest on Eglintoun. 'And if you thought to end this trial by force...' his voice, quiet now, nevertheless carried the length and breadth of the chamber, '...think again.' An answering flurry of movement, other men, swords drawn, thrusting through the press to flank Eglintoun and each of his men, outnumbering them two to one.

Kate's head was throbbing, pain like flashes of light behind her eyes – is there nothing William cannot counter? She met Eglintoun's eyes, shook her head in response to his mute question – one life against many, she would not go to God, now or ever, with that on her conscience. A satisfied nod from William, the sound of swords sheathed, a sigh rippling through the crowd.

Cowper, also visibly relieved, sought to reassert control. 'This is a trial by commission, not combat.' He addressed Hamilton and Fullerton. 'You have heard the witnesses, what say you?'

William was standing to Hamilton's left, Maxwell on

Fullerton's right.

Hamilton looked straight at Kate. 'Guilty.'

Fullerton hesitated, and then, as if aware of Maxwell's hand on his shoulder, echoed, 'Guilty.'

Cowper swept his gaze around the court, paused for a moment at Eglintoun, as if daring any further opposition, addressed Kate. 'Katherine Grant, being convicted by the deposition of sound witnesses, of the horrid crime of witchcraft, of malefice, and of converse with the devil to the intended harm of our gracious lady the Queen Anne and her unborn child, I sentence you to death by garotting and your body after to be burned. The said penalty to be carried out by the Tolbooth on Monday next under the care of the Steward of Saltcoats and his deputies. And that on the Sabbath between, all ministers in the parishes surrounding shall come together for a preaching against this evil, that the taint spread not.'

The crowd were becoming restive, Cowper hurrying to a conclusion. 'And that you be dragged through the town by a horse tail to the preaching, as an example to others that none may likewise be tempted.'

Kate's breath was coming in short gasps, William's face swimming in front of her, his smile a gaping void threatening to swallow her whole. She drew herself up to face him, refusing to allow him the pleasure of seeing her collapse, cried out above the roar of the crowd's approval, 'I am innocent, so help me God.'

Chapter 26

It was a relief to be on a horse with a turn of speed and willing with it, nevertheless it was approaching evening when John Cunninghame pulled up on the grassy promontory overlooking the loch below the palace of Linlithgow, clouds of midges dancing above the surface of the water. Far off to the west the sky flared red, presaging fine weather to come, and he nodded, satisfied. To travel such a distance on the Sabbath wouldn't meet with universal approval, but if pulling a cow out of a pit was permissible, then saving a life surely was. He passed under the gateway, glancing up at the four brightly coloured Orders set above it: his own personal favourite, the Order of the Garter with the three golden lions prancing on a red background, the blue bosses standing proud, surrounded by flowers entwined with gold ribbons. It would be hard not to be impressed.

The courtyard was all hustle and bustle: a cart in the process of being unloaded, its axles creaking as barrels were rolled towards the tailgate, a dog yelping as someone tramped on his tail, the jingle of harness and snorting of horses overlaid by the distinctive honking of a flock of geese flying in formation above the loch. Servants scurried backwards and forwards, voices rising and falling in a cacophony of enquiry or indignation, careless oaths, laughter and good-humoured name-calling, all the accompaniments of a busy household on a normal day. He accosted a boy staggering under the weight of a bag of oats. 'Where can I find Alexander Montgomerie, the King's Master Poet?'

The boy set down the sack, rubbed his chin where stubble should have been, his reply, had John been in the mood to appreciate it, droll. 'He's no my best friend, so a cannae be sure, but there are fine folk lodged in the north wing. If I was you. I'd try there.'

The woman who answered his summons at the entrance was more helpful, if less encouraging. 'He was here, and twa others wi' him, forbye the lassie, but they're no here the now.'

'Do you know when they left?'

'Yesterday, in the forenoon. I ken because they waited out a shower at the gatehouse.' She paused a fraction, colour in her face. 'I was there myself, so...' She broke off, anticipated his next question. 'The word was they made for Bishopton, wi' a paper of some sort from the King.' She smoothed her skirts, glanced up at him through a curtain of hair falling across her cheek. 'It's a long road, and you look as if you've travelled a distance already. You'll no head off again without a bite surely? I can see to you...'

He dismissed her offer, summoning a smile to take away any offence. 'I need to see the King.'

She indicated the west wing. 'My duties are here, but there will be plenty folk able to direct you, whether to the Queen's or the King's chambers.'

He found them enjoying the last of the sunshine in

442

the rare privacy of a turret room, tucked away from the main concourse. It had taken all his powers of persuasion to convince the Queen's ladies, who hovered in the outer room, of the urgency of his message. James turned at the sound of the door, a flash of irritation on his face.

'Cunninghame. I trust there is a reason for this intrusion? If it is but another petty squabble, I have no wish to hear it.'

'It is a serious matter, Sire, and one only you can resolve.'

'Well then, speak out, man.'

'It relates to Mistress Munro, she that serves the Queen.'

A scowl settled on James' face. 'You are on dangerous ground; the Montgomeries have already petitioned me on that account, and my decision made. I will not go back on it, whatever the Cunninghames may wish.'

'You mistake me, Sire. It is to save Mistress Munro I have come, not to condemn her.' He was aware of the Queen's stiffening, of James' eyes narrowing, hurried on. 'A Cunninghame I may be, but I cannot stand by and see injustice done, though it be my own kin at fault.'

'Indeed? This is an unusual occurrence. Well, you can rest easy, the Montgomeries have gone with the order her trial be halted. Though I was inclined to give your nephew the benefit of the doubt and allow that he might be honestly mistaken. A too generous assessment, would you say?'

To wrest another order from James would require something more than his word. 'I would, Sire, though it pains me to say it. William confessed in my hearing that he knew Mistress Grant to be Kate Munro, but being unable to touch her in her true identity, took advantage of her false name to trump up the charge of possession.' A note of bitterness crept into his voice. 'If he put his intelligence to better use, we'd all be the safer for it.'

'He is not the only noble of which that could be said.' James was settling back in his chair. 'But at least in this he has been foiled.' The irony in his voice hardened to steel. 'You and Glencairn may pray it is a lesson to him, else he will find my forbearance stretched too far. Now, if that is all?'

John stood his ground. 'I wish it were. The trial the Montgomeries thought was to be at Bishopton has been moved to Saltcoats. I came from there yesterday to warn them, and hoped to be in time to direct them aright, but that my horse was lamed on Eaglesham Moor and I had to wait out the night until I could find a replacement. They have already left and no one at Bishopton to set them straight. If William's intentions have gone to plan she will already be convicted, with the preachings and the execution to follow.'

The Queen rose. 'Then we must halt the execution.'

John began, 'If I could take a new order to that effect...' but was interrupted by James.

'There will be no order.'

The Queen sank to her knees before him, her voice breaking. 'This threatens our child...'

He lifted her to her feet. 'There will be no order, and no mistake, because I myself shall accompany Cunninghame to Saltcoats to make sure of it.'

They left at dawn, a small company heading south-west under a sombre sky at odds with the promise of the previous night. Ochre and purple clouds, threaded through with strands of black, massed ahead of them, a strengthening wind buffeting them from the west. James, in a typically quixotic gesture, determined to travel light, with no more than two men-at-arms and wearing clothes as plain as John's own. He took leave of the Queen by the courtyard fountain, raising her up from her curtsey and kissing her on both cheeks, his expression set. 'The Master of Glencairn shall learn he cannot best me. I have no truck with witchcraft, but I'm not so credulous as to mistake a personal antagonism for the diabolic.'

As they rode out, John, seeing anticipation sparking in the King's eyes, wondered if it was for relish of the break in routine and an escape from the restrictions of the court, or the pleasure of asserting his authority over a troublesome lord, but didn't much care. Whichever, it was to Kate Munro's advantage and therefore welcome. And as to the possible consequences for himself, that was a thought best buried. The Earl of Glencairn was hale yet, and long might he remain so. Always the pragmatist, Glencairn wouldn't stand against the King in anyone's cause, and as for Lady Glencairn, she was long past the point of caring for William's approval.

As they passed through the gateway, a crow flew ahead of them to settle in the trees at the edge of the loch. John shut his ears to the raucous caws following them as they turned south-west – superstition was for credulous folk. With luck, by now the Montgomeries would also be on their way to Saltcoats, alerted by the messenger James had despatched to Bishopton to track them down, and for themselves, with a full day in hand and a change of horses, they also should have little trouble in covering the ground in time. They were heading for Avonbridge, keeping to the north side of the Almond Water, taking advantage of the wider valley floor, the land on the opposite bank rising steeply. James was in good fettle, encouraging his horse into a gallop, so that John and the two men-at-arms who rode with them were hard pushed to keep up with him. As likely an illustration of the quality of horseflesh as the calibre of the rider. An almost treasonable thought, and a mite unfair perhaps, that nevertheless brought a smile to John's face, lightening the grim reality of their journey. It would be churlish to be other than grateful that James had taken it into his head to accompany him, for no one, not William or Maxwell, and certainly not Cowper, could ignore the King's presence.

Ahead of him, James reined in at the junction between the Almond and the Avon, allowing his horse a breathing space and an opportunity to drink. He was laughing as John pulled up alongside him. 'Out of condition, Cunninghame? Or will you make your mount your excuse?'

John hedged. 'Both, Sire, forbye that my skill cannot match your own.'

James waved away the compliment, but in a manner that indicated it was welcome. 'Well, well, we make good time. A little under an hour to Avonbridge?' It was less question than statement.

They kept to the ridge, the river twisting through a narrow defile far below, treacherous on foot, impossible on horseback. Occasionally it bent close enough to their route that the rush and gurgle of the water rose up from the depths, warning of danger. They were skirting a loch whipped into grey furrows, the surface of the water in constant motion.

James patted his stomach. 'We may trust the fine folk of Gartness are minded to be hospitable.'

As if, John thought, they could be anything else, and the King their visitor.

'By my reckoning we should make it by dinner time. And dry, I hope.'

A hope fulfilled, the rain coming just as they reached Gartness, driving them indoors to partake of a dinner of beef and vegetables, the whole dressed in a herb sauce that carried too much salt for John's taste, though he made the lady of the house a pretty compliment in his thanks. At the first sign of a break in the clouds they were off again, their speed increased.

The first sign of a problem arose at Cleikhimin, the ostler, though it was clear he didn't recognise the King, fulsome in his apologies at the lack of available horses and eager to suggest alternatives. 'Netherton perhaps ... or Bothwell for sure.'

John favoured Bothwell. 'The Douglases will no doubt have horses to spare, and of a quality that will serve us well.'

The ostler winked. 'And no be mealy-mouthed about the Sabbath.'

James silenced him. 'The disciples broke the Sabbath, and with less cause.' And to John, 'The Douglases are aye keen to curry favour, and today will be no different, Sabbath or no.'

And neither it was, the Douglases falling over themselves to oblige, the horses they provided more than equal to the task. John was in good heart as they set out again, and content to follow James' preference to strike south for Hamilton and Strathaven, before swinging round again to the west. It was a long road round, and would bring them in by Irvine, but he'd no wish to risk the upland moor for a second time, daylight or not. It was mid-afternoon when the rain came again, a sudden squall driving them away from the open country into the shelter of the woods. As they dismounted to lead the horses, John looked back, scanning the sky – it had been gey dark earlier when they'd had to stop at Gartness, but had cleared quickly. Pray God they'd be as fortunate now, for with upwards of twenty-five miles still to cover, time was running short.

The rain became heavier, penetrating the canopy, settling into a steady drip, drip from the branches above their heads. The horses were restive, John also, but James reassured him,

'Have no fear, Cunninghame, we'll be there, should we have to ride through the night. And the horses will benefit from the rest.' He leant back against a convenient tree trunk and prepared to wait.

They had been going again for a half-hour or more, following a track that wound in and out of stretches of woodland, when John felt the first twinge of uneasiness. He dismissed it as nothing, for weren't woods aye alive with sound and movement: the rustling and scuffling of small mammals competing with birdsong; the distinctive grunting of wild boar as they crashed through the undergrowth; the ghost-like passage of deer in a whisper and a flash of white scut. And accompanying the thought, the reality, as a mother and fawn, almost full-grown, disturbed the foliage off to their right.

James flicked his tongue over his lips. 'Fine hunting in these parts, I see. The auld religion knew how to look after their priests. Can you claim acquaintance with the present owners? A delay on the road home would not be unwelcome.'

John was nodding when two figures stepped onto the path in front of them, the lower part of their faces covered, pistols drawn. John turned his head, saw that they were surrounded, cursed himself for allowing his guard to slip – outnumbered two to one, a dangerous ratio. The taller of the two was courteous, but John recognised the steel in his request, 'I'll thank you to step down, gentlemen.'

As they dismounted, John slid his hand inside his jerkin, but was halted by a shot into the ground at his feet and the barked order, 'Leave your hands where I can see them.'

James glared, his tone imperious. 'Vagabonds and murderers you may be, but not, I think, king killers. And I am your King.'

The leader removed his hat, his elaborate bow a mockery. 'And I the Tzar of all the Russias. Unbuckle your swords.'

Ignoring the order, James took a step forward, the leader firing again, this time over James' head.

'Do not tempt my patience. Your swords, if you please!'

John said, 'What must we do to convince you of the King's identity? These are his men-at-arms and body-guard, accompanying him on an errand of mercy. If you would allow,' he indicated James' hand, once again straying towards his jerkin, 'he carries the King's seal.'

A hint of a smile. 'Indeed. I haven't had the pleasure of

the King's company before. Nor, I suspect, have I it now. From what I've heard, the King thinks rather more of himself than to traipse about the country in clothes best suited to a parish schoolmaster.' He looked James up and down. 'Indeed I might think you one, if it were not for your sword, but perhaps you have ideas above your station.'

It was clearly the last straw. James drew his sword with a roar and launched himself forward, only to be pinned from behind, the sword wrested from his grasp, John and the men-at-arms similarly taken.

The leader of the group was still smiling, but his eyes glittered. 'You know how to use a sword. I commend your bravery, but not your common sense. You are outnumbered. Do as I ask and no harm shall come to you. We wish no killing, unless forced to it...' The threat was clear. 'But merely to relieve you of some possessions for which we can find a better use. And which ... as the King of Scotland,' he bowed to James, 'no doubt you can well afford to spare.' He indicated to one of his men, who slid a hand inside James' shirt, withdrawing a clinking purse. He held up the King's ring. 'This seal, as you term it ... a pretty piece I grant you. Fraud or stolen? No matter, the price it fetches likely the same either way.'

One moment they were standing facing the leader, the next they were lying face down in the undergrowth, being stripped of their outer garments, their pistols and dirks added to the swords piled at the leader's feet. The final indignity, as they were trussed together in pairs, the removal of their boots. It was clearly a well-practised routine and over in a matter of minutes. One final ironic bow and the men were gone, the plunder divided over the horses. James screamed his fury after them, his intention to hound them down, to make them pay for their insolence. The laughter floating back a final insult.

Night had fallen by the time they managed, working blind and behind their backs, to undo each others' bonds and, standing at last, flexed their stiff muscles.

James queried John, 'How far is it to the nearest habitation where we will find suitable clothing and horses to see us on our way?'

'Twelve miles perhaps to Kilmarnock Castle, Riccarton about the same, depending on which side of the Irvine we go.' He considered. 'I am known to the Boyds, so Kilmarnock would be my choice.' He rubbed his hands up and down his arms, trying to inject some warmth, looked down at his stockinged feet. 'It'll not be the most comfortable of walks, and any cottages we stumble over in the meantime unlikely to be able to oblige us with boots, but I suppose we may be grateful they left us any clothes at all.'

James humphed, evidence that gratitude was the last thing on his mind, gestured to John to lead on. 'Let's get going then.'

It was an uncomfortable journey. Despite hugging the riverbank, the ground underfoot, mostly grass of sorts, was tufted in places by spikes of bog cotton, sharp on their soles, and punctuated by stretches of marshland, through which they squelched, mud oozing around their ankles, occasionally threatening to swallow them up to their calves. It was a weary and bedraggled group that approached Kilmarnock Castle in the half-light preceding the dawn, the twin towers of the great keep dark shadows looming above the battlements. They splashed, knee-high, through the river where the Borland and Craufurdland Waters met, the water serving to remove the worst of the mud splatters from their legs. As they emerged from the wooded glen into the open, John noted the contrast between the stark architecture of the keep, defensive to the last inch, and its more gentle surroundings of garden and orchard and parkland, always the envy of Glencairn.

At the main door, John saw by the grin on the servant's face who responded to their hammering, that bedraggled or not he was recognised, the tension that had been building in him for the last mile or so dissipating. 'Convey my apologies to your master for knocking him up so early, but it's imperative we see him immediately.'

The servant seemed to be struggling to swallow his amusement. 'I'll tell him ye're here. I can see ye're in dire straits, but Glencairn's brother or no, ye maybes best wait below,' he shot a glance at John's feet, 'for the mistress isn't overly keen on mud on her carpets.'

Boyd was apologetic in his turn, though it seemed he too smothered a smile. 'Cunninghame! Muddy or no, I'm sorry you were kept waiting here. But to what do we owe a visit at this early hour, and in such a state...' He half-turned, his expression of welcome for John's companions turned to confusion as he recognised James. He bowed low, his face flooding with colour. 'We are honoured by your presence, Sire, and doubly sorry you were so treated.'

James' response was wry. 'No matter. At least someone among my subjects recognises me.'

'Sire?' Boyd looked puzzled.

John, weariness visible in every line of his face, said, 'We were set upon, over by Priestland way, the vagabonds refusing to accept who we were. They left us as you see us.'

'Save us! You walked from Priestland?'

'We had no choice.'

Boyd clapped his hands and the servant reappeared. 'Hot water and towels for our guests and changes of clothes, and send to the kitchens for wine and hot food.'

James nodded his thanks. 'We have little time to waste, but must needs get to Saltcoats as soon as we can. There is the small matter of an execution to halt.'

John elaborated. 'We are come to rescue a woman miscalled a witch, her execution set for today.'

If Boyd was surprised at the King intervening in a witch trial, he hid it well, ushering them into two guest chambers off the great hall before disappearing to prepare weapons and horses to speed them on their way. As they re-emerged into the courtyard, he said, 'I've sent ahead to Irvine, the wind is in the right quarter and there will be a birlinn ready to sail, it will be your speediest option.' He handed the King up into the saddle. 'Perhaps we can offer some better hospitality on the road back when your business is done?'

Chapter 27

It would have been the speediest option, had not the wind dropped. As they boarded at Irvine, John noted the shortage of crew, but accepted both the sailor's explanation of the order to choose haste over a full complement, and his assurance that the birlinn, sweet to handle, posed no danger. Now, as the sun edged over the hills to the east, painting the sea a liquid gold, they slowed, the sail beginning to flap, the wash, which minutes before had been creaming out behind them, reduced to no more than a ripple. As the lad brought the sail down and set the oars, the sailor in charge approached James, his face radiating apprehension.

'We havna enough…'

James cut him off. 'I can see that.' His gaze swept over John and the men-at-arms, returned to the sailor. 'Will you manage with an extra four pairs of hands?'

The relief was palpable. 'Sire.'

John's arms were aching, sweat trickling down his

spine as they approached Saltcoats, the men-at-arms red-faced, James also. They could hear a bell tolling as they grounded in a scrunch of gravel a few yards from the shore, John seeing his own concern mirrored in James' face. The men-at-arms splashed over the side, straining to pull it up onto the sand. John, impatient, leapt out also, the water cold against his thighs, and added his weight to the task. The King had one leg over the gunwale when the others, combining heave and shove, succeeded in dragging it into the shallows, so that as James alighted he wet his boots, but nothing more.

John ordered, 'Wait here, we may need you again.' He paused at the water's edge and emptied his boots, water arcing onto the sand. 'I'll move faster if I don't have to wade.'

They heard the commotion before they saw it, a mob in full cry, braying their appreciation. The men-at-arms were battering their way through, laying about them with the pommels of their swords, their calls of 'Make way for the King' swallowed in the animosity of the crowd, John and the King jostled and pushed as they followed. In the space in front of the Tolbooth the line of stakes driven into the gaps between the cobbles to hold back the press of people bent under the strain. They were almost at the barrier as the sound climaxed, a collective roar cut off in a moment of silence. John, recognising its significance, felt the energy drain out of him – we're too late. And however useless, his own voice echoed the men-at-arms' cry, 'Make way for the King.'

The people closest to him were falling back in a mix of disbelief, surprise and consternation; the quiet broken by curses as they trampled each other. A whisper of skirts, a shuffling of feet and a creaking of joints spread outwards like a ripple as they settled at James' feet. The men-at-arms had reached the front and were wrenching up stakes to make a way through, John, heartsick, forcing himself to look past them into the space beyond. On the right was an empty tar barrel with kindling laid against it, mounds of coal and wood stacked to the side. Behind them a cart piled high with turfs, and propped against the cartwheel two crumpled bodies. He started forward, the momentary relief that neither was Kate dispelled as he saw her slumped on a narrow chair at the entrance to the Tolbooth, a post protruding above the back, sunlight bouncing off the metal band encircling her neck. Bursting through the gap in the stakes, heedless of the fact he preceded the King, John saw her lips were blue and clusters of tiny red spots peppered the alabaster white of her cheeks. Her head was collapsed onto her chest and she made no sound – to miss by minutes only… If his horse had not lamed, if he hadn't fallen asleep on Eaglesham Moor, if they hadn't been attacked…

Off to the left a high-pitched scream, 'Mother' and the anguished cry, 'Kate!' as a group on horseback likewise fought their way through the press. John looked up, saw Munro flinging himself from the saddle, shook his head. The man behind the chair gave another twist to the iron bar tightening the band and Kate's body convulsed once more, then was still, blood trickling from her ear and nose and the corner of her mouth.

The King roared, 'Stop! This woman is innocent!' as Munro, leaping the barrier, ran forward and, grappling with the executioner, fought to loosen the band. James roared again, and this time the executioner, his eyes widening in recognition and fear, dropped to the ground, prostrating himself before James, who waved at the the men-at-arms to drag him away. The band released, Munro knelt, cradling Kate, her body limp, Maggie beside him, tears coursing down her cheeks.

A figure thrust Maggie aside, wresting Kate's body from Munro.

'Let me.'

He laid her on the cobbles, began to rub vigorously at her cheeks, breaking off to hold his ear close to her mouth. Began again, massaging her cheeks, her arms, her chest. Without effect.

Munro grasped his shoulders, tried to pull him away, his voice ragged, as if he spoke through broken glass. 'It's no good, Montgomerie. Let us be.'

'I'm not giving up yet.' Montgomerie cast about, called to a clerk who hovered by the entrance to the Tolbooth, 'You there. Bring water and salts, a covering.'

John thought – so this is Hugh's brother. The physician. If he had only been here sooner he might have saved her. Out of the corner of his eye he saw William and Maxwell beginning to push through the crowd as if heading for the shore. He felt a heat flood through him, and without thought for the presumption, grabbed the King's arm, jerking his head in their direction. 'Sire?'

James swung round, bellowed, 'Maxwell! Cunning-hame!', ordered the men-at-arms, 'Bring those men to me, alive for preference, dead if you must.' The crowd, now swayed in Kate's favour, scented other prey and closed in, driving them back towards the Tolbooth. John cast a glance over the crowd, saw Cowper on the fringe of it, Hamilton and Fullerton by his side. And close to them the young Earl of Eglintoun with his entourage. It would be the final outrage to his family name, but necessary.

He battled his way towards Eglintoun, prayed his closeness to the King would have been noted, said, 'Eglintoun. You have authority here. The King will wish to have words with Cowper and those with him. Can we depend on you to hold them?'

Eglintoun bowed, gestured to his men 'See to it.'

John fought his way back towards Kate. The stakes lay scattered across the cobbles, the crowd pressing ever closer, and he drew his sword to hold them back. And so missed the slight lift of her chest, her first cough. Munro was repeating her name over and over, as if he feared to forget, as John Montgomerie propped her up, wrapping a cloak around her and, continuing to rub at her cheeks, trickled water into her mouth. His grim, 'She is very far from safe yet,' lost in Hugh's cry of 'God be praised.' A cry that spread like wildfire through the crowd, so that they surged forward again, straining to catch a glimpse of her.

Over Munro's head John could see Eglintoun forging a path for his men, who drove Cowper, Fullerton and Hamilton before them, the crowd jostling and shoving, jeering and cat-calling, tearing at their clothes, spitting on them.

How fickle people are, John Cunninghame thought, how easily swayed, how dangerous their power.

Behind Munro the King was clapping Alexander Montgomerie on the shoulder, expressing his satisfaction. 'Well, well, this return to life is fine evidence, if any be needed, of her innocence. And our intervention timely.'

Munro looked up, as if to comment, Alexander's fractional shake of the head a silent warning to allow the King his moment of triumph. And facing them, two feet away: William and Maxwell, disgorged from the press, protesting their desire had been for the common weel, that they too rejoiced in Mistress Munro's deliverance. James, ignoring their protestations, instructed the men-at-arms, 'Hold these men. I will deal with them presently.'

Eglintoun, with Cowper and the others, had reached the front.

'Ah, Eglintoun,' the King acknowledged him with a wave. 'Ardrossan is but a step from here is it not? This lady is in need of succour and hospitality, she and her family; no doubt you can see to it?'

'With pleasure, Sire.'

The King looked down at John Montgomerie, still ministering to Kate. 'I have not the pleasure.'

'Braidstane's brother, Sire, recently returned from Florence.'

'You are a physician?'

'Sire.'

'Go with them, and provide whatever medical attention is required.'

Eglintoun signalled to one of his men to bring a horse while he and a man pressed from the crowd tipped up the cart full of peat, tumbling the turfs to the ground. Unused to being hitched to a cart, the horse pawed at the cobbles, showing the whites of its eyes, those nearest in the crowd edging back. Maggie, seeing the difficulty, pulled the horse's head down and murmured in his ear until he settled. Eglintoun stretched his cloak over the cart base, Munro lifting Kate in first, then swinging Maggie up beside her, the crowd parting to let them through.

459

Cheated of one spectacle, James prepared to give the onlookers another. He nodded to the men-at-arms who pushed William and Maxwell onto their knees. James addressed William, his voice carrying. 'I am satisfied by the evidence presented to me that you wilfully and in full knowledge of Mistress Munro's true identity, did traduce her character and slander her good name.' The crowd were murmuring in agreement, pressing forward again. William looked about to speak, James silencing him. 'I will hear no excuse, no false protestations. Neither from you,' his gaze swung to Maxwell, 'nor Maxwell, here. Your ill will towards the Munros has touched my person, and that of my Queen.' The crowd's agreement became howls of outrage. 'All that remains is to decide what is to be done with you both.'

Someone shouted, 'Flail them!' Another, 'We have an executioner here, let *them* be wirrit', and a third, louder than the rest, 'Leave them to us, we'll deal with them,' a cry that brought a roar of approval from the crowd.

James, as if deliberately leaving them to stew, turned his attention to Fullerton and Hamilton. 'You, I believe were deceived...'

A low rumble of disapproval, cries of 'Shame!'

'Though such credulity is hardly to be commended. Perhaps you should confine yourselves to the college in Dublin, and to the work I entrusted to you there. It is to be hoped it is more suited to your capabilities.'

Folk nearest the front began to pelt them with turfs. 'Send them back to the bogs...'

James' mouth twitched. 'If I have need of you, I will send, otherwise...' He waved in the direction of the sea, and Hamilton and Fullerton rose, bowed, and stumbled backwards, the laughter and jeering of the crowd following their retreat.

Cowper was wiping his hand on his hose, leaving a damp mark, beads of sweat glistening on his forehead. James fixed his gaze on him, the crowd momentarily silent.

'Master Cowper. You've carried out how many commissions?'

Cowper straightened, perhaps seduced by the mildness of James' tone.

'Upwards of a hundred, Sire,' he looked around at the crowd, 'and most of them successful.'

'Indeed. And what *is* your measure of success?'

Cowper licked his lips. 'To carry out the Lord's work. The conviction of witches for the good of the realm and the safety of all who live therein.'

'And the innocent? What of them?'

Cowper wiped away a trickle of sweat beside his eye. 'Acquittal … of course.'

The crowd were beginning to grumble again.

'Have you presided over many acquittals?'

It seemed a straightforward question, but John, knowing something of James' interrogation techniques, recognised the pitfall. Cowper clearly did not, his voice stronger.

'Very few, Sire.'

'And the Blawearie witch, she has proved effective?'

Now, John thought, we come to the nub.

'Oh yes. Her denunciations the key to my success.' Cowper was attempting to work the crowd, to regain sympathy.

James' next question was deceptively simple. 'And you had no doubts as to the truth of them?'

Cowper shook his head, still clearly unaware of the trap

461

laid for him. 'She oft offered proofs of her ability, miracles and the like.'

For a moment John almost felt sorry for Cowper, but the image of Kate, the breath choked from her, stifled the impulse. Whether or not he was but a credulous pawn in William's game, it had been a close run thing. And who knew how many others had likewise suffered without rescue.

The crowd were becoming restive, and as if aware of it, James closed in for the kill. 'And Mistress Munro? What proofs were offered there?'

Cowper darted a glance at William, as if in entreaty. 'The Master of Glencairn ... and Maxwell...'

'Whose evidence is discredited.'

Cowper was floundering. 'I saw with my own eyes the ill Mistress Aitken suffered when she cried Mistress Munro, her neck scratched to bleeding. How else to explain it, other than the devil's work?'

'Trickery and illusion, as I have found most miracles nowadays to be.' The crowd were muttering and nodding as James continued, 'I myself have examined Mistress Munro and know her to be, in all important respects, an honest woman. And if she be honest, the Blawearie witch is not. What say you, Cowper?'

'In this instance she may have been ... mistaken.'

James' voice hardened. 'In this instance she has been proved a fraud.' He played the crowd. 'The question is, fraud or fool, which are you?'

Cries of 'Fraud' and 'Fool' almost in equal measure rang around the square.

James held up a hand for silence. 'Whichever, your commission is rescinded, and you may consider yourself fortunate I do not throw *you* in the Tolbooth,' a flash of teeth, 'or to these good people here.' The crowd surged forward, but James raised his hand again as if to show he wasn't finished yet. He nodded to a burgess, who grasped Cowper's arm.

Cowper was shaking, the crowd clearly relishing his discomfort. James' dismissal was curt. 'I daresay there is some obscure parish where you can do little harm. I suggest you find it.' He nodded again to the burgess. 'Get rid of him, before I change my mind.'

He motioned to William and Maxwell to stand. Focused on William. 'This business of the Munro's tower by Renfrew. They were your tenants?'

'Munro and his father before him, Sire.'

'It is in sound condition?'

There was a hint of pride in William's voice. 'Recently restored, Sire, at Cunninghame expense.'

'All the more appropriate then that it be returned to the Munros...'

A pause, in which John Cunninghame thought – William may consider himself fortunate: the penalty is light.

James continued, '...No longer as a tenancy, but as an outright gift. You have done them a great disservice, this will be but some reparation.'

William bowed, ground out through clenched teeth, 'Sire.' Made as if to turn away.

'Wait!' James' voice was a whiplash. 'I'm not finished. The furnishings will be some small compensation for the years they have lost, and the surrounding acreage is, I take it, Cunninghame territory?'

John nodded.

'Then that also is in Glencairn's power to gift. See that

he does. And some monetary accommodation … say fifty merks.'

William blanched, began, 'I do not…'

James ignored the interruption, addressing Maxwell and William together. 'There is also the matter of the ill you have done to the peace of the realm, and the distress you have caused to the Queen. For these too there must be a penalty imposed. For the first you will each pay one hundred merks…' There was a roar from the crowd, a rising tide of satisfaction, acknowledged by James. 'To be delivered to the King's treasury by Monday sennight. And until it is paid, your liberty will be forfeit. No doubt Eglintoun can accommodate you. He has, I believe, underground cellars which will be more than adequate.' James waited for the crowd's laughter to subside, finished, 'For the second, you may not travel beyond the bounds of your own lands, nor come into our presence until such time as we deem it suitable for you so to do.' He paused again. 'Do not expect it to be soon.'

'I can't do it.' Kate sat facing the King in Ardrossan's hall. Her face was wan, her eyes bloodshot, though her hair, brushed and clean, shone starling-sleek against the pallor of her skin. 'I cannot live in a house designed by William, furnished by William…'

James was firm. 'I wish your presence here. The Queen wishes your presence…'

Munro, standing behind Kate, pressed her shoulder. 'We are grateful, Sire, but…'

Kate dropped to the floor at the King's feet. 'I beg of

464

you, do not ask it. We have lived six years in William's shadow when he thought us dead; now he knows us to live...'

'He is confined to his own lands. You will be safe at Renfrew.'

'I will never be safe...' she pressed her fist against her breast, 'inside.'

'You will desert the Queen, when her need of you is great?'

Kate's head dropped.

Hugh Montgomerie took a deep breath. 'If I may make a suggestion?' He drew John Montgomerie forward. 'My brother could take Kate's place in treating the Queen.'

James was brusque. 'And will he be any better than the other charlatans around us?'

'I have studied under the best physicians in Europe, Sire, and am not bound either by superstition or tradition. And of late I've had much discussion with Mistress Munro on the best treatments in such cases, and would be more than happy to fulfil *her* instructions to the Queen.'

Kate pivoted and stared up at James, her hands clasped. Sensing a softening in him, she offered, 'We are of one mind on such things, the Queen would be in the best of hands.'

James prevaricated. 'And Broomelaw? Who will look to it? I did not wrest it from the Master of Glencairn for the weather or the rooks to inherit it.'

It was Eglintoun's turn to intervene. He touched Kate's shoulder, as if seeking her approval. 'Montgomerie here will need a place to bide when he isn't wanted at the court. He could rent Broomelaw, hold it in trust for Munro's son.'

There was a pause in which Kate held her breath, not

daring to move, willing the King to acquiesce, her eyes, as she gazed up at him, damp with unshed tears.

He reached down and raised her to her feet. 'Very well, I will not force you to stay against your will, but where will you go?'

She was crying in earnest now, the King still supporting her.

Munro said, 'I have a farmhouse in Picardie which will serve us well while I resume my duties in the Scots Gardes. I don't wish to stretch the French King's compassion too far.' He gestured towards the west window. 'There is a ship anchored off Horse Island. All that is needed is the tide and,' he dropped onto one knee before James, 'and your blessing.'

The King set Kate aside, drew his sword. 'That you will have, and more. You came home plain Munro, I will send you back to Henri a knight.' He laid the flat of his sword on Munro's shoulder. 'Arise, Sir Adam Munro, of Broomelaw. And God go with you all.'

Epilogue

Kate was sitting in the shade of an acacia tree in the courtyard at Cayeux, the bodice of a dress for Ellie, on which she was embroidering bluebells, lying on her lap. Not the most sensible choice perhaps, harking back as it did to the copse below Broomelaw, but thinking of it now, in trust for Robbie, brought a measure of comfort to balance the pain.

It was September, the days breathless, hot and still, sapping her strength, so that she allowed her hands to fall idle and her thoughts to drift. They had been in France for almost a month and no word from Munro. He had delivered Kate and the girls into the care of Madame Picarde. She had taken one look at the bruising around Kate's neck, at her bloodshot eyes set in hollows soot-smudged, and placing one arm around her waist, had led her inside and up the stairs to a chamber under the eaves, and to a bed with a goose-feather mattress into which Kate disappeared, sinking into an unbroken sleep lasting two days. When she awoke she found Munro had returned to Amiens, the letter he left a lifeline that propped on the mantleshelf opposite her bed, was the first thing she saw when she opened her eyes each morning.

She reminded herself daily that he was but two days' journey away, that no sea separated them, that it was only his duty to the French King detaining him, and that he would surely be here soon. A confidence that waned as the weeks passed, though she didn't share her fears with Maggie. She was a problem Kate worried at like a loose tooth, for having had her taste of usefulness as Kate's assistant, albeit short-lived, she took ill to having little to do other than farm chores, and so moped, her usual spark gone.

Kate tried to rouse her, indicating the books John Montgomerie had ensured followed them to France along with Agnes. 'No one knows the future, and perhaps it's just as well. But one day, when you are a little older, you may get your wish, go to Florence to study anatomy, why not start now?' Maggie, unable to see past the current restrictions of her life, failed to respond. Kate sighed – no doubt she would come round in time. As Ellie had. Her sense of loss, her grieving for the Montgomerie girls, had been a consequence Kate found hard to counter, the local child who befriended her a godsend. Kate could hear them now, in the hay-shed, chattering away, one in Scots, the other in the local dialect, apparently understanding each other perfectly. Which is more, she thought ruefully, than Madame Picarde and I do. Her scholarly French as far removed from the local patois as Scots from English. Communication between them remaining a trial and error mix of gesture and mime and phrases, which, though greeted with smiles and nods, she knew must fall very wide of the mark. She supposed that, too, would come with time, but for the moment was content to allow the peace of the countryside, the sense of safety, of distance from all that troubled them, to penetrate

468

her soul and begin to heal the accumulated wounds of the last years.

She reached into the basket by her feet and retrieved the letter lately come from Braidstane, the news weeks old, but cheering nonetheless, Elizabeth's voice as strong as if she sat by her side: *Glencairn, furious with William, left him to stew in Eglintoun's cellar for nigh on a fortnight, waiting until the last possible moment to pay the fine that James demanded. And Maxwell, for all his show, proved short of funds and languishes there still, and to that indignity is added the requirement to recompense Eglintoun for his board.*

She trusted Margaret Maxwell was making the most of the respite.

A whale beached south of Irvine at the last high tide, both Grizel and I in sympathy with its predicament, for we are well-nigh unable to move ourselves at present. We cannot wait for our time to come. John has promised to be on hand, much to Ishbel's dismay. But at least we are safe at Braidstane, for the plague still rages in Edinburgh and the King has proclaimed a fast until it abates. John, and here Kate imagined Elizabeth's hesitation, *already makes a name for himself, both at the court and around Renfrew; Broomelaw, and his stewardship on Robbie's behalf, suiting him well...*

Out of the corner of her eye she caught a flicker of light on the hillside, as if the glint of sunlight on steel. She lifted her hand to shade her eyes, felt her stomach lurch. Surely they were safe here... A figure emerged from a dip, first the head, then the shoulders and torso, then the whole, mounted. She was out of the chair and through the wicket gate and running up the slope towards him before she saw the second rider. They were flowing down the side of the hill, neck and neck, the horses perfectly matched, the men also. They pulled to a halt in front of her, Munro sliding to the ground to lift and spin her round, and behind him Robbie, holding back a fraction as if uncertain of his welcome. From the safety of Munro's arms she reached out and he came to her, limping, but whole, his hair cut short, a scar running from the corner of his eye towards his hairline, a hint of stubble on his chin. There was a shriek behind her as Ellie flung herself past, leaping at Robbie, winding her arms around his neck, saying, over and over, 'I had to tell, they made me tell.'

Robbie hoisted her onto the crook of his arm, his smile for Kate tentative. 'Where's Maggie?'

'She's here just … finding it hard, but now we are all together…'

Munro placed his finger against her mouth, halting her, his expression rueful. 'For a day or two only. Amiens is won, but the war is not,' and as she drew back, 'but when it is, and I do not think it will be long delayed, I promise you…' He turned Kate around, slid his arm around her waist, Robbie and Ellie close at her other side, so that together they looked down on the farmhouse nestling on the valley floor, and at Maggie, hesitating by the wicket gate. 'I promise,' Munro repeated, 'we will make of this place a home.'

Historical Note

In the late 1590s, James VI of Scotland had several main concerns. A king-in-waiting, he was preparing to accept the English crown upon the death of Elizabeth I and wished to subdue the warring factions in Scotland and ensure that the country was at peace when the time came for his move to London. His wife, Anne of Denmark, had produced only two live children in the seven years of their marriage and they shared a desire for more (preferably male) children. Since his marriage, perhaps as a result of the difficulties experienced on the journey to bring his bride to Scotland, James had exhibited a long-standing and public obsession with witchcraft, fuelling the prevailing atmosphere of superstition.

Although most of the characters that appear in this book are historical, the majority of the events are fictional. And those that are rooted in reality have been depicted in a manner that suits the story rather than strictly mirroring known or assumed facts, particularly in relation to timing and details. I have, however, sought to remain faithful to the wider context in which they are set.

The Cunninghame/Montgomerie feud, thought to have its origins in 1488 when control of the bailiwick of Cunningham was given to a Montgomerie, was characterised by intermittent acts of brutality and murder on both sides. It was the most notorious feud in Ayrshire, not fully resolved until well into the seventeenth century.

The Great Scottish Witch Hunt of 1597 was the second of five major episodes of significant witch trials that took place in the latter part of the sixteenth century and the first half of the seventeenth. It is the least documented of the five, but some 400 people are thought to have been charged with witchcraft in the period between March and October of that year. The normal method of execution of those convicted in Scotland was to be garrotted (the Scots term was wirrit), then burnt.

The most famous case involved Margaret Aitken, the 'Great Witch of Blawearie', who, when she was accused, offered to identify other witches in exchange for her own life. She travelled around Scotland denouncing many people, but was eventually discredited. In August 1597 all standing witch trial commissions were revoked, following concerns that many of the accusations made might be false; owing more to a desire for personal revenge than any real evidence of malefice.

The conflicts termed the 'French Wars of Religion' are generally agreed to have begun in 1562 when the Massacre of Vassy provoked open hostilities between Catholics and Huguenots. These continued, almost without pause, for thirty-six years. The siege of Amiens, occurring towards the end of that period, was successfully concluded in September 1597. The Edict of Nantes, which Henri IV negotiated in April 1598, guaranteed certain freedoms to both sides and resulted in the end of major conflict, though religious tensions continued to affect French politics for many years thereafter. Peace with Spain was finally achieved through the Treaty of Vervins in May 1598.

The Scots Gardes were an elite Scottish regiment in the service of the French King whose duties included both ceremonial functions and the provision of a personal bodyguard.

Patrick Montgomerie did die while serving in the Scots Gardes under Henri IV, however the specific circumstances of his death as depicted here are fictional.

Under the terms of the 'Auld Alliance', Scots had de facto citizenship rights in France as well as various special privileges, for example in relation to trade, and could buy, sell and, crucially, inherit property there.

Margaret Maxwell did courageously seek an injunction from James VI against her abusive husband, but was refused and went on to bear him fourteen children before finally leaving him. Patrick Maxwell's mother is reputed to have supported Margaret in her appeal to the King, but the timing and mode of the appeal is my invention.

Glossary

awry (adj): wrong
aye (adj): always
bairn (n): child
barmkin (n): enclosed area within the outer fortification of a castle or tower house
bastle house (n): small scale dwelling, often associated with a tower house
bawbee (n): copper coin, worth six pence Scots
besom (adj): term of contempt, generally applied to women
bide (v): to live
birl (v): to whirl around
birlinn (n): wooden vessel propelled by sail and /or oar
bothy (n): primitive shelter
bravely (adj): well (health)
breeks (n): trousers
byre (n): cowshed
canny (adj): shrewd
chirurgeon (n): surgeon
clack (n): talk, gossip
coorie in (v): to snuggle up
Cordiner (Prop n): leather-worker
cowp (v): to tip over
deeve (v): to bother, annoy

dreich (adj): damp
dug, cow's (n): udder
feart (adj): afraid
fettle (adj): condition
filch (v): to steal
forbye (n): besides
founder 1. (v): to collapse
foundering 2. (v): to be chilled
gawk (v): to stare
gey (adv): very
grub (v): to scrape or dig
guddle (n): mess
haar (n): fog
hunker (v): to squat
ken (v): to know
kilter, out of (n): wrong
lochan (n): small loch
lye (n): liquid obtained by leaching ashes, used in soap production
mair (det): more
maun (aux v): must, may
merk (n): silver coin, worth 2/3 of a pound Scots
mirk (n): 1.darkness, 2.mist
mite (adj): little
Octavians (Prop n): Financial commission set up by James VI
pelt (v): to rain heavily

Prosector (Prop n): a preparer of corpses for dissection

racket (n): loud noise

redd-out (v): to spring clean

reek (n): stench

rummage (v): to search through

smirr (n): fine rain

speir (n): talk

stour (n): dust

strait (n): difficulty

sutler (n): civilian merchant who sells provisions to an army in the field

swee (n): a horizontal bar from which pots are suspended and swung over the fire.

hole (v): to suffer, endure

thrapple (n): throat

thrawn (adj): contrary, ill-natured, perverse

traipse (v): to wander about

twit (v): to taunt

vennel (n): narrow lane between buildings

weel (n): well-being

wheest (imp): be quiet

wynd (n): narrow street or alleyway

wirrit (v): to kill by strangulation

Also by Margaret Skea

Turn of the Tide

Scotland 1586

An ancient feud threatens Munro's home, his family, even his life.

Munro owes allegiance to the Cunninghames and to the Earl of Glencairn. He escapes the bloody aftermath of a massacre, but cannot escape the disdain of the wife he sought to protect, nor inner conflict, as he wrestles with his conscience, with divided loyalties and, most dangerous of all, a growing friendship with the rival Montgomerie clan.

Set against the backdrop of the turmoil of the closing years of the sixteenth century, *Turn of the Tide* follows the fortunes of a fictional family trapped at the centre of a notorious historic feud. Known as the Ayrshire Vendetta, it began in the 15th century and wasn't finally resolved until the latter part of the 17th, the Cunninghames and Montgomeries dubbed the 'Montagues and Capulets' of Ayrshire.

'...a fascinating and engaging read with great visual effect'
Ali Bacon

'I have read some wonderful debut novels this year – *Turn of the Tide* is one of them. I loved it ... a tale of love, loyalty, tragedy and betrayal.'

BooksPlease